SEA OF
TRANQUILITY

Sea of Tranquility

~ a novel ~

Lesley Choyce

SIMON & PIERRE FICTION
A MEMBER OF THE DUNDURN GROUP
TORONTO · OXFORD

Editor: Barry Jowett
Copy-Editor: Andrea Pruss
Design: Jennifer Scott
Printer: Transcontinental
Special thanks to Julia Sway for editorial assistance

National Library of Canada Cataloguing in Publication Data
Choyce, Lesley, 1951–
    Sea of tranquility / Lesley Choyce.

ISBN 1-55002-440-X

I. Title.

PS8555.H668S37 2003   C813'.54   C2003-900344-2   PR9199.3.C497S42 2003

1   2   3   4   5   07   06   05   04   03

THE CANADA COUNCIL | LE CONSEIL DES ARTS   **Canadä**   ONTARIO ARTS COUNCIL
FOR THE ARTS | DU CANADA   CONSEIL DES ARTS DE L'ONTARIO
SINCE 1957 | DEPUIS 1957

We acknowledge the support of the **Canada Council for the Arts** and the **Ontario Arts Council** for our publishing program. We also acknowledge the financial support of the **Government of Canada** through the **Book Publishing Industry Development Program** and **The Association for the Export of Canadian Books**, and the **Government of Ontario** through the **Ontario Book Publishers Tax Credit** program, and the **Ontario Media Development Corporation's Ontario Book Initiative.**

Care has been taken to trace the ownership of copyright material used in this book. The author and the publisher welcome any information enabling them to rectify any references or credit in subsequent editions.

J. Kirk Howard, President

Printed and bound in Canada.⊛
Printed on recycled paper.
www.dundurn.com

Dundurn Press
8 Market Street
Suite 200
Toronto, Ontario, Canada
M5E 1M6

Dundurn Press
73 Lime Walk
Headington, Oxford,
England
OX3 7AD

Dundurn Press
2250 Military Road
Tonawanda NY
U.S.A. 14150

SEA OF TRANQUILITY

Chapter One

A woman's voice rising up out of the silence of the island morning. Speaking the names of the men she once loved, still loved. A lone woman's voice on a morning like this, conversing with no one save the wind, the young spruce trees abloom with tiny globes of crystal clear dew and the cloak of mist hanging from the sky. What better audience?

Sylvie Young. On her eightieth birthday. She and the beginning of summer there in the great big backyard on Ragged Island. To be alive on a morning like this. Summer had finally come to Nova Scotia, damp and cool, but summer all the same. Summer had been on the mainland for a couple of weeks but couldn't find safe passage to the island. Summer holed up in a bed and breakfast in Mutton Hill Harbour, reluctant to make the last leg, but finally, she shook herself and said, what must be done, must be done. Sylvie was waiting for summer to arrive. Never cursed its tardiness. Finally, this.

Sylvie decided this would be the day to walk again to the graveyard. Hadn't been all winter. Take a toothbrush and clean up the headstones of her four dead husbands. At least she could still count them on one hand, she offered to folks when they said how sorry they were that all her men had died. It was a sad thing for Sylvie, but she sometimes pretended it was the same as taking in a bunch of stray cats for pets. Fox would kill them or they'd get run over by one of the Oickle boys in his no-name, pieced-together car. Always something. Not a thing to keep whimpering over for the rest of your life.

The truth was she missed them all and would scrub away the lichen on their gravestones with the toothbrush she'd been using on her own white teeth all winter. Use a little Javex and some Dutch Cleanser — on the headstones. Pull out the dandelions and make room for the grass to grow in sweet and green.

"Eighty. Damn." It was a sort of sweet, melancholy damnation that the nuthatches and cedar waxwings heard her say. The ravens had heard plenty worse and weren't offended. Besides, Sylvie would spread seed in the backyard in about twenty minutes and they would try to get at it before the glib squirrels or the belligerent blue jays. It was just a number, eighty was. Like any other number.

Sylvie looked around. She knew there was no one in her big, empty backyard, framed in by the tall, stately spruce trees, the good ones with deep roots, rare for these parts, planted and then thinned by her second husband, Kyle Bauer. No one was there, but she wanted to check anyway. That done, she sat down on the damp carpet of spring beauties, her favourite of all the flowers because it was the first one to arrive each summer, delicate but brazen as born-again bats. She settled there on the cold, wet grass, clutched at a little green puff of moss, and she cried.

She cried not for all those dead men mouldering on the bedrock with gravel shovelled on their caskets. She cried not for the fact that she lived alone or had dozens of reasons to complain about her pains and minor sufferings. She cried not because she was lonely or destitute or feeling rotten as the floorboards of Kenny Oickle's '59 Edsel.

She cried because she was a woman who needed to cry. Plain and simple. Salt tears, saline as the sea that wrapped its cold, powerful arms around this island. Crying, laughing, saluting the sky, sticking your middle finger up to God. Maybe it was all the same. Life comes at you and you have to make something of it, you have to respond, Sylvie would say. You have to collect all of it and do something with it. Write a goddamn book, pick up a guitar and sing a drunken song. Shout at your neighbours for being who they are. Tell the frigging government to go shove itself up its arse until it's inside out.

Something to do with it. Take life and respond. Cry if you have to. There it is. Eighty. Tears falling on the little spring beauties. That's done with it — for now at least. Off to the next thing. Books to be read. Things to think about. A tea kettle will boil. Birds will peck at the seeds dropped from her hand. Maybe it will be a good garden this year. But not before she wages war against the recalcitrant earwigs and the rapacious turnip bugs. Cabbage moths from hell; she'll have to suffocate them with cold stove ash every day until they give up. All part of it, all part of living.

She did not feel sorry for herself, but it was, nonetheless, for her own singular being that she cried. News of starving children in Africa did not make her cry. It made her angry and embarrassed to be part of the human race. But tears were saved for rare moments like this. Life coming at her like a two-by-four or a low doorway lintel. All at once — not bad, not good, just overpowering, with every blessed thing of this world and the next sweeping through her like a hurricane through a broken window.

Sylvie sniffled, wiped tears from her face with a strong wrinkled hand. A lifetime stared back at her like mighty river deltas. Mississippis and Niles, Mekongs and Ganges. She had named them. Turned her palm over and there was her lifeline, strong and long and wrapping halfway around her wrist, her longevity documented from the time she was a child. Imagine what it takes in the way of courage to think of yourself as old when you are young. Sylvie had read her lifeline and believed what it prescribed. She spent afternoons as a teenager trying to figure out what she could do with all those eighty or more years. Have a couple of husbands. Four had never been considered an option. Men died easily, she knew. They were fragile beings. Men and their trouble: large egos in need of feeding and preening; dangerous work on boats or bridges, in mines and railroads. "I love men," her own mother had once said, probably quoting someone, for she was always quoting something she had memorized, "not because they are men but because they are, thank God, not women."

Sylvie had even predicted that she would spend much of her life alone. Solitude had always been like a mythical Greek god to her. Solitude was geography and body and place and a feeling of closeness — with what she was not sure. Sylvie had tried being in love with God. She had dabbled with the idea of a celestial marriage to God or Jesus or the church or any other masculine spiritual thing worth marrying. But it was a failed attempt. God was in her heart where her father and mother had put the idea and it was neither a *he* nor a *she*, and, as much as she tried, she could not externalize any god and propose marriage.

Marriage was now a thing of the past in all forms. Divorce, the great twentieth-century deception, had certainly never been considered an option. She'd known men with pent-up rage even, but they'd never taken it out on her, not even Doley, her third husband. She would have stuck by him though, good or bad. That's what women should do with their men. Doley had carried with him hurt and pain from one of those "traditional," hard childhoods. No one called it abuse in the old days. They'd just say it was the way some folks brought up their kids. Good parents and bad parents. Doley grew up loving everything that lived, except for himself. He loved Sylvie dearly and was always kind to her. Then he was gone.

Sylvie had stayed right by him and watched as he slowly travelled away from her. She had known then there would not be many more men in her life. She ached for him when he was finally gone. Ached and ached for him, just like the others. And then said goodbye and, with the help of Phonse and Moses, laid him to rest, down on the all-too-familiar granite surface beneath the deepest soil of the graveyard.

Her only crime, it seemed, was her ability to endure. Long lifeline, good blood, heart like a mighty backyard hand pump, set nonstop from here to eternity.

What was there in a day? A book to read. Birds coming to you from all directions, flying out to visit you here because you leave them seed on the ground to find. Mist, soon and certain to lift from the feather tops of those trees. A blue sky waiting for the right moment of surprise. Summer coming out to Ragged Island, off the coast of Nova Scotia.

Summer and the tourists again. Sylvie loved to see the tourists come out on the old ferry boat from Mutton Hill Harbour. Not like Peggy's Cove. Not like that at all. Tourists

could not bring cars here, but they brought families, most of
them. Walked around the island in disbelief. "Like going back to
another time," they'd say, ever and again. They were sometimes
exasperated by the old wrecks of cars, however, driven around
by the islanders. No mufflers, lots of noise. Noise was sometimes
good on an island as quiet as this one could be. No one who
lived here would ever complain.

But she knew the only thing that brought the tourists now
was the whales. Moses Slaunwhite's boat tour out of the little
harbour. Mainlanders wanting real adventure would take the
ferry out from Mutton Hill Harbour in the morning and then
go to sea with Moses, out in front of the island, out where the
big waves rolled and rolled in the deep. And the whales were
there waiting. Every summer. Whales guaranteed. Right whales.
The same whales that had disappeared altogether early in the
century. Vanished. But they'd come back, once the whalers of
this island had stopped killing them.

Sylvie believed that the whales had come back for her,
because of her. She was one of the few who had been around
when island men killed whales. She had seen the butchery
ashore and openly cursed the men who did it. Tried to get it
stopped. And succeeded. Or at least she had taken credit for it.
And then the whales began to come back. Close enough to
shore that you felt you were there with them. Deep water right
up to some of the rocks out near Nubby Point. Deep, deep and
dark and treacherous and secretive in ways that Sylvie understood and the whales understood.

And she did not curse Moses Slaunwhite for his boat and his
tourists. The tourists came and brought children again to the
island. The sound of their voices like choirs of wonderful noise.
Their parents would buy the baked bread and cookies Sylvie
made in her wood stove oven. And they would talk. They would
reassure her that life went on beyond the refuge of her island.

Sometimes she thought the world was coming to an end and it was only the sound of children's voices in the summer that reminded her the cycle was continuing. She loved all the children and tucked candies into their hands and they stared at her in a kind of fear and wonder. Was she an old witch? Was she a sea hag? No one was ever cruel to her, though, and the parents were polite. They would all ask, "Have you seen whales? What do they look like? Do you think we'll get to see any when we go out on the boat?"

And Sylvie would say, "The whales are great and wondrous creatures. Kind and friendly and playful and talkative and you must listen very closely to hear them singing." She would never tell one of the children, or even their wide-eyed, curious parents with their hand-held video cameras, that soon the whales would be gone from the waters around the island. Soon, she knew, the whales would stop coming here in the summer.

For Sylvie knew silence to be a reliable ally, a dedicated friend and advisor who had carried her through many bad moments. Silence was almost always hand in hand with wisdom. And so the children continued to smile for her.

Chapter Two

Phonse's Lighthouse, they called it. But it wasn't a lighthouse at all, more like a mirror. Only worked on sunny days with all that sunlight reflecting off the windshields of maybe five hundred wrecks of cars. You could see it, though, and use it to guide a boat home from as far away as Indian Harbour, Pearl Island, or even Peggy's Cove. Phonse's Light.

Phonse Doucette was forty-six and he was that rare man who had lived his dream. Born on Ragged Island, all through school he pledged to stay there, spend as little time on the mainland as was humanly necessary. He was one of those blessed men who had a dream and knew how to follow it. The dream: his own junkyard. Went through several incarnations: Phonse's Junk Yard, Phonse's Salvage Yard, Phonse's Quality Used Car Parts, and, most recently, Phonse's Auto Recycling and Environmental Control. Well, that was stretching it some, but Phonse thought it might make him eligible for some government incentive programs.

When Jack Zwick looked at his new hand-lettered sign and stated flatly, "Environmental me arse," Phonse said in defence of himself, "I'm hauling junk cars off the mainland, aren't I doing that? Cleaning up the place. Putting some of the parts of them bloody cars back into circulation."

Everybody still called the place the junkyard, though, even Phonse. And there it was: Phonse's Junkyard, on the hill with its beacon of car windshields all facing south, tail lights all pointed toward the mainland, some of the trunk lids propped open like the cars were mooning the people who lived way back in Mutton Hill Harbour. The well-to-do inhabitants who used lawnmowers on their lawns, or hired people to use them. "Lawnmowers kill snakes," Phonse muttered to the ferry captain one day. "I love snakes, 'cause they're natural and they're good for the environment. There oughta be a law." Against killing snakes, he meant.

Right off to the side of Phonse's litter of cars was Oickle's Pond, which had ended up somehow, through an ancestral convolution of gambling negotiations and a bad year of herring fishing, in the Doucette family. Oickle's Pond. Could swim in it once, he remembered, but old transmissions kept finding their way to Oickle's Pond, rusty gas tanks and oil pans, the odd driver's seat from an old Mustang with springs popping through it like so many toy snakes from a Chinese store.

People other than Phonse found Oickle's Pond suitable for depositing old stove oil tanks and oil barrels, other kinds of barrels with warnings about toxic substances all rubbed off or cam-

ouflaged with rust. People used to swim there once. Phonse
remembered that Sylvie did when she was younger. Phonse
talked about cleaning it up, swore that people sneaked in and
threw things in there. Well, that was partly true, but Phonse had
probably started the problem himself. Back before anybody
thought anything about tossing garbage wherever it looked like
it would fit. Phonse was always amiable, trying to please. Back
then, if one of those big American warships had pulled up in the
deep channel out front of the island, if the captain had come off
the ship and knocked on Phonse's door and said, "Excuse me, but
we happen to have several containers of nuclear waste, uranium,
plutonium, and methalonium aboard and we were wondering if
you could take it off our hands," Phonse would have considered
it. Or what's a junkyard for? Sure. Hell. Oickle's Pond would do
the trick. "Dump 'er in there, buddy. Just back up your boat to
the government wharf and I'll bring down the truck for ya."

Since then, of course, Phonse and his recycling yard had
gone green. Someday Oickle's Pond would return to its natural
state, but it would take scuba divers and cranes and some sort of
newfangled toxic sludge incineration plant like the one that
never worked right on the Sydney Tar Ponds. Government
money, big wads of it, would have to be involved. Phonse would
have to wait for that.

Phonse was Acadian by blood. His people had been escorted out
of Grand Pré by the Brits and tossed ashore in various American
locations. The Doucettes had ended up in Virginia and were not
wanted by the snobbish English living there. The Virginia House
of Assembly had been generous enough to provide a ship and a
few crusts of bread to send them back to Nova Scotia. So
Phonse's people were set back down along the shore near
Lunenburg. Not much to work with, but after a couple of gen-

erations they got their pride back intact and handed it down like a cherished heirloom from father to son until Phonse received the gift. Phonse was proud, resourceful, cussed at times, but a guy who, if dropped from a twenty-foot ladder head down while trying to paint the side of his big pink and blue house, would always land on the balls of his feet and be back up the ladder again with a fresh can of paint in no time flat.

"My people knew how to care for this land," Phonse asserted. "The English knew nothing. If we didn't feed them way back when, they all would have starved." Way back when was a muddle of history, mostly bad news for the worthy Acadians. Way back when it took two generations for an Acadian family to build a dyke, say near the Cornwallis River, and create beautiful, fertile croplands and pastures. Two generations and it didn't seem a problem. "They were this close to the land back then." Phonse pinched his finger and proved the point. "Soil in their blood. An Acadian could grow anything anywhere. Set a cabbage seed on top of a rock out there at Nubby Point and make it grow into a big, beautiful thing that'd make five of us a good dinner. Piece of salt pork and that cabbage grown on a rock and we'd be full up, belching and farting like a big happy family."

The Acadians knew how to grow things, while the Englishman would just look at a field and feel sorry for himself, wonder where he was going to find someone to work it or how he was going to find himself a cup of tea for his morning break. That's what an Englishman would have done. Back then. Or now maybe. Not much changes.

No one really complained much when Phonse started bringing the wrecks over from the mainland, one a day on the ferry service. School busses, old hearses, dump trucks gone bad, pick-ups, service vans. One by one until he had that hill filled up with junk. A dream realized. Once the phones were in, people could phone Phonse for a part and he'd send it over on the ferry to be picked up in Mutton Hill Harbour. If it didn't fit or if it was the wrong one, it could be returned or just tossed in the bay, and Phonse would send another one over.

To some people it seemed like a lot of trouble for a car part and they'd end up driving to Bridgewater to get a new or reconditioned fuel pump from Canadian Tire. Often a part from Phonse's yard was seized up pretty bad. All that salt air doing its work. But business was business for Phonse and he didn't mind a little hard work to make a go of it. Hell, none of his people had ever shirked hard work.

"Dirt under the nails, that's what makes any man happy," Phonse said. Caked oil and grease made him happy, but farming, growing cabbages in his little dyked area next to Oickle's Pond, made him even happier. His own little dyke by the pond only cost him two days work with his backhoe instead of two generations, but it freed up some fine little marsh full of rich sediment. Phonse liked working there, puttering on a summer day in his off hours, talking to philosophical red-winged blackbirds who looked at him sideways as they dangled on the sides of cattail plants. And frogs; the dark, oil-stained waters of Oickle's Pond were always full of frogs, as well. Bullfrogs, big as footballs. Tiny peepers, too. Fish in the pond too, of course. Nobody knew what kind. Unidentifiable. Started out as suckers maybe and evolved to survive the change in water quality. Tasted some good, eaten cooked or raw. Phonse was particular to the livers of such fish.

And the cabbages. The big mealtime ones that could have been grown by an Acadian on a rock with just a sprinkling of piss, two ground-up clam shells, and soil cleaned out from under one thumbnail. But these cabbages were even more than that — grown in the Acadian soil of Phonse's little garden, a cabbage was a thing to behold. Big as a beach ball. No holes in the leaves from cabbage flies or other bugs 'cause Phonse always kept them doused in cold wood stove ashes. Seemed to help the flavour of a cabbage. Phonse had no German in him but he knew how to turn that cabbage into sauerkraut if he had a mind to. Enough salt to preserve a mummy. Made your eyes water just to think about it. But a Phonse Doucette cabbage was a prize. Men who pay other men to mow their lawns back in Mutton Hill Harbour would pay ten bucks for one head of Phonse's cabbage and not ask any questions how it was raised. Send one over on a hot summer day to the mainland in a box that's just been used to ship a big boat engine battery over from the mainland. People'd just stare at that cabbage the whole trip back to Mutton Hill Harbour, not even look at the scenery.

All that was in Phonse's blood. Heritage. The ability to develop ("devil-up" as Phonse would say it) a piece of land in the old Acadian tradition. Only this was the modern version of it — if anything at all could be called "modern" on Ragged Island. He had retained a French accent, bestowed upon him by his parents, and he had fine-tuned it while growing up. He sounded more like Jean Chrétien than a true Acadian, but no one knew what a true anglicized Acadian should sound like anyway.

Sure, some men with old junkers did come across on the one-hour ferry ride to Phonse's salvage yard for parts, but these were men who didn't mind investing a little time in finding the right flywheel for an old Oldsmobile, men who preferred talking over working any day of the week. And Phonse could talk the ears off a dead mule if he wanted to. "It's because I have so many ideas," he'd say. "Possibilities. Dreams. If only I could *devil-up* each and every one of them. The world would be a better place."

Better, perhaps, or at the very least, more cluttered. So men would come for the talk and buy something or other, usually a car part that wouldn't fit or, if it did, was seized, chipped, cracked, or otherwise brutalized by the island's weather. No one ever

complained. Yet over the years, Phonse noted the marked decline
in customers, what with the Canadian Tire only a half-hour's
drive from Mutton Hill Harbour, and other competition from
junkyards on the mainland. Men with German names, some of
Irish descent, some from Halifax. Some, it was said, were even
tied in with computer networks telling the world that they had
available for sale the drive shaft of a 1957 Chevy station wagon.
"Computers," Phonse said, and shook his head. "Someday, I'll
show them how that is done. I'll be on that Internet thing. I'll
put some of my ideas on there. Then people will see."

Phonse was not ever discouraged. Like his ancestors, he
adapted to hard times and thrived on adversity. Cabbage seed on
a rock. Spit on it and look at it with kindness and it will grow.
Feed six families.

So the junkyard business was slow. Some of the old regulars
would come, though, and buy something or other. If it was a slow
day, Phonse would get out his guns. He loved guns, all kinds of
guns. But he never, ever hunted. He hated hunters and would love
to see all hunters tied up together in a big huge fishing net and
picked up by a Coast Guard helicopter, taken out to the deepest
part of the sea, right there in the pathway of the whales that
cruised back to this island every summer. He'd like to see them
dropped from the sky and sunk to the bottom of the sea to feed
the fishes or whatever. That's what he would do with hunters.

So you couldn't talk about hunting around Phonse when he
got out his guns. Everyone knew this and was careful. All those
Mutton Hill Harbour duck hunters and deer hunters, men who
shot a thing and paid another man to skin and clean it for them.
Those kind of men. Pale, pasty-faced, and mostly English.

Phonse's gun collection, all unregistered, would have satisfied the Michigan Militia. Not particularly modern, but diverse
and large. Smith and Wesson hand guns. Derringers, snubby little detective guns, old wild west shiny six-shooters, rifles,

Winchesters, German handguns, shotguns. Old double-barrelled ones mostly. He didn't approve of shotguns in principle but he liked the sound they made going off. "Any bloody fool can shoot a duck with a shotgun. Or a goose. Who *can't* hit a thing when it sprays pellets all over the sky?"

Guns, guns, and more guns. Some men made the ferry trip just to admire his guns. Phonse made his own bullets, too. Melted down old lead flashing from torn-down houses and made bullets to fit his many guns. "Something very meditative," he said, "about pouring molten lead into bullet casings. So bright and silvery. Nothing as satisfying as lead." He made buckshot for his shotguns as well.

And it was the gun thing, and all the general interest in his armoury, that launched his most successful financial venture. On slow days, Phonse took out a .22 rifle and shot at things. Old cars, mostly, never at animals. Everyone who came to visit was given a chance to shoot at something. They all agreed at how satisfying it was to shoot at, say, an old postal truck, or a school bus tire, or the side door of a car once owned by the local member of parliament. The feel was satisfying, the sound — *kerwunk* of bullet into metal — was satisfying, other men looking at you like you'd just won an Olympic sporting event. It was all satisfying.

As a result, Phonse drifted into a sideline business. With the auto parts industry going to hell in a handcart thanks to mainlanders and computers and Canadian Tire and whatnot, Phonse slowly but surely allowed his junkyard to develop into a kind of firearm entertainment centre. He referred to it in more grandiose moments as a "theme park." Eventually, people (97 percent of them men) came over on the ferry and paid Phonse an admission charge to use his rifles, handguns, and shotguns to shoot at things. You'd be allowed to pick a vehicle and buy handmade ammo and shoot to your heart's content.

"It's really more like t'erapy, if you want to look at it as such."

And therapy it was. Satisfying *kerwunks* all over the place, or the blast and skrittle of windshields shattering. If a saleable car part like that was to be destroyed, a patron might offer to pay for the price of that part. Phonse didn't ask for the extra money. It was just a code of conduct. The sort of thing men understand when they get together for noble, significant rituals like this. Maybe just the muted thunk of bullets blasting into an old sofa would do for some. Oil barrels for targets, or a washing machine worn down by years of trying to wrestle fish smells out of a man's pants.

Men from Mutton Hill Harbour started bringing over guns of their own, but the ferry operator put an end to that. It didn't look good and seemed dangerous. So everyone used Phonse's rifles; not a one spoke about hunting, and the thing evolved. "She's more successful than Upper Clements Park will ever be," Phonse bragged, referring to the little theme park near Annapolis Royal that had cost the taxpayer millions over the years. Phonse knew that the English had stolen all that land around Annapolis Royal from his French forefathers, and he was proud that his theme park was a success and the other one was a financial black hole. "No government grant, nothing. Just a man who can *devil-up* an idea."

Since they couldn't bring over their own guns, men started bringing over things they wanted to shoot at, and that was fine for Phonse. Some brought their old buggered-up computers that had lost a year's work inside them. Some brought television sets with complaints that their TVs only showed stupid television programs. Some unlikely people came to shoot Phonse's guns and paid handsomely. Do-gooders, peaceniks, Greenpeacers, and aging hippies came to shoot at things. They brought flags, old magazines, portraits of politicians, VCRs, and the like.

A retired computer programmer once brought a case of computer disks. He said they were "five-and-a-quarter-inch floppies" that were no good anymore. Phonse didn't care whether they were good or not — the money was, and that was all that mattered. The disks were tossed in the air and shot like clay pigeons. The programmer came back and donated several more cases of them, and it was a favourite in-between-snack of sorts after the main course of shooting up your old toaster or blasting your mother-in-law's microwave.

Homemade beer was sold too, but only after the guns were locked away. Phonse made excellent "Acadian Bitter," and it slid down the throat like liquid silk. Tree huggers and investment analysts were starting to drink warm bitter side by side after a good shoot-out session, and Phonse knew he had struck gold.

The rest of the islanders approved of Phonse's business, and it was a source of community pride that Phonse had been so inventive and caught on to something new that worked so well and earned him cash flow while being good for the mental health of the large, often pitiable community of mainlanders.

Chapter Three

South of the island there was this: water, deep as deep there is anywhere along these Atlantic shores. One of Sylvie's favoured haunts was the "Trough," also known as the "Trowel" due to some pronunciation quirks locally. The Trough was a long channel of sorts between the island itself and an outer reef of rocks, a jagged shoal known as Rocky Shoal, a double whammy of a name.

The Trough had this deep and fast current that raced east to west like it was an undersea freight train to nowhere but up around Seal Point and the next piece of open Atlantic. Phonse said he could throw a quarter in there and it would travel at least a mile before it would land on sea bottom, where it might rouse a lobster or a dozing, camouflaged haddock. Sylvie knew this place, knew it from childhood. Understood the beauty of this place. But also the danger. Men had drowned here.

Of course, the North Atlantic had drowned plenty of island men. Women had lost fathers, husbands, and sons to bad luck from here to the Grand Banks and beyond. Winds that should've switched over from nor'west to sou'east but hung stiff in the winter and cluttered up the rails with enough ice to topple a ship and spill terrified men to cold, watery death. Boatloads of dead fish encased in steel heading back into the grey Atlantic.

There was no denying that this stretch of shore had been a powerful part of her childhood, and if it spoke of death to her, it also spoke of calm summer mornings like this: a short walk from the backyard, past the blooming crabapples and the green, mossy streams gurgling clear and bright. Sylvie, at eighty (and what of it?), could stand and look out to sea, sail away and be anywhere she wanted to be. Back then or right here. Out past the farthest waves she could see or far inside to that safe place inside her heart. Sylvie loved the world and loved life, and curses on the man who would want to alter that in any way. Despite her age, despite the deaths of four good — well, not perfect, but mostly good — husbands.

The currents of the Trough brought the whales in close to shore. Sylvie had seen her first whale here when she was ten. Alone, glinting up at the teasing sun it appeared, glistening, wet, and magnificent like out of a dream. It blew fountains of salt water up into the sky for her and showed its dark, mysterious eye. And blinked. Did that for her. Blinked as if to say hello, little Sylvie, then dazzled her with another shot of spuming seawater way up into the morning breeze.

She told no one for years, for she knew they were killing whales back then, the men of the island, killing them and stripping their flesh and cutting it into big square chunks as if the only way to civilize a thing was to carve it into slabs with right angles. Then what did they do with the flesh they robbed from the sea? Somewhere over in Ketch Harbour they cooked it somehow, did awful things to it. She did not want any of that to happen to this one.

While Sylvie was growing up, as the island was shaping her into a dreamy, sensitive young woman, the fishermen of the island stopped killing whales and went back to harvesting mere scaly fish. It was not an act of compassion but economy. Whale oil gave way to kerosene, thanks to a Nova Scotian inventor named Abraham Gesner. He saved many, many whales, Sylvie would one day understand. If whales were in heaven, then Gesner was there with them as a hero of humankind. And Sylvie was certain, even now at eighty years into a sometimes disheartening life, that there were whales in heaven. For if there were not, then she herself did not want to take up citizenship in that celestial republic.

Heaven would also have to be an island. An island adrift in an endless sea, a sea with dark, glistening whales all around.

The Trough brought to the island other unusual things over the years. Fish that no one had ever seen before. Some called them prehistoric, flushed up from impossible depths and killed no doubt by their disappointment at discovering that there were worlds other than their own bottomless, dark haven. Fish that turned out to have big, long, absurd foreign names that no one could pronounce. So they were shortened. One was a "Chuck," short for something like Chukensiatosiuk. Another was called by locals a cowfish because it seemed to have hooves. Some called it a devilfish, but there were already too many fish by that name in the sea.

Seals perched out on the shoals to wait and see what the Trough would bring by next. Dead men floated in during a pair of world wars. Sylvie had seen them both and was thankful that it was only one dead man per war.

Oh, before she was born, ships loved to come aground here. Ignorant British captains caught unaware by the zealous current of the Trough and then trying to counter the pull, only to ram aground on Rocky Shoal. Bleached pieces of those ships and a few bleached bones even still littered the shores along here, but once the sea has its way with a thing human or inanimate, it doffs it off its back up onto the rocks and lets the shoreward lift have it: waves and then the work of rust, lichen, and blooming red moulds. Old shoes, washed up, bloomed with life — moss and yellow pan flake lichen, soldier cap fungus and crawling natty ants. A little soil caught in a crust of heel and suddenly sea rocket grows green, then bursts a pale electric blue flower atop. Before you know it, some bird from Antarctica is foraging a meal from the worn leather of the toe and the succulence of a rotten lace filled with bugs only a bird can savour.

An island was a place to live and to die. Few had had the same privilege as Sylvie; she knew that, and felt blessed beyond even her years.

Two hundred and some people lived upon the island now, fewer than in the past, but enough. The peripatetic ferry made two crossings over and two back each day. Older kids would go to school on the mainland while the younger ones hung back a few years, taken good care of by the woman from the States, Kit Lawson, who knew the names of all the stars in the sky as well as the names of great composers, and who sometimes talked about seeing things on the moon with her expensive black telescope. Kit was as bad as Sylvie. Couldn't hold a man and did it by fours. Sylvie had seen it happen. Boyfriends, she guessed, not for marriage but here for the live-in type relationship as they do these days. Seemed serious enough. The first was an island fisherman named Ned. The next one had long hair and smoked a pipe, an intellectual type who spoke to everyone about politics. Having failed to convert anyone to atheism or socialism, some supposed, he fled back to the mainland and a job.

The third one was a dreamer — a poetic sort who lounged along the shores at the Trough sometimes and picked at a piece of driftwood until there was nothing left in his paws but salt. Always had a notebook but never wrote anything down. He too found his final ferry back to Mutton Hill Harbour and headed back to civilization. Then that last one. Nice, sweet boy who came and made friends with everybody. Started growing marijuana in the unused cabbage fields and found himself in trouble with the law.

None of the islanders held it against Kit. Sylvie had sympathized with her when it turned out the dope farmer was only using her, as men do on occasion, for mercenary purposes. His claim to fame was that he was an herbalist, but he had specialized in only one herb, the Mounties asserted.

There were no whales today. Perhaps in another week or two weeks they would return. This was the season of whales, and Sylvie knew that the whales had saved this island from ruin almost brought on by bad decisions on the mainland. Saved it for her.

Things were being cut back in Halifax. All sorts of things. People shoved out onto the streets, it was said, lifted hilly dilly out of hospital beds and told to leave. Women having babies in the morning and being carried over their husbands' shoulders later in the afternoon because things were tight. The government was pinching the pennies, making people feel they didn't deserve it as good as before.

Legislators as far away as Halifax and even Ottawa were trying to make her leave. Make everyone leave. They didn't have to steal your land from you, all they had to do was take away the ferry service and everything would begin to shut down.

But they would not do that. As long as there were whales. The whales brought the tourists, brought them right on through Mutton Hill Harbour and onto the ferry to her island. Moses Slaunwhite had dropped fishing like a hot potato and started taking tourists out to see the whales near the Trough. Moses knew the waters, had a big enough boat, and was raking in the cash. It was a sweet combination for all as it turned out. The mercantile interests in Mutton Hill Harbour scrambled for the money from the passers-through and polished up the town. Motel owners and bed and breakfast people suddenly had loved right whales all their lives, even the ones who had never even seen a right whale.

Hell, everybody loved whales now, and no one owned up to the fact that grandfathers with harpoons once slept ashore in those bed and breakfast beds with their old socks still on, socks soaked in slimy whale blubber. Now, by Jesus, everyone loved whales. And there was this economic link, as they were calling it. Ragged Island was the centrepiece. Jacked the prices up on the ferry but at least she still sailed back and forth. Once the warm months were over, it would go back and forth only once a day, but kids could still go to school each day on the mainland if need be, men would still work there and come home to the island. And Sylvie could still stay here, living alone at eighty, if she wanted.

She would pay no heed to all those well-meaning mainland friends who wanted her "safe and sound on solid soil." As long as she had the island she was okay. As long as the whales were there the tourists would come to gawk and take too many foolish pictures, and her brood of sea mammals would perform with a mere blink or a small geyser and let the mainlanders squint at the sun glinting off a sleek, arching back.

A whale could take the indignation of a thousand Styrofoam cups in the sea or a tossed jelly bean. A whale could handle that. Moses knew how to keep a fair distance, knew how to humour his clients but keep them from drowning on the Shoal, keep them from harassing the whales.

"You keep the whales safe and satisfied and the tourists amazed and the island will be safely looked after," said Moses to Sylvie. "Halifax is up to sending hired actors in oil skins off to Rhode Island and Japan with the news that they can touch the sandpapery skin of the beast if they fly here and bring their dollars and yens. Dollars and yens — that's all that matters nowadays. Perhaps a Swiss franc or two. But the Swiss are not so easily amazed. Remember, they were the shrewd bastards could keep the Nazis from coming over the mountains and disrupting their quiet little lives."

And so, Sylvie was certain, the whales would come back this year as every other. They would return for her because she cared for the island and she cared deeply for them. And now there would be no more men in her life, but there would be sea creatures and clear, sunny, squint-eyed mornings like this to last a person through her winter, snug in memories.

Chapter Four

Lonely without whales, Sylvie craved womantalk. Words to fill empty spaces in her life, chinks in the walls. Kit Lawson would do. It was a Saturday, schoolteacher's day off, and Kit would be alone now that her dope-growing young man was gone off to rehab or jail. Sylvie hoped it wasn't terrible punishment. He'd been a cheerful lad, seemed to care about the bees and the soil conditions. Understood rotting kelp and seaweed, was willing to learn all the tricks of gardening on an island like this. She hoped his motivation had not just been profit.

Kit lived in a large one-room house with a loft area for a bedroom. Once a fisherman's house, it was a dream come true for her. "When I first set foot in here," she told Sylvie, "this place reeked of authenticity. I asked Ned where the toilet was, and he asked if I needed to pee or do the other. I said I just had to pee, and he pointed to a little piece of one-inch black plastic pipe in the wall. I looked at it, then through the window, and saw it went outside and emptied into a little stream that grew ferns and cress. Ned had never encountered the problem of a woman having to take a pee in his old house, owned up to it, said it'd been a lonely several years. Then he built a first-rate outhouse. I had to tell him it had to be away from any watercourse. He said women were funny creatures, but he built it where I wanted it all the same. Built it like he was building a dory. Only certain materials, certain types of spruce wood he cut himself. Enough timber in it to withstand a gale. Guess he didn't want me to come to harm if I was inside one day and a hurricane happened. Men are funny creatures."

"Men are," Sylvie said. "Men certainly are."

"Sylvie?"

"Yes." Sylvie had a dreamy look on her face. Talking about how funny men are as creatures.

"Sylvie, do you know there is something about this place."

"The house?"

"No, not Ned's house, although I think it is special too, but the island. Do you think there is *something* indefinable about this island. I felt it the first day I arrived."

Sylvie worried through the pockets in her loose skirt looking for a handkerchief. "Oh, my dear. Something, yes. Not everyone can feel it, but you can, can you?"

"There's doubt in your voice, like you think I'm teasing. It's because I'm from away, right?"

"People from away don't always understand. Lord, many people who grew up here don't even understand."

"But I do."

"I believe that."

"It's not just the land," Kit said. "It's the sky, too. Everything is much clearer. Clearer up in the sky and space above this island, too. Last night I had my telescope focussed on the moon, on a place on the moon called the Bay of Rainbows."

"You're lying to an old woman. There's no place on the moon called the Bay of Rainbows."

"No lies. There is." Kit picked up, of all things, a teacher's pointing stick and went over to the wall where hung a big, round, blue saucer of a map. The moon. She pointed to a place and read it off: "Bay of Rainbows, just north of the Sea of Rains."

Sylvie was hamstrung. Felt like a little girl in school again. "So there it is," she said, as if the universe was a stranger place than she had ever thought, something like a fairy tale complete with astronomers sitting on mountaintops coming up with exotic names for places on the moon.

"Sylvie, I saw a bright light there as I was looking at the Bay of Rainbows. A flash."

"Moonmen?"

"No, I think not. Another asteroid on impact."

"That's what all the craters are about, I suppose. A wounded old thing, the moon is, isn't it?" She felt a kind of kinship there. All her men dying, belligerent asteroids battering the face of the moon in the night.

"Wounded indeed. Look at that sorry old girl." Perfectly natural that the moon must be feminine. Not a man in the moon at all. Wounded old girl. A couple of million years old. Up there hanging over the earth. No atmosphere to help ward off chunks of rock gamming about in space.

"I've never felt closer to the moon than I do on this island. Back in Massachusetts, back when I taught in Boston, I sat on my rooftop and the moon kept me sane when I felt like I was going crazy."

"Some people used to say the full moon *made* you crazy. Women especially, our blood all controlled by the movement of the moon, our periods and all that."

"Oh, women are tidal, for sure. I'm certain of that. Back then in Boston, I always found myself looking at the big crater called the Sea of Crises — *Mare Crisium*. Everything in my life seemed in perpetual crisis. Men at my door in the night trying to bust through seven locks to steal my TV set. Children in my classroom, high as killer kites on crack cocaine. Air sick as the sea and all the while noise, noise, noise. I'd sit up there on a clear night in my lawn chair on the roof camped out on the Sea of Crises. Thought that was what life was all about."

Sylvie felt slightly dizzy suddenly. The mention of children did it to her. Sylvie had never had any children. Not exactly the way she had planned it. Husbands were like children sometimes. But she knew it wasn't the same. But there were plenty of other people's children out there in the world. Without family, sometimes Sylvie felt totally and hopelessly alone. Not often. But sometimes. It was like she had moved to the moon, camped out in a lawn chair in the sea of whatever — Sea of Sylvie Alone. "What about the children?"

"The ones back in the city?"

"Yes. Did you try to help them?"

"Yes. I did." Kit had suddenly lost her enthusiasm for the geography of earth's satellite. "And almost died trying. Every time I got involved, it would be the parents or brothers or some guy selling the stuff who came at me and threatened me to stay clear. I tried and tried until I realized it was killing me. If I'd stayed I would have gone after one of them, the big dealers, would have gone after him with a can of gasoline in the night and burned him to hell."

Sylvie wanted to ask if she was so dead set against men selling drugs to her students, how did she end up with a guy growing weed on this island. But she kept her thoughts to herself. Knew it was part of life's complications. Nothing simple, clear cut, ever. The idea of children stoned out on something called crack cocaine filled her with a big pool of sadness in the very centre of her being, made her feel ancient.

"The island restored me," Kit said. "The island children too. So polite. Call me 'miss' all the time. The one-room schoolhouse. Boys in big rubber boots. The fact they all cheered when I brought back a wood stove for the middle of the room, to supplement the electric heat. The fifth-grade boys carrying in firewood to feed the stove while we studied ancient Egypt."

"Too bad the school board made you get rid of the stove again. I always liked the smell of softwood burning, brought your mind alive."

"Spruced up your senses, so to speak," the schoolmarm said with a clever inflection. "Oh well, it reminded me I wasn't beyond the leash of civilization. Taught me a lesson. Kids suddenly seemed to be all that much more helpful once they saw I had lost a battle with authority. They were even kinder after John was arrested. I guess I knew what he had been up to, but John had this silly dream, believed marijuana would do no real harm. Felt that if he could bring a milder, more natural, and less harmful drug back into use, sell it cheap — no, not to kids — well, that would keep people from getting all caught up in the dangerous stuff. Mind you, I wasn't fully convinced of this. But he always had a way of putting a good spin on everything. Even this. Something good will come out of it for John. You wait. He believes in lifelong learning. Self-education. Probably learn from his time in the institutions. Write a book about it, rise back above it. I miss him, though."

"I know all about that."

"I'm sorry. I guess you do. I have no idea what it must feel like to lose a husband."

"It takes some practice, but you never get used to it. Men underfoot can be an annoyance, but when they are gone, it seems as if they get themselves all polished up in your memory. Can't remember a bad thing about them. I still find an old shirt in the back of the closet and put it up to my face and it's like he was a prince, a king among men, finest man ever to put two feet on the floor on any morning. You forget the other stuff."

Then silence arrived like an unexpected house guest, didn't knock on the door or anything. Just barged in, took the place over. Silence, a masculine silence. Sort of commandeered the big one-room house, tromped about, rattled the dishes, bumped into things like men do. Silence nonetheless. Two women staring away from each other for an instant and then back.

"John said he'd make some money from his plants and then we'd set up a camp here for kids from the city. A safe place, a happy place. They'd study the moon at night and we'd watch whales in the day. Go back to growing cabbages without pesticides."

"Men have to have dreams, don't they?"

"While women do practical things, is that what you mean?"

"Not always. I just think our dreams are more down-to-earth. At least mine were. But now I don't know anymore. Living alone, you turn a bit inward. A good thing and a bad thing. Winter was hard but now this is summer. It feels good, but I need my whales back out there. They've never failed to show up."

"There's time," Kit said. "Moses'll be in some sour mood if they don't show up. All those tourists coming out on the ferry to get on his boat. If he doesn't have whales, he'll be a sorry captain."

Sylvie looked back at the map of the moon, its big, round, sallow, hurt face. She read the name of the great crater she was staring at: the Sea of Tranquility. She tried to imagine the man who would have named it thus. But Sylvie knew the real, true sea of tranquility. It was here surrounding this island on a summer morning and it took up residence in her heart, kept her tides in check during the hard times.

"It's not just a big dead thing, is it?" Kit said.

"No, it's not. It's alive. Everything is. Everything. In its own way."

Kit saw silence creep back in the room, wandering around, looking into cupboards, thought it wonderful that an old woman who had lost so many men to graves, a woman who must've hurt a hundred times more than what her hurt felt like, could still say a thing like that. Sit there, a little damp-eyed, and just spit it out without question. Everything alive, nothing dead. That was the lesson of the island. You can't really kill a thing. It's all alive, all you have to do is understand that, see it with your eyes, feel it in your bones. Dig deep and the news would always be there but you needed to hear it out loud from someone like Sylvie sometimes. Those few words embraced by masculine silence. And silence finally giving up on its own power, stopping to listen to a woman speak words, words that worked their way into all the important little crevices in the wooden walls. Words, sealing the place up against the cold. Words married to the silence in a good way. Ceremonies like that. Island ways.

Chapter *Five*

Timing was the key to Moses Slaunwhite's life. He was the first child born in Nova Scotia in the year 1951. The very first. His father had watchmaker's blood in him and had a house full of Swiss and German clocks, all set in perfect accord with a short-wave radio report he received regularly from Greenwich, England. The scratchy report would always go like this: "When you hear the long tone following a series of short tones, it will now be something o'clock Greenwich mean time." Then followed annoying radio noises, several short and one long, and that would be something o'clock on the hour on the other side of the Atlantic. Moses' father, Noah Slaunwhite, would subtract several hours to account for time zones and he'd have it precise, then race around the house checking all of his clocks right down to the second hands swirling about their orbits as if they could give a damn about precision.

So from the start, timing was everything, and Moses was evicted from the warmth and security of his mother's womb at one minute after midnight Atlantic Standard Time on January 1, 1951. Just as planned. Moses' father was very proud, especially of the exactitude of it all. Moses' mother was in considerable pain and couldn't wait to drop the placenta and be done with bringing another child into the world. She wanted sleep. Lots of sleep.

Now, it so happened that the newspaper in Halifax had a contest going with dozens of prizes for the first child born in 1951. Why the owners of the paper thought it was such a great thing to be the first baby of 1951, nobody knew. As far as they and the fun-loving public were concerned, when it came to babies in this contest, you didn't have to be the biggest, the prettiest, the happiest, or the smartest. You just had to be the first. Some mothers missed it and failed to achieve the goal, ending up with a really late 1950 baby. Some hung on too long to their parcels of delight and waited until several minutes of the new year had slipped by and other babies had already popped out from North Sydney to Yarmouth.

But Moses arrived at 12:01. The head appeared at midnight exactly and the whole child had emerged, rather perfunctorily, within one minute, tops. The father was proud, the mother was exhausted and near unconsciousness as was the way with women giving birth.

It was New Year's Day in 1951 and Noah Slaunwhite was in his boat frothing his way across the waters to Mutton Hill Harbour to make a phone call to the *Herald* in Halifax. A proud father alone in his boat, having left his wife home to sleep and heal with a neighbour woman named Sylvie who would attend to any worries should they arise.

Now there was the problem that Noah hadn't expected in his precision-laden world of clocks and watches chiming on the hour every hour, even on his boat where the clock was called a chronometer and housed in polished brass. The problem with his timely, successful son was the remote location of where he had been born so precisely.

A cold mackerel of a young man was holding down the baby hotline at the *Herald* office, an unhappy lad who had been forced to miss all the fun of New Year's Eve sitting at the newspaper office taking telephone and telegraph reports of babies being born. If another woman called from New Minas or New Glasgow to tell the news of her son or daughter he would have to report the same sorry tale. It was all too late. Too late to win.

And then this call from a man with a strong South Shore accent, this Noah Slaunwhite on the horn from Mutton Hill Harbour. Said his son was born at 12:01 on the dot at home on Ragged Island, wherever the hell that was. "I'm sorry, sir, but in order to be eligible your child has to be born in a hospital and the official time recorded by a doctor."

"But there are no hospitals and no doctors on our island."

"Then I'm sorry, but your child is not eligible."

Noah Slaunwhite began to curse in German. The young man at the *Herald* had not heard German cursing before except in black-and-white war movies. The cursing was loud and guttural, offensive but interesting, and he held the receiver a short span from his ear and listened until Noah's rage had vented itself over the telephone wires stretched like tense violin strings from the South Shore to Halifax on that chilly January morn.

After the rage was pumped into that thin phone line, probably scaring off any number of birds that had been riding out the windy morning with toes gripped around the wire, Noah slammed the phone back in its socket. It rang, and a phone operator came on the line asking for another fistful of quarters for the long distance phone call. She must have been listening in on the line because she sounded offended.

So Moses' arrival in Nova Scotia was not properly heralded with those seemingly infinite prizes that he deserved for his promptness. There would be no full year's worth of Quaker Oats cereal, no hundred-dollar gift certificate from Mills clothing store, no shopping spree at Simpson Sears, no free baby carriage, no free oil changes for the proud father's car (if he had a car), no parental handshaking with the *Herald* editor-in-chief, the mayor of Halifax, and the premier himself. All down the tubes. Ah, hell.

Noah drank one cup of black hot coffee in Mutton Hill Harbour and then steamed back home with the bad news.

But none of that was little Moses' fault. He had arrived on time like his father had wanted him to. And if the *Herald* could not recognize the bravado of that, oh *Gott*, what did it matter? Moses' timing would remain good ever thereafter.

When he was twelve years old, he happened to be walking down towards the wharf on the mainland for the ferry ride back to the island when young Calvin Whittle fell through thin ice on Scummer's Pond. Moses was there to hear the scream, grab a rowboat oar, and shinny out on the translucent ice to tug the mainland kid to cold safety. Whittle's father owned one of those big, overdone houses that sat on a grassy shoreline, offending most island people who had to pass by it on their way home. Calvin Whittle's father was greedy, ostentatious, and hired many men to manicure his lawn (all of the above offended islanders), but he did like to reward bravery, so he gave Moses Slaunwhite a savings bond worth $500 that would come due when Moses was nineteen. It was a lesson in investment as well as a reward.

The salvaged son of Calvin Whittle, Senior would grow up to be a sex offender and a murderer. None of which Moses could have foreseen. In later years he would ponder the irony that in having saved one life, he had inadvertently killed three innocent women and cost the provincial purse plenty to keep up with the Whittle estate's lawyers, who tried in vain to keep a rich man's son out of prison.

Nonetheless, Moses had made good with his five hundred dollars. With it he bought a boat when he was nineteen. And as soon as he had a boat, island fishermen had found themselves headed into five good years of profit from cod, cod, and lots more cod. Moses married Viddy Grandy, a beautiful young woman he'd sat alongside of in the island schoolhouse when he had been only nine. Viddy was talented — she played piano and flute. She was smart. She knew the names of all the capitals of all the nations on the earth. She had a good business head — could advise any man about selling his cod whole or in fillets, whether to sell it to the restaurants in Halifax or ship it on ice to Boston. She had a gift for many things that would make a man happy as well as profitable. Her only twin afflictions were an affection for large, stylish, but sloppy and frivolous hats, and tardiness.

If it hadn't been for Viddy's lack of respect for the clock and Moses' own good timing, they probably would have never married. One damp, cheerless day in April of Viddy's twentieth year, she had decided to leave the island and go take a job in a factory she'd heard about in Saint John, New Brunswick that made fashionable women's hats for the American market. She was packed and rushing to make the three-thirty ferry but missed it by five and a half minutes — according to Moses' Swiss pocket watch that his father had given him upon graduating from high school.

So there was Viddy, floppy hat in hand, her head bowed, long braided hair down to the middle of her back, sobbing. Clearly, there must have been more to it than a missed ferry ride. But Moses' timing as always was good. He had a clean handkerchief that his mother had ironed. He had just had a shower and didn't reek of cod or lobster. He had to sit down because he had just gotten a cramp in the calf of his right leg. The fog looked like it wanted to lift (but never did fulfill the promise). And the ferry would not return that day due to a bad batch of diesel fuel pumped on at the dock in Mutton Hill Harbour that afternoon by Hennigar's Marine Fuel Service Limited. The rest would be marital island history.

Noah and Moses would argue often about Viddy's tardiness, but never in front of her, and, despite this small canker of family strife, it was a good and happy marriage. Whenever she was ashore, Viddy would drive their mainland automobile to all the Frenchy's used clothes stores up and down the South Shore and buy umpteen hats. Whenever she returned from the mainland on such a day, everyone on the ferry boats knew what was in all those boxes and bags. Moses built many closets. A hat was never thrown away by Viddy. But he didn't mind. She was a wonderful woman and gave him twins — Clay and Dawn. When Viddy went hat hunting on the mainland, their good neighbour Sylvie would mind the kids and tell them stories of the island in the old days. When Sylvie would babysit for a day, all the clocks were turned towards the wall and the household schedule went to hell. Neither Moses nor Viddy cared, and once Sylvie was gone, they would not turn the clocks back to face them for well over twenty-four hours.

Moses was generally healthy, and his only real affliction was the predilection of his body to cramp up in the legs. This was a result somehow of having become soaking wet the time he hauled

young Whittle out of Scummer's Pond. His father made him
carry a cramp knot in his pocket to ward off the problem. A
cramp knot was an actual knot from a tree, a cat spruce in this
case. It was an old German folklore thing and it didn't work, but
he carried it anyway to make his father happy.

"It doesn't work because you don't believe in it. We used to
believe in everything when we was young, but not no more," his
father said.

"I try to believe in it, I really do," Moses said. And he carried it with him everywhere, even to bed to dispel the damn leg
cramps, because Moses would get a leg cramp attack any time,
any place. Hauling up lobster pots ten miles at sea or making
love to his good wife Viddy late on Friday night after a chow-
der dinner and several pints of dark, homemade German beer.
The cramps would always come, reminding him of the irony of
saving Calvin Whittle who killed those poor women.

Moses was always one step ahead of the fishery, it seemed.
Already moving into herring roe or silver hake, red fish, ground-
fish, swordfish, or sea urchins when absolutely necessary, and,
when it seemed that the whole fishery along Newfoundland and
Nova Scotia was ready to go belly up for good, Moses anchored
his boat on the edge of the channel at the Trough and he pondered the future. When the whales appeared like long-lost
German cousins, he talked to them and, although they didn't
exactly talk back, they convinced him they were the future of
the island, perhaps his only hope.

Moses knew that if he was going to stay on his island and
remain prosperous, if he wanted Dawn and Clay to grow up
with a roof over their heads and a chance to go to Dalhousie
University or the Sorbonne or even just business or beautician
school in Halifax, he had to time this thing right.

Whale-watching, it turned out, was already taking off in California, Alaska, Baja, Maine, and Maui. As his left leg began to cramp up and he rubbed a thumb on his shiny cramp knot, he phoned the tourist bureau in Halifax and then a travel agency in New York and told them about his whale-watching cruises that were going to begin in the summer of 1993. In two years, while all the other fishermen were grovelling for government handouts to help them through the death of the Atlantic cod and the decimation of the fishery, Moses Slaunwhite's boat had a fresh coat of paint, and he had on clean shirt and pants and a kind of one-off captain's cap designed and hand-sewn by Viddy. He also had a whole load of mainland tourists crossing on the ferry to the island dock to gleefully hand over a fair sum of Yankee doodle to have Cap'n Moses lead them to the blues, the fins, the minke, and the right whales.

Moses had been kind to the whales. Careful as an Old Testament shepherd to his flock of sea creatures. Never too close, never noisy, always full of respect and caution. How many times had he heard a Brooklyn accent say, "Can't you take us closer so my kids can pet one?"

Moses smiled, never let his feathers get ruffled. He pointed out the barnacles on the backs of some whales, the ones he had named Joshua, Rebecca, Naomi, and David. Although he wasn't particularly religious, there was something about giving whales Biblical names, if they were to have names at all.

"Where's Jonah?" someone would ask.

"Inside one of them, no doubt," Moses would answer.

A specialty eco-tourism agency in Chicago got wind of Moses' operation and made a business proposition that he couldn't refuse. His excursions were suddenly part of a world circuit of tours that sent nature-starved city dwellers to the seven seas to observe whales, dolphins, sea turtles, and flying fish. Moses even came up with a specialty bonus of taking visitors to sea on calm summer nights to see "devil's fire," that brilliant, green, glowing phosphorescence of certain diatoms that turned the Atlantic into something eerie, beautiful, and awe-inspiring.

Some islanders begrudged Moses' success. Some spoke of creating competition, but none followed through. Moses bought a second boat, hired on several island men and a couple of women, paid good wages, and was ever careful not to push his visitors too close to the whales. On bright summer days, when he had his boat anchored near the point, he'd see Sylvie sitting there on the shoreline watching the whales. He gave her free rides to sea but she said, "The whales only talk to me when I'm sittin' ashore. They know me there. I know them."

Sylvie baked fresh bread and cookies for the tourists and set up a table by the docks. People paid her well for her creations — the bread, the cakes, the little cinnamon cookies, the home-made ginger snaps. She loved the children the most and gave them freebies when their parents weren't looking. Sylvie was glad other people came to share the whales with her, glad they came to share the beauty of her island.

The only glitch was that the new wave of tourism brought a lit-tle too much attention to Phonse's Junkyard, his shoot 'em up theme park. The travel office in Chicago received some com-plaints from folks who had returned to Des Moines or Poughkeepsie and told of an environmental time bomb clicking away in Moses' otherwise picturesque island. They'd seen the wrecked cars, the oil laden-pond, and heard the *carwong* of bullets hitting things. Only a matter of time, they said, before toxins would leach into the soil and out into the sea or until the rifle-bearing maniacs would start using whales for target practice.

"We'd like to see if you can bring government pressure on closing that place down," Chicago told Moses. "You need to protect your investment up there. Eco-tourists don't want to hear elephant rifles pumping lead into washing machines. They don't want to see junk cars rusting away in the sun. These people want nature in its purest state. If they wanted junkyards, we'd send them to New Jersey. If they wanted gun fights, we'd send them to Detroit or Washington D.C. They don't want that. They want nature. They want *the real thing*."

"I'll see what I can do," Moses said, and he felt a new cramp forming in his arm this time, the one he steered the boat with. That night, after sending the kids over to stay at Sylvie's for the night, after making love for the second time to Viddy, he discussed the problem with her.

"I can't tell Phonse to close down his place. It's his life. He's not hurting anyone."

Lying in bed with his wife, Moses felt a huge responsibility settle upon him like someone lowering a steel-hulled ship on his chest. Phonse had been his friend since childhood. Phonse had been there to throw a coat around him after he'd retrieved Calvin Whittle from Scummer's Pond. Moses thought his heart was going to cramp up, and Viddy massaged his chest with her hand as if on cue. "The island has to come first," she said. "You have to do what's good for the island."

Right then, Moses didn't think that helped at all. What he thought she was saying was that he should listen to Chicago. He knew that if he wanted to get the government involved, he could have Phonse closed down in the blink of an eye. Phonse's salvage yard broke just about every environmental and safety regulation and statute in existence. And, in truth, to clean up Phonse's hellhole would be cleaning up the island. But it was all wrong.

Sleep came to him like a dull, senseless rain — cold, with pellets of ice collecting on the back porch of his brain.

In the morning, however, he had an idea. He talked to Phonse about fine-tuning his operation and opening the gun range to some of the eco-tourists.

"I'm always open to new ideas," Phonse said. "Innovation has been the key to my success. Acadians were always open to new ideas. We come over here and the Mi'kmaq tell my people to eat this root. We eat it. Prevents scurvy and tastes almost good. They tell us how to hunt the animals, we hunt 'em. We survive good because we always adapt. Now we don't have to hunt the animals no more. And that's a good thing, too."

"You understand the nature of eco-tourism?" Moses asked. He was never comfortable with that large, floppy, uncomfortable word the people in Chicago used when they spoke to him. But somehow he had heard himself say it out loud to his friend.

"I understand it if you understand it, I guess."

"Good enough. I just wanted to make sure you were with me on this."

Phonse probably didn't have the foggiest notion as to what was going on, but yes, he was in. Phonse was always in on a new idea, ready to adapt just like his ancestors.

At first Chicago thought the idea was outlandish. "A theme park showing the ravages of cars and industry and neglect?"

"Yes. And tourists can, if they wish to pay extra, take up firearms and shoot at symbols of environmental offense. Cars. TVs. Absolutely no hunting, though, of course. No shooting at anything living. Only manufactured things worthy of an eco-tourist's anger."

"Shouldn't that stuff all be recycled?"

"This *is* a form of recycling. And I've already convinced the owner to use only non-lead bullets. Simple iron pellets or bullets will work. Won't harm the ecosystem. Put a little iron back in the soil is all."

"I don't know," Chicago said. "This all sounds pretty radical."

"Think of it as cutting edge. Our timing will be perfect."
And he was right. The plan turned out to be a hit. Viddy helped
design the new brochure. Phonse fine-tuned his junkyard tourist
attraction. Pacifists and eco-freaks turned out to love pump-
action rifles and guns with infrared scopes. Oickle's Pond
brought satisfactory remarks of haughty disgust and financial
donations to clean it up once and for all. Locals sat side by side
with tourists from Pennsylvania, all wearing ear protection, and
together they laid waste to products of the industrial world.
Phonse brought in a car crusher on a barge once a month. It
smashed up a considerable amount of the metal goods shot to
hell and shipped off the steel for proper recycling. He was paid
a good fee for the scrap and it allowed room for new targets to
arrive by boat from wherever — Blandford, Shelburne,
Dartmouth, or Lunenburg.

Chicago was somewhat shocked and appalled to learn that
eco-tourists loved to shoot at things. As a result of word-of-
mouth reports, eco-tourism to Ragged Island increased by
twenty percent. The premiere package tour included two days of
whale-watching at the Trough, a day of eco-revenge at Phonse's
salvage yard, and, for an extra fee, you could operate the car
crusher on recycling day, which was the third Wednesday of
every month.

Chapter Six

S ylvie, alone in the late afternoon, collecting her thoughts.
Oh, what a great collection of thoughts. They would fill up
some big old South Shore barn, those thoughts, memories.
Goes a ways back and then some. But the blackflies in the
afternoon, that made her think of her husband, her first
husband. David Young.

It had been March when he'd been away. Two days of
warmth all of a sudden, three maybe if you counted that surpris-
ing burst of warm wind that came in the middle of the night like

a lost Arabian horse running wild with hot breath through the sky. The blackflies came out like it was July, pestered islanders right through the brief freak warm spell, then died right off. It had been the entire great summer swarm of insects — annoying little blood-sucking bastards that some hated much more than mosquitoes. Died off and never returned that whole summer. *The blackflies*: that's what made Sylvie think of husband number one.

Both seventeen when they married. It had all started with the high rubber boots in the old schoolhouse.

"What on God's green earth is that smell?" the old teacher asked. She was a wonderful teacher, that Missus Lantz. But, watch out for yourself when things went wrong and she took after that pointer stick she kept sheathed in the rolled-up map of North America.

"It's the boots, Jesus," David said and ran to retrieve them, his and Sylvie's. High rubber boots set tight side by side like lovers, too close to the scalding black metal of the wood stove, old knotty spruce logs ablaze inside warding off winter in favour of education. David had set his own boots there alongside of Sylvie's. He was always doing nice things for her. "Wants your feet to be warm and dry," he had said. Such a gentleman for a boy.

They were melting. Oh, my God, what a stench. Everyone grabbing their noses and pinching. The little ones taking the opportunity to howl and screech. Missus Lantz opening the door to winter and inviting the old gentleman in. "Everybody out," she finally said. "Can't teach with this!" Melting boots meant freedom.

"Whose bloody Wellingtons?" she asked as David scrimped low across the room to grab the boots and haul them out.

"Sorry, ma'am," he said. "My fault." David grabbed the steaming boots and heaved them out into the snow. The little ones ran from where they landed as if the devil had been thrown to catch them at play.

Sylvie remembered going out to look at her own boots and saw that one of them had melted itself onto one of David's. Lying there in the snow, the two black boots stuck together, the smell still something you could not quite pinch out of your nostrils.

"I was hoping to get them nice and warm for you. And dry inside, you know?"

Sylvie felt weak and shy. Not like her at all.

"I'll buy you a new pair when my dad takes me in the boat to Mutton Hill Harbour this week."

"It was an accident."

"I know," David said, smiling now. "Everything's an accident. That's what my grandfather told me the day he died. I'm named for him, you see, and he was named for his grandfather."

"What do you mean, it's all an accident."

"Everything good and everything bad. All an accident. This snow coming down. Missus Lantz back there trying to air the school out. The melting boots. The fact we live on an island like this. All an accident."

Such a goofy look on a young man's face.

"And you think that's a good thing, do you? You don't think God has a plan for us?" Sylvie had been told by neighbour women over and over, neighbour women out trimming cabbages or drying cod on wooden slats in the sun or collecting summer savoury from their gardens, the words had been oft repeated. "'Tis all part of God's great plan."

"God was the one responsible for making everything accidental. It's a big game for him, I guess. Wondering what accidental thing will happen next."

Sylvie knew that this boy liked to talk strangely at times, but his words made her head and heart feel light, like a pair of swooping herons, she was so out of kilter. Her with burning boots turning to deep religion and philosophy in the schoolyard snow.

Somebody was throwing a snowball straight at David's head, but it missed. A second was thrown. That lout Inglis, always bad intent. Another thrown and missed. David pretended not to see, but Sylvie stuck her tongue out at Coors Inglis. Another snowball, this time thrown harder and with worse aspirations, at Sylvie. David turned, put himself in the way, took it hard on the cheek. Looked over at Inglis, gave him a look but did not go after him.

"Sylvie, don't ever cut your hair."

"My hair? I wasn't going to cut it."

"Great. You have wonderful hair."

"It's only brown."

"Brown hair is the prettiest."

Sylvie had known the boy had feelings for her but those feelings had always been in check. Her own emotions had always been in check, too, the way it was supposed to be. Why did this absurd little compliment make her feel so powerfully changed? "I won't cut it," she said. "I'll let it grow long like summer vines."

"Thank you," he said, and now, for the first time, he touched the cold wet spot on his cheek where the snowball had connected with his face. Sylvie could not stop herself from touching the spot as well. Her eyes went woozy and she had to take a deep breath, then pulled her hand away quickly as she saw Missus Lantz come out to ring a bell, calling everyone back in.

"My grandfather wasn't a hundred percent right about the accidents, Sylvie."

"Oh, how's that?'

"You. You were no accident. You were meant to be."

That was the last year of school for both of them. They could have gone to the mainland for an extra year or even two if they liked, but they did not. Nor did any of the other students from the island school, for the mainland was considered to be a sorry, inferior place. Sixteen gave way to seventeen for Sylvie and for David. The year was 1934. Far away on the mainland of Canada, the Dionne family in Quebec had quintuplets, five girls and they all lived. In Germany, a new leader, a *führer*, was sworn in. This man named Hitler would order the construction of concentration camps in Germany for Jews and Gypsies. Off the coast of Nova Scotia the fishing was good, but the prices were less than they should be.

In June of 1934, young David Young married Sylvie Down. Sylvie liked him more than any other boy on the island but she did not know if it was what she truly wanted to do. Her mother said *she* liked David and so did her father. That was not advice or parental pressure. Sylvie's father spoke thus: "Comes from a good family. Good stock. Father's a reputable man. Respectable family. Can't see the harm." Understatement was Sylvie's father's way.

"Women will have more opportunities in your lifetime, you know," her mother said. Something she picked up at the Women's Improvement Association meetings and in the newsletter that came once a month. "We want what's best for you."

"Can't do much better than David," her father had said, but there was still not a quarter ounce of pressure in his voice.

Sylvie felt herself to be the water in the North Brook — clear fluid, pure, slipping down with the pull of gravity towards the waiting sea. It was not an unpleasant feeling at all. She believed there was little control within her to change anything about this elemental force. Sure as the water drawn down the stream, she would marry, she would become the sea, and then what?

The day she said yes to her David Young, she asked him to go with her to sit on the rocks out by the Trough and be with her there all day. David said he would be honoured. Alone on a day in early June, blackflies held imperceptibly at bay by the cool presence of the open sea, they sat arm in arm. Only one whale appeared. It came up once from the deepest part of the channel, surfaced, spouted, let the sun perform for one silver moment upon its dark, wet back, dove deep again, and fanned its tail in a salute or goodbye.

A flock of tiny shorebirds appeared and settled on the rocks nearby, picked through the rotting seaweed that smelled like something sacred to Sylvie and David. Beach peas and sea rocket grew between the stones. A few fishing boats found their way across the sea in front of the island — too far from shore to make out who they were. Year-old seals came up on the flat stones of the shoal and lay on their backs, then at length slipped back into the sea.

The day made her love David more for his silence, but it also gave her mixed emotions because she didn't know if she loved him or the island more. She wasn't sure she could love both, and even though she would not be moving away, she felt like she was betraying some intimate, profound relationship. But she did not fight the sonorous current within her that would bring them to marriage in the little Baptist church with the bare walls, hard seats, and the endless drone of old turgid hymns cauterizing everything that seemed alive and chaotic and wonderful.

In Sylvie's eighty-year-old imagination, David Young is still alive. Still sixteen, or maybe eighteen. His was the privilege of not growing older like the rest who remained on the island. Sylvie sees him as being yet another gift that the island gave to her. A gift with tenure. Time and memory have polished David, the first husband, like a beach stone, into something hard and true. Born of chaos, a child of a family who believed the world was ruled by chaos, by chance, David had come to her, grew up with her through childhood as if an invisible other, and then crystallized suddenly one winter day into something that would be the centre of her life.

Sylvie sits alone with a cup of cold tea on a summer afternoon in her backyard carved from the forest, her back to the sea, surrounded by tiny flowers of early summer. Spring beauties, blue violets, Indian cucumbers, and the fluted, spore-laden stems shooting up from the furry green moss. She has the great gift of knowing truly where she belongs. Here. Now. Inside her, time can drift. David is still with her and she can smell burning rubber boots and she can feel the pinch of biting blackflies although there are none out at this time of day.

Their first night of marriage, they talked through the darkness. They touched, yes, but only tentatively, briefly, fingertips brushing hair, tracing the collarbone at the neck, palms resting on the other's elbow, hands cupped on the other's shoulder. Sylvie was amazed at David's love of ideas, notions. "Suppose we have children, good children, healthy children, and they lead good honest lives and grow up and they have children, good children, happy children, well-meaning children who have their own after that. And one of those children, our great-grandchild, becomes an inventor or a scientist or something and discovers something truly, truly wonderful, like a way to feed everybody on earth so no one will starve, right? And this is a great wonderful thing."

Sylvie wondered at the odd nature of thinking of this man she had married. Here she lay in bed, expecting to be treated to some kind of new experience, some physical thing that both scared her and fascinated her. She had been warned it could be a harsh thing sometimes, but she was prepared, mentally and physically. But this was not the way at all.

"Now suppose this new discovery gets into the wrong hands and is used to create famines and starvation instead of preventing suffering. Suppose thousands or more die. Just suppose that happened."

"David, what?"

He let out a long sigh. "I don't know. Does that mean it would be wrong for us to have a child that would lead to such a terrible thing?"

"How would we know?" Sylvie asked.

"We can't know. That's it. Each of us, each married couple like us, has the power to possibly change the world for good or bad. And we can't do a thing about it."

"Then why concern ourselves with it? What can we do?"

"We can't and I guess that's my point. I'm sorry. It's my grandfather talking here," David admitted.

"I didn't know I was climbing into bed with your grandfather," Sylvie said, teasing.

"Don't get me wrong, I want to have children. As many as you want."

"I want ten," she joked.

"Ten it is. Why not twelve?"

"Twelve is too many to feed."

"We'll start with one and see how it goes from there."

"I want all of our children to stay here on the island."

"So do I," David agreed. "But once they outgrow us, we can't make them stay."

"No, but we can make sure they love the island like we love the island."

David said nothing.

"Do you love this place?" she asked.

"I do, but not in the same way you do. I could almost be jealous if I wanted to."

"Do you want to be jealous?"

"No. Let's go to sleep now."

Sylvie has a swarm of pictures in her head, the tea some strange, exotic drug now that has catapulted her mind into another place. Things that rule her life: fish and cabbage, the backs of whales in sunlight, that mysterious moon pulling the sea slowly in and out every day, the swimming seals. Generations of German and English and French ancestors, for she could trace her roots to all three. The island had lured all three nationalities together.

And she remembers David, standing in oilskins not a hundred yards offshore, hauling up nets with cold, slapping fish, a great steady stance he had in that dory made by his grandfather. She could still see the silhouette, the slanting posture, the wet net in his hand, back bent under the weight. His steady hand with a strong pull. While David stood there, German soldiers on the other side of the sea were slaughtering innocent families, preparing to slaughter the French and the English. In her memory, though, those two brief years of her first marriage, less than two years really, were a tenured stint in paradise.

March of 1936. Bad news for the fishermen. Almost no market at all for the valuable catch. Hope, however, in the fact that big ships would dock soon by the government wharf and look for men to go to the ice floes in the Gulf of St. Lawrence. Good money to be made from seal pelts.

"I'll be gone no more than a month. Hard work, but we need the money. Save some up, spend some to build up the old place here. Plenty of food on the table after this no matter what the fishing does. Do something nice for you when I get back. Don't fancy the thought of staying on a big sloppy metal boat that long with a bunch of mainlanders, but they say the *Allen Grant* is a good solid ship, steady captain and all that."

And all that. Sylvie did not like the thought of butchering baby seals. The greys, the harbour, the hooded ones. She was opposed to the idea. Did not want to debate the difference between catching fish and killing baby seals on ice floes near Isle Magdalene on a ship captained by a Lunenburg man and owned by Halifax investors, they said.

"Good chance to maybe set a bit of money by and eventually get my own boat. Fish prices will come back. Here's an opportunity at building a thing up. Maybe something better for our young ones down the road."

And like that, one morning, he was gone, and Sylvie was waking up alone in her bed. A March morning. Rain. Eight days of it. Walked to the sea every day, the sea of rains. Pelting, icy, cold, drenching. Her own oilskins and high rubber boots to protect her. Seals right up on the island shoreline, one or two with big, round, dark eyes, not even afraid of her.

Even then she still felt the tug of the current. She stopped and stared at the clear little brook, the wet, glowing moss that looked so vital in any weather. Sylvie dropped a twig in the rapids and watched it get swept away, then catch on a shelf of root, then swirl in a little eddy round and round, then disappear down the watercourse.

When the news came back to her about David, it was delivered by his father. David's father — a stout man who carried a hat in his hand almost always, worrying its brim until the brims wore out. He came without his wife, knocked once, walked in. Winter had completely slipped away in the rain and left a damp, warm procession of days. Blackflies, mistaking it for summer, had come alive. They were in the man's hair and he brushed them away, a dozen of them, tiny black gnats. He caught one, however, and pinched it between thumb and forefinger, then stared at the burst of blood, the red stain like a lost thought on his finger.

"On the ice," he said. "Shift of wind. Up 'til then things'd
been going good. Nearly ready to return. Ice so unpredictable at
that time of year. David was always one to be cautious, you
would know that better than most. But he went in, not much
after sun-up. Too far from his companions, I guess. Couldn't get
a proper grip on the ice, lost his pick, legs and hands going
numb, I suppose."

Sylvie didn't hear a thing beyond that.

"Guess we'll hear the full story when they come back. It's a
sorry thing for all of us."

He swatted at blackflies again as he put his hat back on his
head. "Sorry for ... bringing all this in," he said, waving at the
bugs as he walked back out.

So, at eighty, Sylvie still imagines this scene, created from the
clever guesswork of her imagination.

The sun is just barely up, shining bright. A man, her husband, climbs down from the side of a big metal ship that sits like
a human grey disgrace in all that white, frozen beauty. Her husband rows with the other sealers across calm water laced with
bits of ice stubble, docks besides a solid white sheet, flat as a stove
top. She hates that pickaxe in his hand and can see the dried seal
blood on the sleeves of his coat. She sees him head off away from
the rest. Preferring to be alone at the dirty deeds rather than
talking it through with the others.

She hears the crunch of his rubber boots on the hard snow
atop the ice. A short hike across the frozen expanse and there's a
mother with several seal pups. She sees their dark human eyes.
Sylvie cannot help but think of those eyes as the eyes of children.
The irony, the terrible irony of her David, so fearful of the future
— of inadvertently committing some crime against humanity —
doing this. She will never voice her view that her husband is
some kind of killer, that they all are. It will be a private condem-
nation that she can closet away from the world of speech. For she

loves this man deeply, has travelled every twist and turn of thread of thought in his mind that sent him out onto the ice at sunrise.

David is doing this for her, for their children who will never be born. She will forgive him. She hears his ragged breath as he hurries, stepping across one small space between the ice pans, a distance no greater than hopping across the North Brook. She sees the boot land with a hard thwack on the ice. She sees the axe swing free in his hand. She wants to be able to see his face, but she cannot. Perhaps it's better that way. What would she see in his eyes? Determination? Exhaustion, more likely. Eyes fixed on something a million miles away. Thinking of her, perhaps. Thinking of the island.

David stumbles on a small ice ridge, collects himself, walks on towards the mother seal and her several young ones. The ice is bleached pure and white as white can be. A sound can be heard now as the other men drive axe picks into the skulls of young and old seals alike as their mothers howl and try to defend their brood, only to find themselves butchered too. Something so appallingly wrong with this scene that it is inconceivable to Sylvie that she herself is somehow connected to this. But she is connected, inextricably so. This spectacle is part of her life, will never leave her.

David, she knows, is now sick at heart and exhausted beyond anything he has known before. Aches for his island and home, vowing never to sign on for such a thing as this again. The sun is over his shoulder and he turns to feel the slightest tingle of warmth, warm as the breath of his wife asleep beside him on a winter night when he cannot begin to find the proper channel markers that will lead him to sleep. But he is exhausted still on this morning, his feet are like stone weights in the bottom of lobster pots.

He has learned to read the ice, knows that he can trust even small pans if they have the right texture, the right look about

them. He thinks he knows this frozen landscape, but he is
wrong. He makes a leap onto a small ice pan, feels it tilt and give.
He is amazed as he realizes that his brain had already given him
the signal that it was a wrong step. Old instincts working but a
split second too slowly, failing him. A steady stance in a dory is
not the same as walking on springtime ice. He drops the pick,
feels himself sliding, as if he has fallen onto a big kitchen table
face first and its wooden legs give. He tries to grab onto something and then realizes the small ice island is upending itself and
coming fully over on him.

Cold knives of water fill up his boots and his oilskins and
the hard ice comes down above him, shutting out the light and
the sky. His hands form into fists and he pounds at it, then tries
to push it away, but it has suddenly become a cunning, cruel
thing of immense weight.

Sylvie feels the bursting pain in the throat of her husband as
he tries to scream, tries to claw his way along the underside of the
ice to find the sweet, living air to feed his lungs. She feels the panic,
the fear, things completely new and alien to her calm, cerebral husband. Then suffers the immense sadness and regret that comes with
his final exhaustion and the knowledge of his foolish error.

Sylvie draws a deep breath and tests her own breathing.
With eyes still closed, she can see the surviving seals upon the
ice with the morning sun warming their fur. She hears other
men shouting in the enthusiasm of their bloody work but she
does not turn in that direction. She is looking to the east,
towards the rising sun, blooming warm red and yellow over the
panorama of the ice field. She makes what peace she can with
David's belief that we live or die by chance alone. And envisions
what is left of her husband, floating up in the stream between
two stolid ice islands, his back to the sky, rubber boots keeping
the feet afloat, his face down, as if something is of extraordinary
interest on the bottom of the ocean.

Chapter Seven

Todd Sanger, twelve years old, from Upper Montclair, New Jersey, peered over the side of the steaming ferry boat. "Diatoms," he said to his little sister, Angeline. "I bet there's millions and millions of diatoms in there." Todd was a smart kid who loved science; anything that had to do with science was very dear to him. His father had nicknamed him Beaver after an old TV show, but the kids at Upper Montclair Elementary had shifted it to Beavis.

"Do they all have names?" Angeline asked.

"There are quite a few different subspecies, and yes, they all have names. Scientific names in Latin."

"Wow."

"Some of them glow at night."

"I'd like to meet them."

Todd just gave her that big-brother look. Girls, what did they know?

Actually Angeline knew a lot. She knew they were going to a magic island where fairy-tale people lived in gingerbread houses. She knew they were going to see whales. Whales and fishermen, and now they were sailing over a bay of diatoms, several million of them with Latin names and a lot of them friends with her brother. This is what Angeline knew and she perceived she was in a happily-ever-after story because that's the way that all her mother's stories ended for her.

It was a day like no other she had ever experienced. Sun, sea, gulls like gravity-free dancers in the sky. Angeline's mother and father by the railing, arms about each other. Angeline had only been on one other ferry before in her life— the Staten Island Ferry, where people spit over the side and ground cigarettes into the floor. Everyone on the Staten Island Ferry coughed and so did she when she traversed the dark waters of New York.

No one was coughing on the ferry to Ragged Island. There were maybe twelve other people on board, and they all looked interesting to her for she knew they must be island people, all torn from the pages of a story book.

"God, smell that fresh air," Angeline's father, Bruce, said. The air wasn't really fresh at all but permeated with diesel exhaust from the big engine turning the propeller that churned the harbour waters beneath them.

"Do you think there's much poverty on the island?" Bruce Sanger's wife, Elise, asked him.

"I don't think they have poverty here in Canada, at least not in the same way as in the States. People in rural areas might be poor but they tend to be self-sufficient."

Elise gave him that dubious look wives give their husbands when husbands pretend to know things that they really don't. Elise was very concerned with social issues and volunteered her time to various organizations to stop child labour in Pakistan, to end cruelty to lab animals in Switzerland, and to alleviate educational deficiencies in the inner city in places like Newark and Paterson, New Jersey. "We'll see," she said. She knew that if there was any genuine poverty to be found on Ragged Island, she would sniff it out and rub Bruce's nose in it. It wasn't that she was cruel. She just liked being right.

"This is going to be extremely educational for the kids," Bruce said. "I think it was worth the long drive."

"I wanted to tell the manager of that motel in Maine that the moose head on the wall wasn't appreciated."

"It was kind of spooky. But I'm sure it was just an artifact of days gone by."

"Still. It wasn't appreciated. Killing animals for sport — that's not a matter to be taken lightly."

"I agree." Bruce hadn't told Elise yet about every aspect of this curious eco-tour that the Chicago Internet tour agency had lined up for them. She knew about the whales and the island but not about Phonse Doucette's junkyard. Bruce should not have been attracted to anything involving guns but something about this caught his fancy. He was hoping there would be something else on the island — after the whale boat tour — to attract Elise and the kids and keep them occupied. Poverty might work after all. If there was poverty, Elise would detect it and go to work studying it and he'd have some time to himself. Todd could go with him, maybe, while Angie tagged along with her mom for a look at island poverty. Bruce hoped he was wrong about poverty in Canada, after all. If there was a big junkyard, there must be poor people nearby, Bruce reasoned, but he knew he was far out of his familiar territory.

Familiar territory to Bruce Sanger was his office at Small, Smith and McCall Investments. He had an important job as a stock analyst and advisor for a currently fashionable mutual fund called the Earth First Fund. It was an "ethical" fund, at least as far as anything could be ethical in the investment patch. Right before the trip, he pumped ten million dollars into an environmentally friendly ceramic roofing tile plant in Chile that was reported to be labour friendly. He'd also brought about a big push of the fund's money into a geothermal power source in California and a super blue-green algae health food product company in Oregon. He wondered if there was something in a place like Nova Scotia that the ethical investing world had ignored. Something that did not diminish the ozone layer or rile Greenpeace and yet returned an 8 percent dividend each year. He wondered.

The island grew upon the horizon ever so slowly as they steamed on. "We must be travelling at thirty knots," Todd announced to his sister.

"What do you mean?" In her mind, a knot involved a piece of rope. "How do you know?"

"I just do. It's a nautical term. Nobody ever says 'miles per hour' at sea. You're always travelling at so many knots."

"And we have thirty of them, right?"

"Right. I bet the water's over twelve fathoms deep here."

"It is?"

"Could be deeper. You could tell if you had sonar."

"Who is that?"

"It's not a who, it's an it. Tells distance from an object, underwater. Pretty cool for old technology, when you think about it."

Todd had his doubts about old technology, though. He pondered how his father's generation could have grown up without remotes for TVs. No laptops, no Internet. He was thankful he had been born when he had been and often suffered disbelief over the undeniable fact that people had lived in his parents' time without the basics.

Todd was looking forward to the whales, of course. He'd read a book on cetology and considered a future in research at sea. Diatoms glowing at night. Lots of high-tech equipment. Maybe go down in a submersible and see really ugly creatures on the bottom of the sea. This boat ride was a good start — give him the feel for life at sea. And he liked what he found so far: on a boat (old nautical technology, but that had already been factored in and was to be expected), travelling at about thirty knots in twelve fathoms of clean salt water. If you fell overboard you'd drown if no one scooped you up right away. That added an element of danger, which he liked. Todd leaned far over the side of the railing and peered into the frothing water by the hull of the metal boat.

"Careful, Todd," his sister chastised him.

He ignored her but suddenly felt a hand on his shoulder. For a split second he imagined it was someone about to push him overboard. He'd heard about that happening on the Staten Island Ferry. Instead, the hand gently tugged him back, and he turned around to see a young man in greasy overalls, a small blond mustache and a curious kind of smile on his face. "Wouldn't lean over like that, lad, if I's you. Could fall in. Chilly still, ya know. Too early to swim. Gots to be careful." Alistair Swinnemar was missing three teeth where they had been punched out of his right jaw. He still had a hand on Todd's shoulder.

Alistair lived on the island and often got into trouble, but he was kind and good-natured as a general rule. He feared the little tourist kid might go overboard and he'd have to go in after him. Not much of a swimmer, like most islanders, but what could you do if a kid went splash?

Alistair let go of Todd and laughed at the look on the kid's face. Todd was wondering how this galumph got away with touching him. If this had been New Jersey, and a stranger grabbed a kid like that, he would have been arrested. Alistair saw the goofball look on the kid's face and shrugged, looked at the kid's sister and she shrugged too. Angeline liked the funny-looking islander who had maybe just saved her brother's life. She wondered if they all talked like that on the island where they were going.

"Going to have to hire an interpreter if we want to understand them," Todd said to Angeline after Alistair had walked away.

Angeline saw trees on the island now — tall, dark green evergreens like in the picture books her mother read to her at bed time. She saw a few houses that seemed as if they had come out of the pages of books as well. All brightly coloured, the ones along the shore. It was like watching a Disney movie with a really slow but nice beginning. Arriving at a new place, far from home. Diatoms in the water, gulls making noises like "cronk, cronk, cronk" in the air. The sound of the big engine. A sky big like a huge blue bowl turned upside down over your head. She couldn't help but giggle.

"I've never seen a place like this before," her brother grudgingly admitted. The island slowly grew larger and this reminded Todd of the shots of Jurassic Park in the movie, the helicopter coming in from the sea. If he was lucky, he conjectured, there would be raptors.

Bruce smelled fish as they approached the government wharf on the island. It reminded him of walking past the kitchen at

Tomile's Spanish Seafood Restaurant in Greenwich Village. On the way to the washroom you had to walk past the kitchen and the smell of seafood was not always that pleasant there. Dead fish is still dead fish.

Crates of lobster in seaweed were waiting on the island dock for a trip to the markets on the mainland. Several hundred confused lobsters, kidnapped from their deep private lives and hoisted aloft into an alien world. Lobster intelligence, brain evolution asleep at the wheel for a thousand years. Exoskeletons did not always protect. Some sort of evolutionary trade coming on here: a family arriving from the greater New York area, just getting off the boat as bug-eyed crustaceans from the local sea floor head south to feed the fat faces of businessmen from the same locale. An exchange of hostages. The lobsters getting the raw end of the deal. Nutcrackers, claw crackers, who knows what awaiting them. Pliers maybe, electric cutting tools, vice grips to help get at their meat. Destiny awaiting.

"This place reeks with authenticity," Elise said. Colourful old lobster pot floats hung from a big poplar tree. Cars without mufflers idled on the concrete wharf and greeted returning husbands, wives. Alistair Swinnemar lollygagged, talking to the hangashores, and then threw one leg over his Yamaha dirt bike and started it up, spit broken clam shells under the tires, and roared off, the engine sounding like a bumblebee amplified through an old Marshall amp with a really big stack of concert speakers.

The Sangers disembarked and clung together like they had just gone back in time. Bruce surveyed the shoreline; saw a square white building with particle board walls and a sign: "The Aetna Canteen"; saw people driving big, old, rusty cars slowly up a gravel road. No license plates. Men and women with tanned, creased faces like potatoes left in the bin too long. Bruce knew he had found what he was looking for — something completely unlike his familiar Wall Street world or the claustrophobic backyard universe of his neighbours back in Upper Montclair. Something like this. *Authentic.* All his life he had dreamed of authenticity, felt he was trapped in an artificial world where nothing was true. This was the proverbial real thing.

He walked down the wharf toward land and Angeline picked up a small dried starfish that had been dropped by a passing gull. "Poor thing," she said. "Can we bring it back to life?"

Todd harrumphed. "Sure. If we had the right enzymes."

"Can we buy enzymes here?" Angeline asked.

"I doubt it," Elise said, looking at the marker buoys hanging in the trees and then at the small garden patch behind where aluminum pie plates dangled from spruce posts in the light sea breeze.

"Your brother's not telling the truth," Bruce said.

"I read it somewhere. You can bring things back to life with the right enzymes. Not people maybe, but some things."

"Perhaps. Angeline, I'm afraid it's dead. You can keep it if you want. A souvenir."

"I don't want a souvenir. I'd rather it came back to life." She tossed it into the clear water near the wharf and it floated a second, then sank to the bottom.

Bruce scanned the hill ahead until he saw what he was looking for: sunlight glinting off the windshields of junk cars, what looked like hundreds if not thousands of them. He cupped his ear to listen for the *ting* of rifle bullets hitting car doors but heard nothing. Too early in the day, perhaps.

Elise wondered if the reading levels of the children in the island school were far below the national norm. She considered other assorted problems that might beset an isolated island like this. Incest, inbred families maybe. Already she'd seen signs of a critical need for dental help here. True, it didn't appear to be anything like the urban poverty of New York or Newark, but she was sure there was a quiet desperation here, people in need of help, her help. A report could be made to her club back in Montclair. It was always on the lookout for unsung charitable causes. Some people in a place no one had heard of before in need of real assistance. This could be the ticket.

The Sangers had walked right past Moses Slaunwhite's whale tour boat. The sign was down for painting, touching up. So instead of loitering and asking for information on whale-watching, the New Jersey family sauntered toward the only commercial establishment on the shore: the Aetna. "Lobster sandwiches $4.95," the hand-painted sign read. "With or without Sauerkraut." "Beans and Bread $3.95." "German Food Upon Request." Elise wondered what the German food could be: things made from intestines and ground kidneys, no doubt, or fatty sausages with dry, caked blood. She was not a fan of anything German, particularly their food.

Bruce asked the girl at the cash register inside if she had any bottled water. Niva? Aquafina? Perrier? But the girl shook her head no.

"Got some pop in the cooler. Pepsi, Doctor Pepper, Sprite."

"Any ginger beer?" Elise asked. "Or Snapple?"

"Sorry, just what's in them cans."

But everything in "them cans" was Pepsi, Doctor Pepper, Sprite. Bruce bought four cans of Sprite and they retired to the lawn outside, where they discovered an old woman sitting at a picnic table with a display of home-baked goods in front of her. She had no sign or anything, and Bruce silently asserted that here was the least aggressive salesperson, if she were indeed selling anything at all, that he'd ever seen. It would be worth a laugh back at the office where his colleagues prided themselves on being the most aggressive traders in the ethical stock markets of Wall Street, if not in North America.

The old woman was looking at them. Not begging them to buy with her look, just smiling, being friendly. Angeline ran over to her and looked the old woman straight in her eye.

"How old are you?" she blurted out; to her, the woman looked positively ancient. She had never seen any woman who looked this old before. Both of her grandparents were dead and she had been privately in search of a grandmother for the last year of her life.

Sylvie looked at the child whose parents remained at a cautious distance. "I'm eighty," Sylvie whispered, "but if your folks ask, I want you to tell them I'm a hundred and one."

Angie clapped a hand over her mouth and her eyes burned with happiness.

"Have a cookie," she said, "it's on the house." She handed over a large chocolate-chip cookie, bigger than any Angie had ever seen. It looked brown and delicious and the size of a dinner plate. The surface was all bumps and valleys, crags and flat-bottomed craters. It reminded her of a big blown-up picture they had of the surface of the moon back in her classroom at the Montessori School on Maple Street.

Angie held the cookie up to the sky until it perfectly blotted out the sun, creating a wonderful personal eclipse for her. "I know what this is," she said.

"Shh," Sylvie said. Adults approaching. The Sanger family had decided that if there were things to be bought, money should be spent.

"How much do we owe you?" Bruce asked.

"That one is a gift. But you can help yourself to the rest if you like. Flax bread, banana bread, oat cakes, gingers there. Carrot muffins and some other stuff as you see."

Elise realized that what she really craved was a bagel. A bagel with cream cheese — but she wasn't that audacious as to open her mouth and say it. Nothing on the table came close to looking like a bagel.

"Todd, see anything here you'd like to munch on, kiddo?" Bruce asked his son.

Todd surveyed the home-cooked baked goods before him as if studying Amazon foodstuffs made from smashed bugs, pounded roots, and maybe the lungs of small tropical birds.

Bruce got the point. "That fresh bread looks really good. You make it yourself?"

"I did. I love to bake. Just don't have anyone to bake for."

Elise felt a tug at her heartstrings. *Old woman alone, out of desperation she bakes for the scant tourist trade, lives in a tarpaper shack without sanitary facilities.* Missed the true story altogether, but she now gave Sylvie eye contact as if it was a small monetary offering. Woman to woman. An understanding of the trials and tribulations of life. *God, she must be at least ninety. That face, like tanned leather. Something about her so pure.*

"Give me two loaves of this," Bruce said, picking up a loaf of something that could have been pumpernickel and one lighter brown calf-coloured loaf that might have been made with a high fibre grain. He believed that a woman like this would work with organic goods but he surmised that there was shortening in there too, fats and cholesterol that would clog up his arteries. It would taste good, damn good, and he'd eat it because it was made by this sweet old gal, but he'd lose a day off his life for sure. Price to pay, always.

Elise reached into Bruce's wallet when he pulled it out, gave Sylvie a twenty, said keep the change. She tried to wrestle small bills and change out of her dress but the family was already walking away. Only Angeline hung back, the north pole of the cookie moon chomped clean off as she dribbled cookie crumbs for the shore birds to find later.

The sign was back in place now: "Slaunwhite's Whale-Watching."

"You folks are just in time," Moses Slaunwhite said, as they arrived to study the spotless, shiny cape islander captained by Moses Slaunwhite.

"We the only ones?"

"Looks that way, but not to worry. You get the personal treatment. It's early in the season. We're just getting 'er up to speed."

"Guess we're on board then."

"Watch your feet. There you go. Where you folks from?"

"New Jersey," Elise said.

"Heard of it," Moses said. "Heard all about it. Never been there, though. Lots of places I haven't been. Bet it's pretty down there in the States."

"Sometimes," Elise said. "But it's not like this. This is something."

"It *is* something. We all love it here. Couldn't make me leave the island if you bribed me with a wheelbarrow full of thousand-dollar bills."

"I can understand that," said Bruce, fantasizing what it would be like to have a job where you went out every day in a boat. Not like watching computer screens with numbers, making phone calls to corporate executives of coffee companies in Equador. Not like anything he did.

"You kids like to go fast in a boat?"

Todd shook his head yes.

"Watch this." Moses gave her the gas and the engine roared. The boat lurched forward and dug a deep wake behind them. It wasn't what you'd call speed-boat fast but it was good special effects.

"How fast can she go?" Todd asked.

"Maybe forty knots, maybe more."

Todd smiled and looked at Angie, gloating over the fact he was privy to this nautical terminology.

"Don't want to scare the whales," Elise said, loud enough to be heard over the roar of the engine. Moses winked at Bruce and then throttled back the engine to a dull roar.

"We're gonna come around the southern tip of the island now and be on the open ocean side. See them birds on the rocks drying their wings. Cormorants. Might see a few seals up there too lolling around on the flat rocks. Eiders there off to the left. See the baby ones. The male, he's the one with colour, the females just lookin' kinda dull. That's how you tell them apart."

Elise turned away from the overt sexism of the eiders, stared into the sun, adjusted her Raylon sunglasses, and reached for her zinc sunblock tube in her pocket. *Men and talk.*

"How's the fishing?" Bruce asked

"What fishing? Fish all killed, dragged to death, vacuumed up, gill-netted, what have you. Still some lobsters. See those lobster pots over there. Belong to Gillis Jobb. Yep, still a few lobsters but it's not enough to carry a family through the winter. Cod's been racked and ruined. Mackerel comes and goes and herring — if the big ships find 'em first with their sonar, they suck the bejesus lot of them all up and nothing left for the inshore. I don't know what comes next."

"Sounds like a hard life for a fisherman."

"That it is, me son, that it is. Oh well, naught for it. You folks like a coffee? Cappuccino? Got a cappuccino machine inside, the kind they have in the Irving gas stations."

Elise thought he was joking. She blinked. Bruce wasn't sure. He was way off his home turf where even the whimsy of the stock market was predictable within a margin of error. The very word, "cappuccino," came as a shock to his neural network here on this boat at sea. "I wouldn't want to cause you any trouble."

"No trouble. Here killer, take the wheel." Moses tugged Todd over to hang on to the steering wheel. "Just keep her aimed to sea, that's it."

Captain Moses went below and came back in a few minutes
with two steaming china cups of cappuccino. He had installed
the cappuccino machine last year on the advice of the tourist
agency in Chicago. Up until then he'd never even heard of cappuccino and if he had he would have assumed it to be an alco-
holic drink, something rich people gulped down to get loaded in
places like Monte Carlo or Rome. Turned out, he liked the stuff
himself. And the cappuccino caught all the tourists off guard. The
word of mouth on Moses' cappuccino probably brought him an
extra thirty clients last year, more loot in his pockets. Moses was
a man with good instincts when it came to business. All he needed today was to get in close to a couple of whales, send this innocent family back to Jersey with stories of sea wonder, and more
Yanks would come this summer, almost guaranteed.

He prayed to the sea gods that today there would be whales.
Had to be sooner or later. But it had been a bad year, a real bad
year for sightings, and that had never happened before. The only
whales he'd seen this year were miles and miles off shore, too far to
take the tourist trade, took too much time to get there, much more
dangerous, all wrong. Why were they not coming in this year to
the Trough? Another bloody thing gone wrong with the sea. If the
whales disappeared, what would he do next? Had to stay one step
ahead. Not enough money to be made in a lobster season — too
few of them, season too short. Tried the sea urchin thing but the
starfish population got out of control, ate up most of the urchins,
left the gourmet-goers in the Tokyo sushi bars starved for the little pink mess. Price went through the roof but not an urchin to be
found on the sea floor. So, there *had* to be whales.

Chapter Eight

Well, there was more sun and more sea, a little cooling salt breeze, a fresh slingshot of a wind with bits of saltwater to hit you in the eye or on the cheek every now and then. To Angie it was all magic, every bit of it. Magic Ragged Island, magic sea. A captain of a boat who smiled a lot and looked like he came straight out of a storybook, but most of all she kept thinking about the old lady. Could she have been even older than anyone thought? Angie guessed she might be two hundred years old and that was her secret. She'd been around for a long time. The little old lady who lived in a shoe, maybe. Certainly her skin had a leathery look. Angie hoped she would see the old woman again. Her pockets were stuffed with leftover cookie crumbs. Cookies made from the moon, crunched up and ground around in her pockets.

The real moon had just let go of the tide about two hours ago and the water was rising. The Trough would be full and deep soon, the best time for visiting the whales.

The cappuccino had not been bad at all. Elise would not report it to her friends back home, however, for it detracted from the concept of an island with some kind of endemic poverty or social ills, the story she wanted to tell at her women's group. No, the cappuccino on the whale boat would not do at all. Cars without mufflers, men without teeth — that was much better, and an old indigent woman trying to eke out a living by selling baked goods to scant tourists. Nice.

Bruce Sanger was staring off into the Atlantic, conjuring Jacques Cousteau. Hadn't they just said on the news that Cousteau had died last week? The passing of a legend. Like Cousteau and like this Moses Slaunwhite, Bruce Sanger reckoned the sea was in his blood. This very sort of maritime adventure was what he was cut out for. Maybe ethical funds, even Earth First, were not enough. Maybe he'd missed his calling as an eco-warrior of some sort. There would be Zodiacs to be launched and Norwegian whaling ships to be stopped single-handedly, French nuclear testing to be halted during countdowns, that sort of thing. God, what a life it'd be. Not like Jersey and Wall Street at all.

"See that old house out near the cliff there," Moses said to Todd, who looked a little green around the gills, maybe a tad seasick. "I was born there. Yep, that's the place. Looked out my window one morning and saw a water spout headed my way."

Todd's eyes lit up. "Like a tornado at sea."

"That it was. So I ran outside like a fool. I was just a boy like you, not much to look at, just a thin strip of a lad. I ran out on our little wharf to see it better and *wham*, before I knew it, the thing was upon me. I lay down and held onto the boards and thought I could hear the nails ripping out. I saw my rowboat lift out of the sea and then I felt this pummelling of water and I thought I was a gonner. But just like that, the spout disappeared."

"Wow. Think we'll see one today?"

"Not likely. Haven't seen another since. Freak thing of nature. That's the way the sea is, though. You just bloody never know."

The wind slackened as they rounded the front of the island, and Moses guided his boat into the Trough. He dropped an anchor just this side of the shoal and cut the engine. "Should be some minkes and right whales to see today. Maybe something bigger."

Todd and Angie peered over the side. No whales. Todd spied a big jellyfish that he called a Portuguese man of war but he was guessing.

"What does it eat?" Angie asked.

"Diatoms," Todd guessed. "Plankton, maybe."

Two and half hours slipped by and no whales. Greenpeace Zodiac daydreams had worn themselves out. Bruce didn't want to hurt the captain's feelings, but it was getting late. He cleared his throat. "I think we might as well go back now. We all understand, all of us in this family, that this whale-watching is not like Disney World or something. You can't just make a whale appear, after all."

"Why not?" Angie asked, for she still believed this was an enchanted place. There was the magic island right in front of her.

Maybe the whales were all off somewhere grieving, holding a wake for Jacques Cousteau, Bruce imagined; that would explain it. But he would not say this out loud.

"Right you are," Moses said. "Guess I'll owe you folks a freebie. That's what I do, you know. No whale, no pay."

"We couldn't allow you to do that," Elise said. "We'll pay as agreed. It's been a good ride to sea. The cappuccino was lovely."

"Well, okay. As long as you are satisfied. What say we go back and lunch is on me. The Aetna Canteen. Fresh-cooked lobster all around."

The engine roared to life, the anchor was hauled up, and the boat arced around in a U-turn, headed back to the island's government wharf. Once underway, Bruce sidled up to the captain and quietly asked about the other island attraction, the shooting range.

"Of course. It's part of your package. I just wasn't sure you were a gun man."

"I'm not. It's just ..." But Bruce didn't have the right words for it. A fantasy of sorts, was what he had meant to say. Despite the fact that he supported gun control, donated money to the Lobby for the Elimination of Handguns, voted for congressmen who demanded better gun legislation, Bruce knew that he just had to get his hands on some sort of gun and shoot at things. When he'd read about this salvage yard and the interesting angle — "Get back at the technology you hate the most"— well, it stuck in his head like an old piece of chewing gum on the bottom side of a sixth grader's desk.

Elise would never understand.

"Can we go visit the old woman?" Angie asked. "After lunch?"

"The old woman?" Moses said. "You mean Sylvie. Sure, heck, Sylvie would love to have visitors. She's all alone. Some think she's a bit daft. Not me, mind you. Sylvie is something else. Four husbands. All dead. What a tragic streak of luck for a woman. But she's got the courage to keep on. I'll take you and your ma over there if you like. Remember, I got to make up to you folks for all this disappointment."

"No disappointment," Elise said. "Everything is fine. But yes, why don't I take Angie to visit this woman. Perhaps we can help her with some chores or something." Elise had no real affinity for "chores." She had hired help to clean her house, a top-of-the-line Maytag dishwasher for the dishes, professional men to call when things broke down. But today she would go slumming in the boondocks. Maybe down on her knees with a bucket of well water, a hand scrub brush, and some lye soap. Would be good for her. She was even looking forward to it.

Bruce had just seen the heavens open up and a favour granted from the gods of munitions. "Maybe Todd and I will go look around that old junkyard up on the hill. That'd be a real education for the boy."

Moses winked, understood. Todd endorsed the idea. "Maybe I'll get some good idea for a science project or something."

Sylvie was not there at her table by the Aetna but the family sat and ate cold, cooked lobster. Todd pretended to be dissecting his, collected all the little hard-cased eyeballs on crustaceous stalks and set them together in a pile. Angie could not eat hers, said it looked like something she'd like to keep as a pet, thought it might still be alive. Bruce knew enough to keep his mouth shut and to not report that it had undoubtedly been boiled alive, screaming even as it met its scalding fate.

Elise sucked the lobster meat out of the legs and Bruce wrenched his apart like he was wrestling it, savoured the sweet tail meat and even ate the green stuff that Todd mistakenly thought must come out of the lobster's brain.

They tore off big pieces of Sylvie's bread and ate it without butter. Delicious. Never had anything like it before from the best of the gourmet bakeries in Upper Montclair. There was a raspberry pie for dessert and ice cream. And then the women were off with Moses to find Sylvie. Before he departed, Moses scratched his forehead, pointed a finger up the hill towards Phonse's junkyard, and, cautious that Elise wasn't looking, raised a thumb, crooked a finger, and mimed the firing of a gun. The great conspiracy of men. Todd smiled, although he didn't quite understand.

Phonse Doucette greeted Bruce Sanger like a long-lost cousin, introduced him to Alistair Swinnemar, who looked vaguely familiar. Phonse's office looked like maybe a front-end loader had tipped the roof off temporarily and dumped in a load of car parts and technological junk. It had a chaotic lived-in look that Bruce and Todd both found very attractive. It was the antithesis of their orderly lives. Weapons in a glass case lined one wall. Old World War II rifles, shotguns, handguns.

"Guess you heard about us on the Internet?"

"No. Actually it was the tourist agency."

"Oh, right. Chicago. They think we're onto something here. Cutting edge, so to speak. 'Get back at technology.' They think we need to copyright the idea or patent it or something. Personally, I'm not in it for the money. It's just good, clean, safe entertainment. What's your pleasure?"

"This for real?" Todd asked his dad.

"We'll have to explain it carefully to your mother."

"Can I shoot, too?"

"What do you think?" he asked Phonse.

"Parental discretion advised, but I've seen boys younger than him put a bullet hole or two in an old Caddie and come up smilin'."

"Okay then, but only if it's safe."

"Safety first, that's our motto. Alistair, you wanna unlock the gun cabinet? I think we'll stick with the shotguns today for the first-timers."

"Right, Phonse."

Twenty solid minutes of safety instructions and father and son were deep in the centre of the junkyard in a dug-out kind of quarry adjacent to Oickle's Pond. Bruce had elected to shoot the bejesus out of a faded piss-yellow Volvo station wagon. Todd blasted away at a rusty VW bug with stick-on flowers.

"Lock and load," Phonse said. Nothing he liked more than to watch the smiles on the faces of trigger-happy tourists. Father-son bonding at its best, this time around.

"It's when the windows shatter, that's the part I like the best," Bruce announced.

"I think I hit the gas tank. How come it didn't blow up?" Todd wondered out loud.

"All fuel has been safely removed before using the vehicle as a target," Phonse answered. This lesson had been learned the hard way.

"If you like the sound of glass, Mr. Sanger, may I suggest we move you into televisions if you feel you're ready."

"I think I am finding my range," Bruce said.

"Yeah, Dad, can we? Can we shoot at TVs?"

A curious look to Phonse. "TVs, computer monitors, you pick or mix and match as is your pleasure."

So, while Alistair monitored the guns for safety's sake, Bruce and Todd assisted Phonse in setting a big old Motorola floor model TV in the centre of the pit. Acer and Goldstar computer monitors were also expertly placed, one atop each decimated car. Bruce's ears were ringing pleasantly from all the gunshots. Todd's shoulder was sore from the kick of the shotgun.

Bruce fired away at the computer monitors over and over until they were shredded into a ragged mass of plastic, wires, and riddled electronic fragments. But it did not compare with the magnificent implosion of the old TV screen on the Motorola. Todd brought television to its knees with one crippling blast from his shotgun. After that, the excitement dwindled.

Alistair suggested they fire at old five-and-a-quarter-inch floppy disks tossed in the air, but for these novice gunmen, it turned out to be a bit beyond their skills. Nonetheless, after two hours of therapy in the Phonse theme park, both men were pleasantly exhausted and knew it was time to find the womenfolk.

"Time for a beer?" Phonse asked. "I made it myself."

"No. Just tally up what I owe you and we'll be on our way. You do take Visa?"

"Visa, MasterCard, Sears card, if you have one. I can't do Air Miles, though."

"This has been amazing."

"We aim to please," he said taking Bruce's credit card. "Get it?"

Todd was polite enough to laugh.

"What do you do with all the stuff after it's been used for target practice?" Bruce asked, environmental conscience creeping up on him from behind like a stalker in Central Park.

"A lot of it is recycled. For what's left over, well, Alistair takes the Caterpillar and shoves the junk into a hole. We bury it. It goes back into the earth. It's only right."

Something continued to tug at Bruce's scruples as he was handed back his Visa card and signed his name in the usual place, surprised that the total for the afternoon fun was so much less than he'd expected.

"Tell your friends," Phonse said as they walked away, down the dusty road towards the Aetna Café.

"But not your mother," Bruce whispered under his breath to his son.

Bruce could not stop smiling. Yet he couldn't believe that he had allowed himself (and his son!) to indulge in such a thing. He swore to the sky above him that he was still a pacifist; he would donate even more money to the lobby for gun control. He would work for a cleaner world. He would do these things even as he silently admitted he was a hypocrite. *No.* He was a walking paradox. Everyone was. Better to understand the central ironies of your life and get on with it. Better than hiding them away in a closet. This was something to discuss with his wife when the time was right. Not now. No, not today. He would not destroy the euphoria of the day. A day without whales had turned out to be not a bad day after all.

Chapter Nine

M en, off to do what? Go to a junkyard. Well, that was a first for Bruce. Nonetheless, it was a good chance for mother-daughter bonding. That was an important part of what this vacation was all about, after all. She didn't have to read an article in *Cosmopolitan* to realize that kids didn't spend enough time with their overactive mothers these days. Complicated lives. Who didn't have a complicated life? Certainly, Elise Sanger had one.

Angeline was not only insistent, she was imperative. They would go knock on the door of the old woman, Sylvie. Not hard to find her, they said in the Aetna Canteen. Take the road from the wharf and when it splits, go left, out towards the sea, front of the island. Only a few of the "old ones" living out that way. Most sons and daughters had built homes away from the sea. Newer houses down thisaway, here by the government wharf. Closer to the ferry, easier to get back and forth to the mainland.

Elise thought she heard some kind of a blast off in the distance. "A gun?"

"Only them at the junkyard. Phonse and the rest. Old cars and such. Men and their little odd jobs," the canteen woman said. She wore a little button name tag that read "Binnie."

Maybe it wasn't a gun, some kind of air-compressed tool ripping a rear-view mirror off a car. What did she know about such things? Thought of her husband and son around all those rusty cars. Was it safe?

"The whole island's safe, ma'am," the woman said. "Not like some places on the mainland." It was a stock phrase for tourists. Binnie was working up a number of stock phrases for the summer tourists, if they ever got here. Seems that summer was a little slow gearing itself up. Everyone on tenterhooks, worrying about the whales and whatnot. Some slow returning this year, the whales were. Now these tourists back from Moses' boat tour and no whales. Poor old Moses giving them a freebie on him ... lobster dinners yet (lunches as the mainlanders insisted on calling them). If Moses was buying, she'd give him twenty-five percent off. And of course, there were no tips unless the tourists decided to go the extra distance. This husband had left an American five. Nothing to write home about, but it was a start. Undeclared income. No taxes to be paid on that bit, anyway.

Angeline thought the gravel made a little song underneath their feet. She studied the coltsfoot flowers growing by the side of the road, the pretty green spires of horsetail plants, saw a frog in a pond. Dragonflies the size of model airplanes. Small yellow birds sat on spruce boughs and chirped so loud she thought she might have to cover her ears.

Mother and daughter walking down a dirt road on an island. An enchanted island, Angeline was certain of that. Yet it somehow seemed so much more real than where they lived in Upper Montclair. Maybe that life had all been a dream. She was just now waking up. Waking up to blue sky, shredded cotton candy wisps of clouds. The smell of sea everywhere. Old barns, tilting to one side as if a giant had been leaning against them, taking a rest. Ravens sitting on the ridge posts, louder than the chirping yellow birds, big awkward voices echoing against the forest.

The road looked less and less travelled. Fewer driveways with cars, gravel giving way to grass and dandelion beneath their feet, two tracks and a hump in the middle, little blue flowers in the hump, and a well-placed bony boulder or two that was hungry for the undercarriage of the car of anyone willing to drive here without caution. Then a little driveway off to the left, a footpath really, leading through tall trees and opening up into a clearing.

An old house with weathered grey wood shakes on the walls, the same weathered shingles for a roof. Moss on the roof and lichen. Yellow and orange. A scruffy-looking chimney, tottering. Sylvie's house. Old woman in a shoe. Not quite. But this was better.

Robins hopped around in the early summer grass. A harmless snake lay on a flat slate stone, relaxing, slowly absorbing solar energy to bring it fully back to life. An osprey flying overhead. Angeline noticed it all as if in an instant, witnessed it all and absorbed it, said to herself, "This is me. This place. I am at some special, special place and it will stay with me for the rest of my life." She knocked on the door. They did not have door bells or buzzers or outdoor intercoms here on Ragged Island.

A door swung inward. *Open Sesame.* The old woman, blinking in the light. Slightly surprised. Not many visitors for her, Angie guessed.

Elise cleared her suburban throat. "Hope we're not intruding."

Sylvie adjusting her bearings. The word "intruding" had a funny foreign feel to it. People on the island usually didn't worry about intruding. You were either there to visit or you were not. You did not worry about if it was intruding. But these were not islanders. Mainlanders. Little girl and her mum. Sylvie smiled, opened the door as wide as it would go. "Not at all. Was just sitting alone with a not so interesting book. Close it up. Easy enough at that. Come. Sit. Angeline, isn't it. Cookie, girl?"

"Yes, please."

"Nothing to drink but tea or well water. No pop."

"It's okay. We're both okay. Angie wanted to come say hello."

"Tea, then. I'll make it weak. Won't hurt the little girl. Not much caffeine if you make it weak. Sometimes I make tea from tansy or mint, too. Grows wild in the backyard."

The old woman went to her sink and there was a hand pump. She pumped it up and down in a smooth stroking manner like she had done thousands of times in a life. Water in a kettle, set upon an electric hot plate. *So she has electricity,* Elise was thinking.

This must be what "rural" poverty is like. Elise kept her thoughts to herself, studied every detail, prepped herself for a debriefing with the women in her group once she returned.

Sylvie wore a long, theatrical dress, something clearly from what she thought of as "the olden days." And she was tall. A bit bent over, but tall and graceful. "Sit," she told the mother from New Jersey.

Three of them sitting at an old oak kitchen table, with knife marks in it, chips and dings, rounded edges as if from sheer use, not design. Three rocks positioned on the table for some purpose — or maybe just decoration. Three round, elegant, but common beach stones. The chairs: spindle-legged, flat-seated chairs creaked, thanged, hawed, and yankled with every little movement. Aside from that, the room was stone still and quiet. Outside, though, birds performed soundtracks for nature films.

Angie was still looking at the hand pump, had never seen such a thing or even heard of it. "Can I try?"

"Sure. Oh yes, dear. Please. Lots of water in the well. The island has lots of fresh water even though we're surrounded by salt. You'd think it'd be salty down there below too, but it isn't. Clean. Fresh. They say you should drink lots of fresh water, flush your kidneys and all that."

"You live here alone?" Elise asked.

Angie pumped the handle and water flowed into the sink. She smiled and laughed and held one hand under the flowing water, then touched its wetness to her forehead, a baptism ceremony.

"Alone now. Well, depends how you figure it. Husbands are all dead."

"All?"

"All four. Some died young, some older. Way it is sometimes. All good men. They're all still with me, though. In my heart."

Elise tried to look at the beautiful face of the old woman but could not. She was slightly embarrassed as Sylvie revealed so much so quickly to a stranger. Elise was used to small talk, endless small talk. Her crowd talked around in circles about trivial things for a long time before zeroing in on anything real and worthy of serious woman talk.

"Where does the water come from?" Angie asked.

"Oh, just out of the ground, dear. Free gift from the island. Out in the yard there. I found the spot a long time ago with a dowsing rod. Not much of anyone better than me with a dowsing rod."

Elise tucked her chin in. *Charming. A hundred percent charming. The old lady reeks of authenticity.* Wondered if this was part of the eco-tour somehow. Almost too good to be true.

"You knew where to find water?" Angie asked and stopped pumping, then splashed the last dribble of water onto her face, drew a little circle with it on her cheek like she was face painting.

"Yes, I did. Made the men mad, some of them. If someone wanted a well, they'd call me and I'd cut a bit of alder or willow and go tell them the best place to dig. Never failed. Now they think that's all superstition. Funny, that. No one bothers with using a dowser anymore even though it worked for generations. I did it for free. Now, if someone wants a new house, they call out a drill truck from the mainland, comes over on a barge and drills down through the rock. Costs an arm and a leg but they don't seem to care. The modern way is the better one. Old woman and a stick can't be of any use."

"I believe there has been scientific research," Elise said, coming to Sylvie's defence.

"Yes. Indeed. Somewhere in one of those books. I read it myself." Sylvie pointed to books. A whole wall of books on shelves. No illiterate old island woman here. "Yes. The United Nations workers in Africa still rely on water witches, as they are called sometimes. And it's almost always women who have the touch more than men. Women are more rooted in the earth. More connected with the sea. We're tidal, if you know what I mean."

"Yes."

"So if you ever need to dig a well where you live, give me a call. Not that I'll come up there to the States, but I could do it over the phone with you if you use one of them portable phones and go walk around your own backyard and hold onto the right witching stick. Don't think I'm silly. Did it once for some friends on the Eastern Shore. At their cottage. She in the backyard with a little hand phone. Me on the phone down at the Aetna. Everybody had a good laugh about that one but saved the boy a pile of money. No twenty dollars a foot to dig into the hard rock. No sir. Twenty feet into gravel and pure, sweet water, all they'll ever need and then some."

"Do you know any other tricks?" Angie asked.

"It's not a trick," her mother corrected.

Sylvie smiled, set out a plate of cookies, another one of small cakes, one of crackers, and a jar of relish and homemade mustard. Some preserves, too, then poured tea. "I added some mint and one tea bag. Fine for both women like yourselves. Tricks? Why, yes."

Three cups of tea steamed little twirling wraiths up into the sunlight above the table. Dust motes sailed like tiny hang-gliders in the shaft of light from the backyard window.

"It's not necessary."

"Just one then." Sylvie walked to the bookshelf and lifted off an old mariner's compass. Elise looked at all those books and then noticed the rocks sitting on the shelves as well. She realized, too, there were other rocks on tables or piled up on the floor as if some kind of art or avant garde sculpture.

The compass in its polished copper mounting was placed in the centre of the table. The compass needle floated on clear liquid. It was a relic, for sure, something that would sell for a mint back in a Montclair antique store. The compass needle wobbled, wavered this way and then that, until it found north and anchored itself on its little inland sea.

"So that's north," Angie said.

"North it is."

"Now watch." Sylvie took three smooth stones from the bookshelf and set them on a triangle on the table, framing the compass. She rubbed the palm of her right hand and then held it over the magnetic needle, closed her eyes but then opened one eye in a squint to get a look at Angie's intent face. Next she raised her hand up once and brought it back down on the compass, then fanned her hand left slowly, and then right. The needle moved with her.

Sylvie worked her hand around in a perfect circle and the needle followed her movement like a well-trained dog. Then she fully opened her eyes and showed that she had nothing in the palm of her hand.

Angie clapped her small but enthusiastic applause. Elise smiled, knew there was some easy explanation.

"Do you let us in on how the trick is done?"

"Absolutely, madame. No trick at all really. Magnetism. All basic scientific principles."

Two mainlanders waiting for the punch line.

"The lodestone in that floating needle came from this rock beneath us. I was born here. I live here, grow my food here, drink water from the well. The island is part of me just as that little magnet was once part of the island. We are kin. I belong to this place."

The smell of minty tea in the air. Stillness. No one reaching for cookie or cracker or homemade relish.

Angie wide-eyed. Elise suddenly feeling very remote, far outside of her comfort zone. The peculiar sensation tapped into something that had been simmering on the back burner of her mind. Something missing in her life. Some strong attachment to place. She had never felt like she truly belonged to any physical place, ever. They'd moved from one house to another since she married Bruce. Each time he stepped up in his career, it was always a new car, a new house, a new neighbourhood, and sometimes a new set of friends that seemed to go along with the move. Together as a family, yes they belonged. But no allegiance to geography, adrift in the urban-suburban sea of countless faces. No rudder, no compass with a true north bearing.

Sylvie bit into a cookie, looked at Angie when she saw the far-off drift in the eyes of the child's mother. "These are old skills women had before we started relying on other parts of our brain." Sylvie tilted the sugar bowl and purposefully spilled some sugar on the table. Then drew a picture of the earth in the sugar and curved lines arcing out and down from the north to the south pole. "Magnetic fields. Birds sense them. So do fish. Whales, dolphins. Most animals make use of these magnetic fields in their every day lives. People did too once."

"Is that the earth?" Angie asked.

"Yes."

"Is the earth made of sugar?"

"In a story it could be."

"It would get sticky if it got wet."

"Good point."

"Can I draw in the sugar?"

"Yes." Sylvie poured some more upon the table. Angie trailed her finger around like it was beach sand. She had never played with sugar on a table since she was an infant. "Oops, I messed up your earth."

"It's okay."

The child was occupied dissecting the planet into several triangles like it was a pie. Sylvie looked at Elise, who was coming back from someplace far off. "Ever feel like you know a lot more about some things than you should? Feelings? Intuition?" Sylvie asked.

"Sure. Often."

"Most of us push those feelings away. Replace them with reason. But an old woman has so much time on her hands. She follows some of those things in her head, things she feels. She discovers some interesting notions." Sylvie pointed to the books. "And then she discovers that she's not onto anything new at all. Old stuff. All in the books. Just sometimes hard to know what's true and what's false until you feel it for yourself. The island things, though, I understand. That part is always true. For me at least. Finding water? I just know. Make a compass needle move? My magnetism can be as powerful as the pull of the earth's, if I'm close by. You want me to tell you if it's a full moon, a quarter moon, or no moon at all without ever looking into the sky or reading it in the paper? I can do that too."

"And more?"

"Yes. More. Some of the islanders know. They have respect for these things. Most people do not. Is there any value to these ... these skills? I don't know. I don't think of them as *useful*. They just *are*. I can't imagine leaving this island. I just can't. It would be like shutting off *who I am.*"

Elise was confused. "Why would you have to leave?"

Sylvie shrugged. "An old woman, alone. Talks to the birds, the whales. Daft, they say. Needs to be looked after."

"You seem to be doing all right on your own."

"That's because I never really feel like I am alone. Angeline, what grade are you in?"

"Third."

"On the island, children still go to a one-room schoolhouse. Just like I did when I grew up here."

"Do they have computers?"

"Yes, two anyway. Two computers and one wood stove. My friend, Kit, teaches there. She knows more about the moon than anyone I ever met."

"Does she talk to the moon?" Angie asked.

"I don't know. She studies it. She has names for all the seas. Sea of Rains, Sea of Clouds, Sea of Serenity, Sea of Nectar. Sea of Tranquility is the name I like best. The craters all have names, too. Abulfeda, Catharine and Cardanus. Walter and Pitiscus."

"Pitiscus?"

"He must have been someone famous."

Angie began to smooth out the sugar and then drew a moon, dotting it with the tips of her fingers to make craters.

"Walter," she named one. "Pitiscus," she named another. "Angeline" was next. "Sylvie," she said, and looked up at the old woman whose face seemed to be almost imaginary, like something she would see when she stared into the clouds.

Elise and Angeline met up with Bruce and Todd at four-thirty at the Aetna Canteen as planned. Right on schedule. They would catch the five o'clock ferry back to the mainland and spend the night at the Bay View Motor Inn back near the Number 3 Highway.

Sitting around the outside pool at the Bay View something was wrong. They'd had a wonderful day and were supposed to drive on tomorrow to see Peggy's Cove and then back towards New Brunswick, to take in the tidal bore and Magnetic Hill. Bruce was nursing a Moosehead beer and Elise had a Tom Collins, which she studied more than she drank. A crisp half of a moon had just hoisted itself up out of the bay and you could see the low, dark outline of the island they had visited.

"The moon is so bright," Angeline said. "I can see Catharine and Pitiscus, I think."

"It's not the moon that's bright," Todd corrected. "It's light reflecting off the moon from the sun. That's all."

"Well, that's something."

Angie splashed Todd and then Todd grabbed her and pulled her into the swimming pool, where they horsed around.

"I'm thinking," Bruce began, furtively, tentatively, like he was fishing for something, waiting for the words to form the idea. Elise held her breath. It was the way Bruce had begun any number of conversations that had to do with buying a new BMW or moving into a bigger house. What now? she wondered.

"You know that guy Phonse Doucette who runs the salvage yard?"

"Um hmm."

"He told me about a place to rent for the summer."

Elise drew a deep breath, felt an electric thrill run down her back.

"A house?"

Bruce was cautious. Would she think he was completely out of his mind? He'd have to phrase this delicately, with just the right spin. He would use the same tack he had used when introducing his investment firm to the idea of California Geothermal. One little baby step at a time. It sure did sound California flaky at first, but it had paid off big-time and was one of the most environmentally sound investments going. "Yes. A house. Owned by his cousin, gone to Toronto or wherever. For rent. Dirt cheap. We could rent it. You and the kids stay, if you wanted. I could be there three, maybe four days a week. Been talk at the office of doing this sort of thing — you know, laptop off in the boonies, all wired up to the big system. They have phone lines out there. I'd just have to get at least three days in at the office. Fly from Halifax to Newark and back. Hour and a half in the air is all."

"You're serious?"

Well, serious, but fishing. He had a worm on the hook, but he wasn't sure there were any fish, and even if there were, he might be using the wrong bait. If she was going to laugh outright at him or go in for a big yowling argument, he'd reel in the line, shake off the water, then tap dance his way right out of it. *Just a joke. What are you crazy? Live out there with those people. The land that time forgot?* He decided to add something wistful and then shut up. "Something about the place. Different."

"It's that," Elise agreed.

"It gives you a certain ... feeling. I don't know. Do you think we're too locked into our, um, lifestyle? In New Jersey, I mean."

"Sometimes."

"Do you think it would be good for the kids?" He was pushing it now. Getting ready to bail out if he had to. Checked for the parachute and made sure he was set to jump.

"I think today was the best day the family has had in long time," Elise said.

"Me too. The boat. The water. I didn't even care that there weren't any whales."

"Angie seemed really happy there visiting the old lady."

"Todd loved the salvage yard. Learned more there than he learns in a month of school."

"Does the house have electricity?"

"Natch. Phones too. For my modem hookup."

"Running water."

"I think."

"Hand pump on the kitchen sink?"

"No, I think it's more sophisticated than that." Was she teasing him now? He sucked on the beer, felt a crazy little glimmer of hope in his head, felt like a kid back in university. When was the last time he had done anything unpredictable?

"Darn."

Now he was certain she was fooling him, ready to slam him back into the twentieth century with a thousand reasons why it couldn't be done. Meetings to be missed. School clothes to be bought, social obligations.

"Darn?"

"I was hoping for something really primitive," Elise said.

"But you like the idea?"

"I love the idea," Elise said, spilling her drink as she leaned forward to kiss her husband full on the lips. As if on cue, the kids popped up out of the side of the pool like trained porpoises, gushing chlorinated water all over the concrete apron as the sickle moon sent down its steely white light to sprinkle on the bay like crazy diamonds.

Chapter Ten

It was exactly 11:49 P.M. when Kit Lawson phoned to tell Sylvie that she needed help. She was losing her mind. She was scared to death. She couldn't explain what was going on but desperately needed Sylvie to come over.

"Yes, I'll be there. Now calm down."

Middle of the night, the house seemed to say to her. *One of those middle of the night problems*. More than loneliness. A crisis of some sort. The Sea of Crises in a person's life. Surprised that it would happen to Kit, who always seemed to have such a

positive attitude. Night was her time, too. Moon, stars, looking up at things in space.

Ah, yes, walking the island this late at night. She'd almost
forgotten. Grass all wet with dollops of dew. A distant sound of
some young fool trying to drive his wreck of a car into a ditch
or up a tree. Clear night this, with a big piece of moon like the
half-eaten pie in her refrigerator. Smell of summer in the air.
Invisible flowers. No wind. Sylvie wondered suddenly if she was
really out walking on the worn path from her house to the gravel road. Was it a dream? Some of those dreams had been so real
lately. Old age removing some of the distinctions between
dreaming and waking. She touched her neck and felt the bones
of her chin. Real enough for now. Walk on. Need to go help Kit.

Twin bats above her near the treetops skimmed the air.
What other night creatures roamed this island of hers that she
had not encountered? Hadn't had a bat in her house for over
thirty years. Bats, eh?

Kit opened the door before she touched it. Light spilled out into
the darkness, making it hard for the old woman's eyes to adjust.

"Come in, come in."

"I'm here. Now just settle yourself and tell me all."

But Kit could not settle herself. Her hands were frantic,
independent things working at the air in front of her to make
way for her to pace about. The look on her face was all desperation, confusion.

"I can't ... I can't ..."

"Can't what, Kit? Just try to calm down and let me help you."

"I shouldn't have stopped taking the pills." Kit picked up a
book and leafed quickly through it like she was speed-reading,
but it was all nervousness. The book fell onto the floor and made
a sound ten times larger than itself. Kit stared at it.

"Drugs of some sort?"

"No. No. Not like that. Treatment. Bipolar. Manic depressive, they used to say. Up. Down. Up, down. All the time. Then the medication. Evened me out. But I always felt ... I felt ... I felt ..."

"Take your time. I have all night. I'll be here." Sylvie felt a profound calm come over her, even as she stared into the haunted, fearing eyes of her young friend. Odd. Sylvie always thought of herself as the crazy one. Kit: sane and smart, out to save the world. Old Sylvie, a bit odd in her ways from a solitary life, a little daft, but what of it? Eighty years to cultivate her own proud eccentricities.

Kit was crying now, kneeling upon the rag rug on the floor. "I always felt like the medication, the pills, changed me somehow. I could cope better, for sure. But I didn't feel fully alive. I stopped taking them a month ago. And I've been okay since. But now this. If John was here I think I would be okay, but he's not."

"Do you have some of your medication here, Kit? Could you take it now?"

"No. I chucked what was left in the sea. I told myself I was cured."

Sylvie reached out a hand and smoothed it across the island teacher's head, her long, beautiful, light-brown hair. "You've been doing pretty good, then, I'd say. We'll get past tonight and things will smooth out, I bet."

"I don't know if I can get past this. I'm scared."

"Scared of what?"

"I don't know. I don't feel safe. I feel threatened. And there's no real reason for it."

"But it's in your mind, do you think?"

"I think so. But it feels very real. I can't shake it. God, it's like I need to claw away at something in me, rip open my skin and dig it out. Oh, Jesus. I hate this. I don't know what to do.

Nothing is fixed in one place. I think the room is spinning. Is the room spinning?"

Sylvie looked around and realized that, yes, to her, it did seem as if the room, the whole house had been lifted off the loose stone foundation and was twisting itself around somehow. But she knew better. The power of empathy. *Careful. Don't want to feed off the madness here.* That would be easy enough to do but it wouldn't help anybody. "Yes, the room is spinning. But now I'll make it stop." She put two hands, palms upward, in front of her as if she were a crossing guard in Mutton Hill Harbour, asking the cars to stop and let the children cross.

The room slowed down and stopped. The house was still. A magazine fell to the floor from a precarious perch on the corner of the table. Now what?

Sylvie was thinking about how a mind can project things. Somehow. Breaks down all the traditional rules and limitations, but life gets powerfully confusing then.

"Do you *know* what you need? Right now?"

"I don't know."

"Try to figure it out. Just tell me. I'm here."

"I need a safe place where nothing can hurt me."

"I understand that. Do you mind if we go out for a walk?"

"It's very dark out."

"It is. The moon is low now in the sky. Some stars. You would know their names."

"Some of them. There are millions."

"I can take you to a safe place if you want to walk with me."

"Yes."

Sylvie knew what was wrong with the house. No, not ghosts. People project anxiety or madness and it invests itself in things. Animals knew that. A dog would bark at a stick used to beat it the day before. A cat would hunch up in defence if it came close to an axe, let's say, used to murder. Birds would not sit on the roofs of some houses. With good reason. Kit had taken her dementia and painted it all over the inside of her good house. The house *had* been spinning. Better to be outside, walking towards the open ocean.

Sylvie held her friend's hand. Kit was sobbing, crying in small, fragile convulsions as they walked. The forest trail, though, did not seem frightening. The trees of spruce were tall, steady, silent, and compassionate. Moss grew on this little-used path. Moss the great comforter of stones. Stones asleep beneath such resplendent growth. Sylvie would point this out. *Midnight in a forest is not such a bad thing.*

"My mind is feeling more steady. But I'm still uncertain of everything. I was sure the island was the safe place I was looking for. Away from the pain of the kids in the city. Away from all that craziness."

"I know. But you were right. The island is the safe place. Now try to forget about the mainland. If you listen, you can hear the dreams of the forest." It was a foolish madwoman thing to say, but Sylvie trusted her intuition.

"What does the forest dream?"

Good, Sylvie thought. She is willing to let go of her own madness and move into another sphere of crazy thought. "The forest dreams itself into the past and into the future. Old tree trunks rotting gracefully back into the soil. Seeds asleep. Past, future, and right here now. Going back and moving forward. All at a pace much different than our own. The forest dreams itself into being. It breathes slowly as it sleeps and in doing so cleans the air. There are no single trees, only the forest. The forest is satisfied with itself and sleeps well at night."

"Is this the safe place?"

"Well, it is, but you need open space right now. You need the sea and what it can give."

They walked on and could smell the apple blossoms of the old crabapple tree that grew by the soft, moss-covered knees of an old homestead. Apple blossom gave way to wild rose, and even without daylight there was colour in the minds of two women.

The rounded stones found the feet of Sylvie and Kit and led them towards the edge of the sea, to the shelves of stone, flat as dance floors, which allowed them easy footing. Sylvie did not know if the whales would come for them tonight. She would try, but she knew something had changed. So many things unseen changing around her. Like Kit, she sometimes felt uncertain of anything, less stable than ever before. But the feeling usually only arrived at four or so in the morning and never stayed around until breakfast. Age, she had counselled herself. It was only old age.

"We always think we are at the centre of things, that we have some sort of control, but we don't always," Sylvie announced. Uncertainty confirmed was a way in to Kit's dilemma.

"Copernicus moved the earth away from the centre of the universe and everybody got angry at him. He assumed the centre was the sun and even that was wrong."

Sylvie nodded. "Maybe there is no centre. Just like the way that there is no beginning and no end. The dreaming forest would know this. And the sea. Listen to the sea."

And the sea talked, tongue guided by the moon, translated the effect of storms many, many miles away. Wind talking to water, water sending her story through the waves on and on through the deep, shushing in final syllables on the flat stone and evoking small stones into some kind of poetry along the sandy pockets. Cool water swaying the kelp back and forth. Verse, chorus, dance.

"Copernicus is showing," Kit said. "Look."

Ah yes. The moon, what was left of it. The half-pie about to slip into the sea.

"Where, Kit?"

"That big crater middle and to the left."

"That's him?"

"It is. What's left of him. One of the first things on the moon I learned to identify."

So the moon was with them, as was Copernicus, who had been wrong about the sun being the centre. She could feel the sleep of the forest behind her, could taste and feel the endurance of the patient sea in front of her.

"I like it here," Kit said at last, interrupting the endless announcements of the small waves.

"I knew you would. You've been here before. But not at night, I bet."

"Never at night. This is beautiful. But if we lose the moon, will we be able to find our way back?" Caution but not paranoia in her voice.

"Yes."

"Are we waiting for something to happen?"

"Are you feeling better?"

"Yes, a little. Maybe a lot."

"Then something has already happened, but we'll wait longer."

"Part of me is calm. The other part is still a raging lunatic."

"Which one is more powerful?"

"The crazy one, but I'm trying to keep her distracted with the beauty of all this."

"Good tactic."

"What if I can't straighten myself out? What if I have to leave here and stay in an institution again? What if I can't teach?"

"I don't know, but that's all tomorrow. Or the next day. Right now there is just this."

There was a phosphorescent flush of something on the rocks of the outer shoal. A signal. News perhaps. Sea creatures did not necessarily sleep at night. Diatoms celebrating the evening with their light. Portuguese men of war afloat, entangling their prey.

Nations of fish swimming, travelling great distances on highways marked clearly by rivers within the sea. And something about magnetism. Something about the earth guiding creatures to where they needed to be at the right time of the year. And the moon, with her gentle but powerful tug.

The half-moon grew immense as it prepared to dip into the cold silver bath of the sea. Sylvie was sure there was a sound as the lunar south pole touched down on the Atlantic. Then, it seemed to increase the speed of its descent, anxious for the full bath of night and the sleep that would follow.

"They say Yuri Gagarin went mad before he died," Kit said, "and it had something to do with being in space."

"More likely something to do with being on earth."

Kit smiled. "You're a good friend."

"Thanks. Can I tell you something?"

"What?"

"You are going to get well and you are going to be okay."

"How do you know?"

"I know. And you should believe me because I have been around for a long time and I know some things."

"Women's intuition?"

"More than that." But Sylvie would shroud the rest in mystery. What she knew was that if she could convince this friend, Kit Lawson, that everything would be okay, then it would be. Simple trick of the mind. Earth force, mind power. Healing touch of the sea. Mix and shake, cook it for a while. Spice it up if necessary. Tastes good and cures. She should write down the recipe some time in case she started to lose her memory.

Sylvie was certain she could feel them before she saw them. Four: two of them just small. Dark humps on the sea. Her whales, a few of them at least, returned.

The moon was diminished to a quarter. Ten more minutes of light if that. Then nothing but the afterglow of star shine.

"They're beautiful," Kit said.

"You can't see much but their backs."

"But why are they here? How did you do that?"

Sylvie truly believed that she had brought them here. Called out to them with her mind. An old woman's delusion. The whales would come for her if she needed them. Wouldn't say so out loud. Sound like an idiot.

"Good guess, really. I didn't know they would come, but I felt some connection between your pain and confusion and something going on out there." No, don't rattle on and try to make it sound all fuzzy and metaphysical. Just shut up, she told herself, and let it be at that.

The whales were in as close as they could come now, and, in their wake, the phosphorescent diatoms, stirred back into life.

"Trailing clouds of glory," Kit said.

"Yes, that."

The whales in close, in that deep, deep place that made the island unique and made it possible for whales to commune so closely with life ashore. Reach out and touch them with your mind, Sylvie said silently to her friend, but her lips did not move. Not telepathy, just a tug at a thought. She watched Kit's face, saw her doing just as she had suggested.

"It's amazing."

"It is, isn't it? You would have missed it if you hadn't been losing your mind tonight."

Sylvie studied the dark, moving forms. Felt their motion inside her, experienced the powerful but timid thoughts of her allies. But something else. Something that felt like an apology. Something that felt like a husband dying or someone saying goodbye. The ache of wanting to stay but the tug so strong to leave, to be someplace else where it is necessary to survive.

Then the moon was gone; the eyes of the two women adjusted to the lesser lights of suns millions of light years away. The tide came inching up on the rock shelf towards them. Then, in the new full-darkness, the Milky Way remembered itself and painted a band of soft light across the night sky.

Chapter Eleven

Sylvie was not just a casual acquaintance with madness. The two of them had been around the block a few times together. Old close friends in the 1950s in particular. Husband number four from Halifax. William Toye. Brilliant, restless, highly educated, a man who drank and waxed eloquent upon subjects Sylvie had never conceived of: history of Mesopotamia, John Calvin, calculus, Ernest Cassirer, the pantheistic religions of Aboriginal peoples.

William Toye. She should have known he was at least half-crazy by the look in his eye. Something bright and burning inside him. How could she resist? William Toye was, in a way, her escape from the island when she needed it most. But she would not have to leave.

"I'm through with Halifax," he told her when she asked him why he had come to the island. "I've quit the university — Dalhousie. Oh, they'll miss me when I'm gone, but I'm good and gone. I'm tired of academics. I'm looking for life. Life. Life. Life."

And then he looked into the eyes of Sylvie Young and he thought that maybe he had finally found life after all. And Sylvie had found her own new life off the island without moving a step onto the boat.

William Toye had smooth hands, hands that had never been pierced by a fish hook, never chafed by ropes, never blistered with wielding a tool. He did not mind the idea of work and agreed with Thoreau that work was edifying. "Self-reliance gives a person dignity. I admire all the men on this island more than any of those louts at Dalhousie."

"What of the women?"

"Yes. Them too. Behind every great man is a great woman." A line borrowed and one that Sylvie took as either an insult or a compliment, she just wasn't sure.

William Toye asked the circumference of the island and Sylvie's answer proved satisfactory. "Would you walk it with me, madame?"

Her reply: "Yes." It took the better part of the day. William Toye talked at great length but when he finally flagged, he turned to Sylvie and said, "You have eyes the colour of that sea pool there, hair like the fields of autumn grass. Something about the way you walk. I'm having a hard time not touching you."

Sylvie had not been touched by a man since the death of her third husband, Doley Keizer. She closed her eyes and faced into the light sea breeze, let it decide for her what to do. William

Toye cautiously took her fingers in his hand, then grasped her whole hand in his, took a deep breath and said, "Poetry pales compared to this."

Sylvie knew it was not just her. It was the combination of everything. And she knew she was in love with this William Toye already, even though she had sworn off love, decided that the excesses of grief were not worth it. But she had been expecting that she would mostly have to contend with island men. A Slaunwhite or a Swinnemar, men easy to resist. And she was certain she was way past longing.

Now this cloud in her chest, this summer day, this crazy man with candles in his eyes beneath a pale blue sky and the advice of the sea telling her that life was yet to be lived. And she knew it.

Invited for supper, William Toye could not say no. "I'm living purely by my instincts now. Sylvie, I don't know what you did to me today but I'm thankful. I don't know if I ever want to leave this island. Here I am, only fifty miles from Halifax, and I feel like I've gone far, far away to a Greek island or some village on the shores of Fiji. It's as if I've been asleep all my life. Those dusty classrooms at Dal. Those boring meetings. Old men with opinions. Oh, so many opinions. I was buried and now I'm resurrected. I've come back to life."

Sylvie loved the way he pronounced words. She sat silently, waited for more syllables to spill from William Toye.

"I've brought cognac," he said. "To celebrate."

And celebrate they did. William Toye was a man all of fire. His eyes, his drink, his own animated opinions, his attitudinal knowledge of the world's history: "There is no truth to history, no way of nailing it down. Oh, we try, but we know next to nothing. That is what my own education, my readings, and my knowledge have given me, the understanding that we know next to nothing. Better to give up the past for dead."

"My mother said we should learn from history's mistakes. She was considered a very wise woman on this island." She did not tell him that her mother had been an adamant temperance organizer. The temperance movement had been partly responsible for lifting her intellect. It had been a call to women's rights for many of her mother's generation and she had taken that call. She had fought against booze and then gone on to be quite a free-thinking woman for Ragged Island.

"Your mother was right to an extent. We *should* learn, but we do not. We plunge back into our own errors with glee. We will dream ourselves into oblivion now that we have the weapons to do so. We will kill off humanity with the belief that we are doing some good, some purposeful important deed, standing up for what is believed to be right."

"Dark words, Mr. Toye. Do you really believe this?"

William Toye sipped cognac ambitiously from a glass that had once been a jelly jar. "I don't know what I believe anymore. I believe in reason, perhaps. I believe in the rational mind. I believe in the pursuit of knowledge, but I cannot fully defend any of the above. It is what I know and who I am, but now I'm here with you on this island and I feel like I am becoming another person."

Sylvie sipped her own drink tentatively. Each time she sipped, she thought of her mother. A paradox. Her mother would have loved to hear the words pouring from this man, yet would have abhorred him for bringing strong drink into the house. Sylvie studied the face: fixed muscles in the cheek and chin as if too much time had been spent questioning and criticizing every minutiae of daily life and thought. Hairline receding as if a tide was going out, slowly leaving pallid skin stretched over a prominent skull — like a shiny, light-coloured stone. Longish hair aft and a protracted neck with a prominent Adam's apple that bobbed as he spoke. City clothes and hands, those smooth, lily-white hands, always framing things in the air in front of him. It was as if he were constructing some small invisible building as he spoke his ideas: footings like fists, plane-level floors as the language flowed out, upright beams as fingers pointed rigidly skyward asserting positions of ancient arguments, strong rafters and joists and even a roof in the testing of two opposing ideas with fingertips arched against each other in some kind of contest of strength.

"I've given up trying to make sense out of the world," William Toye said after spilling several thousand words in her room, asserting and questioning the reasons for life on earth, World War II, and the philosophy of Immanuel Kant. Once it had all gushed out and silence collected in the near empty bottle before them on the table, Sylvie wondered if she should talk at all. For she felt so uneducated, so completely different from this man in front of her. But the cognac had made her light-headed and she felt words welling up in her own throat. They would not be satisfied to remain inside of her.

"Death is what makes the world make sense."

"Death is what prevents us from achieving our full potential. Death brings us to our knees and erases who we are just when we are realizing that potential."

"I don't know if that is truly the way it must be. William, have you lost anyone close to you?"

"My parents are both alive. The Toyes tend to live to a ripe old age. I've lost a colleague or two. Accidents. Cancer."

"I've lost three husbands. Death has always been very close at hand for me." Her hands were framing something now as well. She wondered what sort of edifice she was building. Palms upright, opposed to each other. "Death. Life." Then she flattened her hands and waved them in front of her. "Opposites? I don't think so."

"You would deny the duality of things as basic as life and death?"

"They're not opposed to each other, if that's what you mean."

Toye studied this with a frown, then gave it up. "You've studied religion, then. Hinduism, Buddhism, Zen?"

"Not much of that around here, I'm afraid. Mostly just Baptist and Pentecostal. I'm not either one. I have my own beliefs."

William sat silent now, wide-eyed.

"Suppose we did not think of things in terms of opposites? Us/them. Good/bad."

"Brave woman. Tell me more."

She blushed. She had never talked like this to any man. "What did you think of the island, today?"

"I loved the island. As we came back to the place from which we started our walk, I felt that for once there was a sense of meaning and completion in my life. And I was not the same man when the circumnavigation ended. Not the same man at all."

"I understand what you're saying. When we arrived back to the government wharf something had changed. Not just us. But the actual physical place."

"Yes," he said, more fire kindling in those eyes, but tempered this time by a silliness, a softer side of him. "You've read T.S. Eliot?"

"Who?"

"Sorry. I'm such an idiot. For all my adult life I have believed that you only learn from books. Second-hand knowledge. I'm beginning to see I've missed a considerable amount in my education."

"Don't be so hard on yourself."

"Is there someplace on the island I can rent a room?"

"There is, but it won't be necessary. Stay here as my guest. There is an extra room."

"You're very kind, but I fear that it may not be the right thing to do. Your neighbours may want to give you some grief over having me."

"Neighbours talk. That's what they do. Those who know me will not judge. Besides, I like talking with you." She almost said,

It's like talking to some handsome stranger from another planet, but she did not. She had learned over the years that half the art of good conversation was not saying everything that ran through your head. Her remaining reservoir of self-preservation told her she did not want an intimate relationship with another man — any man from any planet — but the cognac and the night were draining that reservoir. William Toye would sleep in the spare room and there need not be more to it than that.

But there was much more. She fell in love with him in a complicated package of emotions. She felt sorry for him, admired him, was attracted to his intellect, repelled by his self-confessed arrogance toward the rest of the common world that he could not seem to shake. But most of all, there was a sense of need between them. Mutual comfort. Some might call it love. And beyond that, there was the matter of Professor's Toye's education, seriously lacking in important particulars that Sylvie could teach him.

Sylvie didn't fully realize that William Toye was slightly mad, perhaps truly psychologically ill, for at least a week. He switched from cognac to rum, the local staple. Rum was much cheaper if bought through the network of bootleggers who could still bring it in duty-free from ships off the coast, a longstanding island tradition that had somehow survived the end of the rum-running era. Drink loosened his tongue and inspired a stampede of speech that galloped forth — about great thinkers and inevitably about history. The Romans, the Celts, the Gauls, Japanese emperors, and the customs of Native tribes in the Amazon. The problem was that some of it was true (if books can be trusted, that is) and some of it was made up on the spot. And William Toye could not distinguish between the two.

Which was why he had been fired from his position as senior instructor of philosophy and history at the university. He had pontificated all kinds of things that just weren't in the books. He made things up and he didn't even realize he was doing it. Much of what he invented was far more interesting than what was factual.

He was a hit among students who reported back on final exams detailed information about wars that had never occurred and great thinkers who had never existed. Toye's favourite subject for discourse was Guilliamo Mellesandro, a seventeenth-century Italian philosopher who had dissected the brains of a living subject without injury and discovered what he believed to be the seat of the human soul, a small, pentacle-shaped organ that could be accessed by a minor incision in the base of the skull. Mellesandro, of course, was scoffed at in his day, especially when he deduced from these surgical experiments that some people had the newly discovered organ (which he called the mellengra) and some people did not. *Ipso facto*, some people did not have souls. Toye admitted to his students that, of course, Mellesandro was wrong. You could not physically locate the human soul. But Toye also professed that Mellesandro the Italian philosopher had set in motion the very basis for our understanding of the physiology of the brain. Yet, he had never been given due credit. If you didn't know your Mellesandro, you were not likely to pass the final exam for Professor Toye's Philosophy 800 course.

There had been a departmental meeting finally when this Mellesandro business was put on the table and Toye was deeply insulted, outraged. The youngest member of the department, a small man with pinched glasses named Smeets who had only recently received his PhD from the University of Toronto, asked Toye to account for Mellesandro. "Pull any book from the department's library shelves and turn to the page," Smeets challenged. William Toye refused to have any man question his scholarship. Certainly, Mellesandro had lived in seventeenth-century Rome, where he had performed medical experiments upon cadavers, and even several living subjects. He had taken a faulty step in the evolution of knowledge but, in the long run, it had proven to be a useful one. All this was explained to a roomful of colleagues who knew painfully well that Guilliamo Mellesandro had never existed and that Dalhousie was not prepared to risk its reputation by keeping Toye on as a professor. Before the hour was up, he had resigned, maintaining that he was being crucified. Free speech and academic freedom were *in absentia* at Dalhousie that day and Toye would leave at once.

It never occurred to William Toye that he could be wrong, and he himself refused to crack open any book to verify what he knew to be fact.

"The English metaphysician, M. John McTaggert, believes that time does not exist," William Toye stated at breakfast on the third day of his tenure at Sylvie's house. Sylvie would have had no way of knowing if McTaggert was real or illusion, but then if time was an illusion, what were the reference points for reality?

"I always thought mainlanders placed too much emphasis on time. When to do this, when to do that. Schedules and such. Did you know this man, McTaggert?"

"Knew him from his writings. Sometimes that is one's most intimate relationship. McTaggert had this notion, shared by others, that nothing exists *outside* of the mind." He tapped a finger ever so gently against Sylvie's brow, and studied the sea pools again in her eyes. "What's up here is all there really is."

"Do you believe that?"

He traced her hairline with his index finger as if reading a road map. "I keep an open mind. I can embrace the idea. It opens up all kinds of possibilities."

"Which kinds are they?" Sylvie was falling in love with this wonderfully curious man. She adored his talk, his intellect, his furrowed brow that had horizontal ridges, like the line of distant waves on the sea. But what was she doing with another man in her house? Hadn't she sworn herself to a solitary life?

"You and I. Here on this island. It may only exist in our thoughts. This is just theoretical, mind you."

Sylvie touched his neck, let her fingers glide over his Adam's apple. *Men, such odd creatures. Comical. Always working away at a thing, never happy to just let it be.* She smiled. "I can believe that I created this place, this island. Or that it created me somehow. It's a connection that I feel very strongly."

"Animism. The idea that a thing like the island is alive."

"But it is."

"Yes." He kissed her. William Toye let the world of ideas rest for a time. He felt her strong body in his arms. If she existed only in his mind, if neither of them had real physical flesh at all, then this was enough. This moment, this room, this woman. This embrace, not of an idea, but of a woman. It was enough. Was there a category for this experience? Was there a school of thought that already articulated what he had just discovered to be true in this instance? If not, he would lay down the basics of it, by God.

Neither the Baptist minister nor the Pentecostal one would have anything to do with marrying William Toye who was already living with Sylvie. There was a justice of the peace in Mutton Hill Harbour, a doddering old man whose office contained hundreds of souvenir bells from tourist destinations around the world. He had yellowed newspaper clippings on the wall about the Dionne quintuplets. Toye had noticed other curious things: books, records, and various framed advertisements where the number five was prominent. Hillory Docker, J.P., had some particular affection for the number five but when asked about it, he'd only answer, "A random interest. As a boy, I picked a number and decided I would collect anything involving that number. I selected number five. It's been a good selection. If I had picked something obvious like seven or something too round, like the number eight, it wouldn't have been the same."

And so they were married, Sylvie to her fourth husband in a room that was a kind of shrine to the number five. It was the first day of a full moon, the second highest tide of the year, and they were the third couple to be married that week by Docker.

It was Toye's first marriage to a woman, although he had been married to several fields of scholarly research before and one or two schools of historical analysis. He was of the opinion, after his fifth night of wedded bliss, that this type of marriage was much more satisfying than the others. He worked hard at being a fine husband although he had poor credentials and had not been properly trained for the job. He needed tutoring.

"You're going to have to coach me on things. What to do. How to interact with your friends and neighbours, responsibilities around the house, that sort of thing. I'm very bad, I warn you, when it comes to anything financial. I just can't seem to lather up any interest in money matters."

There was a small, begrudged pension from the university for all those years spent lecturing about nonexistent events of history and imaginary heroes of philosophy. "And I should be receiving a small royalty soon from my scholarly book. A trifling thing, really, a slim volume on Immanuel Kant, published by Oxford. I have to make sure they have my new address. Of course, I'll have to find a bank that can cash a note in pounds Sterling."

But something must have gone afoul with the postal delivery system and the forwarding of mail, because the cheque from the publisher never did arrive. Sylvie never suspected that there had *not* been a book. Nor did William. He remembered writing it. He remembered posting the manuscript and receiving acceptance. All as if it had really happened. Living proof that McTaggert may have been right.

Other books did arrive, however. A big crate of books from Dalhousie, shipped at the university's expense. Aristotle, Plato, Heidegger, volumes of world history. The books invaded the house and filled shelves, piled in corners, scattered themselves under beds and lounged on chairs. The books did not seem to quite know what to do with themselves now that they had been kicked out of the university and trundled off to this rustic island home. Sometimes, while her new husband was refreshing his memory on Egyptian kings or inching his way through a biography of Immanuel Kant written in German, Sylvie grazed through a book titled *Understandings of Paradox* by a long-winded fellow named Lancelot Vertiges.

Sylvie taught husband number four how to split wood and bake bread and cakes that were sold on the mainland, ferried over and delivered to a couple of small stores there. William tried hiring on with a couple of fishermen but proved to be more in the way than any good and had a poor stomach for choppy days. "He spends most of 'is time feeding the fish," as Moses Slaunwhite's father put it. William Toye had never vomited so much in his life.

So, a hangashore he would be, and do whatever a hangashore was cut out to do on an island. He did not mind the smell of fish or tasks around the wharf so island men, still skeptical of Toye as some kind of mainland gigolo or something, were big-hearted enough to give him the odd piece of work. And odd it was. Toye's favourite job, it turned out, was untangling massive convolutions of rope and netting. Before he had arrived and proved so adept, some fishermen would just cut the mess and let it drift off in the currents of the sea.

"I learned more in one week about logic and problem solving," William told his wife, "than I learned from all those years of reading and research. It's quite incredible, really."

"My father knew all about tangles and knots. Always start with the loose end, he'd say. Follow it. Let the tangle teach you what to do; never force it. Patience wins out."

"Yes, it does."

William Toye drank his rum, read his books, and wrote in a notebook that he seemed somewhat private about.

"Can I see what you write?"

"My handwriting's bad. Always has been. You can't make much out."

She peered over his shoulder and stared into the puddle of light on the lined page. Bad was not quite an accurate description of his writing. Impossible was more like it. Squiggles, symbols, tangles of letters and lines looking like a mass of very tangled nets and rope piled on a wharf in disgust.

"What's it about?"

"Trifles is all. Things that turn through a man's head. Ideas and notions. Half thought out patterns of understanding. Just a mind cast loose with words and images. I always have the feeling that if you put enough down on a page, enough jabbering and rambling of intellectual thought, just one day you'll come up with an idea that will change the world."

William Toye did not change the world. Yet he made his wife very happy. He was ill-prepared for much about life on the island but he never complained. He nearly cut his foot off splitting knotty softwood junks. His hands grew a bit tougher from untangling hand-lines and mending rough nets. He piled eelgrass around the bottom of the old house to help keep out the winds of winter, and, in bed on those cold nights, he kept his wife very warm and made love to her with dignity and passion, somehow blended together just right. He would praise her in Latin and console her when she felt sad in a language that he said came from the ancient Celts.

Those were happy years, and Sylvie shared her own understanding of the deeper things of life with her husband, who was an eager student. She always believed that William's eccentric notions and his wild ideas were somehow rooted in reality. Well, most of them were. She became more convinced he was truly mad when the business came up about Johann Gottlieb Fichte.

"Moses Slaunwhite's father told me the story and I can't quite believe it. Fichte was here." William gave an alien throaty hiss as he pronounced the *cht* sound. "Fichte came here himself at the beginning of the nineteenth century. Part of a wave of German immigrations."

"Many German families came here. Who was this man?"

"Student of Immanuel Kant himself. And famous in his own right. Knowledge, Fichte believed, comes from a free, self-determining mind. Within that mind is the moral code of the world ... well, the universe."

"If you say so." This one sounded like so much gibberish to her.

"Fichte was here in the summer of 1801, if I have the story correct. He came here with the intent of establishing a utopian community. A perfect society."

"But I've never heard anything about this. Usually all the stories about the island filter down to me one way or another."

"Fichte didn't stay. He became disillusioned when no one would pay attention to him. But it was here he formulated some of his most prominent theories."

"Here on Ragged Island?"

"Yes. Isn't that beautiful. He went back to Germany and he did some of his best work."

And to that discovery, they celebrated.

The next day, while visiting with Viddy Slaunwhite, she mentioned the business about the dead German philosopher and discovered that Noah Slaunwhite had been sick in bed for several days with "a raspy throat and a fever like a kettle aboil." He'd had no visitors.

It was the first time that Sylvie had fully doubted her husband on anything. She felt horrible and guilty about sitting down alone in the house and looking for Johann Gottlieb Fichte in the index of one philosophy text after another. And then she breathed a great sight of relief when she found a reference to him and discovered he had lived from 1762 to 1814. She read a chapter in one volume about this man and his ideas but could find no reference concerning his efforts to start a utopian community or a trip to Nova Scotia. She closed her eyes and considered the possibility that her husband was just a bit of a liar, like the men on the wharf who make up great false, entertaining yarns — half true, half fabricated. Maybe that was all there was to it.

She tried to put the worry out of her mind as if it were a bird that had accidentally flown in through an open window. Chased it out of the house. Gone. But it wasn't that easy.

Then William came home one day from his odd jobs on the wharf and he had more to his story. "I talked to old Slaunwhite again. Apparently Fichte got into a fanatical argument with one of the preachers on the island here. It turned into fisticuffs: determinism versus free will. Fichte was a passionate man when it came to the central idea of freedom of the intellect. They fought. He picked up a rock and nearly killed the clergyman. He barely escaped the island with his life. It changed his whole view of the world."

Why this foolish tale was important to her husband, Sylvie couldn't begin to comprehend, but he was very enthusiastic about it all and wrote extensive, incomprehensible notes that evening as he rifled through a pair of books concerning German philosophy.

So Sylvie decided she could live with what William Toye believed to be true. And she began to understand that her husband's beliefs had something to do with why he left the university.

He was a good husband, though, a good man. What exists in the mind, she told herself, may be the only thing that is real after all. Great men and women had lived by such principles before, and an island was a good, safe place for such a high-minded doctrine.

There had been three happy years. She always thought of them as thus. And then, suddenly, he woke up one night and said outright, "Sylvie, I don't know what is real and what isn't anymore."

"What do you mean?"

"I mean that I've discovered that some things I believed to be empirical fact, are not."

"Why should this come as any great surprise to a man who has taught logic and philosophy?"

"It's not that. It's something different. It's like a big tangled pile of that rope on the wharf. I've started with one end and threaded it this way and that, just barely got it free, only to discover that it turns back on itself somehow to lead me to the same free end. And yet the knot is still there, bigger and more tangled than ever."

"Just let it go."

"I don't know if I can. I don't have a clear reference point as to what I know to be true."

"I am real, you know that. And I love you."

She held him and rocked him back to sleep like he was a little boy, but in the morning, she realized that something had changed.

Wild frantic birds for eyes. Like the swallow that had darted into the house. Unable to find a way out. Back and forth.

She walked him to the sea, to the Trough, to sit again and watch kelp sway back and forth in the sweet, salty pools of cold, clean water. She waited for whales to appear. And they did.

"I believe sometimes that I can hear the voices, the thoughts of those big creatures, in my mind," she told William.

He looked at her intently. "Are you serious?"

"Yes. I am"

"It's probably just your imagination," he told her.

"It probably is. Because I can't translate what they are telling me into any language. Yet I learn something new each time I hear them. There are unspoken ideas that cannot be formed into words."

"Yes."

"It doesn't even matter to me if those whale voices are real or not. I would continue to believe in them because they are important to me. They are part of who I am. Do you know what I mean?"

Just then, William Toye began to cry. He hung his head and wept, his wife's arm around him, until salt tears splashed upon the flat slate rock at his feet. "Yes. I do know what you mean. And I know why you're saying this to me. I love you all the more for it."

William Toye became kinder and softer after that, but a great, ponderous uncertainty had set in like a damp, cold fog in his soul. He drank, but without his previous enthusiasm. He sought refuge in the arms of his wife and began to shy away from interactions with others on the island. He required care, and Sylvie was the one to provide it. They ceased being lovers and became great friends. William Toye lost his fervour for books and knowledge for the most part, although he settled into reading anthologies of old poets.

He died in his sleep three years into their marriage. Sylvie woke in the cool, thin, grey light of early morning and realized the man beside her was cold. Icy cold. His two hands were upon his face, covering it as if he'd just seen something that he did not care to look at. Sylvie did not pry his hands loose but held him in her arms and rocked him as she had done in recent months. She tried not to swear out loud or blame herself for the pain that would now re-enter her life. But she could not contain herself. She cursed loud and long and then cried until her tears soaked into the nightshirt of her fourth husband. Grief swept over her like a familiar advancing army, crushing everything of her spirit, trampling her and leaving no room for her self. Leaving no oxygen in her lungs, no hope in her thoughts.

When she could bring herself to move, she walked outside and saw the pale three-quarter moon like a white ghost hanging in the morning sky, fading into invisibility as the sun began to burn off the mist.

She did not call for any assistance until late that afternoon, and soon after, she asked Moses to arrange for a simple burial, a non-denominational service.

Chapter Twelve

The island does not sleep. Not in this century, anyway. Sylvie knows this, feels this in her old bones. Sylvie wakes at five-thirty today. July 15. The summer slipping by so quickly. Wondering how many summers there are left. The brevity of the season makes her love it all that much more. She awakens with the feeling that there are scattered pieces of something she needs to fit back together. She is significant, important. She is the essential connection between the island, the sea, the moon, and the people. Some kind of thread she is: these are an old woman's thoughts rattling around in her brain. And she knows this is not madness at all, yet words will fail her should she try to explain this to Kit or to Elise, the woman from Upper Montclair.

Silence and stillness on a grand morning like this. Some would think the whole island at rest, at sleep, but not her. She feels the life of this place beneath her, all around. She knows the island will sleep again someday, will rest when the world changes. Another ice age, or rising tides from the melting ice caps. Then it will sleep until the moon or sun tugs it awake again. She is grateful that this is her home, as always. Love for this place. No one understands the sustenance of geography like she does.

Sylvie's feet upon the gravel road leading to the cemetery. Old barns leaning into the earth, swallows shooting like rockets from cracks in the walls. Old, quiet houses with families of young children asleep. Clapboard cocoons. Neat lawns mown with gasoline mowers, the grass smooth and sculpted around hillocks and cosy up to the boulders with flakes of silvery lichen.

Rotted fenceposts around the old cabbage fields where now wild mustard blooms yellow in the morning sun. Dew on everything like a crystal clear sugar glazing on baked goods. Her own breathing: a sigh, a gulp of clean air. A step forward. Why, on this morning, is she going to visit her dead men? She doesn't know really. Love, perhaps. Memory and love.

Death is a small impediment to love, she admits to herself. Love collects. Somehow. Never diminishes. Oh, you can put it like a kettle on the back burner once it comes to a full boil, but there it will simmer. She's been simmering for a long while.

A step at a time, a breath. The air into her lungs, the air parting as she moves through it, the island air filling in behind as she moves on. Moving on, each day to connect one thing to the next, to keep things whole. Sylvie's job. This morning, a thread must go out to the past.

Four graves are all in a line at the farthest back corner of the cemetery. This arranged against various misgivings of various ministers. Four husbands in a row. Death uniting them now, but each related somehow to each other, each husband of a woman named Sylvie. David Young, her first love, stiff body salvaged from the icy waters by the first mate. Why was it that the need to see the dead body is so strong that men go to great lengths to retrieve the lost from battlefields, from collapsed mine shafts, from deep saltwater canyons? The row of four, however, gives her a sense of unity. Some would say that she is a victim of all that loss. Some would say she has been punished for something she has done or for who she is deep down. But Sylvie knows the world does not work that way.

Something to do with men that she cannot explain. A thought planted in her head by William Toye in his ramblings. Time, our notion of it, he had advised her, was just a theory, not a fact. *We like this backwards-forwards thing. Time on a single plane, one line. We can look back but always move forward, as if on a train.* Mad William wondered if it was all wrong. *There is only the present and we expand it somehow. We can live in the past or the future. Nothing ends, nothing begins. Things just are. And since that makes life too confusing and too impossible, we create a workable lie to satisfy us and we make beginning and endings. Births and deaths.* And Sylvie was well versed in both.

Her own children — the ones she never had. She missed them all but refused to let the weight of her grief chase after them like dark shadows.

Her husbands, all buried. But all of them still in her heart. She placed a hand on her chest, just beneath her throat, and spread her fingers wide, felt something, felt the presence of these men. All with her here on this pale blue wonder of a morning. The tall, dark spruce trees at the edge of the graveyard had a practised, benevolent look to them. They'd seen her here like this before.

Suddenly the roar of a muffler-less truck up the gravel road and over the hilltop, churning stones. A loud radio blaring from the

window. Moses Slaunwhite, driving down to the wharf. Arm out
the window, waving. Sylvie turns and smiles. Men and trucks.
Surrounding themselves with noise and machines. Chaos. The dust
tries to rise from the road but is too damp and settles again, to sleep
until the sun dries it and gives it the lift of an afternoon breeze.

Moses had seen Sylvie there at the graves before. Early in the
morning like this. Knew not to feel sorry for her. No one needed to feel sorry for Sylvie. A strong woman, had a soul of stainless steel, heart as big as a Chevy V-8 engine. Smart old gal. Too
bad about all those men going away on her. Moses didn't think
he'd ever die. He had a hell of a lot of things to do yet with his
life. A life that seemed to be going just like it was ordered up that
way, all planned out. Up until this summer that is. One thing
always leading to the next. Fishing, eco-tours, etcetera. But that
was washing up stiff now. What next?

Moses had noticed the orderliness of everything moving
into the future ever since he was a kid. The power of the plan,
Moses' father, Noah, had called it. *Plan. Act. Adapt. Learn. Duck
the worst blows and roll with the punches you don't see coming.* But he
hadn't expected that the whales would disappear. And with
them, the eco-tour business would go. And with that demise, his
livelihood. The bank would want the boat soon even though
there was bloody all they could do with it but sell it for a third
of what it was worth.

Moses slammed on the brakes. Loved the feel of an old truck
skranking along to a stop on the loose stones. Backed her up and
made a little whipper turn there on the hill from Up Along —
just like a reckless teenager would. Throaty exhaust talking back
to him up over the rise and then he killed the motor out of
respect for the morning quiet that filled in around him as soon
as he slammed the door shut.

"Sylvie, how'd you like to go for a boat ride today?"

"I'd be honoured, Moses. What would you charge me?" she teased.

"Sylvie, you know I couldn't take an old woman's money."

"You're a practical man, Moses Slaunwhite. I've always known you to be. Must be some reason for you to invite me."

Moses removed his cap that said Clearwater. He scratched the part of his head that had the least hair. "Whyn't you just go ahead and read my mind, while you're at it? You probably know more about what I'm thinking than I do. You've always been like that."

"Are we thinking about whales?"

"Yes. Of course. *We* are thinking about whales."

"I haven't been to sea in a long time. I'm more comfortable here on the island."

"I know you are. But here you are standing around the graves of your dead men and I just thought that you might like to hang around with the living for a while."

"You think I'm morose?"

"Not at all. I'm not inviting you out of pity, darn it. I'm inviting you because I think you can help me figure out what's going on with the whales. Madame, if I don't find 'em soon, I'm up to my earlobes in ox droppings."

Moses was funny. He made her smile. Her love for dead husbands would abide, it was true. She still had time for the living, those who needed her help. A boat ride to sea on a morning like this would be something.

"Who else will be aboard?"

"Just you and me, girl."

"What if people talk?"

"Let 'em."

The government wharf was pretty well deserted. Moses had the biggest boat of the lot, but it felt too modern, somehow sterile. The big engine roared into life, and Moses said there'd be cappuccino in a few minutes. She thought he was joking, but as he found the seaward channel and walked from the wheelhouse, he handed her a steaming mug of something that must have been cappuccino.

"Bought the damn thing for the clientele but now I don't know if I'll have any clientele. Don't burn your lips on it. She's hot."

Sylvie smiled through the steam of her cappuccino and felt honoured to have this voyage to sea.

"Sylvie, you know I'm not just asking you out here to introduce you to fancy coffee drinks, don't you?"

Sylvie smiled and her face recreated itself into a fine display of adventurous wrinkles. "Are you suggesting your intentions are not honourable?" she teased.

"Don't test me now, Sylvie. You know all the men on this island have been in love with you ever since they graduated from grade five. Everybody always figured you were out of our league."

"Or too dangerous." She could joke about her dead husbands. It was one of the things she could do. She could do it with islanders, at least. They knew her. And she even knew there was some truth to the fact that, over the years, men and boys had crushes on her ever since way back when. But she was old now and all the teasing was doing her good. She took a sip of her drink and believed she was somewhere far off — on a boat in the Mediterranean, perhaps.

"All women are dangerous if you ask me. But this isn't what I'm getting at."

They were rounding the island now, passing Jack Zwick's home at the end of the west road. Jack's outhouse still stood on the edge of the land. Seagulls perched on top of it, where they whitewashed the roof with gull shit. Jack was in his garden with a hoe, leaning on it and looking at them as they passed. His house was painted a blazing greenish blue with pink trim and it had a blue shingled roof. Looked like something out of a theme park. Jack's excuse had been a paint sale, but those were the colours he chose, the colours he liked. His wife spent all her time apologizing to everyone for a year and then gave up and decided she could live with it.

Past Zwick's house there was nothing but forest pulling down to the shoreline of loose stones and flat slate outcropping. Sylvie felt an odd sensation, looking at the land from a boat. It had been a very long time since she'd seen her island from this perspective. An island, placed just so in the sea, a thing unto itself. Houses, trees, people. Fully alive. Her place, her world.

"Viddy's been into Mutton Hill Harbour and says there's talk of shutting the ferry service down. Government bloody cutbacks. When we elected Dancy Moxon, he promised that would never happen."

"They wouldn't do that. The ferry's been there for a long time." But Sylvie realized she knew nothing at all about what *they* could do. Or who *they* were for that matter. She had no understanding of the world outside the island. In general, she wasn't that interested in matters of the mainland.

"Still, if the ferry goes, a lot of people'd have to move off the island. I don't see how the government could do that to us."

"Don't worry, Mo. It couldn't happen." As she said those words, the first deep water wave passed under the boat, a wave that had travelled from far away. It lifted them up and casually released them to come back down its back onto the smooth, flat sea. Sylvie found the feeling in her stomach a pleasant sensation. A brief experience of the density of gravity in a lift and then the graceful release and fall. Energy passing under them, created from wind on water maybe five hundred miles away.

"Things change, darn it. Sometimes you just don't know. Like the whales. Which is why I brought you out here, if you don't mind me telling you now."

"I know. I know. I'm not sure what good I'll be to you, but I'll see what I can do."

"Sylvie. Look, I've never been a big believer in some of that stuff people say about you. I reckon you can find water. That dowsing thing's been around for a long while, eh? Mostly just lucky guessing though, right?"

Sylvie didn't answer. She knew people thought her odd.

"But I'm desperate here with this whale thing. Got this whole fancy packaging deal going with Chicago, people coming up here from the suburbs of Cincinnati and Pittsburgh and God knows where, and I haul 'em out here and all they have to show for it is a sunburn and a cup of cappuccino. Well, the news is out. Folks are going elsewhere: Oregon, Baja, California, B.C. Hell, they fly off to Alaska. But that doesn't help me and my family much."

"Well, the whales weren't exactly here because they were waiting for tourists to look at them."

"I know that. But I don't understand what happened. The whales were always around the island. Maybe we scared them off. Wouldn't that be some ironic?"

"No, it wasn't that."

A single gull swooped low and tracked alongside of the boat. Sylvie was eyeball to eyeball with it. As if they knew each other. She reached into her pocket and found a crumb of a cookie, held it aloft, felt the beak touch her skin as the gull took the food. He dipped his head as if in thanks and then swooped off.

"Then you do know something."

Sylvie knew more, much more than she ever let on to people. Deep intuitive things. She had collected knowledge and built upon things that came out of her connection to the island, the sea, the sky. She had never been able to fully harness the knowledge and form it into some orderly package, but she knew there was a powerful wisdom that she had accumulated. William Toye and his books — and even his madness — had been the catalyst for her to begin to harness some of it, to piece together a hodgepodge of science, philosophy, history, and metaphysics into something that, well, made sense. To her at least.

Should she say that some believed the moon was a hole in the night sky with light coming from another dimension, an astral plane? Should she begin by telling Moses that dowsing had to do with the magnetism of the earth, that birds migrated north and south according to their knowledge of the earth's magnetic field, that people were governed by it more than they ever knew? Should she let on that she could read the magnetic field with all of its pulses and variations like a road map? On the island, at least, she could do these things. She could walk anywhere on the island now with her eyes fully closed and know exactly where she was going.

And the dolphins, the fishes, and the whales all travelled in accordance with magnetic paths, the highways for migration. The earth had its own magnetism and the weaker but insistent pull of the moon sculpted those magnetic paths. It all made sense, perfect sense, until you said it out loud to someone and then you sounded like a bloody fool.

"I don't think you can make the whales come back."

"Don't tell me that. Maybe we can attract them with something. I'm sure you know a lot more about whales than a bunch of Bedford Institute experts. Please, Sylvie, help me on this one. I've always, always been lucky in my life. Everything just fell into place, but I can tell that it's not that way this time. I need your help."

"You know what whales eat. You think you can drop several tons of krill each day here like so much chum to attract them?"

"No."

"You say you can tell something's changed?"

"Yes."

"I thought men didn't have intuition."

"We've got something. We're usually just too caught up in other stuff to pay attention."

The boat was in the Trough now, and Sylvie studied her familiar shoreline from this unique perspective. In her mind she could see herself sitting there on her favoured rocks, waiting for the whales. She could see herself as a little girl. She could see herself as a young woman. She saw herself standing there in the spring after the death of her first husband, David Young. She saw all the whales of the past but none of the present or the future.

"Sylvie, where are they?"

Sylvie closed her, yes, and knew the whales were out there, far out there. East northeast.

"Can you take me to them?"

"Just point the way."

Sylvie knew just where the whales were. Four hours from the coast of Nova Scotia, they appeared, three young ones, two old. Moses saw them before Sylvie did but she already knew they were there.

"How did you know?"

"I knew."

Big swells rolled under the hull of the boat as it rose and fell gently upon the spine of the sea. Clouds — fuzzy white ghost ships — were scattered in the sky. It was an innocuous day of little wind. Good thing. Moses had not been this far out in a long time. He checked his global positioner to make sure he wasn't lost, but knew that Sylvie could guide him back if need be.

"Can we go in close to them?"

"Yes," she said. She held onto the railing at the side of the boat, watched the grace and beauty of the sea creatures rising with the swell and then falling back in the water. *They are here and this is where they are supposed to be.* She did not say it out loud. "What can we do to lure them back toward the island? Is there anything?"

"What do you think I can do, talk to them, Mr. Slaunwhite?"

"Can you?"

"No." It wasn't like that. She felt their presence, she even believed that they were aware of her. This was not whimsy. The two older whales, she knew, had been there as she had walked the rocks along the Trough when she was twelve years old. They had always returned to her over the course of many years. They had not fallen prey to harpoons or disaster or disease or collision with supertankers. There was a thread of something that connected them to the island, to her. That was all.

"I'm glad they seem to be doing all right," she said. "I've missed them."

"Me too."

"Moses, we can go back now?"

He looked at his GPS equipment and was about to cut the wheel and turn about but instead he switched it off with the flick of a wrist.

"You wouldn't need this to find your way back, would you?"

"I don't think so, but then there have been generations of sailing men who could find their way back home without the need of electronic equipment."

"Well, I'll be the first to admit that I'm not one of them."

"Can I steer?"

"You betcha. If you run 'er up on some rocks, I got insurance."

"I'll keep that in mind."

Sylvie liked the feel of controlling the boat as she turned her about and knew, just knew, exactly where her island was. Moses

took off his Clearwater ball cap and placed it on her head, backwards. "That's the way the kids wear 'em, Captain."

"How am I doing?"

"You look like you were born to it, ma'am. But Sylvie,
about the whales. I can't bring visitors this far out. Too costly, too
dangerous. Hell, it just won't work."

"I know. But there's nothing you can do about it."

"That's not helping."

"Sorry."

"Hey, not your fault."

Sylvie almost believed she could formulate the words to
share what was in her head. Simple cause and effect, connec-
tions, intentions, actions. Change. But nothing was absolute in
life. Nothing final. Nothing perfectly meant to happen. There
was always flexibility built in, she knew this. She had learned
this during her eighty years. Always something to be made out
of the flexing and shifting of various energies of the world. But
she couldn't bring herself to explain this to Moses Slaunwhite.

After a long journey home, expedited somewhat by a fresh
wind at their back, the island appeared like a green smudge
floating on the horizon. Right where she knew it would be.
Right where she left it. She felt the island pulling her home. It
was a mildly euphoric sensation. She felt the island tug at her,
deep down. It was a wonderful feeling.

"I think you'll want to take her in," she told Moses.

"Like I say, got insurance in case you smash 'er to bits. Sure
you don't want to test your skill? You could probably do it with
your eyes closed."

Sylvie thought she probably could. "I've done enough for
one day. Better the whole world doesn't see a woman driving
your boat. Bad luck, eh?"

"No such thing as luck."

"Glad to hear you say that."

Chapter Thirteen

G reg Cookson was a university student with a summer job. He had been hired by the provincial government to go around the province counting things that some deputy ministers thought should be counted and logging the numbers into a small, state-of-the-art laptop computer given to him by his supervisor, Vance Little. Greg eventually realized that this was a make-work project, but he didn't know that at first. His beat was the South Shore, where the province was fairly certain there were a lot of things that hadn't been counted lately.

For a while, he counted various items of trash along a certain stretch of the Number 3 Highway. He wore shorts and a t-shirt that promoted the Canadian rock band Rush. Not everyone understood that he was a Rush fan, and they couldn't fathom why anyone would wear a t-shirt that stated you should move faster instead of slowing down and taking it easy. Some drivers along the Number 3 actually drove faster when they read "Rush" on Greg's t-shirt. Subliminal maybe.

So Greg counted the trash, then street lights in Lunenberg, mailboxes in bad repair in Bridgewater, and potholes in Mutton Hill Harbour. He fed all these numbers into his laptop and plugged in a modem at night so he could send it all to his boss in Halifax. He wondered what he was going to count next, and he was starting to feel like a character in a play. Something in the Theatre of the Absurd that his St. Mary's University English instructor had taught him about. Eugene Ionesco had written the script for his summer job. But despite the absurdity, he liked the job okay. He had some outrageous games logged onto the hard drive of his laptop for desperate moments of boredom. And he was outdoors a lot, getting a tan, meeting people sometimes. Sometimes young women asked him what he was doing, though, and he felt like a fool trying to explain that he just counted things. Computers had to be fed information and there wasn't enough new information to feed them. Summer job. Help get him through school, that sort of thing. Someday he'd be a lawyer. He didn't know why he wanted to be a lawyer. Maybe he didn't want to be a lawyer, really. He just liked the idea of going to law school. Or at least just telling people that he would go to law school. Something about going to law school seemed cool, but he didn't know why.

Vance Little phoned him at his bed and breakfast, the place with way too many flower arrangements and lots of Victorian stuff that made him gag. "Greg, I need you to go out to Ragged Island on the ferry tomorrow and count people."

"Wow."

"Pardon me?"

"You want me to do the census?"

"Not exactly. But our information is way out of date. And we can't tell from our records exactly how many people live out there. Oh sure, we could guess, but why do that when we have you out there working for us. Department of Transportation wants hard data, as current as possible. Something to do with the ferries. Guess this is really why we hired you. Our man on the scene. Households, family counts, breakdown by age. Probably take you a few days. I'll download the templates for you after we hang up if you want to plug in."

"Sure." Greg plugged in the modem to the phone line and his laptop sucked up the forms it needed. Greg lay back on his Victorian bed and studied the frills and fluff of his room. The B&B, known as Fishermen's Rest, was run by a gay couple, two men from Calgary who made extraordinarily good breakfasts with local German sausages and eggs and enough cholesterol to kill an Olympic runner.

In the morning, the ferry left Mutton Hill Harbour dock no more than thirty seconds after it was scheduled to go. Cormorants dove out of the way of the big iron vessel. It was a bright warm day, and the sting of salt in Greg's nostrils gave him a *déjà vu* feeling that would not go away. He looked down into the cool, greenish water and saw his own wavy reflection. He kept staring at it like a movie of himself pumped through a special effects toaster. He looked up in time to see an osprey dive straight down into the water and nail a fish, then surface, make a difficult ascent back up into the air, shake itself, and fly off toward an island. Something about all this made Greg decide that he wouldn't be a lawyer at all. Maybe go to law school for a year, then drop out and hitchhike around the world. It was that kind of a morning.

On the wharf at Ragged Island, people smiled at him, but no one said hello or anything. He looked like a tourist, a bit goofy with his laptop case slung over his shoulder and the white zinc gunk on his nose to keep it from burning. Zeke, one of the owners of Fisherman's Rest, had insisted he start wearing serious sunblock or he'd end up with a purple nose and terminal skin cancer by the time he was sixty. Greg figured Zeke was probably telling the truth.

So where the hell to begin? It wasn't like counting fire hydrants in Halifax. People. He was counting people. One, two. No. People didn't stay put. He'd have to go door to door, rely on verbal information. Feeling like an encyclopaedia salesman. Oh well, nothing to do but go for it. Do the best he could. Get a tan, enjoy being on an island.

He started with something that looked official. There was a post office, but it had been closed down. There was a school that looked like something out of the TV show *Road to Avonlea*. The door was open. Someone was inside.

"Hello?"

"Hi."

Whoa. Like going back in time. Young woman not much older than him in a long cotton dress, sitting at a desk, cutting out oak and maple leaves from coloured paper. Another *déjà vu*.

Greg tried to explain what he was doing on the island, but suddenly he didn't care. He stared at her delicate hands cutting out the leaves.

"Gotta be ready for fall. Lesson plans, visual aids. I'm Kit Lawson, I teach here."

Greg sat down in one of the desks in the first row, a desk designed for a kid in third grade. "This place is unreal."

"It is. That's what I love about working on the island. It's not like anywhere else. Your first time here?"

"Yes."

"Did you see the moon last night?"

"What?"

"The moon? Full. I can pick out H.G. Wells and Jules Verne now. Grimaldi. Gutenburg. The Bay of Rainbows was like a gift. Daedalus, Doppler — right there, just like they were announcing themselves. Abulfeda, Birkoff, and Botzman."

"Excuse me?"

"Sorry. Craters. Those are some of the craters on the moon. I can finally identify even some of the obscure ones. Telescope on a clear night is all you need. When there's no fog out here, the conditions are perfect."

"They named craters on the moon after science fiction writers?"

"Yes. And astronomers and composers. I love the moon."

"So do I," Greg heard himself say.

Kit stood up and wrote something with chalk on the old-fashioned slate blackboard that had been washed to a dull, clean surface: "The bluebird carries the sky on its back."

"Henry David Thoreau," she said. She gave a curious smile that made Greg think she was a little off her rocker.

"I read Thoreau. Something about a cabin in the woods."

"Yes. Something like that. Welcome to Walden Pond."

She was making those little leaps in conversation that he'd encountered only once before with a girl from St. Mary's he'd gone out with, fallen in love with, then given up on. So much smarter than him, more complex. Greg was a nuts and bolts kind of guy. Get a degree, go to law school, maybe *don't* drop out, get a job that paid good bucks. All there was to it.

Out of nervousness, he unzipped his computer case and set the laptop on the desk. It seemed absurdly out of place. But Eugene Ionesco was writing. Greg inhaled deeply the smell of chalk, of washed hardwood floors, a trace of wood ash. He felt under the desk and there was chewing gum, decades deep.

Ohmigod, he thought. Something going on here. He didn't know what. He knew that it was important. Shit. "I'm doing a kind of census of the island. D.O.T. is looking for the number of people living here."

"Dot?"

"Sorry, Department of Transport. It's a summer job. Better than sitting on my butt at home."

"You'll like this place. Everything about it. This island has saved my life." Kit began to talk as she continued to cut out fall leaves. Words spilled out of her as strips of coloured paper fell onto the floor. Everything right up to her boyfriend being busted for growing dope.

Forty minutes had passed. Greg felt like he'd been hypnotized. He stared down at the blinking cursor on his laptop screen. *One*, he said to himself. So far he had counted one person — a teacher. Slightly mad, very beautiful. He didn't know if he had the ambition anymore to get up and count others on the island.

"Do you remember your dreams?" Kit asked, getting up to erase Thoreau from the board.

"Hardly ever."

"Tell me just one."

"Um. Well, I'm in a boat and there are no oars. I'm in the middle of the ocean, but somehow there are all these people out there. Laughing at me. I don't know what to do and I'd like to get out of the boat but I don't know how. I have no sense of direction. And they keep on laughing."

Kit walked over and ran her hand in a strangely casual way through his hair. He thought he'd maybe faint or something, felt his jaw muscles paralyze, stared at the curser blinking at him. "I know that dream. It takes many forms. Don't worry. You're okay. The fact that you told me the dream is a good thing. Most people are chicken shit to tell you their dreams because dreams are mostly about fears."

"I thought you were going to interpret my dream?"

"Who do I look like? Carl Jung?" She laughed. Greg had a funny look on his face. Maybe she was laughing at him.

"Oops, sorry. Not trying to offend. Sure I'll interpret. No surprises really. You have decisions you have to make about what to do with your life. You don't think you're going to make the right decisions. You don't even know how to begin to get them right. People are laughing at you. You feel insecure. Welcome to the human race."

Greg clicked off his computer. Jesus. Why did he feel like someone had just lifted twenty tons of concrete off his head?

"Is this what you do?" she asked, pointing at the computer.

"Not really. It's temporary."

"What do you want to do when you get done university?"

He would not answer with the lawyer thing. No way. "I want to volunteer for work in Third World countries."

"Which ones?"

He was caught off guard. It was some kind of a teacher's test.

"Australia," he said.

She laughed. "Right. Good choice." She laughed again and he was back in the oarless boat. Now he thought he could see all the faces of people laughing at him from high atop the deck of a big cruise ship. The big ship reminded him of another dream. He had dreamed that he had been on the *Titanic* and gotten off in time — that was one version of the dream. He was in a lifeboat with no oars but he had left the ship of his own accord. The rest of the people on the *Titanic* were laughing at him. And then he saw the name of the ship, not the *Titanic*, but the *Queen Mary*. And it began to move off. He was alone on the ocean. Waiting for the currents and winds to carry him to Australia perhaps.

Greg heard what he thought to be gunshots in the distance, felt that he'd arrived in some strange land where the usual principles of civilization did not necessarily apply.

"Just the men at the junkyard. Not to worry," Kit said. "Harmless fun, shooting at cars and whatnot."

"I guess I better get on with this census thing."

"Go talk to Sylvie. She can give you the run-down on everyone on the island. She'll save you the legwork."

"Is she reliable?" he asked like an idiot. *Oh, frig.* What was he, back to being a lawyer now?

"Sylvie wouldn't lie, if that's what you mean. Sylvie understands the nature of truth better than any of us. Oh, and hey, I'm sorry I laughed at you. I didn't mean it like that. I just thought it was kinda cute."

"Okay."

Greg walked out of the dark school into the blinding sunlight and tried to get a grip on himself. Another gunshot. Men hooting and laughing. A car raced by suddenly with a roaring exhaust and a storm of dust. It had no doors on it and the driver was sitting on a plastic milk crate. He blew the horn and waved. Greg waved back.

Greg was waylaid on his way to Sylvie's house by a twelve-year-old American kid named Todd. Todd had been looking out his bedroom window, daydreaming about a video arcade at Seaside Heights on the Jersey Shore. He liked the island okay but he felt peaceful here all the time and he hated feeling peaceful. He called it being bored, and it was the result of a programming problem in his mind that related to vocabulary and the colouring of words with various meanings. He had phone lines and Internet but it just didn't feel right spending too much time at his computer somehow. Like there was some kind of a force field around the island that made you feel uncomfortable sitting in front of a computer.

Todd's sister, Angie, was getting on his nerves here, too. Hell, she got on his nerves everywhere. And it was a little too much like they were living in some old TV show like *Little House on the Prairie* or something. It was so weird that it was interesting sometimes, but other times he felt cheated out of a *real* life, not being able to ride his skateboard down to a Seven Eleven and get a large watermelon-flavoured Slurpee when he wanted it. Life was passing him by. If it wasn't for the fact that his father was letting him shoot guns at things in the junkyard, he'd hate this place altogether. His mother still didn't know about it. She was all caught up in time-tripping back to life in another century. Even though they had electricity, they had a hand pump in the kitchen. You'd pump it and water came up out of the ground. Spooky or what?

When Todd spotted the mainlander with the laptop, he was out of the house like a bullet. He introduced himself and told the college student how much RAM he had in his own portable Compaq. Like two wolves in the wilderness, the older boy and younger boy sniffed each other out by trading computer specs and knowledge about software programs. There was common ground and so a sense of community was established. Todd said he'd trade his upgraded Duke Nukem and a couple of three-dimensional chess and checkers programs for anything Greg could offer.

About then, both noticed that the sky was getting very dark off toward the eastern side of the island. They were standing by the road on high ground, overlooking the harbour. Greg noticed several boats hurrying back to port. They walked up the steps of Todd's house and sat beneath the sheltering roof of the old porch.

Greg had bootleg copies of several new adventure games and some role-playing stuff that fundamentalist church groups thought was downright satanic. It would be an equitable trade.

Todd was only a kid but Greg trusted him, as an outsider, to provide some inside edge on what this island was all about.

"I don't know, man. It's like voodoo or something. People talk funny, they have weird ideas, and everything is like a thousand years old. You can't pick up TV stations from out here unless you have a dish and we don't. But I don't hate it."

Greg knew that when a twelve-year-old kid said he didn't hate a thing, that this was actually very positive. "Do you know how I can find this Sylvie woman? I think I got the directions screwed up."

"Oh, yeah. Just go to the end of the road. Keep going until the road ends and there's just a grassy path. She's pretty cool, makes good stuff like cookies and cupcakes. But a little strange."

"I'll be careful."

"Right."

Todd brought out his laptop and they swapped software as the sky darkened around them and some lightning flashed off at sea. They ran out of things to talk about except for short fragments of sentences about technical attributes of computers. In another time or place, they might have been trading baseball cards, a Hank Aaron for a Roger Maris, and talking batting averages and ERAs; or further back it might have been kids with whittled model boats showing off a miniature keel or rudder. Instead, it was this. Todd was losing interest after a bit and felt boredom creeping up like a familiar thief in the back alleys of his brain. "The only problem with this place really is that nothing ever happens here."

Nothing, Greg understood, was the thing that drove you nuts when you were twelve years old. What happened today? Nothing. What are you gonna do this afternoon? Nothing. What's bothering you? Nothing. Nada. Inactivity. Lethargy and stasis. He fully understood Todd's dilemma. Nothing ever happened on the island. In one respect.

That's when they heard the hail begin to hit the roof of the porch they sat on. Both closed up their laptops and set them up against the house wall. "Holy Mother of Shit," Greg said suddenly as he saw a waterspout moving up the eastern side of the island from the sea. He'd never seen a waterspout before and neither had Todd. It was a tall dark funnel of water leading from the sea right up into the heavens, a water tornado. Both Greg and Todd were certain it would not turn out to be real, that it just had to be a Steven Spielberg special effect. Nature could never be this cool.

It only lasted about five seconds, at least the part they could see. Then it suddenly disappeared. The hail stopped hammering on the roof of the porch and, as Todd's mother and little sister came out of the house with mouths agape, the hail turned to heavy dollops of rain, each drop seemingly the size of a hardball. Puddles formed almost instantly and those massive clots of rain would hit and flatten, looking like shiny CD-ROMs tossed randomly about on the yard.

And then the fish began to fall out of the sky.

At least fifty mackerel splash-landed in the great sheet of water that was now the front yard. They hit with a splat, flipped and flopped around, along with a few slithery eels, rockweed, kelp, and the odd clam and quahog that cracked upon impact. Then the sun burst out just like that and there was a rainbow over the government wharf, where the tethered boats were rocking back and forth like toys in a tub.

Chapter *Fourteen*

T wo hundred and forty-four. That was the number of living souls on Ragged Island. Sim Corkum at the D.O.T. finally had the figure he was looking for. His right-arm man, Vance Little, had this kid out there on the island; none of this blind government statistics bullshit. Always out of date, the feds' material was. The province had the actual number now and it was lower than they had reckoned. That was the good news. There was a bottom line to this thing that could be nailed down. Vance owed his minister a favour, big time. The Honourable Dancy Moxon. It was his own riding, dammit, but Dancy knew he had to cut back the ferry budget to the bone to keep the minster of finance off his back.

It was all there in logical black and white. The only thing holding them back had been that damn whale-watching thing. Tourism was all over it like flies on shit. For God's sake. You might think they found gold out there or some friggin' thing. Assholes driving their families out here from all over North America. If it wasn't for that, Sim knew they could have closed that island down a long time ago. Close the school, give up on the subsidy to the ferry, the whole shooting match. Save the tax-payer plenty of out-of-pocket expenses. Nice neat package.

Moses Slaunwhite — all his fault. Couldn't leave well enough alone. But that was all over now. The Department of Tourism was getting complaints. No whales were being spotted on the Ragged Island tour. Big-ass company in Chicago fun-nelling all those tree-huggers and fish-loving freaks in; they were ticked off and were bailing out on the whole shebang.

Not one bloody reason left to defend the cost of the ferry service. All over but the shouting and the stink. So it was a done deal. Sim could tough out the clatter. That's why Dancy had appointed him to the job to begin with.

Moses took the call from Chicago with as much dignity as he could muster. Nails in the coffin, he supposed. Boat would have to go back to the bank, he realized. What next? Always something around the corner. If only they could count on a good water-spout once a week, they'd have tons of tourists. Maybe find some dinosaur bones or buried treasure. Jeez, what would it take? Wasn't like the old days when fish was enough, or cabbages. Had to roll with the swells, take the tide as she turned, what?

Nobody really knew what went through a mainlander's mind, especially the mind of some bureaucrat in bloody Halifax.

Up to his ear hairs in patronage and piss. Had Moses had a bit of foresight, he'd have rallied the people of the island sooner, but islanders thought they had seen it all — the good times, the bad times, wars, rum running, sea disasters, and the death of the fishery. But this was different.

It was a damp and mildewy afternoon when Sim Corkum and the Honourable Dancy Moxon stepped off the ferry onto the wharf. Moses saw them sniff the air like a couple of worried Labrador retrievers; he noticed the shoes the men wore — city shoes with a shine. Moxon had a Colwell Brothers suit on. No one wore a suit on the island unless it was funeral. Not even to regular church on Sunday. Only when someone died.

Dancy went to the Aetna with Sim and they ordered clams and chips, sat at the picnic table outside, and talked to a woman and her two kids from New Jersey who were there eating ice cream cones. Sim realized that Vance's college kid had probably counted them since they were spending the summer there. Three, he realized, three fewer year-round residents. Island population down to 241. Can't subsidize a bloody year-round daily ferry service for a mere 241 people. He pointed this out to Dancy after the family left.

Where to begin? Dancy had built a career in a short span of time out of glad-handing the public and then turning around and dropping to his knees at Province House any time the premier or minster of finance wanted him to chop jobs or service. Not that he liked it, mind you, just the way things were. He referred to it as "the government of the here and now," as if that meant dick. Not exactly the fat days of Pierre Elliot Trudeau. Not that at all. Deficit reduction was the name of the game, the ladder to the top.

Where to begin? He knew he was brave to even be here at all. Away from Halifax and here in his own riding to put forward the bad news. Public meeting coming up at four o'clock. Had to be out of there on the six-thirty ferry. Home to the wife by ten if he was lucky. Back to civilization. Clayton Park on Bedford Basin suited him much better than where he had once lived in Blue Rocks. Course, there was still the constituency office in Lunenberg. Two afternoons a week. And now here he was. On a bloody offshore island. Legwork. No one would ever accuse him of not trying to face up to the music. He knew he could ignore New Germany, Hebb's Corner, or Vogler's Cove. As long as he had Bridgewater and Chester in his pocket. And Mutton Hill Harbour. Mutton Hill would understand, he knew they would. People in the town always believed islanders were backwards. There would be resettlement to consider. Think of Joey Smallwood doing what he knew he had to do for his people in Newfoundland. *Come ashore boys and burn the boats. Join the twentieth century.*

Only now it was nearly the goddamn twenty-first century and a province couldn't afford to keep people living on islands like this. Health care. Education. Transportation, the worst of it. Consolidate. Pay some compensation if need be, although there would be an easy away around that. No work on the island. What were you compensating people for? Doing them a bloody favour, was the truth to it. All this swimming through Dancy's head like a school of piranha as he worried his fried clam on a plastic fork.

He nodded to the old woman with the card table beneath the willow tree. He waved and said hello even though he figured she was probably old and deaf. "Look at the old thing," Dancy said to Sim, "sitting there with a couple of cakes and a loaf of bread, waiting to sell them to tourists, but there's no tourists here. Oh hell ..."

Dancy got up and went to the old woman, offered to buy the bread and her cakes. Gave her a twenty and told her to keep the change. She seemed puzzled, didn't like the feel of the money in her hands, knew it to be charity and wondered what

Dancy Moxon was going to do with her baked goods.

Nothing left to sell, she was off home and Dancy gave the stuff to Corkum, who peered around the area like a bloody vandal, and when he was sure no one was looking, he tossed the stuff into a trash bin. But got seen in the act by Moses Slaunwhite running towards the Aetna.

Moses tipped his cap and then tried to smile but couldn't. Saw Dancy Moxon sitting at a picnic table with fried clams and greasy fingers.

"Sim Corkum, D.O.T.," Sim said, trying to be civil.

"The meeting, right?"

"Yup."

"You two aren't really out here to tell us what I think you want to say, are you?"

"It's just an information gathering session. Dancy tries to keep in touch with his constituents. Nothing political about it or anything."

"That's a load off my mind," Moses said with a fresh coating of sarcasm.

The old woman sat in the front row at the meeting. Moses and his wife, Viddy, were there. Viddy had a new haircut from the unisex salon in Mutton Hill Harbour. Short, like the women on the TV shows they picked up on their satellite dish with the illegal decoder. Kind of like English schoolboys. Everybody noticed Viddy's hair. She liked it that way.

Everyone also noticed Sylvie sitting front and centre. Probably so she could hear, they thought. An old woman probably needed to be close to the action to hear anything.

About seventy-five people were in the room, in the dusty so-called town hall, which was hardly ever used. Everyone had given up on committees and meetings. Everybody ended up getting mad at one another over nonsense like what to do with the town hall trash — even though there was hardly ever any. Dump it at Phonse's and pay him a small fee or send it to the mainland or just heave it into the ocean? Another environmental argument that was never resolved. Moses volunteered to haul it to *his* property and put it in a hole and bury it and some people had found fault with that. So they stopped having meetings. And the hall grew lonely, diminished in esteem, and dust gathered for conventions inside.

The dust made Elise sneeze. She was allergic to dust mite excrement and here she was among a whole universe of dust mites left to hatch and feast and roam about. She decided she could handle it. Something important was happening here. Canadian politics. Nova Scotian democracy in action. Something she could talk to Bruce about when he came up from Wall Street — or *down* from Wall Street as they would say on the island. The island was down. Everything else in the world was up. Even South Carolina was "up" from here.

Kit would have sat next to Sylvie but she didn't want to be up front. She sat in the back, and not far away from her, leaning against the back wall, was that college kid, Greg Cookson. Came to the island one day counting things and forgot to go home. The Swinnemars said he could have the fish shack on the front point for the summer and he went crazy fixing it up with discarded lumber and bent nails. Only today was Greg beginning to realize that his final report to the province (before he had quit his summer job) was somehow useful to these two assholes from the mainland.

Everybody in the room knew there was bad news coming. The good news was always *no* news, when everyone off-island left them alone. But now this.

Sim Corkum rubbed back his thinning hair three times when he stood up, as if paving the way for what was to follow.

"I want to thank you all for coming out tonight and I apologize for intruding into your well-deserved free time. I'm not going to talk too long but I just want to say that we've always had good relations with Ragged Islanders ever since the D.O.T. took over the ferry service. I know that Gil Lovelace has done a good job under contract for us to keep your roads in order and plow the snow in the winter, and our department appreciates his work."

A couple of men with reddish sunburnt faces laughed, someone hooted, and there was one set of hands that applauded. Truth was Gil Lovelace did have the contract but did a bad job, or at least a lackadaisical one. Potholes aplenty in the summer. In the winter, snow had to be a foot or more before he'd start up his damn rig and do anything, but people generally didn't like to complain. If you did, you'd end up with some asshole like Corkum down here in the town hall trying to change things and make it worse. Lovelace himself cleared his throat heavily and with significant orchestration, wanted to spit but thought better of doing it in the hall and swallowed whatever he'd sucked up from the back of his throat.

"Now this meeting tonight," Sim continued, "isn't going to be easy for me or you or Dancy here but I hope you'll bear with us because there's a silver lining to this thing and you just have to let him get around to it." At that, Sim knew he better just shut up because he was setting everybody on edge, the very thing he was trying not to do. "So I'll just say it's good to see all of you here tonight and turn things over to Dancy Moxon, your elected representative."

Scattered polite applause, cursory and insincere. Dancy stood up, studied the tips of his fingers, and looked up at the dark space above the exposed rafters. "God, I love this island," he began. "You know, people in Halifax don't understand about places like this. They don't understand the importance of men and women and their families and their honourable traditions of working on the sea, farming the land. They're too detached from all that now and they live in a different world. But I don't need to tell you that."

Men fidgeted in their seats. Phonse Doucette couldn't keep his mouth shut so he blurted out, "Jeezus, Dancy, don't give us none of that sweet shit. Just cut to the chase and save the heavy breathing." Which was pretty polite considering what Phonse really wanted to say.

"See. That's what I mean. You're a people who won't stand for all the foolish diddle daddle of bureaucrats and city talk. So I will 'cut to the chase' as Mr. Doucette said. I'm here tonight to offer you a challenge and a great opportunity. The world's changing out there and I can't stop it. I can't do a damn thing about what they do in Ottawa, slashing those transfer payments, ripping the heart out of our social safety net and taking your tax money and wasting it on pension plans for Quebec senators. I can't change that. But what I can do is keep your voice alive in Halifax. I let the premier know at every blessed cabinet meeting who I represent and he hears me loud and clear.

"So when I hear him tell me that he's cutting the ferry service for good to Ragged Island, claiming that it's too expensive, too shamefully expensive amidst all the belt-tightening and squeezing of our financial resources, I stand up and say, 'Mr. Premier, I'm not going to let you do that to the good people of Ragged Island.'"

"You're damn straight on that," Moses cut in. "You cut the ferry service and you'd cut the lifeline to this island."

Sim Corkum began to worry over a bit of a sunburn scab on his nose as Dancy nodded like he understood ever so well what folks were thinking about. "Well, there it is. I know you don't want me pussy-footing around it. I fought the good fight, friends. But I lost. That decision has already come down and I'm going to tell you what it was. And how it happened. Ottawa cut us back to the bare bones. You've all read the papers. We had a

choice. We either close down hospitals or we trim the transportation budget. We send people with cancer back home to die
or we treat them. And in order to treat them we have to lose
three ferry routes in this province along with cutting back in a
hundred other places. All of which is gonna hurt, I know."

People were on their feet. Men and women were mouthing
curses in English, German, and French. Dancy stood his ground,
took it all in. Sylvie thought his eyes were beginning to water.
Was he feeling hurt at the rage of his constituents or was it well-
deserved heartburn from his meal at the Aetna? She dared not
guess which. Sylvie sat still as a stone. There was an odd numb-
ness she felt in her toes and fingers, a dizziness in her head and
a great hollow sensation in her chest.

"Dancy," Moses said. "We're not going to let you screw us
like this."

Other people were less polite. Epithets were hurled. Sim
looked with glazed eyes at the back wall. He'd driven down this
road before, knew all the twists and turns, knew how to get himself out of a ditch if he had to, knew there would be a smooth
patch further ahead to take a deep breath and cool off. All he had
to do was keep from getting sucked into a public argument. Put
a good face on it like Dancy. Damn, if the man didn't have the
silver tongue of the devil himself. Some truth in what he said,
but there was a prize awaiting Dancy if he could cut the budget. Dancy never went out on a limb like this unless there was
something in it for him, probably get himself bumped up to a
better cabinet posting. That would do it.

"Look, it's already done. By October of this year. And as far
as I could tell, the province was going to do frig all to help you
adjust. But that's when I put my fist down and said no way. So I
fought for you again and now we have a plan."

Everyone was talking to each other now. Chewing over this
inevitable, impossible news. "Look, we've had meetings in

Halifax and stared at this thing upside down and sideways until we were cross-eyed. Your ferry was costing us, each year, over a thousand dollars per person. Unless we raise the fare to fifty dollars a head, each way, we still couldn't make a go of it. There was some hope for the tourism side of things. I argued until I was blue in the face about the spin-off dollars that went into mainland businesses and money coming into the province with the tourists but you and I know that things changed. Who ya gonna blame? Mother Nature?"

Moses seethed with rage. It was as if Dancy was pointing a finger at him. What the hell could he do if the whales stopped coming? He couldn't keep his mouth shut. "We're not going to take this lying down."

"S'right," Phonse said, loud enough to hear the echo in the room from the high ceiling. He was thinking about his arsenal of weapons. A lot of people on the island had become pretty good marksmen thanks to his outdoor arcade (as he was calling it now). And he had a pretty fair loyal following on the mainland, customers who would be cut off from their water taxi ride to his junkyard. Hell, he was about to lose everything he'd worked for all his life.

Dancy held his hands up in the air and offered up a theatrical glum look. "I know what you're feeling and I hear you. The bottom line is this. Nobody has to move off the island. But if you are willing to relocate, we're going to foot the bill. We're going to offer every bit of assistance we can and we'll even buy your property at the assessed value."

Joe Krauss spoke up now. "You and I know that our homes aren't assessed at fair market value."

Dancy shook his head, acknowledging this point. "Funny, nobody's ever complained before about their assessment. Nobody's ever come to the tax office to say they are not paying enough taxes and want us to raise their assessment."

It was a cruel blow. Dancy knew he better cut it out. He was right on that point but he had to be more cautious.

"But what about the older kids who go to school on the mainland?" Kit asked. "How are they going to go back and forth?"

"They'll need to find a place to stay on the mainland if the families don't want to move."

"How's this going to affect my school here on the island?"

Dancy was up against it again. "Education has decided the island school's cost is ineffective."

"So you want us all to bloody move off the island, don't you?" Viddy blurted out. "Who are you, Joey Smallwood? What the hell is going on here?"

"Look. Each of you is going to receive the package of what we can offer. Some will want to stay, some will want to leave. What we're offering, I repeat, is an opportunity here. I'd suggest you don't turn it down. It will only happen once. And if it wasn't for me — I know you don't want to hear this — but if it wasn't for me, you'd all have squat. You'd lose the ferry and be on your own. Now you will have a compensation package, moving assistance, a buy-out of your property if you so desire, and back on the mainland you'll have full services, schools, hospital, the whole shebang."

Moses was silently considering the alternative. What if he took up the slack and turned his boat into a shuttle to the mainland? He thought it through right down to fuel costs and knew that it was a losing proposition. He'd have to work his ass off back and forth each day and he'd have to charge twenty bucks, maybe thirty, or even fifty. It wouldn't work. He wished the numbers added up differently.

Dancy and Sim were walking now toward the back door, ignoring the faces. Somebody tore up paper and tossed it at Dancy; that was as physical as it got. Greg leaned against the back wall and regretted his role, however small, in what was happening here. The ferry was waiting, the very boat destined to be axed for good come fall.

Sylvie sat silently, her hands folded. Kit came up and sat down beside her with hurt and madness in her eyes. Sylvie took her in her arms and rocked her like a little child while others watched them. Sylvie was the oldest islander. In many people's minds, Sylvie represented the island and its past. Now this.

Sylvie rocked Kit and wondered what it would be like to be an old woman, left alone to herself on a deserted island. How long would it take for almost all of them to leave, despite their loyalty, once they were cut off from the mainland, set adrift. What would happen when she needed medical help? She knew she could not leave but that the government would try to pressure her into doing so.

She couldn't bear the thought of leaving her four dead husbands and their graves. She could not even begin to tolerate the idea of *not* waking up in her house, *not* having her backyard, never again going to sit by the sea at the Trough and wait for whales. She knew the world had moved on without her — the mainland world. Her existence, her life, her dreams were inconsequential. Sylvie felt the eighty years of her life collect and push down on her as if the gravity of the planet had just increased tenfold. She began to sink into the depths of the Sea of Cold, the Bay of Despair. Sylvie hugged Kit to her and wondered if she might not be approaching a good time to give up her allegiance to life. Eighty years on. Better to collect it all and say it had been a very good life. The best. Better that than leave the island.

Chapter *F*ifteen

No. She could not live on the mainland. She envisioned the town. Mutton Hill Harbour. And the hospital there. She had not thought about the hospital for a long time. She had not thought about the baby.

Kyle Bauer's father had drowned at sea in a fishing accident, as had his older brother, Taggert. Kyle himself had put in two years working on long liners out of Lunenberg before he found himself one day on the Grand Banks in the middle of his first truly vicious storm. A November hurricane, the last of the season; the first that year, however, to make it this far north.

Kyle came within six inches of going over the rail when one of his shipmates reached out a hand and grabbed the back of his rain gear as he started to go over the side. Kyle fell back onto deck, locked onto something solid, and hung on, barely able to pull oxygen into his lungs, the air was so full of sea water. He lay like that, shivering and crying, until the captain steered the ship out of the worst of the storm, and they had to pry what was left of the young Bauer kid off the deck plates. Whoever had saved his life had gone overboard. Three men in all had fallen prey to the hunger of the sea: Kessel, Hennigar, and Johnson. Kyle thought it was Hennigar who had saved him but he could never be sure, so he prayed for all three and spoke highly of all of them to anyone who would listen. Hennigar was a heavy drinker who kept a knife in his pants and would use it on anyone who he felt deserved it; Kessel was quiet and moody and never had any time for anyone; Johnson was a bully who always liked to pick on the weaker men on the *Good Fortune*. One of the bastards had saved his life.

It was 1942, a bad year for the planet, when Kyle Bauer left the sea for good and took up farming. But instead of moving down to his family's old acreage in New Germany, Kyle was lured to Ragged Island, where cabbage was king.

He held fast to the railing as he sailed out on the ferry, on a clear day in June, to see what there was to see on Ragged Island. An island at sea seemed an unlikely place to have a sauerkraut plant, but there it was — a big old warehouse by the government wharf where island women shredded cabbage heads with knives that looked like sickles and dumped the cabbage into brine solutions. There was a growing mainland market for island sauerkraut. It had a reputation as being the best sauerkraut in North America. It was served in fancy Halifax restaurants. It was shipped by the truckload across Canada and down into the Boston States. Better still, Ragged Island Sauerkraut had landed a massive contract to supply the armed forces. Canadian soldiers would go into battle against German troops with salted cabbage (made from the oldest of German recipes) in their stomachs.

Kyle had never been to the island before. All he knew was downtown Mutton Hill Harbour, the waterfront of Lunenberg, and throwing up on ships bobbing up and down on sickening swells over the Grand Banks.

Even though it was an island, in the middle you could forget the sea. It had a prairie sky, old swayback barns painted with ochre paint, a big empty forty-acre field going to wild mustard, and Kyle had money burning a hole in his pocket.

If he acted immediately, he could still plant for the coming summer season, but he'd have to move quick. So he leased the field and the ancient barn in poor repair. He hired old Mr. Swinnemar to plow the place for him and Kyle began to plant cabbage — just him and a hoe.

And then it rained for nearly a month. Kyle holed up in the barn and read from a stack of old *Weekend* magazines he found there. He made friends with the field mice and thought he was beginning to comprehend the language of the ravens who visited. At night there were owls and even bats. He thought it was all much better than being at sea. He thanked God every single damp night of that month that he was no longer a fisherman.

It was during the third week of the rainy season at about ten o'clock in the morning when he heard someone knocking at the barn door. When he opened it he saw it was a young woman — a tall, elegant slip of a thing with brown hair tied up in a bun. She wore a long dress and had a picnic basket in her arms. "Come in, please."

Lately, Kyle had only been communicating with ravens, mice, bats, and owls and had lost a good grasp of the English language.

He remembered that someone from Lunenburg had told him that most people on the island, cut off as they were, still spoke German instead of English. He could still remember his own grandparents speaking in German when he was quite young.

Sylvie Young walked into the gloom of the barn and smelled the wet hay. It was intoxicating. She saw a bed of straw underneath a tarp slung up over the beam to keep the insistent rains out. "One more week of this and the sun will be out, you'll see," she said.

"I'm not complaining."

"Hungry?"

Kyle felt a little dizzy. Hungry, he was. Hungry for food, for companionship, for something more than the way he'd been living here. Hungry for life to start over for him. He wanted to shout it all out but he held it back, didn't want to scare the young woman. What was she? Twenty-three, twenty-four? Older than him but only by a year or two he guessed.

"I'm Sylvie. Live out at the end of the road. Up Along. Brought you some bread. And cookies. And tea. Do you drink tea?"

"Yes, please."

Kyle lit an old kerosene lamp so he could see her better. The place was like a dungeon but as the warm yellow light came up, it transformed instantly into a palace. *Sylvie, Sylvie, Sylvie.* He took one sip of tea and stared into her dark, warm eyes and his life story spilled out of him. Then he let go a deep, significant sigh that had been trapped inside him for either three weeks or all his life. And he felt so much better.

And Sylvie understood, or at least thought she understood. She believed she knew all about men and their dreams and their intentions. Sylvie, who had sworn off ever getting involved with any man after the death of David, also felt something let go inside her chest. Kyle's story had suddenly reminded her that men were also human.

She had kept herself at a comfortable distance from them for a long time. Now she wondered how she could have done that for so long. She had learned to live fully alone. Men were always polite to her on the island, but always formal with her and she with them. On separate planes of existence.

Now, in a barn, with a fledgling cabbage farmer from the mainland, she felt otherwise. She poured tea, cut off big, thick slices of dark bread, and talked about death for an hour straight. Kyle told her about Hennigar, Kessel, and Johnson. Ugly, selfish, and even violent men, he could attest to that. But one of them had saved his life so he could turn his back on the sea and become a farmer.

"I don't think the rain can keep going much longer," Sylvie said. "I haven't seen the moon in nearly a month now. The moon always gives me a feeling of peace. And I miss that. But even without seeing the moon, I can close my eyes and feel its effect, the tides tugging one way or the other. I know other people on the island have this ability too. I can tell you if it's high or low, mid or whatever. I can see it in my mind even if I'm not there. Isn't that silly?" Sylvie didn't know why she had launched into talking about her personal little quirks, her eccentric tricks of mind and body, but there it was, out in front of them like the food on the blanket spread out on the straw.

"I don't trust the sea," Kyle replied haltingly. "Took my father and my brother. But still I couldn't move inland. I feel like this is where I'm supposed to be — in the middle of this island. I'm safe here."

"You are safe here. And so am I. But why did you come out here?"

"I don't know. I'd never even been here before. Back in Mutton Hill Harbour, everybody talks about this place ... well, you know how they talk." Kyle was sorry he brought it up. *Inbreds, hicks, and loonies was all that lived on the island.* That's what he had heard. Although it wasn't true at all. Mainlanders' prejudice.

"The island can be kind and good. I know."

"Hasn't been too kind so far."

"It's a test."

"Right."

"Yes. Think about it. Water, the thing you don't trust. Lots of it falling from the sky. Is it trying to drown you?"

"You're crazy." Beautiful but crazy, he wanted to say.

She smiled. She'd been called crazy before, and he meant nothing bad by it. "P'rhaps. But you haven't drowned yet, have you?" Sylvie knew all about various forms of drowning. David Young down beneath the ice, over and over how many times in her waking and sleeping. Stories, oh those ungodful stories of all the men who didn't come back from fishing. Of wrecks out front at the Trough. Yes, the sea had its hungers and its taste for humankind.

"No. I'm doing surprisingly okay." Okay meant he was going out of his mind and couldn't bear to read one more magazine with gossip about Hollywood movie stars and what was going on in Toronto.

Sylvie leaned back against a bale of old, musty timothy and looked up into the darkness of the lofty barn. The warm yellow lantern light dancing on the skin of her cheek and her neck made Kyle catch his breath. He moved towards her and could not stop himself from touching her face, gently with the tips of his fingers. Sylvie closed her eyes.

Above them birds — swallows probably — fluttered. Kyle traced his finger across her lips and then pulled back, lay down on his back on the straw that was his bed. Sylvie found herself lying down beside him. They both lay there still and quiet. The rain came on quite strong just then and the kerosene lamp was running itself down to a half-sincere blue flame. It was a little chilly, after all, and the two of them came together for warmth.

Kyle didn't know he was going to kiss her until he was already doing it. Sylvie didn't seem to mind, and Kyle knew he should stop there because this was so far the best thing that had ever happened in his life and he didn't want to mess it up.

He knew that he *was* finally drowning, but it was not as he had expected. He touched her hair, stroked her cheek, and kissed her again, so delicately that he didn't go all the way to the bottom of the sea this time. Instead, he drifted down slowly and patiently and all the while he heard the sound of the thrum of rain on the wooden shakes of the roof. And so did she.

The rain stopped six days later. The sun came out and only a third of the cabbage seeds had rotted in the cold, wet soil. That left two thirds to sprout and poke their way through, eager and waiting for the sun. Kyle and Sylvie replanted the lost third and Kyle never complained once about weather problems. The island gave him back the prairie sky he had remembered from the day of his arrival, and, because he was way up on a smooth, round drumlin of a hill, he could see the waters of the ocean and bay on all sides. There it was. And for once he was glad it was there. He had a high, safe place to live on an island and didn't mind the sea at all if it could keep its distance.

After a few days of working, Kyle noticed he had some problems with his feet, and his back was hurting him, too, just like on the ships where he had worked. Sylvie worked his back and massaged his feet sometimes and that made it all better. Sylvie was the most remarkable, intelligent, and mysterious woman he had even known. But then he'd really had almost nothing to do with girls and women. He had expected to live all his life alone and never marry. Now he wasn't so sure.

By August, Sylvie had invited Kyle to live with her, but he insisted they get married first.

"I made a promise to myself never to remarry," she told him.

"Break the promise. Please."

And she did. A Lutheran minister of German descent named Keizer married them on Monday afternoon in Mutton Hill Harbour. It was a private ceremony. Kyle's mother was there but that was about it. The minister was only half there. He wasn't all that keen about marrying people who were not in his congregation, but he did it as a favour to Kyle's poor widowed mother who invited him to Sunday dinner once a month.

The cabbage crop was a good one, especially the plants that grew from the late seeds. Some heads grew to be big enough to fill a bushel basket, one per basket. The sauerkraut plant was still gong strong making sauerkraut for the troops and so the price was fair and equitable. Kyle and Sylvie harvested cabbage right up to and beyond the first frost in late October. They were already planning for the next season in late November when Sylvie looked up at the quarter moon one night and knew she was pregnant.

Kyle made the mistake of buying a radio to help entertain them through the long winter. Winston Churchill and FDR came into their lives — news of some very important meeting in Casablanca on the far side of the ocean from here. Kyle and Sylvie talked of Hitler, of Mussolini, of Japan and China even, and ravages of war all over the world. It seemed impossible that all of this was happening on the same planet they lived on.

And then Kyle learned that someone had thrown a rock through his mother's window in Mutton Hill Harbour on a Sunday afternoon while she was having dinner with the Lutheran minister. They were both, after all, Germans. Or at least of German descent.

Kyle went ashore to fix his mother's window and some young hoodlums came by and shouted curses at him. He picked up a newspaper later and discovered that German spies had been caught in Halifax and that German subs were regular visitors off the coast. Kyle cursed his own heritage but knew that whatever had happened in Germany was like some kind of disease, something he could not possibly understand: Jews being led into gas ovens, monsters killing babies, burning down villages, trying to rule the world. Impossible things.

And so this was the world he was bringing a child into, he pondered on the ferry back to his island, back to Sylvie. All winter and into the spring, the radio reminded him of what was happening out there. Kyle realized how he'd had his head under a bushel basket. He was blessed with a wife and then a child on the way and he was in the middle of another good and profitable season of cabbage growing. He leased another field to grow savoury for the sausage makers in Lunenberg and also planted blue potatoes, kale, and Swiss chard. The crops were bountiful and life was good, but by August, he was cursing his own good fortune and haunted by the knowledge that there was an imbalance of happiness and tragedy in the world.

It was a personal thing. He had no right possessing such good fortune if it meant that all those others were suffering. The thought grabbed him in the middle of the night and would not let go. Nothing could keep him here.

Sylvie could not hold him back, and on the day when he took the ferry ashore to catch the Halifax bus, she sat in the sunlight on the rocks at the Trough and felt the warm north wind, smelled the sweetness of cut hay and wild roses of the island. She waited for the whales to find her. She dipped her feet into the clear tidal pools that swayed with golden seaweed and asked the vast ocean to give her the proper perspective of time, the belief that time would pass and everything would be okay. Her husband would return.

Kyle failed the physical to get into the army, and the navy would not take him. Problems with his feet and a minor deformity in his spine. Kyle had thought it was all mere aches and pains but it was going to keep him out of the war where he felt he should be. He took the failed physical personally, knew there was some personal and historical connection with being German and believed more vehemently that he must be part of the war effort. He had to end the incalculable suffering once and for all like the other men he was meeting who were willing to make sacrifices of themselves, who instinctively knew they must fight to keep the world free. He did not want any of the glory of war. He only felt duty and necessity. He would do this for his wife and child, for them and for all those of German descent in Canada and America who hated what Hitler's Germany was doing to innocent people.

So he did not give up. The Merchant Navy was willing to take him. Yes, of course, he'd had experience on ships. He would not admit how much he feared them, however.

Kyle Bauer was assigned to an old tanker called the *Piccadilly* with a cargo of airplane fuel to be transported to Liverpool, England. With only half a crew, the ship sailed to St. John's Harbour, where more men were brought on board for the crossing. Kyle was shocked to discover that some of the new crew were as young as fourteen and he went directly to the captain, who everyone referred to as the "Old Man."

"This is unreasonable, sir. They are only children."

"There's a war going on, Bauer. Look, those lads told me they were of the appropriate age. Lots of these outport kids don't even have birth certificates. How am I to say who's lying and who isn't? Hard times, Mr. Bauer. The worst of times. We need capable bodies on board. Navy's got all the good men. We do what we can."

Kyle realized that the world outside of his island was an unfair and inhospitable realm. He stared down into the cold, dark waters of the narrow harbour entrance as they steamed from St. John's and met up with a convoy coming from New York. Safety in numbers, he hoped. They had a military escort. But he knew his ship was a prime target. Airplane fuel — high octane. One good hit.

Sylvie woke to the sound of thunder. She ran outside but it was dark and the sky was full of stars. The wind was sifting through the high branches of the spruce trees and it was a cool, clear night. She had dreamed the sound. But she could not go back to sleep that night and sat up listening to the radio, listening only to the music, always turning it off when it came time for news. She felt panic in her limbs, made tea and tried to be quiet but ended up sobbing and rubbing tears out of her eyes and smoothing them onto her cheeks. She felt the tide ebb and begin to retreat. She could chart in her dark mind the necessary paths of migrating birds and schools of fish, the avenues of whales and dolphins. Wondered at the uselessness of all these things she was feeling and wondered again why she was feeling them.

Kyle saw the first vessel in the convoy take a hit two days into the Atlantic crossing. He was on watch and called the sleeping captain to the bridge. The *Piccadilly* was rear and centre, supposedly well protected by flanking ships, navy ships with weapons to the ready. Within minutes, one of those escorting vessels took a hit that echoed through the night. She did not go down, but Kyle saw her slow her pace. One engine had been damaged. She could not keep up with the convoy.

"Bloody hell," the Old Man said.

Kyle knew as well as his captain that the *Piccadilly* was now perfectly vulnerable. He studied the surface of the night sea, understood the certainty of the hidden danger in the waters of the North Atlantic, felt a hot surge of something forged of anger and fear within him. "We've got kids on board, Captain. Boys. They don't have any idea."

"We tough it out, Bauer. Try to change position to get some more protection."

But there was no protection to be had. Kyle felt the torpedo hit beneath the water line of the ship as if it had just impacted upon the soles of his feet. An explosion ensued that ripped metal plating apart and killed Newfoundland outport boys as they slept. The Old Man was quick to insist they abandon ship. "I don't know why she didn't blow on the first hit," he said. "Nothing for it now but to get in the friggin' water." He gave the order to abandon ship, and his words were barely out when the *Piccadilly* took a second hit and an explosion roared out of her belly with deafening and terrifying force.

Kyle found himself at the rail looking down into the dark sea. Fire swallowed up the sky behind him. A young man with his back ablaze was running towards Kyle. One of the Newfoundland kids. Kyle looked around for the Old Man but he wasn't there. He heard yet another explosion and saw a ball of flame racing towards him. He grabbed the screaming boy and jumped with him into the sea.

The water grabbed at him with icy claws as he hit. He lost his companion, and Kyle felt the sea close in around himself as he went under, but his life jacket brought him back to the surface. He began to swim away from the ship in an awkward stroke. But then the boy surfaced, sputtering, calling for help, wailing, "I don't want to die! Don't let me die!" Kyle could not see him but swam towards the voice, grabbed hold of an arm, felt the hand go into a clenching vice that seemed to want to hurt him. The kid clawed at Kyle's life jacket and Kyle pulled at the cord, undid it and jammed the kid's arm through it, pushed him around backwards and got his other arm in as he screamed. Then Kyle tried to hang on to the boy, keeping himself at arm's length, but all too aware of his own inability to stay afloat without the jacket. In the light of the burning vessel, he saw it had been nearly ripped in half. The *Piccadilly* was starting to go down, and its descent was creating a current that was pulling both of them towards it. He was unable to continue to hold onto the boy now. Reluctantly, he let go of the life jacket and started to swim away from the insistent, invisible force dragging him towards the sinking ship.

All he knew was dark, cold, and wet, oily ash falling on his face, even on his tongue so he could taste it. He swam, pulling himself away, but towards what? The other ships in the convoy were already moving on, trying to get back into formation and out of range of the German subs.

And then the ship was beneath the sea and it no longer wanted him for a crewman. He felt the insistent tug at his limbs cease. Kyle was barely afloat, trying to calm himself, but his legs were numb with the power of the cold water. He reached out his arms to see if the boy was anywhere nearby, but he could not be found. Suddenly he became fascinated with the idea of having been attacked by an enemy that could not be seen. An underwater ship with a crew of men with German blood like him. He wondered what could have lured them away from their homes, their lives ashore. He tried to fathom what he himself had been thinking. How could anything have led him away from the happiness and safety of Sylvie and the island? For a few quiet seconds it seemed that he was floating without effort. A calm presence came over him. He wondered if there was another sailor whose last name was Bauer on board the sub that had attacked them. He wondered how any man could learn to kill strangers with such detachment and ease.

And then he tasted the sweetness of the air. Despite the smell of burning fuels and scorched metals, he realized how good it was to bring air into his lungs once, and then twice. But he was tiring quickly. When the salt water found his open mouth, he thought he tasted something familiar now, the taste of Sylvie, her mouth upon his. The taste of love and life and all that was meant to be.

By sunrise, Sylvie had calmed herself and imagined dozens of ways that Kyle might have died. All of the horrific possibilities that had crowded her overzealous imagination. As the sun began to pull itself up out of the sea and grace her with its warmth, Sylvie, still pregnant with Kyle's baby, huddled within her coat, went back to the tidal pool and slipped her hand into the water, then tasted her fingers, closing her eyes at the powerful sensation of cold salt water upon her tongue.

That afternoon, the anguish she felt in her heart was compounded by a terrible physical pain. At first, she believed she had brought it upon herself, but it was more than that. The sea was rough as she was ushered to the mainland in Noah Slaunwhite's boat, but the nurses were kind to her in the small Mutton Hill Harbour hospital and they wept with her, like sisters, at the loss of both husband and child.

Chapter Sixteen

Brian Gullett had been with the *Halifax Herald* for almost twenty years now. He was forty-three but still envisioned himself as a young hotshot reporter, believed himself to be an investigative journalist, a crusader. Around the office, he was known as "the Gull." He'd staked out patronage in the Buchanan government, gone hard on the real culprits of the Sydney tar pond, and relentlessly hounded politicians of all political persuasions accused of being on the take. He even went after Mulroney once when the great jaw was prime minister. He couldn't peg anything corrupt on Mulroney but had some verifiable stories about him when he was in Dalhousie Law School. Flunked out due to venereal disease, more or less. It wasn't Watergate, but it should have been worth something.

The *Herald* didn't print that one, nor a couple of Gullett's other best pieces. Pity, really. But the Westray Mining tragedy had come along — all those young men killed underground — and that had taught him how brutally cold, hard, and unfair the world really was. He metaphorically buried himself in that blasted-out coal mine and immersed himself in the lives of the victims' families. He nailed it down good: the way government bureaucracy fails, the way corporations try to make a profit at nearly any cost.

In a way, he had dug too deep into the story. Brian Gullett lost his edge. He once had a cheery defiance over exposing corruption, over attempting to right a few wrongs through freedom of the press. But the price had been a high one. He now had few friends. He had never gotten around to investing the time and energy into forging one good, lasting, serious relationship with a woman. Westray had soured him in a way that he couldn't quite recover from. He saw exactly how the whole tragedy could have been avoided. He saw how a hundred business and government decisions that followed were leading down similar paths — offshore oil and gas exploration, government cutbacks in health and education, landfill issues, human rights agendas that were backfiring.

Recently, Brian Gullett wrote about what he saw and how he felt about it. Amazingly, his editor, Trent Stoffler, gave him a pretty long leash. Legal was always on his heels, but he knew how to make them listen and he could get away with ninety percent of what he wanted. Brian should have been smart enough to know that he'd been too long without a vacation, too hyper on every story he got his teeth into. He was getting addicted to his own brand of slash-and-burn crusader journal-

ism, and everywhere he turned in Nova Scotia, he discovered a
deadly seam of coal, a collapsible roof, explosive dust ready to go
off. He saw the world in terms of Westray. If he could only head
off one or two disasters, save a few lives, he'd have spent his time
well on this planet.

He thought he was getting a good lead on a pretty weird but
interesting story when a secretary at the Department of the
Environment called to tell him that her office had decided to
ignore something about a toxic waste site on Ragged Island.
"The deputy minister says we just don't have the staff to deal
with it and it's far enough off the mainland so that it probably
won't do anybody any real harm. Sounds like this island is like
some kind of wild west town. Lawless. No Mounties.
Unregistered cars with drivers who have no licenses. Lots of
guns. Like some kind of militia thing, maybe. The Mounties
know all about it but just want to keep hands off."

Brian knew all about that kind of cavalier attitude found in
Tory and Liberal governments alike. Ignore the problem and it
will go away. Son of a bitch. He punched up Ragged Island on
his computer and got a few old stories about fishing and cabbage, stuff about old boat building traditions, recent clips about
whale tours, eco-tourism, a feel-good piece about a family of
American tourists staying for the summer. Not much to go on.
Gullett began to wonder if the woman at Environment had
some mental health problem. Was she just making it all up?

But he needed to chase it. He couldn't help himself. It was
a wild tale that didn't make a hell of a lot of sense, but then
nothing made much sense to him these days except the funda-
mentals of human motivation: greed and power. If he dug away
the apparently organic topsoil of this island, what might he really find buried beneath the surface?

Gullett had lost track of his true sense of fairness, however, and
stopped worrying about Ms. X's motivation for spilling her inside

information. She was a part-timer at Environment, a pool secretary who spent most of her time at D.O.T. Sim Corkum promised her a good shot at a more permanent desk with some newer computer equipment if she'd make the phone call to Gullett. The task allowed her to use some of her skills as an amateur actress that she'd honed under the tutelage of Jeremy Ackerman and the Dartmouth Players. Sim and Ms. X were both pretty proud of the way she handled herself on the phone and he almost made the *faux pas* of suggesting there was a lot more money for her to make in the dark netherworld of phone sex than in government offices. But he knew when to keep his mouth shut, these days.

As the ferry docked at the government wharf on Ragged Island, Brian Gullett smelled a familiar fecund fishy smell. It was an intoxicating aroma to him. The smell of the real Nova Scotia, not the stench of a room full of computers and body odour and janitorial disinfectants like back at the newsroom. It was the fragrance of life. A light fog hovered over everything and glazed every particular of the island, including the people, who had big drops of mist in their unkempt hair. He took off his glasses and wiped the lenses clear on his shirt. It was a damp day but a warm one. He walked off the wharf and pondered the proper phrasing. *Anybody know of any toxic waste sites? Ever hear of someone trying to form a secret military organization? Weapons training, that sort of thing?*

He need not have worried. "You headed to Phonse's are ya?" a friendly man on the wharf asked him.

"Phonse's?"

"The junkyard thing. That's 'bout all that brings the visitors now. Figured it was what you're looking for."

"Yeah, that's it. The junkyard thing. Which way?"

"Straight up the hill road. Can't miss it. Have some fun, eh?"

Fun? Brian wondered. Junkyards and fun. Damn strange place, this island.

Brian trudged up the hill and walked through the gate with the neatly scripted lettering: "Doucette's Recycling. Welcome." He knew that in the States, the word "recycling" often meant out and out environmental decimation. It was always the worst environmental rapists who called themselves environmentally friendly, and wasn't it the Mafia that owned half of the waste disposal operations of North America these days?

Phonse had a glass of home brew beer in one hand and a rifle in the other when Brian walked in through the door. The man with the gun smiled broadly. "G'day, my friend. What's yer pleasure?"

Brian looked off toward the field of old cars and the crazy assortment of washing machines, dryers, and various rusty appliances. "I, ah, well, I'm just getting into rebuilding old cars. Classics, you know. Late sixties, early seventies. Thought I'd just see what you have here in your yard, ya know, in case I need some parts."

Phonse nodded, winked an eye. "Wonderful hobby, restoring old cars. Had a Pontiac once that I'd give my eye teeth to still have in one piece. A sixty-five, she was. Big-bellied beast with a good engine and a nice smooth ride. I was young then, though. Drove it to hell. Straight away. Wrecked the transmission and then drove it right into the ocean just to be done with 'er. Young and foolish. Should have kept her, bunged-up transmission and all. If I'da put her in a shed and hauled her out nowadays, car buffs would be green with envy. Young and stupid was all I was. Worked hard at it, too. Nowadays we appreciate the old things better."

"Some of us do, it's true. So it's okay if I just wander for a while? Be like a kid in candy shop for a guy like me."

"Oh, Jesus, please, wander all you like. Stay off to the left there. Down to the right, might get a little noisy with the practice range and all. Safe to stay up thataway, though. Make a day of it. C'mon down for a drink or a sandwich from the Aetna if you get hungry."

"Thanks." Brian liked Phonse immensely. The guy reminded him that he'd spent way too much time around city people — editors and proofreaders and other journalists as cynical as he was. He wandered off, but already began to wonder what the "practice range" was. And what should he think of a man with a beer in his fist at this time of the morning? Hmm.

The fog was thinner here up on the hill and he could see above the bulk of it, like he was on some great mountain peak, above the clouds. But instead of pure, snowy white mountains, he was surrounded by junk cars. Hoods up, doors half pried off, engines disembowelled, tires piled into ugly foothills. Visions of the future. The world as junkyard. Chevy. Ford. Toyota. Nissan. Bronco. Jetta. Shadow. Taurus. The hulks would all eventually rust and crumble into the soil and all that would be left would be the nameplates of cars, stainless steel or chrome-plated, to be found by future generations. Code words from the past, as meaningless as television.

Brian sat near a pile of pancaked wrecks at the top of the hill, looked out to sea, saw the mists below his Kilimanjaro thinning out, disappearing. It was quiet here except for birds and squirrels chasing each other across front seats and into the glove compartments of GMC trucks. A couple of convertibles had young spruce trees growing right up through the upholstery. Apocalyptic and peaceful. Made him feel like he was missing something in his life and he didn't quite know why.

The place was much bigger than he had thought at first and Brian wondered how all these old automobiles had found their way to an island. Completely illogical to haul junk out to sea like this. Stolen cars, perhaps. Most of what was left here looked unsalvageable, though. Couldn't be much of a market for pure rust, seized engines, bent wheels, hammered hoods, and carburetors that had moss growing in their throats. What the hell was going on here anyway?

Brian walked on until he came to the gravel lane that snaked down to Oickle's Pond. Ringed with weeping willow trees, Oickle's Pond might have almost looked beautiful except that it was covered with a thick, tarry oil: almost looked like a frozen dark pond in winter. An old Rambler station wagon, a '58, was nosed in at one end of the pond, and there were dozens of unlabelled, rusty barrels, some along the edge, some floating like ugly fat swans. Frogs burbled up through the muck, and there was a great blue heron standing with blackened legs and tar-stained feathers across from him. Whatever had been dumped here, Brian knew that it was an unpardonable sin against nature.

He took his old reliable Pentax out of his bag and snapped photos, the sort that Greenpeace would have loved to use for posters. *Save the world before it's too late!* A pile of shopping carts stuck out of the muck on the other side of the gooey, black pond water. Random household garbage had been dumped along part of the sorry shoreline and looked like it had been set on fire once. Big gobs of plastic had melted into a convoluted mass that had flowed partly into the pond, like lava spewed from a volcano, until it had set. Brian turned over a couple of the barrels near where he stood to try to read the contents, but they were too rusty. Some clearly had the skull and crossbones, however. He'd found his toxic dump. Wondered how that charming and friendly chap was responsible, then didn't give it a second thought. People'd do anything for a buck. What better place to dump poisonous waste that would otherwise cost you a mint to legally dispose of properly? He took a full roll of thirty-six pictures and reloaded for more.

That's when the first shot rang out. Brian put his camera away and waited. A second shot and then a third, then a full volley of blasts and the echoing racket of bullets hitting metal. It sounded like a war had begun. Brian couldn't tell how close or how far away the shooting was, but he hid behind the willow tree that seemed surprisingly healthy, given its proximity to the sludge pond.

As soon as Brian decided that he was more or less safe and that he was not going to die, he realized that he liked the feel of imminent danger. Decided again that he'd missed his calling, should've been a war reporter spending his days in Sarajevo, Cambodia, or Northern Ireland. Instead, this would have to do.

He got his bearings, tried to get a fix on where the shooting was coming form. The "practice" apparently had begun. He hiked back down past the archives of automobile wreckage until he found a place to post himself behind a Bluebird school bus that was lying on its side. Poking his head around the side of the front of the bus, he saw six men in what looked to be duck hunting outfits shooting at items dangling in the air. On a clothesline strung between two sturdy posts hung what appeared to be a portable hair drier, a toaster, a telephone, a laptop computer, and a portable CD player.

Men were shooting at the objects, occasionally scoring a hit and laughing. And among them was one boy who couldn't have been more than eleven or twelve years old. It didn't quite make a whole lot of sense.

When the shooting stopped for the men to reload, Brian saw the proprietor he had met earlier. Phonse walked out from a shed towing something on a little kid's trailer. It was a large TV — 36-inch screen, was his guess. He parked it in the middle of the gravel clearing and walked back to the gunmen. Brian saw him hand a double-barrelled shotgun to the boy, who loaded it as if he'd been doing it all his life. Then the kid walked out into the middle of the clearing and let go a mighty double blast with both barrels. The TV glass shattered, the tube imploded and gave off a very satisfying report in its unlikely demise.

All the men cheered.

Brian sat down on the automotively littered soil and reached in his pocket for a cigarette, momentarily forgetting that he had quit smoking over two years ago. He fingered his pockets nonetheless, gave up, torqued a telephoto lens onto his Pentax and clicked off a good twenty pictures of the men while they were still holding their rifles. Got one of the kid holding his shotgun aloft. There was a story here, but he knew he didn't have all the pieces yet.

The reporter waited twenty minutes until he was sure that practice was over. Then he sauntered on down to the rattletrap building that appeared to be the junkyard office. Phonse was alone now, his feet up on a pile of old *Car and Driver* magazines.

"Guess you heard the racket," Phonse said.

"Yeah, wondered what that was."

"Oh, you didn't know?"

"No."

"Sorry, my friend, I would have invited you, too. Just the usual routine. People come from all over to have a go at it. Good clean fun. Although business is slacking off now the eco-tourism thing is down the tubes. Should have known you couldn't trust whales to do what you wanted them to."

With little prodding, Phonse gleefully and generously explained the nature of his little theme park, noted that even a few off-duty Mounties from the mainland came out to practise. "Hard to keep up with appliances and computers and whatnot though. Still, it's one last use for all the junk manufactured on the mainland."

"What do you do with whatever's left?"

"Oh, bury it or throw it in the pond."

"That kid looked like he was having some fun."

Phonse nodded. "He'd had at them little computer monitors before but I'd promised him a full screen Panasonic. His father said it was worth double the price of admission."

"You charge people."

"Not much. Twenty bucks an hour plus ammunition costs. Beer, if they're interested. But I only let 'em drink after they shoot. And I never let kids have more than a couple of sips."

"Guess you have to have some regulations."

"Absolutely. I run a tight ship. Wanna have a crack at anything before you go? First-timers usually just like shootin' the windscreens out of cars."

"Thanks anyway. Maybe I'll be back another time and take you up on it."

"Bring your friends."

So there was no Michigan militia here. But there was a deadly pond and some wacko with a junkyard where people came to blast away at the paraphernalia of civilization. If Brian had given himself a day to cool and consider things, he might not have let the words take over and write the story themselves. He might have considered that this bad publicity for an otherwise respectable island was going to do more harm than good. And he had kind of liked Phonse Doucette. The man seemed genuine, sincere, fun-loving. Certainly no guerilla groups practising for the upheaval of the state here. Just some good old boys with a sightly off-kilter sense of entertainment. Sure, the kid shouldn't be there with a gun. But he was blowing up a TV after all. Commentary on the electronic media.

Brian unfortunately decided to trust his initial instincts and believed that if he cracked the lid on this thing, there'd be

shit a mile deep. God knows what kind of vile toxic waste
melded with pure, raw gun culture. Pollution and violence.
Nifty news combination.

Trent Stoffler, his immediate boss, was out of town and the
stand-in editor, a rookie, was easy to manipulate. The story ran
page one. People all over Nova Scotia were outraged. Ragged
Island had proven itself to be some kind of horrible place, not
the eco-destination it had once been thought to be. How the
hell could all that go on unnoticed, unregulated, and unlicensed
here at the tail end of twentieth century, anyway?

E-mail flowed, phone calls were placed, editorials were written, and, worst of all, inspectors started to show up at Ragged
Island within days. As did more reporters. Phonse told them that
he felt like Jesus Christ in the Garden of Gethsemane now that
some damned mainland asshole from the *Herald* had published all
that horse shit in the paper.

The island was warped and wanked by TV, radio, and
newsprint for several days until a building under construction in
Bedford collapsed and killed eight workmen, taking all the wind
out of the Ragged Island story for a while. But the damage was
already done. And D.O.T. had no problem getting the cabinet
approval to kill the island ferry for good come October and
began offering very modest financial packages to bring Ragged
Island families back to the mainland and home to civilization.

Chapter Seventeen

People on the island began to bicker. Their home had made the national news. The province was trying to figure out what to do with Phonse Doucette, what to charge him with, how much to fine him, whether to put him in jail or what. The government had all the PR (and then some) that they could possibly need to do their good deed by moving as many families ashore as possible, bringing the islanders screaming and kicking into the civilized world of the late twentieth century.

On the island itself, everyone blamed one other for the crisis. Fights broke out over beer, rum, or just a lobster sandwich.
Many blamed Phonse, some blamed Moses for his failed tourist
business. Moses blamed the whales. While all this was going on,
Sylvie was working on some kind of cocoon inside herself.
There were only two things that were keeping her sane. One
was Kit's mental instability — a kind of roller coaster ride that
required the proximity of one solid and sane woman to hold her
down to the ground or to pull her back up from under the sea
of despair. And the other thing was this: kids. The two American
children. They visited every day, told impossible tales of life in
Upper Montclair, where people had money to burn and spent it
freely and frivolously on junk. These two, even Todd, who could
be arrogant at times, were great fun to be around.

Todd offered to bring his laptop over and hook it up to
Sylvie's phone so she could try out the Internet for recipes, but
she declined. Angeline asked for stories, and Sylvie was happy to
comply. Todd pretended that he wasn't interested but he was. He
listened while playing some kind of joyless little pocket electronic game.

A favourite was the story about the moose that Sylvie's parents raised from an orphan. Way back there in the early part of
the century. An orphan moose with long, gangly legs swam
ashore one summer and had to be fed milk from a baby bottle.
Sam they called him, and Sam he was. A moose made a fine pet.
(Todd thought she was making it all up but she was not. He
would report the story in a chat room on the Internet and get
spammed by other users who also disbelieved.)

Yes, a moose was a fine and loving pet. Sylvie's father, a big
man of few words with a long beard and few teeth, loved the
animal dearly and allowed the moose in the house sometimes
until it just got too big to fit its antlers through the door. "I rode
bareback on the moose, you know. And we borrowed a saddle

and rode Western style. Sam took me everywhere. He had kind eyes and a good heart and didn't mind people.

"My dad hitched up a plow to Sam and Sam didn't mind that either. He liked to work, Sam did. And we fed him well. In the winter, we'd hook up a sled and he'd tow us around Up Along and whatnot. Not a thing wrong with a moose for a pet.

"In the winter we had to keep a big, red blanket tied onto him so that a hunter wouldn't shoot him. You know how people like to kill things for sport. Sam lived a long and happy life, I guess, for a moose. He died the day after Dad did. Was his time, I suppose. We weren't allowed to bury him in the cemetery but he was planted in the field. Deep under. Bones are still there, I reckon. Old Sam, he was. You don't see many people have a pet like that anymore."

And that just sort of took the wind out of all the fine things in Upper Montclair. Old stories began to grow on the kids like those round globs of fuzzy, soft moss. Old and soft. Old stories and Sylvie, who didn't want to be thinking about any damn future. And she refused to get into blaming her neighbours for whatever the hell was going wrong. Let 'em all leave. She'd stay, figure something out. Maybe all she needed was another good, faithful pet like old Sam was.

Angie and Todd were given free rein of the island after their first couple weeks. As long as they followed the rules. *Don't go swimming in the ocean. Stay out of the way of young men gunning the engines of their ratty cars. Don't fall off the wharf. Watch out for poison ivy.* (But there was none.) *Don't talk to strangers, only people you know.* (But that's all there were at that point on the island — people they knew. Not many mainlanders or tourists.) *And, oh yes, stay out of the way of TV camera people and don't talk to reporters.* They'd misquote kids as sure as they'd misquote a politician.

Make a twelve-year-old boy look like some poverty-stricken juvenile delinquent for the sake of the dinner hour news and completely miss the fact that he was the son of a financial advisor from Upper Montclair.

Todd and Angeline knew all the trails inside the forest and along the coasts. They were careful around the rocky cliffs of chunked-up brown shale and cautious with their footing around big boulders gummed up with green algae from the sea.

The dreams of children are elastic and the island was an ever-expandable dream world of possibility. Todd carried around a video camera, sometimes working on what he called his "documentary." Angie filmed while he held up a sea urchin or a starfish or a tiny blue and orange crab and spoke at great length about the creature's eating and mating habits. He made most of it up but it sounded very convincing, the result of having watched too many science documentaries on PBS and the Learning Channel.

Near the old, fallen-down house in the clearing by the spring there were butterflies and a mountain of wild roses. Todd documented the place this way. "The Angioderm butterfly arrives here from Paraguay every summer to feast upon rose nectar and copulate with its counterparts who have flown here from .... um, the Marshall Islands. They bask in the glory of life in this haven and then, as the coolness of fall approaches, they leave for the southern hemisphere, and ride the Jet Stream south." That sort of thing. Todd had a nearly endless supply of words and fragments of unrelated knowledge that he jury-rigged any way he saw fit.

Angie, even as she filmed, remained in dreamland. She absorbed sun and sea and sky and salt water soaking through the pores of her skin and her thoughts. She never wanted to return to New Jersey. Rose petals sometimes fell like pink snow onto the ground around her. Butterflies were being just butterflies. Seals would pop up in the sea like Charlie Chaplin comedians several feet from where she sat on a smooth stone perch by the Trough. She thought often of Sylvie. Sylvie, with her stories of older times, better times. "I want to adopt you, Sylvie, as my grandmother and take you back to the States," she had told the old lady.

"No, child. I don't want to move. This is my island. But I can be your grandmother while you are here and when you are gone, we can write to each other."

"All right."

"Now we're family." And there was plenty of truth in that.

"In some primitive countries, extended families are extremely important and often family members who die can be replaced by others chosen from the community," said Todd.

"I'm very sure that can happen," said Sylvie.

The sea caves at the base of Signal Hill were always a bit of a tempting mystery. You could see them from across the little bay and you could try to look at them from above on the hill, but they were, alas, facing the open sea, and without a boat you could rarely view them head on. Todd and Angie had messed about that area. Sylvie had told them to be extra careful and to never ever go swimming there because a wave might wash you into the cave and under the hill. Sylvie was the one who had shown them the existence of the caves in the first place and told the tales to go along with it. Todd would create his own private pseudo-scientific essay about the caves and send it off anonymously on the Internet, where many people would believe it to be true.

Then August and a different phase of the moon. Lowest tide in maybe three years or more. Todd and Angie out on the prowl, looking for adventure, when they discovered that the shoreline in front of the caves was exposed. They scrambled down and landed on a strip of smooth, sandy beach — and saw a tunnel going back under the hill. "Too dark in there," Angie observed.

But Todd's tug of curiosity was a powerful thing and did its usual trick. Todd and Angie, hand in hand walking into the sea cave on a floor of smooth, damp sand, listening to the sound of their voices echoing. "This is way cool," Todd noted.

"I don't know."

"It's okay. Our eyes are adjusting. The pupils are dilating to allow in more light. See? It's not so bad."

The sea cave veered a bit to the left, the result of the weaker band of sedimentary rock that had been eaten away by the ocean over the years. And there was a low part where they had to duck down, but then it opened up again into a kind of room with a higher ceiling. Todd had a tiny flashlight attached to his collection of keys that unlocked things left back in New Jersey. He carried it everywhere, and it afforded a small, delicate ribbon of light.

But the stubborn moon was at work on that low tide. Water was seeping in. Todd was already practising the narration for a potential video documentary about this amazing place, trying it out on his usual audience of one. "We're here inside the sea cave of Ragged Island and, as you can see, well, it's very dark."

They sat on a small ledge about three feet off the floor, and, as long as Angie focussed on the bright sunlight creeping into the tunnel, she could keep herself calm. While Todd pontificated, Angie silently sang a Spice Girls song to herself, one that she used to hear on the radio in New Jersey.

Todd was wondering if there were any cave paintings or gold or buried treasure or maybe stalagmites. "Stalactites are usually formed by calcium and they hang down from the ceiling. Stalagmites are the ones that come up from the floor."

"Can we go now?"

"Sure. I'm hungry."

"Me too."

Splash.

Ankle-deep water and creeping up. The moon busy calling back the tide from the other side of the Atlantic Ocean.

Todd held onto his little sister's hand and urged her forward, but she wouldn't move.

"Damn," Todd said out loud. "Come on, Angie."

"It was dry when we came in."

"I know. I guess the tide is coming in."

"Let's wait until it's dry again."

"Not a good idea."

"Why?"

Todd wasn't sure how long it took tides to cycle. He also didn't know that there was a tropical storm sitting a couple hundred miles off the coast and even though the weather was perfectly fine in Nova Scotia, the distant waves were creating an unusual storm surge that was pushing the incoming tide.

When Todd finally convinced Angeline to jump into the water she screamed. It was only three feet deep, but that was almost up to her chest.

"We've got to get out of here now," Todd insisted.

"I can't."

"You can."

"No."

"It's no big deal."

"It is."

Todd said he'd check the passageway. Maybe the water was shallow there. He checked and, much to his despair, he discovered that in the passageway, with its low ceiling, the water was almost up to the top. There was only about a foot of air space.

When he sat back down on the ledge, Angie was crying. "I'm not moving," she said.

Todd felt panic rise up like some kind of acid taste in his throat. He shone his tiny flashlight around the cavern. It had a high ceiling. He was sure the tide would not fill it up. He didn't know what to do but heard a sound that sent a shiver down his spine. A wave had broken at the shoreline and water was rushing into the cave. He heard it slapping the top rock of the low passage. Damn.

"Here. Take this." He handed her his keys and flashlight. "I'm going out and I'm getting help. You stay put. Don't be scared. Move up higher onto those ledges, if you have to. Stay calm, Angie. I'll be back as quick as I can."

"Don't leave."

"I have to. I'll be back. You'll be okay." Todd could not look at his sister's face. He knew he'd start crying. When he jumped in the water this time it was already deeper from the waves pushing the sea in. Angie was still high and dry. She'd be okay. She had to be okay. He was almost swimming by the time he came to the low overhead. Inches of air left in the passage. He banged his head on the rocks several times. Blood trickled down his face. He took a mouthful of water when a wave washed in. Swallowed it and coughed but yelled to Angie that it was all okay. Just water up his nose. And then he was out in the bright sunlight, blinding him. He didn't know if he was doing the right thing. He couldn't think straight. Should he go back in and drag her out? He didn't think he could do it against the current sweeping in. An adult could. He'd have to find someone.

With blood running down over his forehead, Todd ran. His lungs felt like they were on fire. He wished they'd never come to Ragged Island. He wished he'd never woken up today.

Sylvie's house was the closest to shore. Todd banged hard on the door, then opened it and roared into the room. Sylvie stood calmly in the kitchen by the hand pump, washing dishes.

"Todd?" She saw the blood on his head first.

"Sylvie, Angie needs help. We found this cave down at the foot of the hill and there was no water and we went in." He couldn't get the story right. No air in his lungs. His head was spinning. "But then the tide came up kinda quick. I couldn't get Angie to come back out with me. She's in there."

Sylvie closed her eyes for a split second. *The sea cave.* Yes, she knew. *The low tide.* Yes. She understood. The tide was coming up and she knew there was something brewing at sea. A storm somewhere. She had not read a newspaper or heard anything on the radio. She just knew. Things of the sea, things of the moon. The tide would only get higher, waves would wash in there. Angie, inside the rock womb of that cave. Sylvie had been there once herself, as a teenager. Same low tide. No problem. In and out. An exquisite adventure. As long as you understood the tide business.

"You okay, Todd?"

"Yes. Help Angie."

"I will." Sylvie picked up the phone and called Moses.

"Moses, one of those little children from the States is in the sea cave. Tide's coming in fast. I think she's trapped. She's eight, Moses. Do you still have your diving gear?"

"Damn. Sold it when the bottom dropped out of the sea urchin business. But I can get down there with the Zodiac."

Sylvie could see the problem fixed in her head as clear as if it were a photograph. "Yes, bring the Zodiac, but it won't be enough. Call the RCMP and Coast Guard. Explain it. Tell them we need divers. Now."

"You know about Freda?"

"Who?"

"Freda. Tropical storm. Off Sable. It's staying put, but they're calling for heavy surf."

"Moses, I'm going out there. You get some help and get out there. Please, Moses."

"Yes, ma'am."

Sylvie knew Moses would do all the right things. But she also knew it was not enough for the immediate problem. She also knew that divers could not bring a little girl back out through the tunnel if it was filled with water and getting hammered with heavy waves.

"Todd, go get your mother. Bring her out there. I'm going to find a way to help your sister."

"She's going to be okay, isn't she?"

"Yes."

Todd left, running.

Sylvie split every second into four parts and made sure she was using her time wisely. *No, she could not swim underwater and get inside the chamber.* But she could see the tunnel in her mind. She could see the chamber inside. Back then, she had lit up a kind of torch made from a cattail. The tunnel could fill, but there was air space inside the inner chamber Todd had described. Ledges to be climbed. Tough it out till low tide again, a long twelve hours away. She shuddered at the thought of a little girl all alone in there. She put four chocolate chip cookies into a plastic bag and wrapped it in two more plastic bags, grabbed a flashlight and put it in three bags, sealed each one with a knot but didn't think it was enough. What else?

Negotiate with the sea, with death.

She hurried out the door of her house, towards the headland. She would stop for the college boy, Greg Cookson. The one who had quit his government summer job to live in the fish shack up along the shore. He'd said something about being a swimmer. Long distance, laps in a pool. She didn't know. He was bragging, maybe, a liar. No, he couldn't bring her out. It was twenty yards underwater.

There would be help, yes. But RCMP divers would be at least forty minutes in getting here at the best of times. Coast Guard rescue craft? What could they do? They couldn't get in there.

Sylvie felt betrayed by her sea, by the moon. But she knew she had some hidden knowledge, some special arrangement with death. Four good men, buried. She understood something of death, something to toss back in its face, maybe.

She walked fast and purposeful, her mind racing. *Death, take me, please.* She would not abide the drowning death of an eight-year-old girl. Gladly give her life several times over. *Take me, dammit. God, if you exist, bloody take this woman from the earth and spare the child.*

Anger rose up in her veins. Who was she negotiating with? She didn't even know what she believed in. Could she pull the tide back out to sea, make the waves from Freda move off in another direction, move the clock of earth ahead twelve hours to the next low tide? She kicked at a rock in her path and looked at the hopelessness of a small supply of cookies and an old flashlight in a couple of Ben's Bread bags.

Sylvie knew there must be something in the crazy mix of beliefs and understandings within her, something of value and use right now. Her personal relationship with the sea, with the island, with the way the planet talked to her. But there was an intrinsic logic that kept telling her that some things cannot be changed. Some things, even horrible things, were meant to be.

No. They were not.

Chapter Eighteen

Greg Cookson had slept in. He'd been feeling depressed for a few days. He wasn't used to living alone. He had quit his summer job, a good one that paid well. He'd decided not to go back to university. He'd started to fall in love with some woman on the island who turned out to be totally nuts. He'd screwed his life up in some grand way and didn't even quite know why. Twenty years old and living alone in a fish shack. No job. No real friends. Swimming in the ocean, staying up late and reading books by a kerosene lamp, collecting mosquito and blackfly bites. Sleeping late and waking up drowsy.

Someone banging on his door, opening it and walking in. He sat up quickly, pulled the sheet over his nakedness.

An old woman full of anger. Why was she angry at him?

"Sylvie."

"Greg. I'm going to ask you to do something for me. I'm going to talk you through it. I won't allow you to say no."

Greg's mind was a jumble.

"Listen. Carefully." Sylvie explained haltingly. She stumbled on words and regretted the loss of each second. She threw Greg a pair of canvas swim trunks she saw hanging over a chair. He slipped them on, still feeling funny about sleeping naked and having a woman, even an old woman, walk in on him.

"That sounds crazy. Why would they go in there? I saw the place but it always seemed too spooky to me."

"Kids. It doesn't matter. You're a swimmer, right?"

"I was."

"How long can you hold your breath?"

Greg laughed out loud. He had passed out and nearly drowned himself once in his own bathtub when he was thirteen. *One thousand and one, one thousand and two ... one thousand two hundred and ten.* He had counted. His father had had to break the door lock and haul him out of the bath. Greg could hold his breath. Not forever, but it was one of those idiotic skills that boys hang onto, and it had helped him win a swim meet or two — one less bob of the head to catch air.

"You want me to swim into this tunnel?"

"Yes. You have to do this for me."

"But I can't possibly bring anyone back out of there that way."

"I know. You have to go in and wait."

Greg couldn't bring himself to say what he was thinking. He was a swimmer, yes, but he was deathly afraid of drowning at sea.

When he was young, he'd been caught in a river current once at Lawrencetown Beach and swept to sea. He and his father both had nearly drowned. It was after that event that he had begun to practise holding his breath and swimming long distance, but he never had gotten over the terror of being swept a half mile to sea and expecting to drown. "I don't know if I can, Sylvie."

Sylvie said nothing, closed her eyes. Stood there in the morning sun with the door open, sunlight spilling into the room, washing the wood plank floor in bright, cleansing light. She didn't know what to say.

Greg had heard the words come out of his mouth and felt ashamed. He rubbed his eyes, recognized the depth of his fear, wondered at the horror of swimming underwater through some kind of a tunnel to a cavern inside a rock headland. Swimming blind and unable to come up for air if he needed to. But as he rubbed his eyes, this other thing came into his head. What had he accomplished in his whole life? Sweet nada. Nothing he had ever done had mattered very much. Swimming medals, good grades at school — what was the point? All his life, he realized, he'd been waiting for a chance to do something worthwhile. It was like a powerful, cold wave washing over him. He stood up.

"Do you know the distance?"

"Twenty yards. Wait for an incoming wave, stay deep and go with it. The tunnel turns halfway. You'll have to feel for the wall in front of you and veer left."

"What if I don't make it?"

"You will. You swim. I'll guide you."

"Shouldn't we wait for backup or something?"

"No. Too long. Her name is Angeline. She's eight."

"I've seen her with her brother collecting sand dollars and shells."

"Then you know."

"What do I do once I'm in there?"

"Stay with her and wait."

Greg knew that there would be no way out of there for ten or eleven hours. It would be dark in there. If he made it. If he tried to turn around and come back out halfway down the tunnel, it would be much, much harder to swim against the incoming surge and there was a good chance he'd be pushed back. He wouldn't make it. One-shot deal. Greg decided not to think too much on it. All his life, right, waiting for a chance. Go for it.

"Take this with you."

Sylvie held out the small packet of cookies. It seemed like a ludicrous gesture. He almost laughed but didn't. He put them into the back pocket of his swim trunks and pulled the Velcro tab over. She tried to hand him the flashlight too, but he knew he couldn't swim with it. "It's going to be completely dark in there, isn't it?"

"Yes. I thought this might work."

Greg grabbed something off a shelf above his bed. A silly thing. A glow stick he'd bought in Mutton Hill Harbour. Cold, chemical light. You break something inside it and it glows for thirty minutes. You toss it around with a friend at night, on a beach maybe, and it'd look cool. But he never had the right chance to use it. He put that into the other back pocket and snapped the clasp.

Angeline cried for ten minutes and flicked the tiny penlight lamp on and off to try to keep herself focussed but gave up on it and instead concentrated on the diminishing light in the water, sunlight that could find its way only so far into the cave. She heard waves smacking against the rocks outside and heard them enter the tunnel before she saw the foaming white come spilling into the larger chamber. The water splashed against her legs and, as she tucked them up and under her, she felt the cold snap of the wave upon her. She was shivering and she was more scared than she had known possible. But she refused to believe she would die. She was eight years old and death was not real for her. Fear and pain, however, were very real.

Why wasn't her brother coming back for her? It seemed like forever. Every minute seemed like an hour to her. But she had only been alone for fifteen cold minutes.

Just as she was about to start crying again, something popped up in the water near her. She screamed and pushed her little body back into the rock face behind her until the sharp rocks hurt her. Something was there in the cave with her. It made a sound like it was spitting and then it moved away from her, circling in the water that filled the bottom of the cave. When she got up the courage to turn on the little light for a split second, she saw it was a seal.

A young seal with that funny comedian's mustache and big, curious, dark eyes. He came within arm's reach and remained upright in the water looking at her. Angeline was not afraid of seals, especially a small one like this. Young seals, she knew, were very curious.

"Hello," she said. "Can you help me? Please?"

The seal dipped sideways, splashed and went under, swam around the cavern and came up a little further away. Angeline was still shivering but the seal gave her new hope. She did not feel alone.

The seal came back close to her and lifted itself half out of the water, eyes open, watching her.

"I bet you know all about this place," she said. "I'm glad you're here. I'm going to be okay, aren't I?"

The seal blinked, flopped sideways in the water again, and looked so foolish that it made her laugh. The seal had some gift for making the minutes slide away more quickly. He made the waves coming through into the cave seem less hostile. Something had brought him in here for these brief moments. Maybe it was just a favourite feeding place where small fish were driven by an incoming tide. Maybe it was just curiosity. And then he was gone. But even then it wasn't quite as bad as it had been before until a big wave plowed through the opening and drenched her completely, almost knocking her off the small, flat ledge. Angeline began to cry again, feeling this time even more hopeless than before. She was sure a bigger wave was coming and if she fell into the cold, dark water beneath her, she didn't think she could scramble back up.

Greg forced himself not to think of the logic of what he was doing except that he was buying time. He trusted Sylvie implicitly even though he had thought she was mental. Not as bad as Kit, but mental just the same. Old and crazy like that. And now he had to trust her completely, believe she was right. Hell, maybe there wasn't even any air inside there. How was he so sure there was this cavern she was talking about? What if there was no little girl in the there at all? Maybe she had made it all up or hallucinated it? Then what? Maybe he'd get inside and find no help coming for him. Maybe there was no open cavern inside, just a dead end tunnel. Fishermen might find him later, flushed out of there on a dropping tide, and wonder why he had a glow stick and a smashed pack of sea-soaked cookies in his pockets.

He looked at Sylvie for some kind of signal, but she was staring off to sea. There were waves for sure and they were building. Freda out there with high winds. Maybe there would not even be a normal low tide in twelve hours, maybe the push of the storm would keep the sea high. That happened sometimes.

"Greg. Ten yards and reach out for the wall. Veer left. Just save your strength if you can and let the wave push you in. If you hit backwash, you're going to have to hang onto something until it passes."

Greg looked at her and suddenly realized how beautiful the woman's eyes were. For an old woman, she had an extraordinary look about her. But mingled with the beauty was fear. "I must be out of my mind," he said out loud.

She touched his face then, held out her two hands and put them flat up against his cheeks and suddenly realized this was something she had done in the days before William Toye had died. And she had sworn never to have anything to do with death again. She had convinced herself that she had suffered enough loss in her life, believed there was some silent pact signed with the great decimation of her men and that she would be spared any further tragedy. For an instant, she almost changed her mind, was certain she was sending this good-intentioned boy to his death. But no. "Try to keep your eyes open, Greg. But if you get confused, close them and trust what you feel."

She meant it, Greg realized. That sounded crazy for sure. Just what he needed. Hell. It didn't matter. Nothing mattered but this. He was going in. He tried to stop the thoughts wrestling around in his head. He walked into the sea near the foot of the cliff, swam into the choppy waves, pulled a good lungful of air, then dove and swam underwater into the entrance of the flooded cave. His body was tugged about by the surge of waves that seemed to want to dash him up against the rocks. And then came the backwash sucking him back out, diminishing his progress. Stiff currents both ways seemed far too powerful for him to fight against. He imagined himself in the emptying river current again at Stoney Beach in Lawrencetown. Not good at all. *Think bathtub.* Warm bath water. *One thousand two hundred and ten.*

Greg gripped his fingers onto the rock wall, tried to perceive the give and take of the waves pushing and pulling at him. Began to reconstruct his confidence, and failing that, bolster his determination. He reached up and his fingers broke the surface of the water. He surfaced inside the cave and sucked quickly at the air beneath the rock above him. A thin seam of air, mere inches at the top of the tunnel. The next wave would steal it away. He felt the seaward tug first and prepared for the next wave that would return. He got his bearings. The walls of the tunnel, the ceiling. He realized that he could turn back right now if he had to. He wasn't that far inside. The backwash could carry him out.

The water was clear with a greenish blue tint to it, and loose seaweed whipped back and forth in a way that did not seem threatening at all.

Gulp of air, enough to get him through to wherever the hell he was going. Dive down and *wham*. The wave arrived, having gathered tremendous momentum as it squeezed itself into the narrow tunnel. There were too many bubbles to see much of anything clearly. He closed his eyes, waited for Sylvie's voice inside his head. Heard nothing. Fortunately, he had his arms stretched out in front of him and jammed his fingers hard as the turn in the tunnel found him before he found it.

But he quickly turned his body and kicked his feet with all his might so he would not lose the momentum of the wave. Then he felt something slide past him and he nearly burst the air from his lungs. It was smooth and dense and, whatever the hell it was, very much alive. He felt wet fur against his side and dared not think much of anything at all. He kicked his feet harder, took a couple of breast strokes and felt the wave give out a little. He reached up but there was still solid rock above him. He kicked again, sensed the burn begin in his lungs. One thousand and how many? No, it was different here. He couldn't hold his breath very long doing this. Different altogether. He took two more big strokes, kicked harder with his feet, reached up again. Rock. A third time, rock.

Swim, Greg. Can't go back now, he drilled himself. I'm doing the best I can, Coach. What if I can't make it? You can. What if? He had all the doubts in the world now. This was a very stupid thing to attempt. Then he jabbed his fingers upward for a fourth time.

And then sliced up out of the water into air. He rose up out of the deluge with his mouth wide open. It was dark, he couldn't see a thing. He got half a gulp of air, then the wave that had carried him slammed against the rear of the cavern with a roar and the backwash drove back at him like a sledge hammer, pushing him against the front wall while trying to suck him down and under, back into the tunnel. His fingernails clawed at the bare rock face, and he screamed.

He was still clinging to it and feeling the wave relent when he realized someone else was screaming. The voice of a child. He continued to gulp air.

"What are you?" she screamed, crying at the same time.

"Greg," he said, barely able to speak at all. "I'm Greg. Where are you?

"Here. Please help me."

Greg cautiously clawed his way along the wall until he found her. He reached out in the darkness, touched her, and Angeline grabbed onto his two outstretched fingers like a vice grip. He found the ledge, but it was awash in seawater. Another wave came through just then and both were nearly swept off. He was holding onto her wrist at that point and having a desperate time keeping his footing. But when that wave had passed, he put an arm around this little kid and said nothing until he could get his lungs to work right again.

"Where's Todd?"

"Who?"

"My brother."

"Oh, right. Todd and Sylvie sent me. I'm here now."

"I'm scared."

Greg did not say that he was too. He knew you could fake some stuff with little kids, although he knew next to nothing about child psychology. His ruse would be to present a clear game plan. And only eleven hours and twenty minutes to go.

Chapter Nineteen

Sylvie knew that Greg had made it through into the cavern. She saw the seal pop up outside of the cave and understood that his presence inside had been a good thing, a purposeful thing. Now Angeline had Greg. There were ledges inside high enough to keep them out of the water. Low tide was ten o'clock tonight. Everyone from the island would be out here. There would be help aplenty. Just a matter of time now. Suddenly the negative events of recent days — politicians, ferry closures, newspaper reports — all seemed insignificant. This was what mattered.

Todd and his mother came running down the shoreline. Todd pointed, and Elise began to shake her head and lose control. "Easy, girl," Sylvie said. "Your daughter is not alone. I had a champion swimmer handy. You remember Greg, the college kid? That's why he stayed. He didn't know why. I didn't know why. But this was it."

"She's okay in there?"

"Yes. It'll just take time."

The size and power of the waves was definitely on the increase, but the weather itself was even-tempered. It was a warm, sunny day. Light onshore breeze with a scent of the tropics in it. Freda, off Sable Island. Sinking ships, as it turned out.

Elise wrung her hands and held tightly onto Todd. "It's my fault," he said.

"Doesn't matter now."

They walked closer to the shore and stared at the cliff with the underwater cave. And waited.

A half-hour later, Moses' boat rounded the front of the island but stayed offshore. Sylvie saw him wave, pointed to the RCMP Zodiac ready to beach itself on the pebbled shores. A four-wheel-drive truck could be heard as well, grinding its way over the rubble towards them.

The battery on Todd's little penlight had gone dead as Greg helped Angie climb further up the rock face, seeking the ledge that Sylvie had promised was higher up. Greg felt overwhelmed by responsibility now and worried again that he was not going to be able to cope with this. Nothing in his life had prepared him for this immense responsibility.

And then they found the ledge. Waves still splashed them but they were way up there near the roof. Unless a really monster swell slammed its way through, they'd be okay.

They sat and Angie snuggled close to him, making him feel uncomfortable. He didn't have a sense about kids. He was just never around them much. She shivered, and he wished he had something warm for her, but he didn't. He remembered the cookies and pulled the soggy bag out of his pocket.

"You brought cookies?" She started to giggle.

"Here."

"Sylvie made these."

"Yup. She sent me in here. I didn't think I was going to make it." He shouldn't have said that, but she giggled some more.

"Then why did you do it?"

"I don't know. She asked me. I'm not good at saying no." Then he started to laugh. He liked the sound of his laughter inside the sea cave. Wow. It sounded cool. He laughed again out loud because he suddenly realized he was so fully alive. About ten minutes ago, he figured he was about to die. Now this. Unbelievable. The soggy cookies tasted like nothing he had ever known. He gave Angie most of what was there and then he tried to explain about the tidal problem.

"It will be night. Might be a little light left."

"I've never done anything like this," Angie said.

"Me neither, so we have to figure it out as we go along."

"Most adults wouldn't say that."

"I'm not most adults. Besides, I'm only twenty."

"But you're old."

"Yes. Don't worry, I know what I'm doing."

"Liar."

"Well, okay, whatever."

"Did you see the seal?" she asked.

"I think he nearly smashed into me on my way in."

"He kept me company until you arrived."

"No kidding?" Greg didn't believe it. He figured she made that part up.

"He had beautiful eyes and a mustache."

"Seals are like that."

"When you came through, I didn't know what you were."

"That's what a summer job dropout looks like when he comes up for air."

"I'm glad you came."

"Me too. You still scared?"

"Yup. And cold too. But it's the dark that bothers me most. It's really spooky. What happened to the sun?"

"Still out there. We'll see it again." And then he told her about the glow stick, which was still in his pocket. Said he didn't want to use it unless he really had to. It was going to be a long day without light.

Just then a thunderous sound made them both flinch. Angie held onto Greg and Greg braced his feet between two rocks. A wave compressed and surged through the tunnel into the wider opening and then slammed the back wall where they sat. It sounded horrific, but all they got was a blast of spray in the face and the tug of both air and water as the backwash headed back to sea.

The RCMP divers stood on the rocks, talking to Sylvie and Elise. Sylvie explained about the tunnel and the cavern and they talked about the tide. The diver seemed worried most about Freda and the storm surge. Could the girl be taken out underwater somehow? Could she swim and share an oxygen mask? Definitely not, her mother said. She now had her husband on the cellular phone she carried everywhere. Bruce was in his office in New York and insisted he speak to the divers.

It was an intolerable situation for a husband far off at work in another world. He shouted at them, insisted they go in and save his daughter.

"We're going in, sir, but we're not bringing her out until it's safe," Corporal Dan McGuire insisted.

But they'd never ever done anything quite like this before. And of the five emergency dives McGuire had undertaken with his men, the best they could ever do was pull up dead bodies from lake bottoms and rivers.

Island people began to arrive. Kit, Phonse, the Slaunwhites. Everybody offered to help but nobody knew what to do. There was no bickering today.

"We're going in," the corporal said. "Two only. We've got an underwater light. I don't like the way those waves are rolling into there but we should be okay. We'll take an emergency pack with a space blanket, some dry food, and water. One of us will be back to report."

Two men with black neoprene suits, face masks, air tanks, and goggles walked backwards into the sea, turned on their bellies, and began to feel their way along the rock cliff. In unison, they dove deep and found what they were looking for.

Angeline saw the light before Greg did. Only one diver, Corporal McGuire, made it through. His backup man had been hammered by a wave into the turn in the tunnel and it knocked loose his air valve. He'd turned and wrestled the sea back to sun and safety, but McGuire was luckier.

"Look, it's a sea monster," Angeline shouted.

"Hang on," Greg told her.

Another wave slammed up against their ridge. The sea monster came into view, the light shining straight at them. He held out an arm and bounced off the rear wall and then was spun around in a furious whirlpool. Greg didn't reach for him but held onto Angie and kept his feet braced securely.

McGuire was finally released by the whirlpool and shone the light around until he saw them up on the ridge. Before the next swell arrived, he swam towards them and hoisted himself up out of the maelstrom, popped off his mask, and then shone the light straight up on the ceiling, where it lit up the place with an eerie but welcome glow. "Everybody all right?"

"So far, so good," Greg said.

"This is quite a hideout."

"Can I go home now?" Angie asked.

"No. But I have a blanket for you. And this inflatable life thing. You have to put it on. I gotta tell them you're okay."

McGuire tried to get his waterproof radio to work but it was pretty fuzzy. He got the point across that he was inside and everyone was okay. Did his buddy get back outside? Yes. What next? Sit tight and wait for Mother Nature to drop the tide. A long way off. Given the sea state, they'd have a very narrow window. Marine weather and the RCMP were working on a precise time frame. Sit tight.

Angie was warmer with the life jacket and the blanket. Greg was shivering like crazy but insisted he was okay. It would be a long, weird day. If they were lucky, they'd have headroom above the water in the tunnel, but they'd still have to fight the waves the whole way out. McGuire insisted another diver round up a survival suit for Greg and a hastily adapted kids' version for Angie. When his man brought the gear through he dropped it off, along with a new light with fresh batteries, and then McGuire insisted he get the hell out of there. The corporal told Greg he could ask another one of his men to bring him in fresh tanks and a wetsuit. A quick scuba lesson and his man could probably lead him out, but Angie asked him to stay. Greg said he'd hang tough for the whole show. He was in it for the long haul, and besides, he didn't like the idea of learning a new skill under these conditions.

After that the stories began.

Dan McGuire had grown up in Toronto and run away when he was twelve. He slept in a dumpster. One time he woke up and he was being toppled head over heels with a bunch of supermarket garbage into a garbage truck and he barely got out with his life.

"What about you, mister?" Angie asked.

Greg said he'd led a really boring life. Nothing ever happened. Until this. Something about this was ... he didn't know, a turning point, maybe.

"A crisis is always good for an adrenalin rush," McGuire confirmed. "If you like it you should be a cop."

"Jeez, I never thought of being a cop."

"There's worse things."

"Maybe a child psychologist. I might be good with kids." He was still holding onto Angie, or she was hanging on to him. They were locked onto each other. He knew that Angie had taught him some serious stuff already. It was like a wake-up call for the dismally brain-dead.

"In order to understand children, you have to be able to think like a kid," Angie said. It was borrowed from her brother's analysis of TV shows.

"I could go with that."

Greg found some good second-hand stories to add. Close calls his college buddies had on fishing accidents and drinking binges. That sort of thing. McGuire said he'd jumped from a plane once while learning how to parachute. Something happened and he froze. His instructor saw his problem and dropped down out the sky right beside him, yanked his lead, and he landed okay, but he never quite got over it.

Angie said she got bit by a dog once in West Orange. It was only a small dog but had sharp teeth. West Orange, everyone agreed, must be a very dangerous place.

Plumes of water from the crashing waves washed right up over them a couple of times, but Dan had rigged some ropes along the rock face to keep them stable. It worked. They ate all the emergency rations in the dark as McGuire was keeping his under-water light off to conserve batteries. By around seven o'clock at night they were feeling tired and drained and Angie started to squirm and cry.

"Almost there, kid. Gotta sit tight."

"But I hurt all over."

That's when Greg decided to go for the green light. He crushed the end of it and the cool glow lit up the cavern with a truly wonderful green light show.

"It's like Mars or something." Angie said.

"It's something, all right," said Dan McGuire. And it took the edge off for a good twenty minutes. You could see the top of the tunnel to the sea now, but it was still completely filled. Another RCMP diver arrived with wetsuits, and it wasn't easy to get out of the survival suits and into the new gear but the warmth of neoprene was welcome. The food was gone, the green glow had disappeared, and there was maybe eight inches of air space showing in the tunnel at eight-thirty that evening when McGuire got a raspy call on his two-way telling him that Freda had changed course. She had come across Sable Island and was heading towards Nova Scotia tonight. Low tide simply was-n't going to happen.

Greg understood and so did Angie.

"You can't sink in the wetsuit, honey," Dan told her. "You don't have to dive but you're going to get a lot of salt water in the face."

"I can't go through there."

"Yes, you can," Greg said. "Dan and me, we're going to hang onto you. You've got a wetsuit. You'll be okay."

But just then another wave rolled through, filling the space to the top and roaring into the cavern. McGuire got on the radio and said he needed to know when there was a good lull. Word came back that Moses Slaunwhite was on his boat, still anchored offshore. He could watch for a break in the sets of waves and the news would be sent to McGuire's men, who'd pass it on. It looked like the swell was building, Moses had said. The word was now or never.

But just as Moses gave the word that a lull was upon them, Sylvie insisted they wait. Greg and Angie heard it all from McGuire's radio.

"I say we go," Dan said.

"No, we wait," Greg insisted.

Forty seconds later, by McGuire's watch, the biggest wave of the day came roaring through and Greg held tightly onto Angie as the water seethed up around them.

"Now. Go." They heard Sylvie's voice over the radio, choked with static.

"Yes," Greg said, and in the wake of the backwash, the air space left in the tunnel increased significantly. Both held onto the girl and swam like maniacs. McGuire had detached his tanks before they left. He'd worried the logic of it over and over until he decided the girl could not get out of there underwater, that's all there was to it. He'd have to stay up and keep her up too, no matter what.

They made it past the bend and could see faint evening light outside but they could also see the next set of waves — four waves in a row —, coming at them. They couldn't exit in time. McGuire forced Greg and Angie to the side of the wall and slammed himself against them both, gripping onto a crevice above his head. Angie squealed as the first wave tried to rip them away and she screamed as the second tugged harder. The third was not so bad but the fourth one knocked them back into the water. Greg still had Angie in his arms and McGuire was trying to keep them from being dragged back further into the tunnel. Then came the backwash and McGuire guided them to the centre of the tunnel, let it draw them towards safety. They made good headway but by the time they were at the mouth, the girl was coughing and sputtering and both men were near exhaustion.

It was then that the Coast Guard Zodiac engine roared into life. The craft was steered in close, and a man pulled the girl up into the boat, but before Dan and Greg could get aboard, the helmsman was forced to turned seaward into a six-foot wall of white water. The Zodiac shot up into the air and over a mass of turbulent water and then headed back to sea. Just about then, Greg was slammed up against the rocky cliff and had the wind knocked out of him. He watched Dan trying to find something to get a grip on as the following wave tried to force him back into the cave like a spider being swept down the drain of a sink.

McGuire cursed but held on. A second Zodiac made a run for them and nearly capsized. It tried a second time and was hammered up against the cliff as Greg felt himself dragged up into the boat. Then it turned, plowed hard into another frothy wave, engine screaming as it shot skyward over the wall of water, then made a U-turn and raced full throttle towards McGuire while the waves continued to pummel him against the rocks.

Finally, the weary diver was yanked aboard and the Zodiac headed back out to sea and the relative safety of deep water.

Angie had been landed ashore and was carried up the rocky beach to her mother's arms just before a massive shore break overturned the Zodiac on the rocks. Greg and Dan were put aboard Moses' boat and sent the seaward route back around the island to the government wharf.

Angie and her mother were immediately packed into the waiting four-by-four and taken to meet an ambulance helicopter on the other side of the island, as islanders wiped tears from their eyes and patted each other on the back. After the sun had disappeared, Sylvie sat for a long while in the dark as the winds began to howl and the waves grew larger. She stayed alone there, despite the many offers to take her home. She remained until a torrent of tropical rain spilled down upon her. Then she stood up and slowly began to walk back home. An old woman, tired, alone. Thankful.

Bruce Sanger arrived on the first morning ferry after a bumpy flight from Newark to Halifax. He had been in a state of frenzied panic for his daughter for over twenty-four hours, and even though he had been told she was okay, he had to see for himself.

Once he was absolutely sure that Angie was fine, he announced, "That's it. We're getting all of you back to someplace safe."

"I'm not leaving," Angeline asserted.

"We'll be more careful, I promise," Todd said, still feeling it was all his fault.

"Somehow, I don't feel like we should leave just yet," Elise said.

"Jesus." Bruce felt like he wanted to hit somebody or something. His family had gone insane on him. He looked at them. They had that unified Sanger family look he'd seen before — when they all wanted something very badly. It used to be just ice cream or a new TV or the movie channels, or maybe a trip to the Jersey Shore. Now this. "Okay, dammit. But I'm not going back to work until September and we're all back in Jersey and the kids are safely back in their seats at school."

And that was the end of the family discussion.

Chapter Twenty

The storm named Freda did come ashore and hit fast and hard, but there was no one in the cave, and by then the rescue workers had all gone home and Moses had his boat snug back at the government wharf. Two barns that had been waiting patiently for a good hard blow of ocean air toppled in upon themselves and brought a final end to long, honest careers of housing farm animals, hay, thoughts, and sweet memories of many island youths.

Sylvie's mind seemed to dance with the wind in the night. She did not mind its intensity and savoured the sound of the swooshing treetops, the groan and creak of the walls of her old house. In her bed alone, she felt perfectly safe and warm and incredibly light. She felt as if she could fly or levitate if she so much as dared to dream it so.

Sylvie was certain she had tampered with the basic rules of the universe, the most fundamental principle of nature: the one that says it does what it does and pity the man or woman or child who gets in its way. But she had changed all that. Once, anyway. As the wind pushed and shoved at her house and all things on the island, some gave up grip: roots of small trees, shingles nailed to walls, children's toys laying about in a yard. A wheelbarrow upside down became a gymnast, did a back flip and landed upright and filled to the brim with sweet hurricane rain. Birds hunkered down — tiny goldfinches and sparrows on up to the shrewd and powerful ospreys, wings pulled tight to the sides to avoid the hazards of accidental night flight into the chaos of the tumultuous sky.

Waves pummelled the shale spit and gouged the land. The seas swept over the barachois ridges of loose stone here and there and fed new salt water to the ponds near Phonse's "lighthouse." At the top of the hill in the middle of the junkyard, at least three car hoods left open — "engine bonnets" as the islanders called them — were ripped from their rusty hinges and sailed off like a small battalion of alien space craft, leaving the island altogether and splashing down in the bay where they floated on choppy seas for a brief instant and then sank to the bottom.

Freda would take a full six feet off the front of the island that night. She knocked down big trees along the shore, stole the soil of the bank, and laid claim to the ribbon of real estate that was now nothing more than bare, exposed rocks where once stood twenty-foot spruce trees at the edge of a forest. The tumble of ravaged trees spilled over the rocks, their roots sticking up into the air, the root system of each toppled tree stripped and polished by the waves. It looked like a jungle of vines, a thousand medusa heads.

As Sylvie tried to go to sleep that night, she saw Freda as a perfectly satisfactory hurricane. Some kind of signal of beginnings or endings. A solution to an all-too-dry summer. A reminder of the power of things beyond themselves. Had Freda come ashore earlier, had the little girl died without the mercy of the winds and tides, all would be different. But it was enough to read portent into a day like this and carry it in your mind and heart.

Sylvie knew she was the link in the chain that saved this young one's life, and her actions seemed like the most important thing she had ever done. Maybe it was why she was still alive after all those years with husband upon husband dying on her. Some great, inexpressible lesson here about a woman and the art of living, a crazy thing that involved intimate dancing along a threshold of thoughts concerning death and life.

Sylvie had never been willing to accept the notions of death doled out by the churches. Too facile, too easy. Always the request that you did not try to understand God's higher purpose; it was not for mortals. Amazing that this little bit of whimsy satisfied some, but not her. Upon the burial of several of her men, clergy had come to give comfort, only to find their platitudes unwelcome. Sylvie had a personal relationship with death and it was not something many could even begin to comprehend.

Tonight she had sweet confirmation of the intricacy of the pattern — beyond understanding, yes, perhaps, but at least there was room to manoeuvre caring and compassion into the picture. There was the hard weaponry of free will against the absolute conspiracies of death and nature. Large thoughts on a windy night. Rain pelted against the glass and became a symphony. It had a beginning, a middle, and an end. There was crescendo as well as diminuendo. Harmony and dissonance. Structure and chaos. But mutability as well. Sylvie recalled her husband William Toye once referring to a big, blasty September storm as a "philosopher's gale." That applied aptly well to this night.

Sylvie understood why she had linked the impending tragedy to the young man, Greg Cookson, who was required to fight his own fears and go into the cave, stay with the girl until further help arrived. She was the link in the chain of events that had saved the girl. It was as if she had gone into the cave herself.

A thing of beauty.

This lightness of being. The weight of history sloughed off. The burden of responsibility diminished for now at least. She felt the return of a familiar aching within her — not the loss of her husbands this time, but the absence of children in her home. But she had given up, long ago, the notion that she had been somehow punished for a crime she was unaware of. No, despite everything, she felt blessed, not damned. She had immense love for all children. One of her greatest fears now was that all the island children would be moved to Mutton Hill Harbour to be closer to the schools.

The island was about to change; the province had already made an offer on her house and land, assured her of a place to live in the Cedars Retirement Community ashore. A room of her own with a shared bath. TV in the rec room, meals in a cafeteria. Old men and women fumbling about together and doing arts and crafts in the afternoon or watching soap operas. Social events. All planned and scheduled. Imagine.

Just before Sylvie woke, she was dreaming of a sea at sunset. An old woman was rowing a dory alone far from land across dark blue water that was like a sheet of glass. Each oar stroke sent calm, controlled ripples away from the boat as it slowly progressed through the placid, even benevolent, waters. The old woman's rowing was slow and sure. Sylvie could not see her face but she knew the old woman was herself.

In the morning Sylvie discovered that her old outhouse, which was in semi-retirement but still functional, had blown over in the night. Spruce boughs were scattered about her lawn, and the grass was like a sopping sponge. The island had been sea blasted, spit-polished, drenched good, and it would now drip dry and be good as new.

Greg Cookson did not sleep hardly at all that night and it was not just the fact that the old fish shack leaked like a sieve. He sat up all night with a cup of hot tea in his hands, refilled over and over, although he almost electrocuted himself on the old electric tea kettle as the rain dripped on his wrist when he went to unplug it for the third time.

Unlike Sylvie, Greg felt anchored by the density of purpose in his life. He pondered over the fact that people do not go out into the world craving to do good and dangerous deeds. He had swum underwater down a long, dark tunnel of the sea because an old woman had asked him to help a trapped child inside. How could he have mustered the will to do such a thing? He had been training himself for at least the last six years to be, above all else, a rational person, a controlled individual who would not allow others to manipulate his life. Each decision was to be made in a rational and orderly fashion. And in doing so, he now realized, he had robbed himself of both passion and compassion.

What was his true purpose? he asked himself over and over. Certainly he was not put here to provide data for some bloody computer, to take a government job or become a good corporate employee. Nor was he destined to be a lawyer.

No. Nothing like that. Now he had an island. He had a great storm raging out there all night to remind him that he had just barely removed himself from harm's way. He had a thankful family of islanders and this glow inside his head that he wished would never go away. He heard the old, loose cedar shingles on the roof rattle and thrum with wind and rain. A few took flight as if all their lives they had waited to become brittle birds on one dark, turbulent night like this.

Drenching bombardment of the island. Dark sounds. Sounds of war but, thankfully, no bodies to be counted.

Greg did eventually fall into a fitful sleep. And when he woke up, he burst outside into the sunlight and heard the birds. Nothing, nothing had prepared him for this feeling. It was like he had been asleep all his life.

Greg sat, then lay down, on the bright, wet stones along the shoreline and stared up into the empty blue sky. Life loomed grand and large and yet he knew that he needed to fix a plan for extending some degree of the euphoria he was feeling. Life could not always work in such a burst of risk and reward, but the events of yesterday were a trigger of some sort. He now realized he liked saving things. He helped save the girl. Now he needed something else to save. It was a big planet with a lot of problems. Where to begin?

He found some clean clothes in a bottom drawer and put on the blue jeans, the faded black cotton shirt, white socks. He slipped his feet into his damp shoes and splashed out into the puddles of the old road that led from the fish shack to the rest of the island community.

His feet found their way to the door of Kit Lawson, and he knocked a short tattoo.

She opened the door looking very sad, very tired, a bedraggled beauty with darkness about her face and that crazed look in her eyes. "Ocean of Storms, Sea of Rains, Sea of Crises, Seething Bay," she said.

Greg recognized the names of moon geography, understood it had something to do with Kit's brand of madness. Could he love a woman this crazy? Did he want to get involved with all the baggage of her mental and emotional instability? He held out his hand to her. Yes, he did. Kit needed saving lest she drown herself in her private Sea of Crises or Ocean of Storms. Greg understood that he was diving headlong into Seething Bay as he invited himself inside.

Kit had learned about Angeline, trapped in the sea cave, and it made her all the more afraid of the world she lived in. "It's a very untrustworthy place. Nothing is fixed, nothing stays put. Everything is in danger of losing itself. Did you feel the storm try to destroy us all last night?"

"No, I felt the storm challenging us, and, realizing we were strong, it moved on."

"Why did you go in there?"

"Because Sylvie asked me to."

"Sylvie is a strong one. And good."

"Yes. That's why I had to go in."

"Sylvie is the Sea of Tranquility."

"Is she?"

"She is. What was it like underwater?"

"I didn't think about it. I just swam. I didn't think I had enough air but I did." He told her about holding his breath in bathtubs all through his childhood. "It paid off big time." Then he paused. "Kit, are you all right?"

"No. I need help. I've been like this before but never on the island. I thought I was safe here."

"Safe from what?"

"From everything. I thought I wouldn't feel the pain again."

"I want to help."

"How old are you?"

"Twenty."

"Twenty is very young."

"How old are you?"

"Twenty-six."

"Only six years' difference between us. If I were eighty-six and you were as old as Sylvie, there wouldn't be much difference, would there?"

"Right, but if I were seven, you'd only be one year old, and that would be a big difference."

"Would it ever. You'd have to learn baby talk to communicate with me."

Kit smiled. Doors were opening. "You had any breakfast?"

"No. I was going to have cornflakes but they got drenched. Turned to mush. Leaks in the roof."

"Can I make you something?"

"Yes, if you don't mind feeding a younger man."

"Do I have to speak baby talk?"

"Only if you want."

It was a large breakfast and a good one. Everything in it was organic. There was ground coffee with honey and goat's milk, Gouda cheese, apples, granola that she had made herself, orange juice. And a story.

"You know I'd been living with a guy. John. He was a great person. When he got busted for growing marijuana he tried to explain that he was going to put the money into a good cause, a school for inner-city kids. A safe place for them to learn and to play and all that. Back in Boston. It didn't seem to matter. He'd been busted before. He took it okay, even tried to convince himself that the two years in prison would be like a learning experience. He really is that kind of a guy."

Greg saw some thread of connection between him and John. Kit handed him a tattered photograph. Lovable looking, long-

haired hippie type with a goofy grin. Good intentions, bad plan
of action. Wanted to save a bunch of kids in the Boston States.

"I missed him something awful. He writes and tells me jail
is not so bad. Lots of new friends, new ideas. Says he's realizing
how messed up the legal system is. Pot growers like himself side
by side with guys who have committed violent crimes. He's
reading law books, even taking a course of some kind. Says he's
got it in his head that he wants to get involved with the movement to legalize marijuana. It has to be done, he says. When he
gets out he's going to Vancouver to work with the people there."

"What about the kids in Boston?"

"They don't seem as important to him anymore."

"What about you?"

"I don't know. He says I can go out and live with him if
I want."

"Do you want to?"

"No. I don't think I want my life dedicated to legalizing
dope. I think it's an okay thing. I just don't think it's for me."

"John's a crazy guy. He'd let you go?"

"He already has."

"Quite a sacrifice for a cause."

"I don't hold it against him. I just wish it didn't hurt
so much."

"You still love him?"

"I think so. But most of the time now, I don't know what I
think. You can tell I'm kind of around the bend, can't you?"

"You seem distraught. I want to help. I like you a lot." Greg
heard himself fumbling with simple words. The way he used the
word "like." As if he were a kid in grade six. Emotionally, he figured, he hadn't advanced much beyond that, never given himself
the chance. Never been *willing* to take the chance. Always kept
to the safety of the sidewalks when it came to emotions. Never
jumped out into the traffic.

"I need someone to like me a lot right now."

"I'm your man."

"Soft landing in the Bay of Rainbows."

"Is there really a Bay of Rainbows on the moon?"

"Yep." She led him to the map on the wall. Damn. There it was. Just south of a crater called Pythagoras and east of one known as Plato.

Chapter Twenty-One

Sylvie believed that the war had changed the sea somehow. The island had seen oil slicks on the waters of every shore. Smashed crates and rusty metal barrels had washed in. The North Atlantic had played a vital role in the war of ideologies. Sadists and heroes had died at sea. Sylvie had lost Kyle to the waters as well. Sitting alone yet again on the shoreline, selecting one stone and then another to hold in her hand as companion, she considered an end to her relationship with the sea. She considered taking the ferry to Mutton Hill Harbour and then going somewhere else. Halifax maybe, or Boston. Or Toronto. Or further. Into the mountains of the west. To lose herself. To lose this place and the hurt that went with it. But she did not act on the impulse. She went home. She let warm seasons disappear and she hardly noticed.

Time does not heal all wounds, she believed. Wounds become part of your life. And you live with them each day. December of 1945 seemed like the coldest it had ever been in her life. Sylvie closed off all the rooms but one. She lived in her kitchen and fed the wood stove with softwood she had cut herself with the ragged-blade handsaw. She felt great pity for herself. She endured immense sorrow for the world. January was also an appropriate month to continue to suffer. Sometimes the fire burned down in the wood stove, water froze in the sink, and she huddled beneath blankets. She lost her appetite and finally became ill. She had a high temperature and felt dizzy through most of the day, then slept for fifteen hours at a stretch.

Sylvie was twenty-eight. Her life had been an abysmal disappointment. She did not want to die but she did not have any wish to go on living. Could there not be some other, third alternative?

The fever was at its worst on the fifteenth day of January. Wind blew wisps of snow in under the door. She had mustered a low, begrudged fire from damp kindling. A woman in a bundle of blankets, eyes red, hair asunder, face pale as plaster of Paris one minute, then flushed with red the next. A body at war with itself, resulting from a strain of influenza that had found its way here all the way from Europe.

Wind raged on from the north with cold, cold, cold. Snow sifting and sculpting into little piles outside. Spruce trees bending under the weight, branches snapping off. The old grey sea slapping on stones, turning snow to slush. And a single man, hunched over, face into the wind, walking along the island road from the wharf. Unshaven, but fully dressed for the weather, gloves with holes, a scarf the colour of molasses, huffing as he trudged. Finding the courage in his own desperation to knock on the door to the house at the end of this forgotten road.

Sylvie did not answer.

He knocked again, and a third time. Nothing. Turned to go on his way. Not much luck today. A bad stroke for sure. Better to have stayed on the mainland than try a hunch that people on the island would take some pity on him and give him some work. Wind. Curse it. Sucking snow through his teeth, trying to whistle as he spit it back out. Bloody weather, anyway. He wasn't even sure anyone was living here. So what's the point?

But as he was turning to leave, he thought he heard someone crying inside this old house. Whimpering, maybe. Not his business, whatever it was. Better to move on than to get concerned in someone else's misery. Every time Doley Keizer ever tried to get involved in any damn thing it turned bad on him. He didn't know how to help others with their problems. Jeez, he had so much heartache of his own, how could he muster enough brain power to help another living soul? He trudged on, back to the wind now. Knock on another door or give up and go back to the boat, bum a free ride ashore. He tried to leave the sound of the woman's crying there on the doorstep where he'd found it but it stuck to him and kept gnawing at him with each step.

"Damn it all." He went back. Knocked again. Nothing. He opened the door and set foot inside.

It was dark. He stood on the bare wood floor and cleared his throat, stamped one foot and then another to loosen the snow, let whoever was in there know someone had walked in. Finally, he closed the door behind him as a puff of snow spilled in like unwanted confetti through the door.

Sylvie felt the rush of cold air and saw the silhouette of a man in her doorway. Tried to speak but found her mouth dry as dust, her voice gone.

Doley didn't know what to do. He held his hands out in front of him and tried to form some kind of a question or a greeting as he focussed on the poor woman hunched over in a blanket by the cookstove. She was shaking, and he didn't know if she was cold or scared of him or what. Finally he swallowed hard. "You all right, miss?"

Sylvie shook her head no. She knew she was not all right. She did need help.

"Cold in here, miss. Whyn't you let me get the fire goin' for ya?"

Sylvie blinked her eyes and nodded ever so slightly.

Yes, Doley would get a fire going, warm the place up. It was the least he could do. He reached for a light switch on the wall by the door so he could see better but there was none. Of course, many people on the island didn't have electricity yet. He saw a kerosene lamp on the table and lit that with a wooden stick match. He nearly singed his eyebrows as he was leaning over it when the wick took the flame.

"You're sick, aren't ya, miss? Don't worry, I'll get the place warm and I'll help ya."

Doley was a large, clumsy man and he banged into a chair, knocked it over, looked around for kindling but saw none. Found an axe by the door and went back out into the snow. Stack of cordwood by the porch. All wet. He set a few logs on the frozen ground and quartered them and split each piece again. Dry enough on the inside. He gathered the wood up into his arms, went back into the house.

Doley balled up an old copy of the *Halifax Herald*, shook the ashes from the grate and set it down, placed some dry wood from the heart of the log, the splintered thin kindling on top, pawed a

match until it came to life, bent over it, sucked the sulphur fume,
lit the paper, opened the flue at the back of the stove and then
the air supply. Whoosh of flame. He dropped in two more logs
and let the wind above the chimney pull the smoke from the
flame up the chimney. The fire roared to life and Doley felt like
he had performed a miracle, done one thing right in his life.

Doley managed to cut his hand pretty bad trying to open a
can of chicken soup, discovered it was frozen inside, but scooped
it out with a big *thunk* into a pot and listened to it hiss. Couldn't
get any water from the hand pump at the sink so he went back
out and collected snow in a clean bucket, added it to the soup.
Started talking to her, the woman in the blanket with the sick-
ness, didn't know what else to do.

"Doley Keizer is who I am. Came out here looking for odd
jobs today. Bad weather, though. Pretty stupid of me wastin' my
time like that. No takers. So here I am. Don't worry, you don't
have to pay me or nothin'. This is just like a neighbour helpin'
out. How long you been like this anyway?"

The room was warm now. Smell of soup in the room. Sylvie
didn't know how long. The man handed her a cup of water that
he had just melted from the snow. Placed the cup awkwardly to
her lips. She tried to look him in the eye, but he couldn't look
straight back at her. She swallowed, let the cold water trace a
small, blessed river down her parched throat. She took hold of
the cup with her own hands and drank some more.

"That's a girl," Doley said, and realized that he sounded like
someone talking to a pet dog.

"Thank you." Sylvie smiled at him and the blanket fell
away. She had been wearing an old flower print dress and it had
been on her for three days. The room was warmer now. She
shivered and noticed that her skin glistened with sweat. Doley
picked up a dish towel on the table and dabbed at her forehead. She was very sick but he also found her very beautiful.

His breath caught behind his teeth and he couldn't let it go. "You're going to be okay."

Doley stayed on through the rest of the day, and, after putting Sylvie into bed, he sat at the kitchen table and fell asleep. He woke up several times to re-stoke the fire from the supply of firewood he had split and piled inside. In the morning, he cooked breakfast from eggs that had been frozen. He made a clear broth that Sylvie sipped off and on and he made some tea from the melted snow. "Snow tea," he called it.

There was sunshine on the next day but the wind roared on and on until it stopped all at once at noon. Just gave up and went home. The outside temperature went up a notch and snow began to melt from the heavily weighed boughs of blue-green spruce.

Doley was a massive, homely man by most people's standards, although it wasn't so much his look but the way he carried himself, the way he shuffled when he walked, all hunched over, the darting eyes, the unshaven face. Underneath, Sylvie knew there was not a brute but a man with a big heart. Doley had nursed her back to health, acted with great gentleness. She didn't quite know what to make of him. Once he had settled in, he fussed about the place, cleaning up after himself, making her tea or broth, putting order to the kitchen, washing dishes but then always retreating to sit at his seat at the kitchen table as if not to intrude in any way further into the privacy of her home.

Sylvie got better but did not ask him to leave. Told him he could stay in the spare room. He obliged and asked no questions. At first, she did not tell him about her two deceased husbands, for she had spent so much time feeling sorry for herself that she did not want more sympathy from this man who had already been so kind to her.

When they ate meals together in the semi-darkness of the early evening, Sylvie wished she could tell him that he need not be so uncomfortable. Poor Doley was awkward with a knife and fork and shovelled food as he fed himself and then apologized for his rough manners. She insisted he give her his entire story — his life. But for now, she herself was offering up none of her own. She didn't know why she was being so stingy. Maybe she wasn't ready to give up the perimeter of her inner pain and loneliness. Whatever it was, Doley was a welcome guest in her house.

Doley's story, as it was revealed, in bits and pieces, tattered fragments of a life spilling out of him at random and unpredictable intervals, went something like this.

He'd been the youngest child in a large German family — the Keizers of Blockhouse, not far from Lunenburg. He'd always been told he'd amount to nothing much and believed the news that was delivered to him by his older brothers and his parents. Believed it as if it were law. There had been a pair of oxen that his father raised, and his father had taken better care of them than he took care of his kids. The oxen were harnessed by a colourfully painted wooden yoke and there was a cart drawn behind them. For some reason, the children were never allowed to ride on the cart. It was used to haul firewood and even to transport large stones from the middle of the potato field to the edge, but it was not for kids. Mr. Keizer rode proudly in his ox cart at the yearly exhibition in Bridgewater and he entered his oxen in the ox pull, winning it one year and never letting anyone forget that.

Doley did poorly at school and dropped out after his grade eight teacher called him "a stupid Kraut, the dumbest boy in all the school," in front of the class. His father said he had expected as much from this son and put him to work in the fields in summer and in the woods in winter.

Doley left home at fifteen and went to work delivering coal in Bridgewater. On a Friday night, sometimes local boys would lure him into a fight, and Doley was an easy target, big but not at all capable when four or more bullies ganged up on him. He would wear a pinkish blue scar across his chest from where one of his more vicious adversaries took a broken beer bottle to him. On that night, Doley thought he was about to bleed to death, and he sat on a dark street by the LaHave River waiting for death to take him, but it did not. In great pain, he staggered to the police station and was rudely shuttled to the hospital, then later charged with "disturbing the peace," fined, and let go.

After several years of working hard at hauling coal or lumber at the mill, Doley convinced himself he was ready to move up in the world and succumbed to his desire to be a salesman. He lasted only three days at a hardware store in Lunenburg before it was discovered he couldn't read, write, add, or subtract with any accuracy. In the wake of that humiliation, he doubled it by becoming a door-to-door salesman of cookware, and then later, vacuum cleaners. An awkward, socially inept soul at the best of times, Doley did poorly but felt that the work was better than going back to hauling coal. Occasionally, a housewife would take pity on him and buy an Electrolux Queen with personal money she had saved for a rainy day.

The war arrived and, despite the significant German population of Lunenburg County, certain individuals of German descent were singled out for derision. Doley Keizer was a prime target. "Dirty Nazi," "Baby-killer," "Hitler lover." He heard them all. His looks were all broody and he had a trace of an Old Country accent: these were the only gifts his parents had given to him, the only family assets to take off into the world. He tried to enlist but even then, there was some reason why he was turned away. Fear, maybe, that he would turn traitor on Canada, sneak secret messages to his good friends working for *der Führer*.

It was insanely illogical but there it was. Maybe some actually believed poor Doley was sitting in his basement at night with a wireless radio, sending coded messages to submarines offshore, telling them how to sneak into Lunenburg Harbour at night and blow up all the mackerel boats.

Doley went back to work in the woods, swatting hordes of blackflies in summer and suffering frostbite of nose, ears, and fingers in winter. When the war ended, there was a flood of men returning to Lunenburg County wanting jobs. Doley, even though he was a fine and sturdy woodsman, was given the boot, and he suffered the indignity of going from home to home begging for odd jobs. And one day, fed up with the way people treated him each time they opened a door, he thought that, perhaps if there was no kindness, compassion, or a shred of yard work on the mainland, he would go to the island and see what manner of folk they be.

Doley stayed on for a week and then came to his own conclusion that it was not his place to take advantage of a poor widowed woman. He had already fallen desperately in love with her and knew this to be a hopeless situation if ever there was one. Sylvie was a beautiful woman, all of twenty-eight, in the prime of her life. Doley was nearly forty and nobody's idea of a prize catch of a man. He would do her a great favour and move quietly out of her life.

He moved himself to a small cabin in the woods on Noah Slaunwhite's property. Noah used to call it his hunting cabin, but there was no hunting anymore on the island. The deer had all been killed, rabbits pretty well wiped out by kids with wire snares. Nothing left to shoot at but tin cans and junk that washed up on the beach. Noah gave Doley some work and a serious lecture about how important it was for a man to "shave the grunge off his face." Noah bought him some fresh Gillette razor blades and gave him some old clothes from his attic. Noah tapped him twice between the shoulder blades and told him that if he wanted to stay on, he had to stop stooping like that. Doley tried the best he could to stand straight and, as result, hit his head almost every time he walked into the door of his cabin.

Noah made up work for Doley to do: things that he'd never really planned to get fixed in his lifetime got fixed, buildings never expecting repair found new boards. Shingles got nailed down. There was enough firewood cut, split, and piled into immaculate structures so that some of it would have to rot before it ever had a chance to kiss the flames of a wood stove.

Summer took Doley out on the boats, where he was slow to learn, but he was a good, faithful worker who never complained.

From winter on into spring that year, Sylvie tried to reconstruct a definition of love. What she had felt for David and what she had felt for Kyle. Similar but different. Two versions of love. First you are attracted to a man because of his smile, the way he looks at you, the way he moves. Then you get to know the way his mind works, what his dreams are, and you discover you can share those dreams together. But do you fall in love with a man just because he loves you? Or do you fall in love with a man because he's kind to you, because he maybe saved your life? Do you fall in love with a man you don't find particularly attractive? Is there some relationship between love and simple compassion? Can love be based on pity?

The crabapple trees near the fallen homesteads bloomed late in June. After the hard winter, the land was slow to recover, but something let go in the last week of the month and summer arrived without the precursor of spring. The whales came back to keep Sylvie company upon the sunny shoreline

of grey stones. The aching in her heart that was the lingering love
and grief for Kyle Bauer seemed only to stop when she recon-
sidered again and again taking Doley Keizer into her life. But
why had he not continued to come visit her? She had to ask him.

The wharf at 2:30. Boats back from a day at sea. A good catch.
Fish stink, slime, noisy talk. Men with sharp knives at grisly grey
planks, slitting belly to head, spilling guts into the sea where waiting gulls scooped the entrails and fought each other time after
time. Sylvie standing back a bit, watching Doley at work, watching the men making jokes at him, jokes about his size, his intelligence, all fairly benign compared to what Doley had known in
his life. Sylvie standing there on a soggy, mild day with beads of
mist caught like jewellery in her hair, looking at Doley, trying to
attach words to what she was feeling.

"How come you don't stop by anymore?" she asks him,
while everyone listens. The knives stop clicking. Motion of fish
from tub to board ceases. Doley looks up, dumbfounded. The
other men stand gawking. Jaws drop. Doley swallows hard, as
usual doesn't know what to say. Someone begins to laugh but has
the goodwill to stifle himself. Then Sylvie understands. Doley
believes he's not good enough for her. He's doing her some kind
of favour by not coming by.

"I don't know," he says, and Bill Pleasance lets out a hoot, but
then turns his head away when Sylvie gives him a look that
would snap the head off a shark.

"Come for dinner, would you, when you're through?"
"Yes."

Doley was clean-shaven and well dressed, something just short of
handsome, as he arrived back at Sylvie's house. Sylvie was healthy

this time and radiant. She had resolved her definition of what love was, had decided love was many things. Pity, compassion, gratitude were part of the package. But they were only words — small harnesses to yoke onto large ideas and emotions. There was much more to it than that but she would be obliged to no one to explain it.

Doley married Sylvie in August on the island at the Baptist church. A fill-in minister from Cape Breton was holding down the church for the month while the regular clergyman, Reverend Snelling, was having his appendix out with ensuing complications in a hospital in Halifax. The young Reverend Steele had no problems with marrying these two fine people and gave them his blessing. Later he would weather a blast of insulting remarks from Reverend Snelling, but it would not trouble the Cape Bretoner a great deal, only convince him to change his stripe to a more liberal church.

Doley's dreams were simple dreams and Sylvie understood that they were worth sharing. He always referred to their house as "Sylvie's" and never felt any rightful ownership. Doley was a quiet man, and Sylvie learned to spend entire evenings in near silence. Sometimes he carved small figurines with a sharp knife, carefully scraping the blade across soft, wet spruce wood. Sometimes he just sat and looked at her or into the flame in the lamp. Doley liked doing housework and this always made Sylvie laugh. A big man washing dishes or folding clothes. Doley enjoyed that as much as he gained satisfaction from splitting wood or rebuilding the shed from the ground up.

Doley had a secret that he kept well hidden until one night three years into their marriage when some young roughnecks from Mutton Hill Harbour came over one night. Wayne Dorsen and some of his cronies he ran around with. Beached their Boston whaler at Front Bay and went looking for an empty house to torch or anything worth stealing.

Lights were out early at Sylvie's house and it seemed empty, so they entered, shoving open the door and smacking it against the wall even though it wasn't even locked. Doley was sound asleep after a hard day of working at sea. Sylvie got up to see what was going on when one of Dorsen's friends, a twenty-four-year-old good-for-nothing named Teazer, shone his flashlight on her and called her a name she'd never been called in all her days alive on the island. The scoundrel started to move towards her when he saw another dark figure come through the doorway of the bedroom and reach out towards him. The next thing Teazer knew, he had something that felt like a bench vice squeezing his Adam's apple and he couldn't breathe. Dorsen and his other ally grabbed hold of Doley, but Doley elbowed him hard in the gut and smacked the other backhanded with a fistful of knuckles hard as beach stones. Then Doley proceeded to lay his intruder flat on the floor and pound his head onto the floorboards with a regular rhythm like he was beating a drum to some ancient, primitive chant. A sound came out of Doley, but it was not words from any language.

Dorsen and the other one fled but Teazer lay motionless on the floor. Doley looked like he was ready to hit him again. Sylvie screamed out for him to stop. He stopped and let go of the man, sat back on his haunches and shuddered.

Sylvie had never believed Doley was capable of such rage, such violence, and it frightened her more than the fact that their house had been broken into and a stranger in the dark had made dangerous advances towards her.

Sylvie helped Teazer to sit up and wiped blood from the corner of his mouth. She leaned close to him and could hear his breath in her ear. "He's alive."

"I'm glad you stopped me."

Teazer found his way back to the mainland in the morning on the first ferry. Neither he nor his two buddies would ever return to Ragged Island.

Doley tried to explain that he had a violent temper, even though she had never seen it before this. He explained how his father and nearly everyone else he knew had made him feel so hurt and angry as a kid. He'd never gotten over it. He had, however, devoted a great deal of his energy to developing the distinguished skill of containing the violence that was within him. He wasn't a hundred percent sure he could hold it in forever. He said that, now that she knew, if she wanted him to leave, he would.

"Can you promise me you'll never be violent again, even against someone like that?"

"Yes, I can promise you that. But can you trust me to live up to it?"

"Yes. I know you, Doley. I know this is part of who you are. Maybe you can't get rid of it, but you can control it and you can live with it."

And so Doley kept his promise. He kept his violence, his throttled engine of hurt and anger, under control. Because he believed he could do anything at all if he still had Sylvie. He loved her deeply.

The next day, Sylvie walked the property with a willow dowsing branch and pointed to the ground. Together they dug a new well, a fifteen-foot-deep hole in the ground. She helped him shovel. He broke stones with pickaxes, lifted boulders from the pit. From the shoreline he brought other stones that fit together as if preordained for this purpose, and the walls of the well were rocked in to the surface. The water was clean and pure, and the old shallow well was given over to frogs. Doley put in a pipe below the frost line so it would not freeze in winter and talked about getting electricity soon — power for lights but also for an electric pump.

Doley began to speak a new dream to Sylvie about moving to Lunenburg and opening up a hardware store. He didn't exactly know why it had come back into his life, this idea of being something other than a labourer, of selling things, of being a proprietor of his own business on the mainland. Mainlanders had never been anything but cruel to him.

He talked about it often and then, realizing how it upset his wife, he stopped. But one day, at the dinner table, he heard himself speaking his foolish aspirations out loud again and saw the look on Sylvie's face.

"How stupid can I be?" he said out loud.

"You're not stupid."

"I'm sorry, Sylvie. It was all talk. We're not moving. We're doing just fine. I don't know what got into me."

Sylvie knew that her husband would make any sacrifice for her and now he would make this one as well. He stopped talking about Lunenburg and about selling hardware to a store full of eager customers. He stayed put in his mind and in his life with what he had and did not feel sorry for himself in the slightest.

Sylvie began to teach Doley to read. It was both humbling and rewarding. Sylvie admired his efforts to learn something that seemed to her so simple, yet proved so fundamentally difficult to him. Words of three syllables appeared to him as the most complex puzzles, requiring him to test one piece of sound with another over and over until he got it right. Sometimes he would give up for a short while and sit stroking the cover of the book. Then he would pick up where he left off. She knew he was not stupid but it would be more than thirty years before she would understand that her third husband had been afflicted with a learning disorder, a common condition known as dyslexia. But that wasn't Doley's only ailment.

Doley was reading at a grade three level when he began to lose weight. He was only forty-eight, but his hair turned grey over a period of a few months. His skin took on a greyish yellow colour, and there were more trips to the Mutton Hill Harbour doctor. Although the doctor had no fixed name for whatever was wrong with Doley, he insisted that the big man check himself into a hospital in Halifax. Sylvie pleaded with him to go, but Doley insisted there was nothing really the matter with him. He was going through a "spell" of some sort. He would get better.

Instead, he aged as if something had taken the timepiece of his life and made the hands of the clock rush ahead on him. Sylvie watched him slip away, slowly but steadily.

When he was gone, Sylvie fought her impulse to curse and rage against such a sinister world that played such malevolent tricks on her over and again. She missed Doley and everything about him but stored his lessons in her heart. Even anger, hurt, and suffering can be tamed and channelled into something sad but beautiful. And Doley, Sylvie decided, had been a very beautiful man.

Chapter Twenty-Two

L egal action was levelled against Phonse Doucette and his junkyard. The place was condemned. Old cars and God knows what seeping into the ground and water table out there. Guns confiscated. Fun sucked wholesale out of this part of the world. Mounties came and issued summonses to anyone driving around the island without a license or with an unregistered, uninspected vehicle. Took all the dangerous kids off the road but a whole whack of their parents as well. Island became quiet for a bit. Health inspectors arrived. Problems with the hall, the school, the post office, the Aetna accused of serving bad scallops.

Welcome to Hell Island, Phonse was thinking. *Downsize this, you friggin' Halifax politicians*. How had they swooped down all of a sudden and ruined them? And why? To save the province some money. Try to pressure everyone off the island. Already a dozen families had jumped at the price offered for their houses. Good riddance. Let 'em go. Not true islanders in the blood. Couldn't be.

Phonse, alone in his junkyard office, sipping homemade John Bull bitter in a Big Eight pop bottle. A man's livelihood yanked out from under him. Not a fair thing to do. Curses on the graves of the mother and father of that little do-gooder pissant writer from the *Herald* who came sneaking around to sniff out his little pissy story. Like some kind of mongrel dog, no better. At least a dog would never be quite so vicious. Words had teeth. Phonse hadn't known that before.

Still, something left of value in a man sucking on a warm bottle of home brew, down and out but not dead yet. No sir, not by a long shot. Phonse was fairly unrehearsed at feeling sorry for himself. He walked outside to take a pee and surveyed what he still had. A big acreage of scrap metal still there. Stored in every bloody wreck and rusty hatchback out there were legends, too — lives, tales of what went on in those vehicles. Graveyard for automotive scrap and then some. Good to have them all togeth- er like this. Old friends, cousins — kissing cousins — made in Detroit, Windsor, Oshawa. Some straight from Japan, a couple of Ruski cars in there and Yugos, Skodas. Cars that outlived nations as they split asunder or fell apart.

"Everything, every bloody thing has a soul," Phonse said out loud. A place and purpose to everything in its season, under heaven, or something like that.

Phonse would not move off to the mainland. Not unless he had to do it for his kids. They were gonna close the school for sure. Fire regulations, health regulations. Arseholes, the lot of them. With arsehole regulations. Something else they came up with about the teacher, young Kit, being unfit. Leave it to mainlanders to screw it all up good, turn it all into lies or whatever it is they teach 'em to do in college and business school.

Nope. Mainland would be a hard scrape for the likes of Phonse. His life was falling apart into little scrap metal pieces around him and still he kept thinking that everything had a soul. And that was worth remembering. The island had a soul and he was part of it, it was part of him. If he moved ashore it'd be like taking your hand out of your pocket and not knowing what to do with it.

Bright guy like Moses should be able to figure something out. Moses always rolled with the punches. Phonse just never even felt the blows, never saw 'em, never felt 'em, and never swung back, always just stood his ground and kept doing what he did. Acadian away. All that good blood of Acadie swirling around in his veins with the alcohol from the beer. That's the ticket. Rely on the cultural tradition. The early Acadians, it was well known, were willing to listen to the Mi'kmaq, and therefore they learned from the land. Whatever was necessary to survive through a cold, hard winter. Eat the roots, store the berries, dry the meat and fish. Build a place that was safe and warm for a good, healthy Acadian family.

Phonse would go for a walk out through his yard and listen to the wrecks speak to him in person, listen to the voice of their many metallic souls. Listen to the sky and the wind and see what the island had to say for itself today.

As he made his way to the top of the hill where those old Ford and Dodge windscreens were splashing sunlight right back up at the sky like a furnace of light, Phonse had a curious feeling that he couldn't put into words. It was a sensation that cut through the beer and the verbal razzmatazz rattling around in his brain like loose change in a fish bowl. Phonse stopped and looked down at the soil, where old radio wires, lug nuts, and parking lightbulbs were scattered — as if on purpose, as if part of some quirky but honest work of art. This thing that he was feeling was larger than he was, but he didn't have any words to attach to it, although he knew there was beauty in there, and sadness, and it was tied into history and Acadie. Loss and allegiance. Perseverance. Blind purpose in the face of adversity. Cheerful defiance. The full meal deal of something that made him feel small but not unimportant. What was going down was part of a grand scheme of notions, as if it was the very essence of truth, the marrow in the bone of life.

Phonse chose an old GMC pick-up truck. Opened the creaky door and sat down on the driver's seat. He put two hands on the steering wheel and felt the truck's history, a proud one, and he sensed that it had been a good machine and that the owner had taken good care of it until salt stole all the strength from its steel undercarriage.

The near tragedy of Angeline and the rescue had changed Bruce Sanger. He had a little room now in his head: panic, fear, desperate love for his family were all camped together in that room in close quarters and he'd open the door a peek and study those elements of his life until he could bring them into focus one more time.

While his little daughter had been in that cave, he had been sitting at a desk in an air-conditioned, windowless office in Manhattan. Phones going, computers threshing out numbers. People talking about the Mets and the Yankees somewhere over by the water cooler. He had a coffee in one hand when the phone rang. French roast. He dumped it straight into the keyboard. Sent off a hot, wet, caffeine message that hammered the hard drive. Oh, that long, agonizing trek by cab to the airport, then on to Nova Scotia. He had sworn to himself he would haul his family back home safe and sound to Upper Montclair, that the whole summer was a fiasco. What had he been thinking?

But then as he arrived and saw Angeline safe and sound, heard the whole incredible tale, he collected what was left of his frazzled self and settled into that little old house where women once made sauerkraut from bushels and bushels of cabbages. And after that, he began to really open up his eyes and ears to things going on there on the island. He heard the language of the rain on the roof, and the soft winds in the trees. He listened to the sea as it settled itself back to normal after Freda was diminished to nothing at all. He smelled the sea everywhere. At night, all four of them in a dark living room with the lights off, with nothing but a candle burning, they sat around on the rag rug on the floor and just talked. Then they'd all tuck into their own sleeping bags and sleep there on the floor. This place, this place, something about this place that Bruce kept trying to formulate into words. But Elise had caught onto it long before. She knew she didn't have to trap the feeling with words. She just knew.

First there had been the relief that Angeline was alive, then the argument. They would all go back to New Jersey tomorrow, then the darn kids, not wanting to leave. His bold statement that he would stay until the end of summer. And Elise talking about the old woman. There were invisible threads tying the whole lot of them together. That goofy but brave college kid, Greg, and all the island people who came out to show support.

By the end of the week, Bruce wasn't sure New York even existed. He thought about his job and wondered why he bothered. What was he, after all, but a kind of truck driver for other people's money, shuttling it here and there over electric wires. Was he really helping the planet or was it just a kind of con job he'd done on himself and his clients? Holy shit. How many wineries can you buy in Chile and still say you are doing it for the environment and then turn over a yearly profit of 21 percent to your smiling investor? Face it, if the investor wasn't turning a tune of percentages, he'd be out of Chilean grapes and coming up with a good ethical excuse to be strip mining bauxite in Malaysia.

And now here he was, with his family — that's all that mattered. The island had nearly taken his daughter, but the island's people had conspired to bring her back. Elise snuggled into his neck. He felt her breathing upon him, heard his children breathing too and listened to them squirm. All the while, the language of a soft evening rain, like poetry, like music.

Monday morning rolled around and Bruce snapped out of the spell. He decided he had said things he couldn't live up to. He convinced himself that it was safe to leave them here yet again and go back to Wall Street, sort out whatever snarls there were from his absence. How many of his ethical investors would be able to have some empathy for him and his family crisis? He wondered. His boss was relatively sympathetic, but that was his style, after all. He had good people working for him and knew they needed physical hugs and perks and room to sort out personal problems when they arose. He only hired solid performers and then treated them with respect and kindness. The bottom line was that it worked well and his traders remained loyal to the company and the bonus at the end of each year.

And then Bruce was back in New York. City streets of lower Manhattan on a summer day, a swelter of cabs and men moving merchandise on rolling racks, on trucks, on trading floors at the Exchange. Everything hot and sweaty and being hustled from one place to another unless it was jammed up on the crosstown

streets or backlogged on a mainframe with a fancy virus stuck
up its ass. And back in the office, the big trouble with Bruce was
that he knew he had lost his edge. He had missed the Icelandic
geothermal company going public on the NASDAQ entirely. So
little of this mattered to him now. Now that he'd stared down
the thought of his daughter drowning in a dark cave with himself sitting here in New York screaming inside his brain — paralyzed by time and distance to do anything. He was a prisoner
trapped between two worlds. He would last only a few days
before begging the jailer — begging himself — for release.

Bruce Sanger flew into Halifax from Newark yet again that
summer, and it felt like he was coming home. This a surprise to
a man not easily surprised by much of anything. Plunked himself down in another rental car, a white Taurus like the last one,
and drove for two hours, parked her by the harbour, didn't even
lock the doors. A few minutes later he was on the ferry. The
ferry that would soon be no more.

The wind was clear and dry, even out in the harbour, over
the water. North wind, a fair breeze, sky and sea all around like
they owned the place. Ragged Island out there on the horizon.
He undid his tie and wondered at the fact that he'd left it tight
around his neck all the way here. He slipped it off and held it
out over the water, noticed how much it looked like the noose
of a hangman. He looked left and right to make sure no one was
watching and he dropped it in the water. Red stripes on blue,
floating and then catching the wake as the ferry cruised seaward.
Bruce made a tiny salute. Why did it feel so good to drop a
forty-five-dollar tie into the sea? He was overcome by a foolish,
teenage desire to strip naked and drop everything into the drink.
Instead, he pulled out his wallet. No. Not the whole thing. Just
the American Express Executive Card. He had cards aplenty

there in his wallet. He tried tearing it once, but the American Express card was made of tough plastic. He bit into it, though, and left teeth marks, then pitched it like an old baseball card into the wake of the ferry, where the little sucker floated.

A gull dropped down from the sky and poked once at it but, finding it unsavoury, didn't scoop it up.

Moses and Viddy sitting at their kitchen table with hot coffee cups. Talking about selling the boat. If they sold the boat they'd have enough money to stay on the island and not work. Then again, if they sold the boat, they couldn't go ashore for supplies once a week or haul the kids back and forth to the boarding school ashore. But if they kept the boat, they'd have to move ashore so Moses or Viddy could find regular work. A fine fix that was.

"Jesus, I don't want to be separated from the kids each week. We'd be like strangers on weekends."

"But they're closing the school for sure. Wiring. Mould, they say. Mould in the walls. They're talking of tearing it down."

"Mould. Mould and dust mites and anything they can use. I'd rather my kids suffered a little mildew in their lives than have to move ashore and suffer all that."

"We're screwed, Viddy old girl. Funny, I thought you'd be the one to say you didn't mind moving ashore. Stores and such."

"I know. I'm surprised too. Something about old days and old ways."

"Tansy and wormwood to cure whatever. Jigging from a dory. Winter haul-up, kraut and summer savoury. Mending nets. How can all that stuff just fade off into the past?"

"You sound like you're a hundred years old."

"And then some," Moses said. "I'm my father's son and his father's grandson. I got their stories fixed in my head to the point that I think I've lived all those lives. I know all the nooks and crannies of the past, but I don't have a clue about the future."

"Nobody does, I guess."

"They all laughed at me, you know. With the whale-watching thing and all. When it worked out, they hushed up, but when the tours *didn't* work out, they were all down at the wharf saying they knew it was gonna turn out like this. They thought I was a fool, but a couple of them men quietly thanked me for saving the ferry and the island for a while. But then when it all turned to gull shit, even they started blaming me. They did that you know. All those ones we call our friends and neighbours."

"Yes, I believe they did. But they'll forgive you and you'll forgive them. And we move on."

She didn't mean it that way, but he picked up on it. "Or we don't move on. We hunker down like it's just another big winter haul-up. Wait for the weather to ease. Wait for the fish to come back, wait and worry with the tides."

Moses found the words unsatisfactory to express what he was feeling, so he got up and went outside and began to split some cut logs. He upended several big chunks of birch and maple and then split them clean and hard until his wrists ached and his jaw muscles kind of locked up. He whacked one last piece with a big knot in it and the splitting maul got stuck good and hard.

Moses left it that way and walked down to the wharf, fired up the engine on his boat, and steered her straight to Mutton Hill Harbour, cursing every minute he was on the water. He docked her and went to talk to the bank about the value of his boat. He felt bad all of a sudden that he had let everybody down. How was he to know the whales would move off? He couldn't blame the blasted government for that, could he? *Eco-tourism*, the word made him want to laugh or kick at something really hard. A lifetime of building himself up. He'd been good at it. Him with his good instincts, his perfect timing. Pure, unadulterated bullshit.

Just before he walked through the door of the godforsaken branch of the Royal Bank, he tried to conjure a picture of him and Viddy and their two boys in some nice little house near the water here in Mutton Hill Harbour. He tried to see himself sitting on a screened-in porch, looking out at rich folks' sailboats bobbing at their moorings. He saw it all, clear as day. And it made his throat go dry as dead, grey ashes in his old wood stove.

Chapter Twenty-Three

August was coming to an end. An end of many things. Families had already moved ashore. Others were still in a quandary. As if it wasn't really going to happen. Everyone was worried about the kids the most. Come September, some believed, it would be discovered that it was all a bad joke. Life would go on as usual. The school would stay open. Kit would teach. The ferry would continue on into the next century. This was what some wanted to believe, despite the fact that they knew politics had failed them, not that it had ever done any good. All manner of Halifax appeals and phone calls to Mutton Hill Harbour lawyers and even sit-down visits with more provincial advisors and government men in Halifax. None of it had done any good. Phonse shouting at the premier, throwing a beach stone through the man's window on Hollis Street. Moses acting more civil. Kit and Greg together proposing one alternative scenario after another to save the island community. Greg with a laptop showing a workable cost analysis of keeping the island alive.

But it was as if the government wanted to wipe the place off the map of Canada. The eco-tourism was a gigantic embarrassment after all that media mess. Another failed enterprise that, in retrospect, seemed farcical: travel agency in Chicago sending down tourists from Minneapolis to go look at whales off Ragged Island with no whales to be seen. And now all those Halifax men in suits who knew how to keep their cool when families and lives were being ripped apart.

And back on the island. Hot and still. Humid, salty sea air in every room. Kelp lying in big, gnarled piles along the shoreline everywhere. Sylvie's dory, paint still drying in the sun — upside down on the round stones beyond her house, facing out towards the sea. Sylvie had bought the dory years and years ago from Noah Slaunwhite, Moses' father. She had rowed it around now and again when she needed freedom or wanted sheer physical exhaustion. But it hadn't been used since she was sixty years old. Sixty to eighty had gone by in the blink of an eye. Twenty years like that. Snap of the fingers, a huff of air through the lungs in and out once or twice. Babies turned to grown men and women around her and having kids of their own. If you lived to be a thousand, she reckoned, a century would be like a burp after dinner.

How or why the idea got into her head, she wasn't sure. It took a full moon night to pull the idea out and set it down on the cotton tablecloth in front of her. The idea. If others knew her thoughts, perhaps they'd put her in some horrible institution with a snap of the fingers, but they would not find out. If she was old and crazy, so be it. Things rooted deep down in her being, powerful swelling emotional things, were swimming through her consciousness. Not much room for pure reason and logic, was there? William Toye would understand this business. The mad philosopher was with her often now, as was the young and gentle David Young. And the others. All her good dead men were with her as she painted the dory blue-green on those calm, hot days on the shoreline. Sanded, repaired, and corked the seams with new oakum. She ran her hand along the smooth deep keel. Studied the spruce knees to see if they were cracked with age or not. Decided the old boat was fit as fun could be. Painting felt like renewal. Some of the boatmen about would not trust an old boat even if it had been inside and dry for years. Old wood could get too dry and start to soak up anything once set upon the sea. The sea had no sympathy for anyone with a craft that was not in good repair.

Sylvie did not worry. Noah's little boat was a blue-green, glossy prize shining in the sun. They both had age as an ally, she was certain. Both lacked fear. Not a speck of it.

Paint dry now. Cured for a couple of good dry days before the humidity set in. Not a blister, not a peel. Oar locks greased. Fresh oars, ordered in from the general store. Questions about what for and why, all answered with vague allusions to lawn ornaments, hobbies, an old woman and her ways. Small knot of men, old but younger than she, laughing. At her. Men who had given up their sea legs for over a decade. Men who would hang around the small general store and complain, never do much else with their lives. Complain and grow lines on their foreheads, watch their hair thin and blame the world for being unkind.

The world was not unkind, Sylvie knew. She was part of it, not separated from it. Connected. To island and sea. And in her connection to these things beneath her feet and surrounding her in the ocean of air, she believed she was some kind of hinge or oarlock or pivotal capstan. Which was why she had this task before her. And still trying to make good common sense out of it.

An old woman was not a weak woman. The two were not synonymous, never were, except in the minds of people who didn't know any better. Two arms and a strong back to lift on the gunwale, roll it over and see what the dory looked like right side up. Wobble and then balance. She had lines on her, yes. Sweet curve of the earth. A good arc of a keel. She sat in it, alone. Testing the feel of the new oars. Remembering something William had taught her: "Man named Buridan, a French philosopher from the early fourteenth century, believed that a person must do only what is of the greatest good. Nothing else. Cuts through all the seeming complexity, doesn't it? Only problem is that philosophy students for the next six centuries became more interested in what became known as 'Buridan's ass,' and they weren't referring to his posterior."

God, she missed him. William Toye. Loved that talk. Still singing in her ears. Madness and wisdom that she carried like a tool kit in her head.

"So the dilemma of Buridan's ass is this," William had said. "You have a very hungry animal, an ass, standing in a field. Starving he is. Before him are two perfectly good piles of hay and each is the same distance from where he stands. By Buridan's principle of choosing the greatest good, the poor creature would starve."

But Sylvie knew Jean Buridan need not be laughed at. She'd whittled away at all those books of philosophy left in her care and found Buridan's notion noble and simple, his starving ass not withstanding. And it had something, something to do with her plan. An image embedded deep in her thoughts, cropping up now almost every night.

A woman in a small boat alone on a wide, empty sea. A tranquil, serene ocean without a ripple. Every time she peered at the face in the dream, tried to make it come into focus, she was always surprised that it was not herself. It was someone different each time. A woman even older than herself with a face of sagging flesh over sturdy bones. Another time it was the face of a young beauty, with blushing cheeks, white teeth, eyes like summer skies. Another time it was a woman crying, the face of anguish, and yet again it was a teenage girl laughing and laughing. She saw her there in her dream — the one that kept coming at her night after night, but a dream always beginning a different way. Started as pure chaos but then grew more focussed, and, each successive time, there would be the woman in the boat on the serene waters, far from land. Sylvie's point of view always came in from above and from the back and passed *through* the person sitting on the boat until she was in front of her and looking back at who she was. Sylvie was sure the woman in the boat *should* be herself but it was not. She even got out old photographs of herself when she was young and they did not quite coincide.

Until one night she could not see the boat or the woman at all in her dream. She could not find them even though she was at sea and scanning the horizon in all directions. She was not above looking down, however, and she could not move forward or back. Then she felt something tug at her arms and looking down realized she was rowing a dory. She couldn't see any woman in the boat now because, at last, she had become that person. She woke up satisfied and confirmed.

Sylvie was old-fashioned in that she believed in patterns of things. Unity, beginnings and ends, and threads or similar colours running through a fabric. She had learned the logic of quilts from her mother and the precision of needlework and the creation of patterns that made sense and pleased the eye. Order out of chaos. Even though her life became rich in complexity and often confusion, even embracing ideas or principles that seemed counter to each other, she still held onto some sense of the rightness of things. She would say that she grew up in an age when right and wrong were instilled in children, but she knew that was mostly hogwash.

The world was a mess in 1917, the year she was born. Europe a tangle of bodies and military hardware, blood and bones on farmers' fields. Sense and purpose of history and beliefs had created what was up to then the ultimate horror and chaos.

The greatest paradox of her own life for Sylvie, however, was the realization that she was not born on the island. She was born in Truro, on a kitchen table among women who had gathered there from all over the province purportedly to come up with new ways to stop men from drinking alcohol. It was a Women's Christian Temperance Union meeting. Even though Sylvie's mother was weighted down substantially by pregnancy, she ferried ashore, took a bus to Halifax and train to Truro, and there she was.

Women had been gathering in groups like that for decades, trying to figure ways to blot out the evils of alcohol. They had some success here and there. Sylvie's mother, Grace, was not obsessed with eradicating booze, nor were many of the women who had gathered. Instead, they talked of many things. Most were rural women and felt a deep kinship. Some were bold enough to speak of new rights for women and ways to help women in trouble in rural areas of the province. What to do with men who beat their wives and got away with it. (Part of that was the alcohol problem, of course.) What to do to help women who wanted to fish, to teach, or to work in factories. Certainly they were being treated unfairly, as if unfairness was the way of the world and couldn't change.

Grace and the others around her believed the world could be changed. And they talked about it until tears streamed down their faces. They sang old Christian songs and cried some more, even though most admitted that they weren't there to have anybody saved by Jesus. They wanted to save themselves.

Grace was there with her husband's strong approval. A rawknuckled fishermen and cabbage farmer, Sylvie's father, known locally as Crib, was a simple believer in possibility. "Anything is possible if you have spunk and the right equipment," was his favourite saying. He drank some but not enough to do him much harm. Heck, Grace drank some homemade raspberry wine now and then too. So did many of the women at the temperance meeting. Only a handful of the hardcore purists were left in this faction of the women's group. The really hardliners had split off to form an organization that would debate whether or not the death penalty was appropriate for men who abused alcohol.

So there was this political, socially-minded backdrop for Sylvie's birth, ten days earlier than expected, on the kitchen table in Truro. Tears of joy fell on her forehead as she was cuddled and swaddled and passed around for everyone in the room to see. There were three midwives attending and they did good work. No men were necessary. Grace stayed on for five more days after sending a message by telegram to Crib. Crib would later say that he hated the wait to see his new little daughter, that he felt like a man who had ants all over every part of his body, he was that restless. But he respected Grace on this one count.

Before Crib arrived to take Grace back to the island, the women had each bonded with Grace and with the baby. They would never see one other again, as it turned out, but Sylvie's birth meant something. Meetings and discussions had continued from early morning to late night. The world was a mess, the worst of it was war and the men who waged war. And the women who let it happen. The world needed saving, it needed fixing. God would not do it for them in the twentieth century. Men were too stubborn to change. Women would have to do it and they would need power and, as Grace would add, "the right equipment," which to her meant education and attitude.

Grace and Crib talked all the way back to the island. A year later, Crib signed up to fight in Europe. Crib agreed with Grace and everything she had to report about the Truro resolutions concerning peace and world justice. "The damn problem is we have to finish this damn thing first and get past it. Then we can talk about peace." Crib left his baby daughter and went to a war where he never fired a bullet or suffered anything worse than dysentery. But he had seen the brutality and ugliness of war close enough and was damaged by it in some way he could never frame into words. He had helped carry hundreds of wounded men in and out of hospitals. He returned home vowing never to leave the island again. And, aside from a few jaunts into Mutton Hill Harbour, he kept that vow.

Grace and her newsletters from the women's group. Her father and his nets, his knife blade "nibbling off" the outer leaves of cabbages. The smell of summer savoury grown for the Lunenberg sausage makers. The pet moose that she would never let go from her thoughts. Rocks on the shore. Seals lying in the sun, whales watching for her in the mornings of spring. An island life. And yet, she had not been born on the island.

On the day Sylvie left for sea, she baked as usual and took her breads and muffins and cookies down to the Aetna, where they were too polite to remind her that there were not enough cus-

tomers to hardly keep the place open. She dropped off some
cookies and zucchini bread with Bruce's family. Bruce talked
nonstop on a telephone to people in all parts of the world. What
was it that he did? It didn't make much sense to her even though
he had tried to explain it. And even though Bruce knew what
his work was all about, each time he tried to explain it to someone on the island, even he ended up admitting that it didn't
sound plausible. Sylvie hugged Angeline to her and shook Todd's
hand when she said goodbye, not letting on what she was about
to do. Elise gave her a long, cool drink of water from the hand
pump at the sink.

She would have visited with Kit Lawson just to make sure
she was keeping herself sane, and she would have liked to have
one last good look at Greg, the boy who had had enough faith
in an old woman to risk his life. But the door to Kit's house was
closed. Even from outside, she could hear bed springs squeaking,
and that was enough to make her smile and feel nostalgic about
all the passions of youth.

Sylvie went home and took a long nap, woke around five
o'clock, made a meal of Swiss chard, rice, ham, garden salad, and
brown bread. She drank a glass of her own homemade raspberry wine and toasted her mother and her father. After dinner she
gathered all of her dead husbands together. The kitchen felt very
small and full indeed. She allowed them to counsel her one by
one and accepted their gifts of wisdom, patience, tolerance,
imagination, mental stamina, and curiosity.

By eight in the evening, as the sky towards the west
expressed its own opinions with vermilion clouds and other
famous colours upon the water, Sylvie settled her supplies into
the stern of the dory and rolled it down her ladder of spruce logs
until it kissed the dark calm waters of Front Bay. Sylvie set her
dry shoes in the boat, not sure why she was taking shoes along
at all, then she lifted her skirt and waded into the water, tugging

the boat until it was fully afloat. Then, bracing herself with a hand on the gunwale, she got in, fixed a good grip on each oar, and took one full stroke. This made her suddenly feel like a small child shaking hands with an old gentleman who wasn't afraid to give a solid grasp to a kid's hand.

Then she was gliding on the calm sea, looking down at the forest of kelp and other seaweed swaying in the dark, cool waters like the long, flowing hair of her mother.

A fish jumped. One and then another. And then all was still again. The sky above was perfectly clear. One star off to the east. Venus, rising. Then another off to the south. The moon would not appear tonight. Stars would celebrate the event. Many things rushed through her mind, but she tried to keep the questions from crowding out what she felt. And Sylvie was glad her muscles felt strong, glad her heart was healthy and pumping blood to every part of her old woman's body.

The shoreline was empty. Rowing seemed almost effortless. She pulled at the oars in a slow but serious manner. She passed by the fisherman's shack where Greg had first stayed. Someone was there, a boy, it seemed. He waved to her. Sylvie waved back, but she was sure she was too far away and that light was too dim for him to see who was in the dory. Then she scooted past the sea cave, tonight looking exotic and benign, and then her boat found the deep current of the Trough. She felt the tug of the current, the pull of the unseen moon, and the graceful, immense power of invisible guiding forces. She propped the oars for a while and let the boat drift away from the island until it was a dark silhouette with a faint red glow of sun behind it. And then it was a smudge until it was erased by distance.

When darkness swallowed what was left of the sun's light, the stars had already grown restless and extravagant above her head. Sylvie arranged her small luxury of needlework cushions on the bottom of the boat and on the hard edge of the seats, and then she lowered herself to the slat floor of her dory, flung her head back, let her mouth fall open, and looked up into the night sky until she felt like she was being drawn up into it. Not a ripple upon the sea, not a breeze. She felt weightless, free, and happy. What she felt inside her chest was like music, but there was no sound save a kind of internal vibration. And with it knowledge akin to what it was like to dowse for water. You just kept quiet and waited and you eventually knew.

Floating now, alone on a dark night with a canopy of brilliant suns above her, she knew that she had chosen the right time to finally leave her beloved island. She thought of old native women of the north, setting themselves adrift on ice floes, old Mi'kmaq women going to the woods alone for spiritual resolution. And she also thought of old women dying in nursing homes.

Whatever it was she was doing, she knew somehow it was the right thing for her and for the island.

Chapter Twenty-Four

When Yoshiteru Kojima stepped out of the taxi at the Mutton Hill Harbour wharf, he was surprised that the long ride from the airport had been so inexpensive — only a hundred and fifty dollars Canadian. He gave the driver a twenty dollar tip. Yoshi stood stone still for a minute after the taxi left. He closed his eyes and breathed the air, smelled the sea, heard the sound of hammers and saws. Men working nearby, building something, boats maybe. Honest work. A Ben's Bread truck was parked in front of a store and a man was carrying in a large rack of baked goods. Cars passed by and the sun glinted off their windshields. Children were laughing somewhere nearby.

Yoshi had grown up in such a town, a world away, on Hokkaido, the big northern island of Japan. Something welled up inside of him. Why had he spent all those years in Tokyo? Why the great drive, the great ambition? His father had been a much simpler man, a fisherman, satisfied with his small, orderly life, content with his work, his wife and only son. But not Yoshi. And because Yoshi was willing to make so many personal sacrifices for his job, he had done extremely well in Tokyo. His employers were always pleased with his work. But he had been growing restless, waiting for some kind of signal that it was time to change.

The phone call from his friend Bruce Sanger in New York had been too great of a temptation. An *island*. With an untouched resource that was in great demand in Yoshi's country. Yes, there was profit to be made — but there was also something else. Profitable deals had been the basis for a long-distance, main-ly-business relationship with Bruce Sanger. And they shared a belief that profit and good work, good deeds even, could go hand in hand. Yoshi found that few of his colleagues, his late-night-heavy-drinking-in-the-Ginza buddies, understood why this combination of seemingly disparate elements was so impor-tant. Why things like resource renewal were better than rape and pillage of the land or sea. Yoshi knew it was a deep-seated belief that his father had given him — like a thorn it was sometimes, but like the flower of a rose as well.

Bruce Sanger had started out as cynical as the next trader on his floor about ethical investing. Investing in a company because they had a good working relationship with a union? Was that enough to qualify for a hefty chunk of their mutual fund invest-ment? Yes, it was. Even if they made automotive parts for the military governments of a dozen countries around the world? Geothermal was better, however, and profitable as well. It was a sorcerer's brew of ethics and profit where performance always outweighed moral issues if it came down to the crunch. Leading investors to those vineyards in Chile and oil recycling plants in Philadelphia. And Bruce knew deep down that his co-workers were still sharks — sharks with teeth as sharp as any of the best traders on Wall Street. He knew the calibre of those teeth because he brushed his own set of them every morning.

And then this thing that happened with Angeline. The world went cockeyed and for weeks afterwards he was still trying to get his equilibrium. The story poured out of him one day when he was on the phone to Yoshiteru Kojima. Business had linked them initially: Japanese fish farming with environmentally appropriate methods. Non-intrusive hi-tech scallop farming in Malaysia and the Philippines. For mutual profit in several mutual funds they helped to administer, they had traded information. With good results. But neither trusted the security of e-mail and both despised the clinical nature of faxing back and forth, so they had resigned themselves to the old-fashioned luxury of the telephone. And over the phone lines their friendship had grown.

Once Bruce was back in New York after Angeline's near tragedy, he was trying to carve away at the pile of work on his desk. It all seemed so trivial. He gave up and phoned Yoshi instead, realizing it was very early in Japan but that his Japanese friend was already likely to be at his own desk in Tokyo. And he told Yoshi everything that had happened on the island.

Yoshi and his wife, Taeko, did not have children, and it looked as if their window of opportunity was closing fast. It had been a conscious decision on his part, on their part. Career obligations for both. Now that they were older, they both regretted it very much but rarely could bring themselves to speak of it. Late last year Bruce had mailed Yoshi a Christmas letter with news of his own family and he'd sent a photograph as well: Bruce in his backyard with his arms around Elise, Todd, and Angeline. Yoshi had not shown the photograph to his wife because he knew how it would make her feel, but he had folded the photo carefully and placed it in his wallet. He looked at the picture now and again. And he had taken it out and studied it as the Air Canada jet was touching down on the runway in Halifax. It made his eyes burn, and Yoshi knew it must be the stale air in the airplane cabin or the physical and emotional debilitation that came with jet lag.

Yoshi knew that he looked out of place. Still dressed in his dark business suit, carrying his Samsonite hard-shell luggage out towards the end of the wharf. The tourist books had said there was ferry service to the island. He had been uncertain about actual departure times and decided to make his own way to the island and then find Bruce on his own. He didn't want to put his friend to any inconvenience, and besides, he liked figuring out things on his own.

He saw the ferry but there was no one on it. It did not seem to be active. Then he saw the sign: the times of departure and arrival, but another board with neat government printing diagonally across it: "Ferry Service Cancelled."

Yoshi looked out towards sea, again sniffed at the fishy smells of the air, like an elixir in his lungs. On the other side of the wharf, a man was loading groceries into his boat.

"Excuse me, I was hoping to catch the ferry to Ragged Island but it appears ..."

"It appears to be dead, my friend. Done for. Kaput. The ferry has ferried its last." Moses Slaunwhite said the words with a mix of cynicism and mild humour. He knew a lost tourist when he saw one. "It wasn't the whales you were looking for, was it?" He'd hate to have to crack the bad news about that as well.

"I didn't know there were whales."

"There were, but there aren't anymore, I'm afraid."

Yoshi was unsure where the conversation was going. He was pretty good at American customs but knew Canadians were different. Could he offer this man money to take him to the island on his boat?

Yoshi handed Moses Slaunwhite his business card and bowed. Moses wiped some winch grease off his hands and accepted the card, nodded. *Yoshi Kojima, global investment analyst.* Moses blinked, looked up at Yoshi — the clothes, the fancy black luggage, the goddam shoes.

"Oh shit," he said out loud. "You want to buy the frigging island, I bet." What else could it be? It would be the last straw.

Yoshi waved his hand in the air. He smiled. Something about hearing a man he just met say "shit" made him feel more relaxed and comfortable. "No. No. Nothing like that. I'm looking for my friend, Bruce Sanger. He lives on that island."

Moses swiped a dirty hand across his face, pulled down on his chin, embarrassed. "Sorry. Didn't mean to be such an asshole. Of course. Bruce is living out there on my island."

"Your island?"

"I don't own it. But I live there with my family."

"Ah, family."

"Wife and a couple of kids. See all that food? My kids eat like horses. Viddy stuffs all of us real good."

Viddy. Family. Yoshi liked the sound of all of it.

"Hop in. Give you a ride."

Should he ask about the fare? Perhaps it would be the thing to do. "How much would you charge me, sir?"

Moses couldn't help but laugh. Snot accidentally flew out his nose and that made him laugh harder. "Sorry, bud," he said, "Didn't meant to blow boogers on you like that."

"It's okay, you missed. What did I say wrong?"

"Ah, nothing, man. Nothing at all. Just the way you said it. So formal and everything. I didn't mean to be a stupid herring choker but I guess that's what I am."

"And what can I pay you?"

"There you go again. Nothing, pal. I gotta take these groceries home anyway. It's on my way. Wouldn't be right to ask for anything. Sit down and enjoy the ride."

And Yoshi did enjoy the ride. Immensely. He felt free of everything that had tied him down, everything that was dragging him down in his successful life in Tokyo. A man named Moses was carrying him across the water in a fine, foreign place called Nova Scotia.

School began the day after Labour Day as usual. The class was smaller. Fourteen students. The school was officially closed. Some parents had followed the direction of the government and sent their kids ashore to board in town and go to Mutton Hill Harbour Consolidated. Several families had moved ashore altogether, some gone to greener pastures in Ontario and B.C. Said it was time to go.

But many stayed for what was turning out to be a fine, fine September on the island. Cloudless days, very little wind. Kit and Greg held some classes outside, took the kids on hikes. Science lessons by the shore with rocks and living things. Kit was impressed with how much Greg knew and what a good teacher he was. Kit was feeling pretty good about herself, but she had begun to worry about Sylvie. She had not seen hide nor hair of her old friend for five days, and it seemed like she had just upped and left. And that seemed impossible. It was rumoured that she'd just gone ashore to visit some old friends who had moved off already, but no one had actually seen her leave the island. This wasn't like her. But Kit knew Sylvie was okay. The old girl was smart and resourceful and was her own woman. Sylvie had certainly pulled Kit back from the brink of madness before Greg had come along to keep her sane.

Now the two of them taught side by side. Unpaid. Unofficial altogether. As far as the province was concerned, the school was permanently closed. Kit's contract was terminated. Island parents, however, had backed Kit's ideas about keeping on as if nothing had happened. She said she didn't care about money, about pay. Everyone said they'd work something out. Barter, or whatever. Food and firewood could be provided. Phonse and Moses said they'd both work at providing whatever else the pair needed. Greg had told islanders he was really happy to be able to stay on and help. He hadn't graduated from St. Mary's but he was close. He'd be a good teacher, he promised. Hell, after the cave thing, all those who kept their kids on the island trusted Greg. They admired the son of a gun and most even approved of the fact that he'd moved in with Kit Lawson. He was sure to be a better catch than the dope grower.

Most of the kids thought school was very cool. Greg had invented a bunch of games for teaching math. Kit had little kids creating fantastic, goofy poems. There were videos and computer labs and music. The American family had donated VCRs and computer gear. A typical day ran the gamut from nature hikes to Internet research. The old and the new mixed up and shook up like some fancy pedagogical milkshake, and the kids loved it.

Sure, island people were still hurting in any number of ways, most of them financial. Not much money coming into or going out of Ragged Island. But there you had it. Not so different from the old days.

September, September, September. A gift of weather, a long last pull at summer. The hum of bad news always in the background, though. A cold, dark November to come. Blasty weather of December and the ice and snow of the dark months. Days already getting shorter. Nights cool, though — good for sleeping. Some fishing activity, but hardly worth the price of fuel. Just take one day after the next. Like the old times. Not much sign of anybody from the province since several families sold their houses. Boarded them up like something gone out of business. Sad. Sorry, sorry thing. But it was chin-up for the rest. Bloody stay put and forge on with a life. See how she sails. Weather it out. Or watch it get worse. Not such a bad thing to be cut off from the mainland, really. Cut off from the world.

Moses cut the engine and let the boat thump gently up against the big truck tires nailed onto the dock. "All ashore that's goin' ashore, bud," Moses said. He hopped off onto the dock and seemed to be walking away.

The quiet settled upon Yoshi until Moses fired up an old, cut-down Chevy Nova parked at the Aetna Café across the road and roared out onto the wharf. Moses set Yoshi's suitcase in the back and said he'd run him out to see Bruce Sanger in this contraption that he referred to as "the truck." When he dropped Yoshi off at his destination, the Japanese man gave him a small lapel pin, an unlikely gift, with an image of Buddha on it. "For good luck," he said.

"Right on. Thanks, bud." Moses had no idea that the pin was solid gold and made by a famous metal sculptor in Kyoto, that Yoshi had bought the pin for something like $300 American. Moses liked it okay, but studying it in the glinting sunlight, decided it was something more for Viddy than him and maybe she'd think it exotic or whatever. Never hurts to come home bearing gifts, even if it was just a little trifling thing like this.

Yoshi had already decided he did not like the island. He loved it. He wanted to give up life in Tokyo and move here. No, he wouldn't buy it, but he knew that he could probably afford it, backed by some of his friends. If he wanted to, he could own this whole amazing, lovely place, create a world there, bring his wife. Forget about Tokyo and the sewer rats he worked with. But as he sipped English tea and ate zucchini muffins with Bruce and his lovely wife, Elise, he absorbed the sorry tale of what had recently happened to the island and knew that he had not come here just to do something selfish; he had come to do something much larger.

"I'm not going back to New York," Bruce told his good friend. It was only his second ever face-to-face encounter with Yoshi, although they had talked on the phone for many years. Once they had crossed flight paths in Honolulu, spent an evening drinking at a bar in Waikiki, become close allies in the crazy world of commerce, then flown off in opposite directions. But here they were on this island. For a reason. Insane as it was. "I'll have to fly down once a month and do the office thing for a few days, then come back. We're renting the house in Montclair. In the end, we let the kids decide."

Todd was at his laptop in the corner, in a chat room with some kids in Germany and Florida. They were discussing the pictures recently beamed down by the little rover thing creeping around Mars. Angeline was standing behind him trying to read the screen, fanning herself with an exquisite paper fan from Japan that this visitor had just given to her.

"How long can you stay, Yoshi?"

"Five days. Then I must go back. But I will return. Often."

"Maybe you could bring your wife."

Yoshi lit up. "Yes, I will bring Taeko." Twenty hours or so on a plane and three more hours on ground and at sea did not seem so great an inconvenience if it meant coming back to a place like this.

Elise wanted Yoshi to meet Sylvie.

She hadn't even seen Sylvie for a while and wondered why she was keeping to herself. Maybe she was sick. Worth checking to make sure she's okay.

Elise knocked at the door. No answer. Went in and discovered how quiet the house was. Everything in order. Door not locked. Dishes washed and stacked. Floors clean. No note on the table or anything. Nothing felt wrong. Since moving here, Elise had begun to trust her intuition more. That was Sylvie's doing. She'd taught her this. Actually, Elise was relearning something she had once been good at. As a little girl, Elise had believed herself to be psychic, but later she convinced herself she was not. She just wanted it to be so. When she gave up on her metaphysical hopes, she had closed down her female intuitive skills. The island and Sylvie had helped bring them back. Once she was out of the loop of her smartass friends from the glitter sector back in northern New Jersey, it was amazing how much more perceptive she was.

So she sat at Sylvie's table and let her mind work at this. Had Sylvie moved ashore as some believed? It did not seem likely. What then? She felt like she was overstepping her bounds when she went into Sylvie's bedroom and sat down on her bed. Again, nothing felt wrong. Elise plucked three strands of long, grey hair from the pillow and held them in her hand. On the small table by the bed was a glass of water, half full, not much to go on either. Beside the glass was a small guidebook to star constellations. The spine cracked as she opened it to a page with a bookmark made from what was locally called "fish leather." On the open page were two maps, one of the dark side of the moon, one of the side of the moon that faced earth. With ink, Sylvie, or someone, had circled the designation "The Sea of Tranquility." And someone had marked an exclamation mark after the name.

Near sunset, Elise, Todd, Angie, and Bruce accompanied Yoshi Kojima to the seaward side of the island, where the sea had indented the land with the large basin known simply as Front Bay. "Front" because it faced out to the open sea. Angie pointed to the place on the headland where the sea cave was. Because the story had a happy ending, the cave was now a proud and exciting part of her personal history. Todd, however, always wished she wouldn't repeat that story. He felt the stinging guilt of his bad judgement that had almost killed his sister, and it sobered him whenever it came up. Sometimes he still cried late at night, but he did it silently so no one would know. Todd reached down and picked up a starfish, still alive, that had been left high and dry by a retreating tide. He hobbled across a few slippery rocks and set the creature back into the waters of the bay.

Yoshi watched the boy and his sister who followed him and felt a profound happiness for his friend at having a son and daughter. He also felt a searing ache in his heart that he had chosen career over family, as if the two could not coexist. But he would not dwell on anything negative. The bay was beautiful. Broad and deep, unspoiled, untouched. North Americans were virtually unaware of the richness of this place, the resources right beneath their noses. He brought that line of thinking to a dead end. Remembered going to the shrine at Nakamura to pay homage to the Big Buddha there that had survived typhoons and even tidal waves. He had thrown change into the grate for good luck, lit incense for good measure, and added his most sincere request to the prayer wheel. And Buddha had been kind to him, despite the fact that he was never a devoted follower of Buddhism. For he had travelled here, all the way to Nova Scotia, not really because he expected it to be profitable, but because his heart told him to do this thing. Now he was amazed to discover that *he* had something to offer the people who lived here. It would not be a matter of just taking. Balance would be achieved, yin and yang. Passive and active. And what was to be taken would be put back in some way. It would be restored. In his own way, Yoshi thought, he would become a kind of bodhisattva.

Gulls swooped in the sunset. As they walked onto a small, sandy length of beach along the bay, Yoshi was astonished at the way the washed-up seaweed was splayed out on the delicate sand as if arranged by some artist. Swirls of angel hair, DNA twists of kelp, rockweed, and dulse arranged in some perfect, perfect pattern. The golden lighting of the setting sun gave everything an enhanced colour. Reds, browns, purple and yellow. Greens of sea lettuce almost explosive. If you weren't careful you'd end up stepping on and ruining priceless art. But wasn't that the way of the earth itself? He turned, and Bruce saw the curious, indecipherable expression on the face of his Japanese friend. Yoshi wanted very much to explain, but he discovered that he'd forgotten how to speak English. Perhaps he should at least utter something in Japanese, but even his native tongue failed him just then and so he remained silent as he watched Todd and Angeline remove their shoes and wade carefully into the shallows of the immaculate, darkening sea.

Chapter Twenty-Five

Sylvie rowed the old dory until the sun had set and her arms ached badly. Her breathing was ragged, but all of the elements of her fatigue were pure pleasure. She had allowed the current to pull her far out into the Atlantic on a dropping tide. She watched the sun set over the waters to the west. There was absolutely nothing about being alone at sea this night that brought fear. There was not a whiff of loneliness about this venture. Purpose and pattern and something close to instinct. But it would not be examined deeper. All she knew was that she was doing a thing that would ultimately be good for the island and good for her. Some kind of pilgrimage. She was alone and would not have to explain to anyone what she was doing this for.

She had supplies. Several gallons of fresh water. Bread. Some tins of herring for bait, a hand line to fish. Blankets for warmth, rain gear for foul weather. There was no life jacket, however. Even Sylvie laughed at the thought of an old woman, alone at sea, after some misadventure, falling into the drink and bobbing around for God knows how long with a floatation device. Like the stubborn fishermen before her on the island, she believed such a slow, malingering death in icy water would not be for her if it came to that. She'd rather go quickly.

In the morning, the sky was grey but not threatening. If there was rain to spill from those pregnant clouds, it would not bring wind or waves. The sky had many soft layers of differing textures tending from palest grey to darker tones near blackness. Sylvie liked the fact that she could not distinguish the line between sea and sky in any direction. No land was in sight. She sat upright, afloat on a calm sea in the middle of a grey world.

A lone gull landed on the bow of her dory before she woke. An old herring gull, large for his breed, with silvery wings and a white torso. A yellowish beak and alert eyes. A gull accustomed to following fishing boats to sea, no doubt. Fewer of those boats in the water these days. The bird made himself comfortable beside an old woman alone with her thoughts in a dory. Sylvie broke a loaf of dark pumpernickel bread that she had made and fed pieces to the gull, who wolfed down the bread with no sign of gratitude whatsoever. Yet the company was welcome, and even when she decided to quit feeding him and save the food for herself, the gull did not seem to mind, but closed one eye, lifted one leg, and appeared to have fallen asleep like that. Sylvie, too, closed her eyes and tried to concentrate on the images of whales from her youth. She still believed she was in the current that would send her in the right direction, but there was no reference point out here and it was sometimes impossible to tell if she was moving anywhere or standing still. She closed her eyes again and waited until she could feel it. Taking the oars into her blistered hands, she began to row very gently in long, smooth strokes and let the wood dip into the water so gracefully that it was as if the surface had been pierced by two very sharp, long knives.

By the third day, she felt tired in her bones, and it was a lovely feeling. Sky and sea, sea and sky. The sun breaking through the clouds occasionally with a brilliant copper slash. Sunrise and sunset were explosive theatrical performances of light, but cloud covered up the sky through most of the days, sparing her from being baked by the sun like dark bread in an oven. She had dropped her fishing line several times, but there appeared to be no fish left in the sea. Or they had no taste for canned herring or soggy pieces of pumpernickel. Lots of water left, though, and some tinned meat. Somewhere up ahead, there would be fish.

Tired, tired, tired. Eighty years tired and sleep was her soulmate on this voyage. A monarch butterfly passed by on the third day, alighted on the gunwale, resting. The wonder of it all, a thing like this so far at sea, making its way back to land, knowing which way to go. Geese high up in the sky in a ragged V, or W sometimes, heading west along the coat before turning south. Something zipped by her face one day when her eyes were closed so she missed it, but she thought it was a hummingbird, departing for South America from Nova Scotia. She was out here on the wide, wide sea among many other travellers.

The sea and sky became all the things of her life to her. She could look up into the muted ripples of clouds and see herself as a little girl, see her dreams, see the faces of the men she loved. It was quite a crowd really. Talk filled her head. Men's talk. Their ambitions, their shared wisdom, their own fears. Philosophy crowded the boat for awhile and then simpler things. What was real and what was not real seemed entirely irrelevant. Not once did she regret having taken up the oars and leaving the island for this journey. Her head was filled with a pattern. Something like patches of lives all being unified together into a big, grand quilt. Each patch was colourful and had its own pattern, yet, when stitched in with the next one, it seemed even grander. Sylvie saw each patch as the life of someone who had been part of her life, and she was the old, widowed quilt-maker. Without her doing the stitching, all those lives would not make the unity. Each would be important unto itself, but she was the one who had the task of completion.

The quilt in her mind was simply the lives of people on the island. And in order to restore what was once the island, she must do this thing. She must row out to sea and search. Search and think. Let the current take her where it must until something is restored, until something is achieved. That's where her thoughts would stop. She knew this was not logical or rational, and she would not try to explain it to anyone. If, that is, she ever saw anyone again. The motivation came from deep within her. And it was a form of knowledge, not unlike her ability at dowsing. Things she knew. She knew it was wrong to try to hammer it into place with fences made of words.

By the fourth day, she had renamed the North Atlantic several times: the Sea of Love, the Sea of Clouds, the Sea of Serenity, the Sea of Fertility, the Sea of Nectar, the Lake of Dreams, then the Sea of Crosses, the Sea of Cold, and finally, yet again, the Sea of Tranquility. She felt herself drowning in all that sky around her and treasured the small irony of the emotions that went along with it. And when the first real taste of wind came up, she began to row into it. But her effort did not last long.

On her fifth day at sea, Sylvie felt light-headed. There was not a sign of a fish for food or a whale for companionship. Her food had run out. She had been less cautious than she thought. There was still some water left. Sylvie was stunned at her bad luck. Maybe the news stories were right. The sea itself was dying.

Sky and sea. Sea and sky. As if it was all she ever knew. She guessed she was twenty miles out, maybe more. Nothing to be afraid of, really. The worst that could happen was, well, not so bad. Some act of completion was what this was all about. Time to start rowing again.

She fit the oars into her hands. The wood felt good against her palms, despite the blisters, despite the fact that she had no idea exactly where she was going. She knew that something in her brain, in her thoughts, in the sum total of the memory of who she was — that was what was driving her to do this. She tested many words to see if they fit: madness, divine intervention, instinct, whimsy. The word "suicide" surfaced and she worried over it for a while, slowing her pace at the oars. Did she believe this was some kind of useful sacrifice for the island? Would her exodus, her demise, appease the bad luck gods of sea and government and restore hope for the island? Maybe that was somehow part of it, but she did not feel motivated by self-destruction.

Sylvie looked up at the grey sky and searched in vain yet again for the line that was the horizon. Sky and sea were all the same. She had rowed herself into some serene, pleasant limbo world, neither earth nor heaven. A watery halfway universe. She would continue to test other words. It was search, yes. That was certainly part of it. She had expectations. She would find the whales. Perhaps she could persuade them to return. Someday they would visit the island again, as they had in her childhood. Maybe that alone was the single, necessary act of completion. But what good would it do? She knew she was too far to sea to ever row herself back home and even now she was still probably rowing away from land. Only a fierce blast of wind from the east and south would send her back home, and she was sure she could not handle the dory in a such a rough sea.

But why was she not afraid?

It was the middle of the day when she first felt nauseous and dizzy. She pulled once more upon the oars and then set them at rest, propped against the gunwales. She felt her vision blur and then darkness began to beckon her. At first she thought it was mere exhaustion. She was falling asleep. But then her mind flooded with confusion. It didn't feel right. Then she felt her right leg losing feeling, and then her arm. For the first time on her voyage, fear overpowered her. She was losing her ability to control her arm. She slipped sideways, falling into the bottom of the boat as she curled up into a fetal position. Holding onto the briefest fragment of consciousness, Sylvie tried to convince herself this was all a dream. All of it. In the morning she would wake and she would be young again. David would be asleep beside her in the bed. There would be mist on the panes of glass by her bedroom window. Outside on the lawn, the spiderwebs would be laden with jewels of morning dew.

By nightfall, an extended family of right whales that had travelled thousands of miles in the Atlantic Ocean arrived at where the dory floated upon the dark mirror of the sea. There was no great hurry to move on to any other place than this. Deep below were krill and small fishes to feed upon. Here was this boat afloat upon the water with a woman asleep. A tug at something deep inside a sea creature's consciousness may have acknowledged something familiar about the person inside and quickly become aware of her vulnerability.

When the phone rang in Brian Gullett's little cubbyhole of an office at the *Herald*, he let it ring three times before he picked it up. Nothing was going to surprise him. What was the hurry? But it *was* a pleasant surprise. The PR person at the Sea Guardian headquarters in New York said they had some of Gullett's stories in their clipping file. One of their research vessels was leaving Boston at six that evening. They wondered if he wanted to go along on the twelve-day cruise.

Brian was ready to jump and wanted to know how high but he contained himself. "Some kind of confrontation at sea?" The Sea Guardian Society was world famous for its fearless confrontations with the Norwegians, the Japanese, and the Russians over whale killing. For Gullett, sullen and shackled to a desk in Halifax, this was a dream come true.

"'Fraid it's not that glamorous. We've been doing some independent research about fish stocks and about whales, right whales in particular — their migration habits. We're going out to verify what's going on. The American and Canadian governments are lying. We want to get at the bottom of the things. Are you in?"

"Yes."

He'd simply insist that his boss let him do this. Let the chips fall where they may. He left e-mail messages for the editor and a couple of other people, said nothing to anybody, grabbed his laptop, and, realizing he had no time to go home to shave, pack, or feed his budgie (he'd call his neighbour to take care of that), he split for the airport and caught the afternoon flight to Boston.

Gullett was licking his chops when he found out he was the only Canadian news guy on board the *Belize*. Three Yanks were on hand. Steve Neffler from the *New York Times*, Mary Soucoup from the *Boston Globe*, and a sole PBS reporter with a Betacam. Gullett was hoping that the Sea Guardian PR guy had lied to him and that a real at-sea faceoff was in the brew.

At an informal briefing in a sparsely appointed but expen-
sive-looking stateroom, the legendary Gale Jardine, current CEO
of Sea Guardian, offered them all a Heineken and gave a low-key
lowdown. "We're certain it's mostly global warming. But there's
more. We've been shovelling data, hard data, into a computer at
MIT for about a year now. It's indisputable. Toxic concentrations
distributed by the Gulf Stream into critical areas. That plus the
obvious: overfishing. Overfishing has been a nightmare. Up and
down the food chain it's a mess. And it's a mess worldwide. We've
been going for the emotional appeal of nailing Norwegians in
their bloody torture fest and harassing the Japanese with their
drift nets choking the dolphins, but some of us finally woke up
one morning and realized that it's bigger than all that and more
deadly. Trouble is, on paper it all sounds a little too boring.

"I mean the ocean temp goes up a degree in one place and
down a degree in another, how the hell you gonna get Joe Cool
to lift an eyebrow? That's why we need you."

"Mind if I have another beer?" Neffler wasn't trying to be
rude. Like the others, he was probably just a bit disappointed.

Gale rolled her eyes. "Help yourself."

"You've taken on a big job," Gullett told her to bolster her
spirits. He liked her immensely and it wasn't just the tan and the
body. He had wrestled with really important stories throughout
his career that never got the coverage they deserved. There
always had to be a hook. An easy hook. Kid hit by a drunk driver. Politician caught with his pants down. If it was really deadly
and dumped in a river, it wasn't even of interest unless someone
who was rich and famous rolled into the hospital on a gurney
as a result. But he knew the real stories were in the big picture,
in the number crunching and the research.

Neffler popped the cap on the beer, as did PBS. Gale
looked directly at them and continued. "Global warming —
now there's a dull thud for the public, I know. Fossil fuels. Cars.

Cities. All to blame. The ice cap is melting and it's still a big yawn. Water's colder off Nova Scotia from the melt, warmer farther south. Fish could have bounced back once the moratorium came into effect but they didn't. They lost a generation — teenage cod, so to speak. There's the lead, boys and girls. 'Teenage cod lose their way.' Can't teach the younger ones where to go and when. Same with other fish. And as a result of the warming trend, the Gulf Stream and the Labrador Current have shifted ever so slightly. It's like someone screwed around big time with an Interstate highway and you never know for sure which lane is going which way.

"The beauty of it is — if I can stretch the meaning of that word — that it's happening in our own backyard. The North Atlantic. Nobody can get excited about the death of the poor old tommy cod anymore. But now we have whales in the picture."

Brian cleared his throat, set his half-empty beer down. "They were a no-show all along the Atlantic side of Nova Scotia this year. Any connection?"

"Give the man a cigar."

"Don't tell me the automobile killed the right whale?"

"Not quite. Just confused him as much as the codfish. The right whales aren't off Peggy's Cove this summer and nobody's seeing them off Cape Cod, that's for sure, but they're out there. Mind you, the entire North Atlantic population is down to less than three hundred. We lose a dozen more each year that get tangled in nets or plowed into by container ships. But I'm going to take you to see some of the survivors." She was all fired up, but Brian could tell his media chums were looking at what they thought was a real waste of their time.

"So who's out there killing them this time? The Icelanders?" Neffler was still sure there was a kicker in here. The Sea Guardian didn't get its rep from backroom nerds on computers studying tide charts and water temperature. They kicked ass.

"No, don't you see? We are. They're confused about where to be and when. If they can't adapt to the changes, and I'm not sure they can, they die. Same thing might happen to us in the long run if we don't get this problem nailed down."

Gullett had swallowed hook, line, and sinker, but the rest were less than thrilled. Gale registered the lack of interest. "Well, folks, we got you here now. Unless you want to foot the bill for your own helicopter flight back to Boston, I'm hoping you'll want to find the sexiest angle you can possibly spin on this. We've got people here to help you. Please," she said. She was almost pleading now. "It's damn important." Then she let out a big sigh. "Don't worry. We'll feed you good. There's lots of beer. Movies if you need 'em."

She left, not fully certain she had done her job. Was this just going to end up being a very expensive whale-watching cruise or what?

Brian tried to get eye contact with her but she was gone. Neffler sat shaking his head. "I had Knicks tickets, too." But Brian was taking the whole thing very seriously.

On the third day out, boredom settled in among the press gallery like an unwanted companion. Neffler had already wired a very negative story back to the *Times* about how the Sea Guardian had lost its edge. He didn't seem to mind that he'd be treated like an enemy on board ship. PBS was holding off on airing anything yet. Nothing but a calm sea to show. No whales, no nothing but grey sky and a gunmetal sea, flat as piss on a plate. Mary Soucoup had tried to muster some enthusiasm and at least some feminist support for Gale and her cause but all she ended up with was a half column buried in the back of the Sunday paper with the headline, "Environmental Group Studies Problem With North Atlantic." With a headline like that it would never get read.

Brian was at the rail around twelve-thirty in the afternoon when he put some borrowed binoculars to his eyes. He saw the little boat first and then realized it was surrounded by a pod of whales. It was a long, long way from shore. The boat looked empty.

Chapter Twenty-Six

The PBS cameraman, Corey Giles, propped his Betacam on his shoulder and began to film. A pod of seven right whales surrounding a dory in the middle of the ocean. Curious. Intriguing visual image.

The engine of the *Belize* was cut and the big metal ship drifted towards the whales. As they came closer to the boat, Brian suddenly realized there was something in the bottom of it — a person. Looked like a woman, and she was lying there unconscious. He shouted to the crew. "In the boat! There's somebody there!"

A rush of adrenaline shot through him. He was breathing hard and he could hear his heart pumping blood. PBS was still filming. Brian could see her more clearly now, saw the woman curled up on the floor of the boat. "Somebody, do something!" he shouted. The crew was preparing to lower an inflatable over the side, but there was a slow, studied way about it that seemed all wrong to him. It didn't even occur to Brian that maybe whoever was in the dory was dead.

Brian Gullett had been an observer all his life, had turned the skill into a profession as a reporter. Other people's problems, other families' tragedies. That's what he wrote about. What went wrong and how people reacted. But he'd been bloody tired of just putting words on paper and trying to make people listen. Tired of it for a long time.

His hands gripped the railing and he squeezed the metal as if he could break it. Then he nearly scared Corey Giles to death by yelling a single, loud syllable as he leaped over the side of the *Belize*. Brian felt something let go inside of him, some linchpin in his brain, some key device that always before had kept him cool and sane. It was a short, gravity-driven trip down through the air and a terrifying crash into the sea. He went under, flapped his arms, and slowly bobbed up to the surface, spitting sea water and shocked at the cold. Not the world's best swimmer, he wallowed, wet clothes impeding him, towards the dory.

He could hear people yelling at him from up above. Floundering in the water, it was both frightening and energizing, like he suddenly had become some other person. He felt the first whale, a young one, slide under him, perceived the compelling wake of even a small whale tugging at him. The little one was followed by its mother, much larger and more brazen. Taking a heavy, clumsy stroke, Brian felt his hand land on the back of the whale, and it slid across the wet, leathery skin. Brian wondered why he was not fearful in the slightest.

Several more heavy strokes and his hand found the gunwale of the dory. He steadied himself, watched the whales circling about him now, felt his sodden shoe accidentally kick against the back of the small one going beneath him. He peered into the boat and saw her again, lying dead or unconscious on the wooden slats of the flooring. A woman. An old lady. A very old lady. Had he expected to be saving some beautiful young woman in distress? Brian wiped the saltwater out of his eyes and carefully, so as not to upset the boat, heaved himself up, then into the dory. Got his bearings. Huffing and trying to make his lungs work normally again. He heard somebody on the *Belize* yelling to him to avoid getting too close to the big ship, saw them still having trouble getting the inflatable lowered down to the waterline.

Gently he touched her shoulder. Nothing. "Come on lady, don't do this to me," he said out loud. And then he wondered, do *what* to him? Something vaguely familiar about this scene, like it had already happened before in a dream.

He knelt beside her and lifted her body. She felt lifeless, but he prayed it to be otherwise. He wanted it so bad he could taste it like something in the back of his mouth. "I'm not going to let you ..." and he almost said it again, *do this to me.*

He closed his eyes for a brief instant. Get a lock on yourself. Get your bearings. Is she breathing? He cradled her against him. An old woman, old, beautiful face. Peaceful. What the hell was she doing way out here? He leaned over and put his ear up to her mouth, tried to concentrate. He heard a whale sliding up out of the water nearby, heard another breaking the surface then diving again.

Concentrate. All he could hear was his own ragged breath. He tried again. Felt it before he heard anything. Warm air upon his cheek. She was alive.

He shifted position, sat down on the planks, lifted her body and cradled her like a little child in his arms. Saw a dry blanket behind the seat and pulled it up and around both of them. He hugged her to him and studied her face. Yes, he had seen her before. He somehow knew her. Who was she?

He held her to him as if she were someone he had known all his life, as if she were the most important person in the world to him. His heart began to come back to normal. She was not conscious. Something was wrong, very wrong, but he had no way of knowing what. Two men from the *Belize* had the inflatable in the water now and paddled to them, nearly getting dumped by the surfacing whales. One of the Sea Guardian men decided it was best to tow the dory to the ship, told Brian not to move, to keep her warm. Alongside of the *Belize*, a sling was attached to both of them and they were raised up on board. The ship's cook, who doubled as a medic, took her into a room below deck and examined her.

Brian followed. "Is she going to be all right?"

"She's had a stroke. That's all I can tell. I think there's some paralysis on the right side of her body. With something like this, it's hard to know if she has brain damage or what. We've got a Coast Guard helicopter coming."

"I want to go ashore with her."

"Sure. Your call. You jumped in. Guess she's yours."

Gullett knew now where he had met her before. But it didn't make any sense. The island. Ragged Island. She had been selling cookies and bread outside the Aetna Café. She had smiled at him. An angelic smile. A lovely old woman with lines etched in her tanned face. He'd not said a word to her, but walked on to that damn junkyard to get his story. In the end, he knew he had brought the wrath of the bloody government against those folks who didn't deserve it. He'd heard the news about the can-celled ferry. And he knew all about the failed whale-watching business. What else? Threads here. All loose ends. And he was one of them. Like it should all make sense but didn't.

An old woman at sea surrounded by a pod of right whales — creatures on the verge of extinction. He felt goosebumps. Up to now he had believed he had a good understanding of the way the world worked, thought he understood people, the order of things, events, calamities, disasters, crimes, corruption. He was so sure he had it wired. The Gull's instinct. He'd sniff out a story and get right to the bottom of things. Sniff it out and pounce. That was exactly what he'd done to the island. He was a predator and he got his prey.

Gale Jardine and Corey Giles came in. "Watch her," the medic said. "I've got to get on the horn to the hospital and see if there's something more I should do to prep her for the flight." Then he turned to Brian. "You all right?"

"Yeah. Go. I'm okay." Dazed, confused, in shock, he supposed. Brian wrapped the blanket more tightly around himself, focussed on the unconscious woman. All he did was jump into the middle of the Jesus ocean, swim through a pack of whales to find an old woman in a dory. She looked like she was sleeping peacefully like a child, but there was a good chance she was dying. A stroke robbed your brain of blood and oxygen. Left you speechless or paralyzed or both. Turned a normal human being into a vegetable. Whatever came next, Brian knew that she was somehow his responsibility. And he would not take that lightly.

Corey Giles sent the video footage to Halifax along with Sylvie and the mysterious Brian Gullett. The Gull saw her safely to the Queen Elizabeth II hospital, and, once she was settled into intensive care, he refused to leave her room. When someone from CBC arrived asking for the tape, Brian said no. He knew better than to trust the media.

It was a producer named Susan from CBC TV news. "PBS asked me to take a look at Corey's stuff, and feed some footage to New York. He said we could use it too, if we were willing to pay. So far I'm not sure there's even a story here. All I know is that a woman tried to kill herself by setting off to sea."

"I don't think that's what happened here."

"How do you know?"

"I know." Gullett felt his throat tighten. He knew that the Sea Guardian people were chomping at the bit to make some kind of story — anything that would grab the public — out of their painstaking but oh-so-boring research. Global warming, dead fish, missing whales. Now they had an old lady in a boat, far at sea, "protected" by a clan of right whales. Nice touch. But how was it going to affect his friend here — unconscious, paralyzed? Did she want to be part of some media circus?

"Brian, I've read your work. I know where you're coming from. I've got a hunch something good is going to come out of this. You're part of this story yourself, you know. I hear you jumped into the water and got to her first. He's got you on that tape swimming among the whales. Then in the boat, holding her. Maybe you saved her life. Somebody'll give you the Order of Canada."

"I don't want the Order of Canada. And I don't think I saved her life."

"Yeah, but you acted. And you had compassion. Works well for the camera."

"Bullshit."

"But what do you have to lose? I can get a lawyer in here and take the tape."

"I can shred it before that."

"But you won't. Look. Let the Sea Guardian people run with this thing. I think they have a point. They may be bang on. A big pile of boring statistics is all they had, but now they have the tools to tug the heartstrings. Come on, Brian, I don't want to have to run back-to-back clips of Preston Manning arguing with the Bloc Quebecois, or news about some hockey player caught with steroids in him. Give."

But Brian didn't want to give. He saw that look in her eyes. He'd lived with it, seen it in the mirror. Hot to trot for a story. And a story was all that mattered. Three good minutes of TV news that didn't make people turn the channel and you could stake a career on it. A dog on a rooftop during a flood in the Midwest. Unknown man swimming people to shore after a plane crash in the Potomac. Brian had a brief, shuddering fear that this whole thing was a hoax somehow staged by the Sea Guardian Society. Maybe he was the ultimate dupe.

But he was tired. He let his guard down and suddenly hoped to hell she wasn't bullshitting him. If she didn't screw it up, three good minutes of TV news could do some good. It was a gamble. "Run with it," he said, handing her the Betacam tape. "If you turn it all to shit, I'll come back to haunt you."

Susan smiled. Victory at sea. When she left, he leaned over close to the woman who now had a name. Sylvie Young. They'd phoned the island and discovered Brian was right. Their eyes had met that once. Hers had been soft and welcoming. His had been shrewd and guarded. Big lesson, there, bud.

He leaned close and listened to Sylvie breathe. Eighty years old, she was. Born around the time of the Russian Revolution, the Halifax Explosion, the First World War. He wanted desperately for her to return to consciousness. He needed her to live. He craved to hear the whole story from her. Let the media skew her persona in all the usual ways, but if he had his chance, he'd learn to understand who she really was. He closed his eyes, listened to her shallow breathing, and said a sizeable, sincere prayer to a God that he almost never believed in.

Chapter Twenty-Seven

When Sylvie woke up she was not at sea. She was in a hospital bed and she had a tube running up her nose. She could not feel her right hand or her right leg and wondered if some horrible accident happened and they had been cut off. But there was no pain. A fog, yes, like a heavy spring cloud settled upon the island. She tried to move her mouth to form words. Questions. How did she end up here? All she remembered was sky and sea. A peacefulness beyond anything she had felt in her life. She wondered, naturally, if she were dead but ruled that out as soon as she turned her head and saw a man, a young man — well, a man of perhaps forty years of age. He was asleep. He had not shaved in a number of days.

She had seen him before. On the island. He was the reporter, someone who had brought trouble to the island. Why was he here? There was a haphazard array of images in her head. It was like her memory had been cut up into many fragments where once it had been a whole, complete picture. A big puzzle, a jigsaw puzzle where none of the pieces seemed to fit together. All the images, all the fragments were there, but in a great jumble. She wondered who could help her begin to fit the pieces back together again. The confusion cascaded into fear. Her eyes darted back and forth, and then, as if someone had just swept a cosmic hand through the chaos to dispel her frenzy, she experienced a feeling of order again. Calm at least. She would discover a way to fit the pieces together.

She remembered going to sea. But she wasn't clear on why. It would come back to her. Give it time. Sylvie knew who she was and where she was. Her identity was her anchor now. Location was not significant. She understood she was not on the island. That much was obvious. Hospitals and Halifax, she knew, went hand in hand.

She closed her eyes and remembered drifting at sea. She remembered the sensation of not being alone. Doley and David, Kyle and William. Each of them, in his own way, keeping her company. This had become more and more frequent towards the point where her memory stopped. Where whatever happened had happened. All of the men had coalesced into one voice — a calming, reassuring, masculine voice. The men who had loved her.

Sylvie opened her eyes again and studied the man in the chair. She had no name to attach to him. In fact, as she looked around the room, objects that should have had names seemed nameless. She struggled with her thoughts until she found the word "chair." The young man was asleep in a chair. Beside him was a table. One entered the room through a hole in the wall with a movable slab of wood. A door? She tried to say the word out loud but there were no appropriate sounds she could create. It was as if she were being choked in some way. Something was choking her brain. Relax, old girl, the collective voice in her head soothed her. It was not the voice of her husbands, however, but her own familiar voice. Almost singing. The song of herself. And it began to sing something soothing and wordless until she felt calm again.

She would study the man beside her and see what she could learn from just looking at him. She breathed deeply of the oxygen and it had a pleasant, cool sting in her nostrils and in her throat. It reminded her of the tart ozone aroma of the shore after rain.

With close concentration and attention to the lines in Brian Gullett's face, she could read in him a deep disappointment with life and a profound sadness. Great compassion blanketed over by injury to a man's ego leading to despair. She also understood that whoever he was, he was supposed to be here. This consoling theory cast itself like a net around her confused thoughts and pulled them together. Two people in need of healing. Very different maladies, but both looking for a cure. Sylvie smiled, or tried to smile, and discovered her facial muscles were intolerant of her will. And then the full weight of understanding her physical debilitation settled down upon her like a dark, heavy cloud.

As the big jet lifted off from LAX in Los Angeles, on Yoshiteru Kojima's final leg back home to Tokyo, he fit the headphones to his ears and watched a pre-recorded version of the midday news. Violence in Miami. A building collapsing in Cincinnati, a very volatile day indeed on the markets in London, Wall Street, and the good old unreliable Nikkei Index was down two hundred points. Problems for the boys back in the office, for sure. But it didn't churn his stomach the way it used to. He felt released from previous distress about the day-to-day twists of the markets after his regenerative time on the island in Nova Scotia. He could not wait to see Taeko and tell her.

After the sports, something else. The bar cart bumped down the aisle. Yoshi leaned left to see the screen and saw a curious thing. A rowboat at sea, surrounded by whales. A man swimming in the water. Yoshi turned up the volume for his headset. Gale Jardine of the Sea Guardian Society was explaining something about global warming, about fish, about whales. Then, amazingly, as if he were dreaming, a camera shot of an island. His island — or so he had come to think of it. "Sylvie Young had travelled over a hundred and twenty miles from here," a young woman reporter said. "This tiny island, with fewer than two hundred people left residing here, has been plagued by disappointment layered over with disappointment for nearly a hundred years. Fish stocks in crisis and failed eco-tours were only two of the most recent events that led to the government cancelling a ferry service that was the lifeline to this idyllic place." Next Yoshi saw a very short clip of the premier of Nova Scotia, clearly embarrassed by the negative attention, trying to put a good face on it. "We're looking into it," he said. "We expect something can be done."

"Meanwhile, an eighty-year-old woman, who has become a powerful focal point of attention for environmentalists around the world, is believed to be in fair condition after a major stroke in a hospital in Halifax." The final shot was a repeat of Sylvie, curled up in the bottom of the dory on a glassy sea, surrounded by seven whales.

"Would you care for anything to drink?" the attendant asked Yoshi.

"No thanks."

"Nothing from the bar?"

"Oh, no. Nothing." He looked at her and smiled, but she had already turned him off. She moved on and repeated herself to a man in a cowboy hat sitting behind Yoshi.

There was an empty seat beside him and he slid across to the window and looked out at the pattern of clouds beneath the plane. The missing woman that Bruce had told him about. That was who she was. He could not remember her name. She must have been crazy. Old and crazy like what happened to his father. Yes, it must have been just that. But then what about those images of the little boat, surrounded, as if protected, by those whales, cousins to the whales that fishermen from his country were still slaughtering despite protests around the world and within his own nation.

Perhaps she was not crazy. The people he had met on that island were completely unlike people he encountered everywhere else. She was one of them. He would like to hear her reasons for going to sea. The TV images of the island reminded him how powerfully the place had affected him. He was tied to the fate of the island. Yoshi picked up the skyphone, made a couple of inquiries, and then located a florist in Halifax who would deliver a great array of flowers to the Queen Elizabeth II Hospital in Halifax. He felt confident she would be taken care of in the hospitals of a country that had universal health care. Someday Japan would be so wise. Later, he would ensure that if she needed anything, he would make funds available.

Concern gave way to a familiar shrewdness that Yoshi was never able to shake. He could use this somehow to convince his loyal investors that investing in Ragged Island's new economy was not just financially prudent but that something much, much grander was going on here. He would get video copies of the news report. He would have his researchers see if it had played in Japan. This was the sort of thing that might allow him the high profile that would nudge this project into something

very successful indeed. But he would have to learn how to protect the island as well, to set up the harvesting and processing
so that prosperity did not destroy this island that he had grown
to love.

Yoshi continued to observe the blue-white clouds beneath
him as he raced home at five hundred miles an hours, six miles
above the planet. And he decided that in order for him to ensure
that his project did not harm the island in any way, fragile as it
was, he would have to move there. He was ready to make the
sacrifice of his Tokyo career if necessary. He would tell Taeko
this, tonight when they were alone in bed. Taeko, who had
longed to return to her little fishing village on Hokkaido,
yearned for it every blessed day of her life in Tokyo. She would
understand. His prayers for good fortune at the Buddha shrine
had been answered.

Brian left Sylvie's room not long after a massive delivery of daf-
fodils, roses, and tulips. He needed to shave, he needed to clean
himself up. She was sleeping peacefully. The nurses said she was
stable. There was paralysis, and the loss of speech was to be
expected. But she was far from death's door. What she was going
to need was physical therapy and retraining. Despite the phone
calls from his editor, Brian decided he was not going to write a
word about his part in all this. In fact, he was prepared to tender
his resignation. The endless spewing of contemporary events, the
rattling on and on of news was a version of reality that was very,
very far from truth, no matter how you sliced it. The endless trail
of carnage, disasters, and human error, punctuated by brief bubbles of good news, would continue without him. He was no
longer a player in that game.

Brian wondered why he had hung in there so long. It was a
sort of addiction, he supposed. Ever since he had jumped from

the *Belize* and felt the cold water of the Atlantic, he knew that he was no longer the same person. His future was now tied to Sylvie and her island.

The first frost of October glistened on the grass in Sylvie's back-yard. She awoke and tried to work her right hand and felt a tingling sensation. Her fingers folded over. Her thumb could bend. She wiggled toes on both her feet and arched her right foot. She had become a child, relearning how to move her limbs. She formed words with her lips, but often no sound came out at all.

The jigsaw of ideas, images, and words rattled around in her head. Each morning, the puzzle needed putting back together yet again, but it was a little easier each time. She felt her energy coming back to her ever so slowly. Her bedroom door was open a crack and she saw Brian Gullett in her kitchen, making coffee in some kind of modern coffee contraption. Another man, a complete stranger, who had moved into her home. A good man.

Today she would sit again and write. It was a much slower task than before the stroke. She now wrote with her left hand instead of the right. Her handwriting was no longer beautiful to look at. And the English language itself did not always work properly for her. But the words would pour out of her and she would put them on paper and Brian would help her rearrange them to make sense. Todd or maybe even Angie would come to visit and use their computer to put the words into the machine and then print them out at home to give back to her. Her story, her ideas.

Brian was surprised at the public's continued interest in Sylvie and her recovery. He was even more shocked at the genuine outpouring of concern for the island itself. The Sea Guardian Society, having lucked onto a gold mine of publicity, had milked the old-woman-and-the-whales story for everything it was worth. Global warming and mass destruction of sea life was back on the public agenda. A recent Gallup poll suggested that it was an issue that was now running ahead of "concern for government deficits." They called it the "Sylvie Factor."

Sylvie needed help getting up but then she could walk on her own with the aid of a walker. She smelled Brian's French roast coffee as she dragged her right leg and stood firm with her left. She kept her right arm rigid but worked to move herself and her walker with her left. She sat herself down at the kitchen table and looked at the frost outside on the grass.

At night while she slept, her dreams allowed her better footing for walking, running, dancing, and even lovemaking. David Young, Kyle Bauer, Doley Keizer, William Toye. In her dreams she always had news for them wherever they were. They were still younger men than her, and good men. Vigilant for her recovery. Once fully awake, Sylvie was uncertain if they were somehow real (spirits alive after death) or purely imagined (existing only inside her imagination and memory). She fussed over that for a few days, writing down questions for Brian, who would, in turn, ask his own questions that led her to her own conclusion: it was more or less one and the same.

She laughed every time someone reminded her of what it was that was restoring the economy of the island. When the new Japanese neighbour and his very delicate wife came to visit her, they brought Brian green tea and left small packages of Oriental herbs to help in Sylvie's recovery.

Sylvie heard the island sing every day. Wind in the trees, ferry boat arrivals, cars without mufflers driving too fast to Up Along. The rattle of stones buffeted by the sea. Sylvie could feel the tug of the moon at night, the push and pull of the ocean's tide. She knew the whales were out there, distant, but safe for the most part, and following the paths they needed to follow until some time in the future, when they would return.

Chapter *T*wenty-Eight

B rian Gullett reads books about whales, about the surface of the moon, and about philosophy. In *Creative Evolution* by Henri Bergson, he learns that instinct is sympathy. Or in Sylvie's case, empathy. Something has transformed her. The stroke took away her speech and gave her this heightened sympathetic awareness. She can read people like words on the page of a book. Brian wants to learn that skill from her as well.

He has taught Sylvie to squeeze a tennis ball with her right hand, to lift her right leg and move her right foot. She can bend her knees. Sylvie is a good student and a quick learner. She is learning how to make the muscles of her face work again, to try to form words with the shape of her mouth. Sounds come out, but they are not always words.

Brian reshapes his own thinking. She is teaching him. About himself. About time, about memory, about island ways. About living with a woman. There was a time when Brian used words to formulate thoughts rather than the other way around. Now he prefers that freedom of idea over the continual regimentation of language. He laughs at his own former stupidity. Several decades of it — being a good reporter, a cynic, a non-believer. Now Brian believes in just about everything. He believes in possibility. He would like to say he believes in miracles, but that implies a set of other beliefs. Nothing is fixed. All things are possible. That is enough to sustain him in a time frame of *becoming* instead of *having been*. He wants Sylvie to train him in sympathy, empathy, and intuitive action. Where should you dig a well and be guaranteed to hit the clean, cool gusher of water beneath? How do you do that mind immersion thing with the sea? What happens when you learn to ride with the solar reflective energy of the moon? Where does it take you? Why is it better to fall prey to madness and return to sanity rather than being sane for an entire lifetime?

Brian now knows, the world knows, that the whales that had come to Sylvie on the open sea were right whales. Only a few hundred left in the Atlantic Ocean, where there had once been thousands.

Sylvie is writing in her journal, slowly and carefully with her left hand. Brian touches her hand, smiles, and goes out into the fall afternoon to sit with Phonse Doucette, to drink beer with him and listen to his jokes. Aside from Sylvie, Phonse is his closest friend on the island. It's because Brian had to work so hard at winning his trust. Today, Brian will tell Phonse about his discussion with Yoshiteru, about the arrangement.

Yoshiteru Kojima wakes up in a cold room in an old wooden house on Ragged Island. It has electric heat, but he and Taeko prefer sleeping in a cold room with the window open, tucked beneath heavy layers of quilts. The air is pure and clean. The sting of salt is always, always there, and it is something they love. Everyone, everyone back in Tokyo thought he was crazy. Except his own father and Taeko's widowed mother. Two important anchors of understanding left on the north island of Japan.

Yoshi wraps his arm around his wife who sleeps so peacefully. He studies the pattern of the quilt upon their bed. The relationship of all the pieces. The quilt was given to them, as was much of their furniture. Things were given to them even before the people of the island knew that Yoshi's plan was part of their own economic salvation. Yoshi, however, imagines himself as part of some grander plan. It's some kind of Buddhist thing, but he doesn't quite know how it has led him to Nova Scotia. In North America, his enterprise is considered somewhat of a joke. But Bruce believed in the idea, and the people of the island, when asked if they wanted to work on the project, said they would give it a try. Even though it sounded pretty far-fetched.

There was a market for seaweed in Japan. It was no joke. Rockweed, sea lettuce, dulse, Irish moss, laver for making okazu, alaria esculenta — edible kelp for making kombu. All harvested from the Front Bay, dried beneath glass panels, using solar heat. Preserved, packaged, and ready for shipping there in the new "factory" up the shore. But it is nothing like a factory. It is more like a family of people working, laughing, telling jokes, with kids playing in the daycare centre there.

The sea is full of wealth to be harvested as long as it is harvested with great care. Protect the resource and it will sustain generations. Everyone is amazed that it is profitable. Yoshi knows that others will dare to ruin the valuable food source by over-harvesting. But he will explain this to his contacts in Japan. He believes they will understand. He will explain about the people of his island. He will convince them to buy only from him or from the Nova Scotian entrepreneurs who can guarantee they will not damage the ocean floor and kill the sea. He believes he can do this. He gained great respect and power as a senior invest-ment trader. Although he shuns that former life, he can still make use of the respect he has earned. Do some good with it.

Yoshi cannot stop being an analyst at heart, but he can shift his point of view. Do the ends justify the means? Will the process and the product share integrity? He is glad that he and Brian Gullett discussed the dilemma of Phonse Doucette. It will be a break-even at best. Crushing old rusty cars, hauling them on a barge to the ship in Halifax, shipping the metal scrap to Osaka. Some risk, no profit for him. But it will allow Mr. Doucette to turn around a failed business. The island will be cleaner, health-ier in the long run. Pieces of the pattern. The quilt that Buddha stitched for him.

Moses Slaunwhite. Standing on the dock in Mutton Hill Harbour. The very man most suited for managing the seaweed plant. Right place, right time. They still laugh at the pot-bellied Buddha statue in the factory sun room. Some put wildflowers in Buddha's lap, others light incense sticks. Gautama Buddha on the Atlantic. It's a fat, jolly Buddha that doesn't seem so out of place here anymore.

December holds back from fully fledged winter this far at sea on an island like this. Soft, wet snow melts before it lands. Grass is still green this year and proud enough of morning frost, but white gives way to green again by late morning. The island is an active place. The ferry shuttles back and forth. Not many tourists, but visitors.

Sylvie can make her own way now to the Aetna, takes along baked goods to sell. Stays for a while. Sometimes mainlanders arrive, hoping to have a chance to speak with her. Pilgrims of sorts. Some find her fascinating, some are a little disappointed that she seems so frail and human. Her speech is slow and she still has trouble with pronouncing words. Those who really care are patient; they wait and they listen. Others return to the mainland feeling they wasted their time. After all, what Sylvie has to offer is very simple, conventional, and old-fashioned.

Sylvie thinks more clearly now, with the right side of her brain compensating for the damage to the left hemisphere. She has found a way to balance strong and weak. Brian stays on even though she can manage on her own. He's involved in the work down at Front Bay. Working with the men, young and old, in boats. Many had been disbelievers from the start. Money from seaweed. Never in a million years. Dollars for dulse? Right.

But then the paycheques began rolling in. A Japanese businessman with a taste for kombu, a yearning to live by the sea, an astute business mind, and a big heart. Sylvie sees the thread of things and it amazes her: a little girl gets trapped by the sea and is saved and her family is transformed, decides to stay on an island. Her father has a friend. The friend has a dream. The dream has a reality and people have jobs. Children stay home on the island. They do not have to attend mainland schools until grade ten. Greg and Kit continue to teach in the island's school. Generations will continue living on the island. Others will move here.

But nothing is linear. Not for an old woman close to eighty-one. She reads their lives in their faces and words and gives something back with a look or with her own halting words. She still mistrusts speech, knows she sounds funny and even scary to some. She's weeded and nourished the flower garden of her handwriting until it has been restored to some beauty. Carries notebooks and tears out pages with messages to show people sometimes. For the children. For visitors. Draws little pictures for her friend Taeko, who then paints over her drawings with watercolours and puts them in frames.

When January arrives with a vengeance, the cold drives like hard nails straight into her bones. The wind howls and yelps and wants to carry off her house with her in it, but she has a certain amount of faith left in gravity. Brian keeps the fires going, writes some on his own when he isn't reading. The plant is closed for a month due to the conditions on the water. No need for men in small boats to risk life and limb. Yoshi had taken this into consideration. Plenty of stock on its way in container ships. "Lots of dulse burgers for the Japanese," he says, picking up on the local joke.

Dulse burgers. Soups from kelp and rockweed ragout. And a livelihood for all involved. Plenty of notches up from catching fish or, worse yet, whales. And steadier work than a summer cabbage crop. What next? Sylvie wonders. Someone will decide the pebbles on the shoreline are each worth a dollar.

Sylvie does not think she will live long enough to see the whales return. This is not a troublesome matter. She has a few more years in her, a few more good years. The stroke was not some kind of error. Her trip to sea, not some kind of mistake. The events are like the man in the moon. Sea of Rains and Sea of Serenity for two eyes, a Sea of Moisture and Sea of Clouds close enough together to appear like a mouth in the night sky. But the Sea of Tranquility, nearly invisible, large as it is, unless you use a telescope.

The winter wind so angry you'd think someone had a grudge against humanity. It blows nor'east for three days, then stops. Just like that. So quiet that silence is like a refugee on your doorstep. The sky quits all that dark, grey brooding and gives up.

The sun cracks clean through at sunset with a big sword blade of horizontal light that throttles the impending darkness.

Sylvie bundles up into two or three coats and old rubber boots, goes outside alone. Snow up to her ankles. She makes her way down to the shoreline, studying her frosty breath in the air as she proceeds. Looks out across the water. Dark stones are capped with white fluff. The sea chop is dying down and waves lap against the rocks. It is an old, familiar song. Across the bay she sees the snow on the winter spruce. Dark green and white.

Sylvie feels young. She still has dreams, waking dreams not of the future, but of the present, stirred around with the past. She knows that lives are imprinted upon the things she can see, just as the sea is imprinted upon the shoreline. We are shaped by the geography of our place and our heart. We collect raw energy and give it form and meaning. And it goes beyond the mere naming of things. Names and language always, always fall short of true meaning.

Sylvie can feel the heat of the sun on her face even though the cold is all around her. But the sun is dropping quickly now. She hears footsteps from behind, turns and sees a little girl bundled in a winter coat, with a long scarf wrapped around her face. The girl is waving, and in the dying light Sylvie thinks that she is some kind of illusion. Sylvie is observing herself as a little girl, recently bundled up by her mother, let out into the snow by her father who has opened the door and told her to be careful. Is it getting darker or is it just her eyes not adjusting well to the dying light of the sun?

When the girl is right before her, Sylvie sighs and realizes that this is Angeline, the beautiful child from away, spending her first winter on the island. How unfamiliar it must seem in some ways to her. All that wind and cold. Sylvie wants to reassure her that it's just part of island life, nothing to be feared, but right now she's having a hard time forming words again.